新托福系列丛书

新托福

考试综合指南

A Practical Guide to iBT TOEFL

（美）Howard·Lynn·Jessop（审）

主　编　侯新民　姜登祯

编　著　新托福研发小组（按姓氏笔画排序）

牛　玮　　王维刚　　王　楠

乔　晶　　刘文华　　朱云汉

张　瑞　　张　璐　　李海霞

赵　予　　锁马莉　　鲁利萍

樊春玲

世界图书出版公司

西安 北京 广州 上海

图书在版编目(CIP)数据

新托福考试综合指南/侯新民,姜登祯主编.—西安:世界图书出版西安公司,2007.11
ISBN 978 - 7 - 5062 - 8651 - 0

Ⅰ.新... Ⅱ.①侯...②姜... Ⅲ.英语—高等教育—自学参考资料 Ⅳ.H310.41

中国版本图书馆 CIP 数据核字(2007)第 167439 号

新托福考试综合指南

主　　编	侯新民　姜登祯
丛书策划	李　丹　李林海
责任编辑	李林海　门莉君
视觉设计	吉人设计

出版发行	世界图书出版西安公司
地　　址	西安市北大街 85 号
邮　　编	710003
电　　话	029 - 87214941　87233647(市场营销部)
	029 - 87232980(总编室)
传　　真	029 - 87279675
经　　销	全国各地新华书店
印　　刷	西安建筑科技大学印刷厂
开　　本	889×1194　　1/16
印　　张	21
字　　数	420 千字
版　　次	2008 年 1 月第 1 版　2008 年 1 月第 1 次印刷
书　　号	ISBN 978 - 7 - 5062 - 8651 - 0
定　　价	30.00 元

本书听力部分可免费下载　网址:WWW.wpcxa.com
☆如有印装错误,请寄回本公司更换☆

前　言

托福考试(TOEFL)由美国教育考试服务中心(ETS)开发,用于测试母语为非英语的考生在校园环境中理解和使用英语的能力。托福考试是一种标准化英语水平测试。目前全球各地约有 4500 多所大专院校和相关机构要求学生入学时提供托福考试成绩。托福成绩也是获取奖学金的重要条件之一。对于准备出国深造的人,托福成绩将是获得签证的重要依据。

托福在中国已有二十多年的历史,从 2005 年开始,托福考试作了一系列重大改革。改革后的托福测试,在时间、题型、考试方式及计分方法等方面都有相应变化。为了帮助参加托福考试的考生尽快熟悉新的托福考试,掌握必要的应试技巧,提高应试能力,我们特编写了此套新托福考试系列丛书。这套丛书由《新托福考试综合指南》、《新托福听力突破》、《新托福阅读突破》、《新托福写作突破》、《新托福口语突破》、《新托福全真模拟测试题集》六册构成。

这套丛书的特点有以下几个方面:

1. 循序渐进,由易到难

本套丛书,除《新托福全真模拟测试题集》外,每册均有托福试题简介(包括试题形式、内容、要求等)、基本功训练、专项训练及讲解、应试技巧及模拟测试等部分组成。语言简明扼要,深入浅出、内容由易到难,循序渐进。考生可以逐步了解考试全貌,并逐步提高应试能力。

2. 内容丰富,覆盖面广

本套丛书,包括了托福考试的方方面面,既有听、说、读、写,又有全真模拟测试题集。考生可先进行单项训练,再进行专项训练,最后进行综合模拟测试训练,以期达到扎实的语言基本功和较高的语言运用能力。

3. 有的放矢,实用性强

本套丛书主要针对托福考试的四个部分,即听、说、读、写的内容、任务、要求进行细致的讲解,所提供的应试策略方向明确,易于操作,实用性强。

本套丛书选用的资料涉猎英国、美国、加拿大及澳大利亚等国家的社会、文化、历史等方面。资料来自英语国家的多种媒体,如广播、报纸、杂志等。

本套教材不但有助于在短期内提高托福考生的应试能力,同时也可以作为英语专业学生的专项训练丛书。

参加本套丛书编写的人员都是长期从事英语出国考试研究与教学工作的一线骨干教师,他们对托福应试培训有着丰富的经验。

由于我们的时间和水平有限,在编写上难免有疏漏和不足之处,恳请广大读者和同行提出宝贵意见,以便日后对本套书作出修订,使之更加完善。

编　者

2007 年 11 月 20 日

CONTENTS

CONTENTS

Chapter One

A Brief Introduction to the iBT TOEFL
新托福考试简介

Part 1

An Overview
概　要

The Test of English as a Foreign Language (TOEFL) is an examination used to evaluate a nonnative English speaker's proficiency in the English language. Many North American colleges and universities, as well as a large number of institutions, agencies, and programs, ask for official TOEFL score reports. TOEFL score is also an important criterion when considering whether a foreign student is eligible to apply for scholarships. Meanwhile, US embassy in China will refer to your TOEFL score when he or she makes the decision whether to satisfy your visa application. Therefore, TOEFL is the first step that you must take if you wish to study in the United States of America.

托福是专门针对非英语国家英语学习者英文掌握程度的一项测试，很多北美的大学以及大多数机构、组织都会要求查看官方托福成绩。托福成绩也是判断一个外国学生是否有资格申请奖学金的重要标准。同时，美国驻中国大使馆在是否同意您的签证申请时，托福成绩也会被考虑在内。由此看来，如果您想在美国学习，托福考试是关键的第一步。

TOEFL test has undergone a series of changes. Before 1988, TOEFL test centered on knowledge and language sub-skills. For example, the test measured how students knew facts about the language, their vocabulary as well as their grammar knowledge. The test then belonged to discrete-point test for each item tested something very specific such as an idiom in a vocabulary test. The test did not show how well students could use the language in actual exchanging ideas and information. In the year of 1998, ETS (Educational Testing Service) introduced a new kind of TOEFL test. That is computer-based test(CBT). This test contained items which were designed to directly elicit the students abilities and skills in using the language. It is a pity that CBT was not introduced in mainland China. Instead we used the old TOEFL test format, that is paper and pencil-based test (PBT). In September 2005, the TOEFL Internet-based test (iBT) came into being. It was first used in the US and Canada. Then in August 2006, it was introduced to China. The iBT TOEFL test is a totally new version of the TOEFL test. It is an internet-based test delivered in secure testing centers around the world. The new TOEFL test has the following characteristics:

托福考试在这些年来已经有了一系列变化。1988 年前，托福考试偏重考查知识和语言上的技巧。也就是说，考试会考查学生的语言能力，词汇量以及语法知识的掌握。此后，托福考试变成每一个部分的分离性较强的考试，就像词汇部分的一道习语题一样具体。事实上，那时的托福考试并不能很清楚地体现一个学生的实际英语表达能力。到了 1998 年，ETS 推出一种新的托福考试体系，那就是机考（CBT）。这种考试所包括的部分都是为能够了解学生对语言的掌握能力和技巧所特别设计的。当然，CBT 没能在中国大陆推广的确是一个遗憾。所以，那时我们仍然延续以前的托福考试形式，即为笔试。2005 年 9 月份，基于互联网的托福考试成为现实，在美国和加拿大首先试考。这种互联网考试对于托福考试来说是一个全新的视点。它由安全测试中心负责传送给全世界。这种新型托福考试有以下特点：

1. It can measure students' ability to communicate successfully in an academic setting. The new test will better measure what colleges and universities need to know: a prospective student's ability to use English in an academic setting. The new Speaking section evaluates a person's ability to use spoken English, and the new integrated Writing evaluates a person's ability to combine and communicate about information from more than one source.

这种考试能从学术环境的角度上成功的考查学生的沟通能力。这种新型托福考试会更好的帮助大学了解他们真正需要知道的：一个学生在学术环境中出色运用英语的能力。全新的口语部分能全面的考查学生的口语运用能力，还有综合写作部分着重测试学生综合以及沟通信息的能力。

2. It reflects how language is really used. The new integrated tasks that combine more than one skill are designed to reflect how people really use language. By preparing for the new TOEFL test, you will be building the skills you need to use language in an academic setting and communicate with confidence.

这种考试对语言究竟是怎样运用的做了好的诠释。全新综合的题目要求多方面的技能，它是为反映人们究竟是怎样应用语言而精心设计的。在新托福的备考过程中，您将会逐渐掌握在学术环境中使用语言的技巧，并且在实际沟通时满怀信心。

3. It can keep up with the best practices in language learning and teaching. In the past, language learning focused on learning about the language(especially grammar), and students would receive high scores on tests without having the ability to communicate. Now teachers and students understand the importance of learning to use English to communicate, and activities that focus on communication and integrating skills are very popular in many English language programs.

这种考试它能够随时与语言学习和教学上最好的实践齐头并进。在过去，语言学习的重心在于对语言的学习(尤其是语法学习)，学生完全可以在没有任何沟通能力的情况下得到很高的分数。如今，老师和学生们都开始认识到如何使用英语沟通的重要性，随之而来是在很多英语语言节目中，强调以沟通和综合能力为主的活动也越来越流行。

The new TOEFL test consists of four sections: Reading, Listening, Speaking, and Writing. All sections are taken on the same day, and the entire test is about four hours long. The test is not computer-adaptive. Each test taker receives the same range of questions. Instructions for answering questions are given within each section. There is no computer tutorial.

The following chart shows the range of questions and the timing for each section. The time limit for each section varies according to the number of questions.

新托福考试共包括四部分：阅读、听力、口语和写作。每个部分都在同一天完成，考试所需的时间大约为四个小时。这种考试不是计算机适应性考试。每位考生被问到的问题都属于同一范围。关于问题回答的说明会在每部分给出。没有教考生如何使用计算机考试。

下表所表明问题的范围以及各部分考试的时间。每部分时间限制会根据问题的数量而定。

Test Section	Number of Questions	Timing
Reading	3 – 5 passages，12 – 14 questions each	60 – 100 minutes
Listening	4 – 6 lectures，6 questions each 2 – 3 conversations，5 questions each	60 – 90 minutes
Break		5 minutes
Speaking	6 tasks；2 independent and 4 integrated	20 minutes
Writing	1 integrated task 1 independent task	20 minutes 30 minutes

分项技能	内容	时间
阅读	3 – 5 篇文章，每篇 12 – 14 道题	60 – 100 分钟
听力	4 – 6 个讲座，每个讲座 6 道题 2 – 3 个对话，每个对话 5 道题	60 – 90 分钟
休息		5 分钟
口语	6 道题；2 道独立题和 4 道综合题	20 分钟
写作	1 篇综合论文题 1 篇独立写作题	20 分钟 30 分钟

The iBT TOEFL Score Scale

Listening	0 – 30
Reading	0 – 30
Speaking	0 – 30
Writing	0 – 30
Total Score	0 – 120

Note: The total score is the sum of the four skill scores.

新托福分数分布

听力	0 – 30
阅读	0 – 30
口语	0 – 30
写作	0 – 30
总分	0 – 120

注：总分由 4 部分成绩相加得出。

Part 2

A Brief Introduction to the Listening
听力考试简介

The listening section measures your ability to understand spoken English from North America and other English-speaking parts of the world. In academic environments students need to listen to lectures and conversations. Listening materials in the new test include academic lectures and long conversations in which the speech sounds very natural. You can take notes on any listening material throughout the entire test. The following is a diagram containing the necessary information about the listening section in the new TOEFL test.

听力考试部分主要考察考生理解在北美以及世界上其他地方用英语交流的能力。在学术环境中，学生们需要去听讲座和一些对话。在新托福中的听力材料包括一些语速自然的学术讲座和长段对话。你可以在整个测试中做笔记。下表提供一些对新托福听力部分的必要信息。

Listing Material	Number of Questions	Timing
4 – 6 lectures, 3 – 5 minutes long each, about 500 – 800 words	6 questions per lecture	60 – 90 minutes
2 – 3 conversations, about 3 minutes long, about 12 – 25 exchanges	5 questions per conversation	

听力材料	题数	时间
4 – 6 个讲座，每个 3 – 5 分钟，500 – 800 字左右， 2 – 3 个长对话，每个 3 分钟左右， 12 – 15 交替	每个讲座 6 个问题 每个对话 5 个问题	60 – 90 分钟

The lectures in the new test reflect the kind of listening and speaking that goes on in the classroom. In some of the lectures, the professor does all or almost all the talking, with an occasional question or comment by a student. In other lectures, the professor may engage the students in discussion by asking questions and getting the students to speak. The pictures that accompany the lecture help you know whether one or several people will be speaking.

A picture where the professor is the only speaker

A picture where the professor and the student will speak

在新题型中的讲座是对教室里听力和口语的一个重现。在一些讲座中,教授的讲话基本上占大多数时间再加上学生的偶尔提问或者发表看法。在其他讲座中,教授可能会以问问题的形式来要求学生们参与到讨论中来。图片中你会了解是否有 1 个或很多学生会参与其中。

The conversations on the new test may take place during an office hour with a professor or teaching assistant, or they may be with the person in charge of student housing, a librarian, a bookstore employee, a departmental secretary, or the like. Pictures on the computer screen help you imagine the setting and the roles of the speakers.

在新题型中的对话或许会选取发生在办公时间里不同人身上的事情。比如一位教授或者教师助理,负责学生住宿的人,图书管理员,书店员工或者部门经理,如此等等,类似的情况。在显示屏上的照片会对你了解场景以及场景中的人物起到帮助。

Things to be noted

1. Conversations and lectures are longer than those on previous versions of the TOEFL test, and the language sounds more natural.

2. One lecture may be spoken with a British or Australian accent.

3. One new multiple-choice question type measures understanding of a speaker's attitude, degree of certainty, or purpose. These questions require you to listen for voice tones and other cues and determine how speakers feel about the topic being discussed.

||| 提 醒 |||

1. 新题型中的对话和讲座会比以前题型中的要长,语言听起来也会更加自然流畅。

2. 其中一个讲座可能会带有英国或澳大利亚口音。

3. 一种新的多项选择题测试您对谈话人的态度、肯定程度或者谈话目的的理解。这类问题要求您听懂语调以及言外之意的暗示,并由此判断出谈话人对讨论话题的感觉。

Part 3

A Brief Introduction to the Reading
阅读考试简介

There are 3 – 5 passages in the reading section. Each passage is followed by 12—14 questions. The length of each passage is about 700 words. You have 60—100 minutes to finish this section. First, you must read through or scroll to the end of each passage before receiving questions on the passage. Once the questions appear, the passage is located on the right side of the computer screen, and the questions are on the left.

You do not need any special background knowledge to answer the questions in the Reading section correctly; all the information needed to answer the questions is contained in the passages. A definition may be provided for difficult words or phrases in the passage. If you click on the word, a definition will appear in the lower left part of the screen. This is how the reading passage and a question look on the computer screen:

阅读考试部分由 3 – 5 篇文章组成，每篇文章会有 12 – 14 个问题，每篇文章约在 700 词左右，时间为 60 – 100 分钟。首先，在拿到问题之前您必须通读或跳读每篇文章。若问题出现，文章会在显示屏的右侧上出现，而问题会出现在左侧。

您不需要特别的背景知识便可以正确回答阅读部分所提出的问题，所有关于问题需要的信息都会包含在文章之中。在文章中还有可能出现对生僻词或难的短语的定义。如果你点一下那个词，在显示屏的左下方将会出现该词的定义。以下图片是阅读中的文章和问题在显示屏上展示：

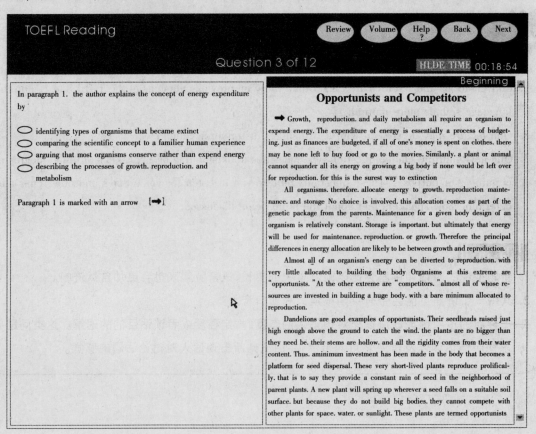

Part 4

A Brief Introduction to the Writing
写作考试简介

There are two different writing tasks in the TOEFL iBT Writing section:

1. An integrated task in which you read a short passage for 3 minutes (about 230 to 300words), you listen to a short lecture that directly addresses the points made in the reading (2 minutes), and you write a summary of what the speaker said about the reading passage.

2. An independent writing task in which you are asked to give an opinion about a general topic or a topic of interest to students. You are asked to support your opinion with specific reasons and examples. This task is very similar to the essay on the TOEFL CBT and the paper-and-pencil Test of Written English (TWE).

Compared with the old test, the new one has been expanded. To be more specific, the new test requires test takers to type a response to material they have heard and read, and to compose an essay in support of an opinion. Trained and certified human scorers rate the responses to the Writing tasks via ETS's Online Scoring Network.

在托福 iBT 写作中有两个不同的部分：

1. 一道题为综合写作题。首先用 3 分钟阅读一篇短的文章（230 – 300 词左右），然后在听完一段短的讲座之后立即记下刚才阅读的要点（2 分钟），最后写一篇关于谈话人对阅读文章看法的总结。

2. 另一道题为独立写作题。它要求您对一个总的话题发表意见看法或是一个关于学生们兴趣爱好的话题，您必须为你所支持的观点提出具体的原因和事例。这道题类似于以前托福 CBT 和 PBT 的写作部分。

同旧托福过去的试题相比，新托福的试题有了更好的拓展。更具体地说，新型的试题要求考生对他们所听到或读到的材料做出回答，而且要为支持的观点写一篇文章。经过培训并取得证书的人工评判员会通过 ETS 的评分网络对写作部分的分数做出评判。

Part 5

A Brief Introduction to the Speaking
口语考试简介

The speaking section is about 20 minutes long, including questions and answers. It includes six tasks. The first two tasks are independent speaking tasks that focus on topics familiar to the test taker. The remaining four tasks are independent tasks, and you must combine more than one skill when responding. You first listen to and read some brief material. You can take notes and use those notes when responding to the speaking tasks. Then a question is asked that requires you to relate the information from the reading and the listening material.

For all speaking tasks you use a headset with a microphone. You speak into the microphone to record your responses. Responses are digitally recorded and sent to ETS's Online Scoring Network. The following is a chart with detailed information on Speaking test:

口语测试部分的时间在20分钟左右,包括所有的问题以及答案,共有6道题。前2道题应是考生们熟悉的独立题。其余的4道题为独立题,它要求你在回答时综合多方面技巧。首先你会听到并且读一些简短的材料,你可以做一些笔记用来回答问题,之后将会提出一个关于你所听到和读到材料的问题。

口语部分使用耳麦,要求对着麦克风说出答案后并把它们录下来。答案均为数字式录音并且传输给ETS评分网络。以下表格是关于口语部分的详细信息:

Tasks	Number of Tasks	Timing of Each Response
Independent—answer short questions on general topics about your opinions	2	Preparation time: 15 seconds Speaking time: 45 seconds
Read/Listen/Speak-answer questions about information you have read and listened to	2	Preparing time: 30 seconds Speaking time: 60 seconds
Listen/Speak-answer questions about a discussion and a short lecture you have listened to	2	Preparing time: 30 seconds Speaking time 60 seconds

题目	题数	时间
独立题——对一些话题作简要回答	2	准备时间:15秒 回答时间:45秒
读/听/说——对读到和听到的信息作出回答	2	准备时间:30秒 回答时间:60秒
听/说——对一个讨论和短讲座作出回答	2	准备时间:30秒 回答时间:60秒

Chapter Two

Basic Skills Needed for iBT TOEFL

新托福考试必备基础技巧

Because the TOEFL iBT is designed to assess the actual skills you will need to be successful in your studies, the very best way to develop the skills being measured on the TOEFL IBT test is to study in an English program that focuses on communication using all four skills, especially speaking and integrated skills (e. g. , listening/reading speaking, listening/reading/writing).

However, if you have no opportunities to attend an English program, another way is to build up your basic skills in listening, reading, writing, and speaking through systematic self-study and practice. In this chapter, you will be provided with sufficient examples to help you lay a solid foundation for your English so that your performance can be improved step by step.

因为托福 iBT 考试是专门用来评估今后在学习中必备技巧的一项测试，所以为准备托福 iBT 考试而要提高这些技巧的最好办法就是在重点为培养交际四项技巧的英语学习班进行学习，特别是侧重提高口语和综合能力的地方(例如听/读说结合,听、读、写结合)。然而,如果你无法参加此类学习,那就要通过系统的自学和练习来提高听、说、读、写四方面的基本功。本章将会提供一些有效的实例来为您今后英语水平的逐步提高打下坚实的基础。

Part 1

Basic Skills Needed for Reading

阅读基础必备

According to the Bulletin of the new TOEFL test, in the reading section, candidates will have to demonstrate their abilities to read textbooks, learned articles and other sources of information relevant to academic education. Candidates will be expected to show that they can use the following reading skills:

1. skimming
2. scanning
3. getting the gist
4. distinguishing the main ideas from supporting details
5. distinguishing fact from opinion
6. distinguishing statement from example
7. deducing implicit ideas and information

8. deducing the use of unfamiliar words from context

9. understanding relations within the sentences

10. understanding relations across sentences and paragraphs

11. understanding the communicative function of sentences and paragraphs

依照根据新托福考试简章中的阅读部分,考生须充分展现其阅读课本,专业文章以及其他跟学科教育有关的信息的技能。希望考生们对以下技巧熟悉并掌握:

1. 泛读

2. 浏览

3. 抓住要点

4. 区分中心意思和细节

5. 区分事实和观点

6. 区分陈述和事例

7. 判断隐含意思和信息

8. 根据上下文判断生词意思

9. 理解各句间的关系

10. 理解句子与段落间的关系

11. 理解句子与段落的交际功能

The best way to improve your reading skills is to read frequently and to read many different types of texts in various subject areas (science, social sciences, arts, business, etc). The internet is one of the best resources for this, but any books, magazines, or journals are helpful as well. It is best to progress to reading texts that are more academic in style, the kind that would be found in university courses.

In addition, you might try these activities:

1. Scan the passage to find and highlight key facts (dates, numbers, terms) and information.

2. Increase vocabulary knowledge, perhaps by using flashcards.

3. Rather than carefully reading each word and each sentence, practice skimming a passage quickly to get a general impression of the main idea.

4. Choose some unfamiliar words in the passage and guess the meaning from the context (surrounding sentences).

5. Select all the pronouns (he, him, they, them, etc.) and identify which nouns each one refers to in the passage.

6. Practice making inferences and drawing conclusions based on what is implied in the passage as a whole.

In the following, you will come across a variety of reading passages. Each passage is followed by some multiple-choice questions. These questions cover a wide range of reading skills that are involved in the test. The purpose of offering such exercises is to help you familiarize yourself with the basic skills required in the reading section of the new TOEFL test.

最好的提高阅读技巧的方法就是经常性的阅读大量不同类别、涉及领域面广的文章(如科学,社会科学,艺术,商业等)。互联网是最好的资源之一,同样的,像书籍,杂志,刊物也有很大帮助。最好在选择文章的过程中多读大学课程中那些学术风格较强的文章。

另外,还可以尝试:

1. 浏览全文找出最重要的事实(如:日期,数字,术语)以及关键信息。

2. 可以用小卡片的方法扩大词汇量。

3. 与其选择一词一句的读,不如锻炼泛读每篇文章,了解它们的大意的能力。

4. 选择一些较难的词然后猜测它们在文章中的意思(通过上下文)。

5. 选出所有的人称代词(他,他们,等等)并且弄清每一个在文章中都指的什么。

6. 练习通过全文来作出推理判断,根据文章的隐含内容下结论。

在接下来的部分,准备了很多不同类型的文章供你阅读,每篇文章后都会相应的有一些多项选择题。这些问题都比较全面的涉及到阅读中所应具备的技巧。提供以下练习的最终目的就是为了让你更好的熟悉在新托福阅读题部分所应掌握的技巧。

Passage 1

It is said that the mass media are the greatest organs for enlightenment that the world has yet seen; that in Britain, for instance, several million people see each issue of the current affairs program, Panorama. It is true that never in human history were so many people so often and so much exposed to so many intimations about societies, forms of life, attitudes other than those which obtain in their own local societies. This kind of exposure may well be a point of departure for acquiring certain important intellectual and imaginative qualities, width of judgment, a sense of the variety of possible attitudes. Yet in itself such exposure does not bring intellectual or imaginative development. It is no more than the masses of a stone which lies around in a quarry and which may, conceivably, go to the making of a cathedral. The mass media cannot braid the cathedral, and their way of showing the stones does not always prompt others to build. For the stones are presented within a self-contained and self-sufficient world in which, it is implied, simply to look at them, to observe—fleetingly—individually interesting points of difference between them, is sufficient in itself.

Life is indeed full of problems on which we have to—or feel we should try to—make decisions, as citizens or as private individuals. But neither the real difficulty, of these decisions, nor their true and disturbing challenge to each individual, can often be communicated through the mass media. The disinclination to suggest real choice, individual decision, which is to be found in the mass media is simply the product of a commercial desire to keep the customers happy. It is within the grain of mass communications. The organs of the establishment, however well-intentioned they may be and whatever their form (the State, the Church, voluntary societies, political parties), have a vested interest in ensuring that the public boat is not violently rocked, and will so affect those who work within the mass media that they will be led insensibly towards forms of production which, though the skin to where such enquiries might really hurt. They will tend to move, when exposing problems, well within the accepted cliché-cliché not to make a disturbing application of them to features of contemporary agitation of problems for the sake of the interest of that agitation in itself; they will therefore, again, assist a form of acceptance of the status quo. There are exceptions to this tendency, but they are uncharacteristic.

The result can be found in a hundred radio and television programs as plainly as in the normal treatment of public issues in the popular press. Different levels of background in the readers or viewers may be assumed, but what usually takes place is a substitute for the process of arriving at judgment. Programs such as this are noteworthy less for the "stimulation" they offer than for the fact that stimulation (repeated at regular intervals) may become a substitute for, and so a hindrance to, judgments carefully arrived at and tested in the mind and on the pulses. Mass communications, then, do not ignore intellectual matters; they tend to castrate them, to allow them to sit on the side of the fireplace, sleek and useless, a family plaything.

1. According to the passage, the mass media present us with _____
   A. insufficient diversity of information.
   B. too restricted a view of life.
   C. a wide range of facts and opinions.
   D. a critical assessment of our society.

2. The word "disinclination" (line 3, para. 2) implies that _____
   A. mass media are not capable of giving real choice and individual decision.
   B. mass media do not feel like giving real choice and individual decision.
   C. mass media do not manage to give red choice and individual decision.
   D people do not expect to get real choice and decision from mass media.

3. The author uses the comparison with building a cathedral to show that _____
   A. worthwhile results do not depend on raw material only.
   B. the mediaeval world had different beliefs.
   C. great works of art require good foundations.
   D. close attention to detail is important.

4. Radio, TV and the press are criticized here for _____
   A. widening the gap between classes.
   B. assuming that every, one's tastes are the same.
   C. failing to reach any definite conclusions.
   D. setting too intellectual a standard.

5. What is the author's final judgment on how mass communications deal with intellectual matters?
   A. They regard them as unimportant.
   B. They see them as a domestic pastime.
   C. They consider them to be of only domestic interest.
   D. They rob them of their dramatic impact.

Passage 2

For the past six years, crime rates have been falling all over America. In somebig cities, the fall has been extraordinary. Between 1994 and 1997 in New York city violent crime fell by 39% in central Harlem and by 45 % in the once-terrifying South Bronx. The latest figures released by the FBI, for 1997, show that serious crime continued to fall in all the largest cities, though a little more slowly than in 1996.

Violent crime fell by 5 % in all, and by slightly more in cities with over 250,000 people. Property crimes have fallen, too, by more than 20% since 1980, so that the rates for burglary and car-theft are lower in America than they are in supposedly more law-abiding Britain and Scandinavia. And people have noticed. In 1994, 30% of Americans told pollsters that crime was the most important challenge facing the country. In 1997, only 15% thought so. Some cities' police departments are so impressed by these figures, it is said, that they have lately taken to exaggerating the plunge in crime.

Why this has happened is anyone's guess. Many factors—social, demographic, economic, and political—affect crime rate, so it is difficult to put a finger on the vital clue. In May this year, the FBI itself admitted it had "no idea" why rates were falling so fast.

Politicians think they know, of course. Ask Rudy Giuliani, the mayor of New York, why his city has made such strides in beating crime that it accounts for fully a quarter of the national decline. He will cite his policy of "zero tolerance". This concept, which sprang from a famous article by two criminologists in Atlantic Monthly in March 1982, maintains that by refusing to tolerate tiny infractions of the law-dropping litter, spray-painting walls—the authorities can create a climate in which crime of more dangerous kinds finds it impossible to flourish. The Atlantic article was called Broken Windows if one window in a building was left broken, it argued, all the others would soon be gone. The answer: mend the window, fast.

The metro system in Washington D. C. was the first place where zero tolerance drew public attention, especially when one passenger was arrested for eating a banana. The policy seemed absurdly pernickety, yet it worked: in a better environment, people's behavior improved, and crime dropped. Mr. Giuliani, taking this theme to heart, has gone further. He has cracked down on windscreen-cleaners, public urinators graffiti, and even jaywalkers. He has excoriated New York's famously sullen cabdrivers, and wants all New Yorkers to be nicer to each other. Tony Blair, visiting from London, has been hugely impressed.

But is this cleanliness and civility, the main reason why crime has fallen? It seems unlikely. "Zero tolerance" can also be a distraction, making too many policemen spend too much time handing out littering tickets and parking fines while, some streets away, young men are being murdered for their trainers. It is localized, too: though lower Manhattan or the Washington metro can show the uncanny orderliness of a communist regime, other parts of the city—the areas of highest crime maybe left largely untreated.

William Bratton, New York's police commissioner until Mr. Giuliani fired him for stealing his thunder, has a different explanation for the fall in crime. It came about mainly, he believes, because he reorganized the police department and restored its morale: giving his officers better guns, letting them take more decisions for themselves, and moving them away from desk jobs and out into the streets. Mr. Bratton made his precinct commanders. personally responsible for reducing crimes on their own beaks. There was no passing the buck, and those who failed were fired. Within a year, he had replaced half of them.

1. What can we conclude from paragraphs one and two about America between 1994 and 1997?

A. Its crime rates have been falling only in big cities.

B. Violent crime falls by 39%.

C. The rates for burglary, and car-theft are lower in America than that in Britain.

D. Violent crime falls by more than 20%.

2. In the last sentence of the 2nd paragraph the word "plunge" can be replaced by _____

    A. sudden fall.   B. pluck.

    C. increase.   D. rise.

3. Where in the passage does the author give a definition?

    A. The last sentence in the 1st paragraph.

    B. The 2nd sentence in the 2nd paragraph.

    C. The 4th sentence in the 4th paragraph.

    D. The 2nd sentence in the 5th paragraph.

4. In Washington D. C a passenger was arrested for eating a banana in the metro system. This cage later shows that _____

    A. the police are fussy.

    B. In a better environment, people's behavior improves.

    C. zero to tolerance is a failure.

    D. Mr. Guilioni disagreed with it.

5. According to the passage, what are the main reasons for the falling of the crime rates?

    A. Social and demographic factors.

    B. The efforts of FBI.

    C. The policy of zero tolerance.

    D. It is difficult to find the vital clue.

Passage 3

Until men invented ways of staying underwater for more than a few minutes, the wonders of the world below the surface of the sea were almost unknown. The main problem, of course, lies in air. How could air be provided to swimmers below the surface of the sea? Pictures made about 2, 900 years ago in Asia show men swimming under the surface with air bags tied to their bodies. A pipe from the bag carried air into the swimmer's mouth. But little progress was achieved in the invention of diving devices until about 1490; when the famous Italian painter, Leonardo da Vinci, designed a complete diving suit.

In 1680, an Italian professor invented a large air bag with a glass window to be worn over the diver's head. To "clean" the air a breathing pipe went from the air bag, through another bag to remove moisture, and then again to the large air bag. The plan did not work, but it gave later inventors the idea of moving air around in diving devices.

In 1819, a German, Augustus Siebe, developed a way of forcing air into the head-covering by a machine operated above the water. At last in 1837, he invented the "hard-hat suit" which was to be used for nearly a century. It had a metal covering for the head an air pipe attached to a machine above the water. It also had small opening to remove unwanted air. But there were two dangers to the diver inside the "hard-hat suit". One was the sudden rise to the surface, caused by a toe great supply of air. The other was the crashing of the body, caused by a sudden diving into deep water. The sudden rise to the surface could kill the diver; a sudden dive could force his body up into the helmet, which could also result in death.

Gradually the "hard-hat suit" was improved so that the diver could be given a constant supply of air. The diver could then move around under the ocean without wowing about the air supply.

During the 1940s diving underwater without a special suit became popular. Instead, divers used a breathing device and a small covering made of robber and glass over parts of the face. To improve the swimmer's speed another new invention was used: a piece of rubber shaped like a giant foot, which was attached to each of the diver's own feet. The manufacture of rubber breathing pipes made it possible for divers to float on the surface of the water, observing the marine life underneath them. A special rubber suit enabled them to be in cold water for long periods, collecting specimens of animal and vegetable life that had never been obtained in the past.

The most important advance, however, was the invention of a self-contained underwater breathing apparatus, which is called a "scuba".

Invented by" two Frenchmen, Jacques Cousteau and Emile Gagnan, the scuba consists of a mouth-piece joined to one or two tanks of compressed air which are attached to the diver's back. The scuba makes it possible for a diver-scientist to work 200 feet underwater or even deeper for several hours. As a result, scientists can now move around freely at great depths, learning about the wonders of the sea.

1. In 1490 or so, the main progress mentioned in this passage was _____

    A. an Italian professor invented a large air bag.

    B. men invented the best diving devices.

    C. an Italian painter designed a complete diving suit.

    D. an air bag.

2. An invention of an Italian professor _____

    A. gave later inventors the idea of moving air around in diving devices.

    B. can "clean" the air.

    C. was used to remove moisture.

    D. was nothing but a plan.

3. The German, Augustus Siebe, invented the "hard-hat suit" which was used _____

    A. for nearly a hundred years.

    B. for almost a thousand years.

    C. for over a century.

    D. for a century.

4. Siebe's invention was not a perfect one, because _____

A. too great a supply of air could result in a sudden rise to the surface.

B. a sudden dive into deep water could cause the crashing of the body.

C. the air pipe attached to a machine could be above the surface.

D. both A and B.

5. The word "scuba" is _____

A. a certain diver's name.

B. an original English word.

C. named by the inventor.

D. the first letters of five English words.

Passage 4

Personnel changes at the International Monetary Fund and proposals for changing the fund have been reported lately. After a lengthy public debate, the leading countries settled on another German, Horst Kohler, to replace Michel Camdessus as the IMF's managing director. Unfortunately, the circus-like process began to resemble an affirmative-action procedure when it became clear that a particular nationality—German—was a prerequisite for the job.

Calls for changes at the IMF came in the report from Congress International Financial Institution Advisory Commission, led by Alan. H. Meltzer. (I was a witness before the commission on issues related to inequality.) The Meltzer Commission's report surprised me by not advocating abolition of the IMF. The report said: "The commission did not join the council of despair calling for the elimination of one or more of these institutions."

The commission came close to recommending abolition, however, by proposing a net IMF that would be limited to short-term-liquidity assistance to solvent economies, collection and publication of data, and provision of economic advice. The short-term-loan facility would represent a reasonable return to the IMF's role under the Bretton Woods regime that prevailed until the early 1970s. However, that role expanded greatly in the 1990s, and it is not clear how such further expansion would be avoided under the new setup. So long as the IMF retains access to lots of money, it will be difficult to say no to lane, insolvent countries, such as Mexico in 1995 and Russia in 1998. Past mistakes will probably be repeated, and the elimination of the IMF would have been a better choice.

I agree that the IMF's role in the collection and distribution of data has been useful. An advisory role might also be satisfactory (and some of my friends and former students perform these tasks admirably). This function could be served just as well, however, by nongovernmental institutions. In any event, the demand for the IMF's economic advice is likely to be low if it is no longer tied to qualifying for some of its loans.

The irony is that the IMF had available the ideal candidate in its deputy managing director, Stanley Fischer. Fischer not only is an outstanding economist but also has a pleasant and effective management style, together with experience at the fund. He also seemed ideal on political grounds because he was born in Africa, previously held a British passport (related to his residencies in the former British colonies of Northern and Southern Rhodesia), and now holds a U.S. passport. Apparently, Fischer's British passport was not enough to make him European, much less German. Anyway, since my opinion of the IMF's social value is unfavorable, I probably ought not to back the most capable candidate as managing director.

1. The word "abolition" in the 2nd paragraph is closest in meaning to _____

    A. elimination.

    B. disappear.

    C. abundance.

    D. advocacy.

2. What is TRUE about Alan H. Mehzer?

    A. He advocates the abolition of the IMF.

    B. He calls for the elimination of one or more of these institutions.

    C. He is the IMF's managing director.

    D. He is the leader of the International Financial Institution Advisory Commission.

3. In the 4th paragraph, what does "this function" refer to _____

    A. IMF's advisory role.

    B. Non-government institution.

    C. Qualifying for some of its loans.

    D. Short-term-liquidity assistance.

4. What happens to IMF after a lengthy public debate?

    A. Horst Kohler works as the managing director.

    B. It is abolished.

    C. Michel continues his leading over IMF.

    D. It is managed by Stanley Fisher.

5. What is the author's attitude towards Stanley Fisher as an ideal candidate?

    A. Ironical.

    B. Favorable.

    C. Negative.

    D. Neglectful

Passage 5

    Evolutionary theories. The Belgian George Iemaitre proposed the idea that about 20,000 million years ago all the matter in the universe—enough, he estimated, to make up a hundred thousand million galaxies—was all concentrated in one small mass, which he called the "primeval atom". This primeval atom exploded for some reasons, sending its matter out in all directions, and as the expansion slowed down, a steady state resulted, at which time the galaxies formed. Something then upset the balance and the universe started expanding again, and this is the state in which the universe is now. There are variations on this theory: it may be that there was no steady state. However, basically, evolutionary theories take it that the universe was formed in one place at one point in time and has been expanding ever since.

Will the universe continue to expand? It may be that the universe will expand for ever, but some astronomers believe that the expansion will slow down and finally stop. Thereafter the universe will start to contract until all the matter in it is once again concentrated at one point. Possibly the universe max' o scillate for ever in this fashion l expanding to its maximum and then contracting over again.

Developed at Cambridge by Hoyle, Cold and Bodi, the steady-state theory maintains that the universe as a whole has always looked the same and always will. As the galaxies expand away from each other, new material is formed in some ways between the galaxies and makes up new galaxies to take place of those which have receded. Thus the general distribution of galaxies remains the same. How matter could be formed in this way is hard to see, but no harder than seeing why it should all form in one place at one time.

How can we decide which of these theories is closer to the truth? The method is in principle quite simple. Since the very distant galaxies are thousands of millions of light years away, then we are seeing them as they were thousands of millions of years ago. If the evolutionary theory is correct, the galaxies were closer together in the past than they are now, and so distant galaxies ought to appear to be closer together than nearer ones. According to the steady-state theory' there should be no difference.

The evidence seems to suggest that there is a difference, that the galaxies were closer together than they are now, and so the evolutionary theory is partially confirmed and the steady-state theory—in its original form at least—must be rejected.

1. What do both theories assume to be TRUE?

    A. That new material is continually being formed.

    B. That, in time, the universe will contract.

    C. That the universe is expanding at present.

    D. That "a big bang" started the expansion.

2. According to Lemaitre, the separate galaxies formed _____

    A. during a pause in the expansion of the universe.

    B. at the time of the primeval explosion.

    C. and will continue to form for ever.

    D. about 20,000 million years ago.

3. What is the basic difference between the two classes of theories?

    A. It concerns the place and time of the formation of matter.

    B. It is whether the universe will continue to expand or not.

    C. It is the current state of the universe.

    D. The variations on evolutionary theories cause the difference.

4. According to Hoyle and his friends at Cambridge _____

   A. the explosion occurred much earlier than Lemaitre suggested.

   B. it is hard to see how matter could be formed in this way.

   C. the expansion of the universe is not a real one.

   D. new material is continually being created.

5. We see distant galaxies as they were long, long ago because _____

   A. they were close together then.

   B. the universe has always looked as the same.

   C. their light takes so long to reach us.

   D. they have traveled such a long way.

Passage 6

At 67, CEO Toshifumi Suzuki has enjoyed a distinguished career as the retailing visionary, who made Seven-Eleven Japan CO, the country's No. 1 convenience-store chain. But just when other execs would be winding down, Suzuki is gearing up for his next big challenge: to turn Seven-Eleven into an online shopping behemoth. In February, he gathered seven partners, including Sony, NEC, and Mitsui, the giant trading house, to develop e-commerce services ranging from book and ticket sales to online distribution of music and photos. By June, 7 dream. com will be a reality. "With our large network of stores and distribution base, we're attracting powerful partners," Suzuki says proudly.

Suzuki has long been a pioneer. In 1974 he opened the first konbini, as convenience stores are known in Japan. He was first to install an electronic inventory and sales system and to offer fast foods. In 1987, Seven-Eleven started accepting payments on behalf of utilities. Last year, it collected some $ 6 billion in such fees—earning commissions as well as increased traffic.

Suzuki and his partners are putting $ 375 million into 7 dream. com. The concept is simple: After placing orders on the Web, customers pick up and pay for them at any Seven-Eleven shop. Seven-Eleven attracts 2. 6 billion customers yearly—a daily average of 950 per shop. And polls show that as many as 70% of Japanese dislike using credit cards for online purchases. "The Japanese would rather pick up their goods and pay for them at a konbini," observes Morihiko Ida, head of equities research at Century Securities. "So they could boost Net sales. "

There's no guarantee the model will work. Konbini accounted for a tiny part of Japan's $ 3. 2 billion in consumer e-commerce last year. And if the idea catches on, it may not last. "In the short term, they'll be major players because of their networks," says Hirokazu Ishii, analyst at Nikko Salomon Smith Barney in Tokyo. "But the Japanese will begin using electronic cash and home delivery, like Americans."

Maybe so. But Seven-Eleven's competitors certainly aren't waiting to find out. Lawson Products Inc. the No. 2 convenience store chain, now plans an e-commerce group, as do five other chains, led by third-ranked Family Mart.

Stilt, Suzuki's allies, which include top media, travel, retail, and Net technology companies, give him an early lead. And while he has no plans to go into such activities as lending, he has drown interest from a number of prominent institutions. Suzuki isn't betting the store on his new venture. But he thinks he has at least one more big coup left in him before taking it easy.

1. Which of the following statements about Suzuki is TRUE?

    A. He has enjoyed an outstanding career and is winding down.

    B. He refuses to turn Seven-Eleven into an online shopping behemoth.

    C. He set up the first Konbini.

    D. He was last to install an electronic inventory and sales system.

2. In the 2nd sentence of the 3rd paragraph, what does the word "them" refer to?

    A. Orders.

    B. Credit cards.

    C. Customers.

    D. Suzuki's partners.

3. How will 7 dream. com work?

    A. The customers will buy goods through credit cards.

    B. Customers just place orders on the Web.

    C. Customers will pay for the goods on the Web.

    D. All of the above are included.

4. What's the reaction of Seven-Eleven's rivals towards e-commerce services?

    A. They show indifference.

    B. They are angry, about it.

    C. They are following it.

    D. They are critical about it.

5. In the last paragraph, what does the word "prominent" mean?

    A. Leading.

    B. Prohibitive.

    C. Private.

    D. Liberal.

Passage 7

In January 1995, the world witnessed the emergence of a new international economic order with the launching of the World Trade Organization. The WTO, which succeeds the GAIT, is expected to strengthen the world trading system and to be more effective than the GAIT in governing international trade in goods and service in many ways.

First, worldwide trade liberalization is expected to increase via the dramatic reductions in trade barriers to which the members of the WTO are committed. Under the WTO, members are required to reduce their tariff and non-tariffs on manufacturing goods. In addition, protecting domestic agricultural I sectors from foreign competition will become extremely difficult in the new WTO system.

Second, rules and regulations governing international trade will be more strongly enforced. Under the old system of the GAIT, (there were man), cases where trade measures, such as anti-dumping and countervailing duties, were intentionally used solely for protectionist reasons. The WTO's strenghened rules and regulations will significantly reduce the abuse of such trade measures by its member countries. The WTO is also equipped with an improved dispute settlement mechanism. Accordingly, we expect to see a more effective resolution of trade disputes among the member countries in this new trade environment.

Third, new multilateral rules have been established to cover areas which the GAIT did not address, such as international trade in services and the protection of intellectual property rights. There still are a number of problems that need to be resolved before international trade in services can be completely liberalized, and newly developed ideas or technologies are fairly compensated. However, just the establishment of multilateral rules in these new areas is a significant contribution to the progress toward a global free trade system.

Along with the hunching of the WTO, this new era in world trade is characterized by a change in the structure of the world economy. Today, a world-wide market for goods and services is rapidly replacing a world economy composed of relatively isolated national markets. Domestic financial markets have been integrated into a truly global system, and the multinational corporation is becoming a principal mechanism for allocating investment capital and determining the location of production sites throughout much of the world.

1. Between WTO and GAIT _____
    A. WTO and GAIT govern the international trade at the same time.
    B. WTO is the pre-existence of GAIT.
    C. GAIT is the pre-existence of WTO.
    D. GAIT is more effective than WTO in some aspects.

2. According to this passage, under the WTO, _____
    A. measures of anti-dumping and countervailing were solely used for protectionist reason.
    B. it is still easy to protect domestic agricultural sectors from foreign competition.
    C. the people can enjoy better life.
    D. members should reduce their tariff and non-tariff on products.

3. Which of the following is NOT true about the WTO?
    A. WTO has made good preparation for the liberation of international trade in service.
    B. WTO ensures effective settlement of trade dispute.
    C. Under GAIT, regulations concerning international trade can be more strongly enforced.
    D. WTO covers the issue of intellectual property rights.

4. It can be inferred from this passage that _____

A. under GAIT some measures can not be effectively enforced.

B. under GAIT, the intellectual property right cannot be properly protected.

C. It is not easy for a country to become a member of WTO.

D. WTO cannot change the structure of world economy totally.

5. Which can be the best title for the passage?

A. The Launching of WTO.

B. The Influence on WTO.

C. The superiority of WTO.

D. The Influence Caused by WTO.

Passage 8

Interest is steadily spreading from a minority of enthusiasts in developing renewable sources of energy-wind, wave and solar power, tidal and geothermal energy. Additional support for them has come with a proposal to explore the untapped sources of hydro-electric power in Scotland.

The details are provided by Mr. William Manser in a study provided for an expert committee to look at the developments possible for hydro-electric sites and, more important, for means of financing them.

There is a clear industrial connection in Mr. Manser's study because it was done for the Federation of Civil Engineering Contractors; hydro-electric schemes, by definition, have a large civil engineering component in them. Mr. Manser estimates that wind power could theoretically provide more than 7 percent of electricity supply in the United Kingdom, provided suitable sites for generators could be found. However, the practical viability of wind power generation is not likely to be understood until 1990.

Other developments using renewable energy sources are also at an early stage as far as their commercial possibilities are concerned, he believes.

The best developed and most suitable form of renewable energy is, in his view, hydro power. The technology has been developed over centuries and is still progressing. At present it is the cheapest form of electricity generation.

Mr. Manser studied past surveys of the north of Scotland and identified several as suitable for hydro-electric generation. Those are in the remote areas, usually of great natural beauty.

But Mr. Manser says a well-designed dam can be impressive in itself. It is also possible to make installation as unobtrusive as possible, to the point of burying parts of them. Hydro generation involves no water pollution, smoke creation or unsightly stocking-out yards.

Thee main trouble, which appears from his report, is financing an undertaking which has a heavy initial capital cost, and very low running costs.

However, Mr. Manser does not see that as an unfamiliar position for the electricity industry. He cites the proposed construction of the new nuclear power station at Sizewell in Suffolk, which will have a high initial capital cost.

The argument at Sizewell that the reason for the expenditure is that the capital will provide a benefit in lower costs and higher returns in the long-term, applies equally to hydro-electric generation.

1. The main subject of this passage is the _____

    A. conservation of energy.

    B. high costs of energy sources.

    C. recycling of resources.

    D. energy generated by waterpower.

2. From the passage we understand that Mr. Manser's study was _____

    A. presented by a financial committee.

    B. part of a civil engineering contract.

    C. commissioned by a professional organization.

    D. written in conjunction with an expert committee.

3. What drawback is there to the provision of wind power generation?

    A. The supply method is not yet understood.

    B. It's a non-viable proposition.

    C. There is a lack of suitable sites.

    D. Theoretical application is still needed.

4. The advantage of hydro-electric power is that it _____

    A. does not damage the environment.

    B. is relatively easy to install.

    C. requires little or no maintenance.

    D. is more suitable for remote areas.

5. In Mr. Manser's opinion, the main stumbling block to the development of hydro-electric power is the _____

    A. capital outlay.

    B. running cost.

    C. public expenditure.

    D. financing risk.

Passage 9

Steve Courtmey wrote historical novels. Not, he was quick to explain, overcolourful love stories of the kind that made so much money for so many women, writers, but novels set, in historical periods. Whatever difference he saw in his own books, his readers did like seem to notice it, and his readers were nearly all women. He had studied at university, but he had been a particularly good student, and he had never (afterwards let an): academic knowledge he had gained interfere with his writing.

Helen, his wife, who did not have a very high opinion of her husband's ability as a novelist, had been careful to say when she married him that She was not historically minded.

Above all, Helen was doubtful whether her relationship with Steve would work at all in the village of Stretton, to which they had just moved. It was Steve who had wanted to move to the country, and she had been glad of the change, in principle, whatever doubts she was now having about Stretton as a choice. But she wondered whether Steve would not, before very long, want to live in London again, and what she would do if he did. The Stretton house was not a weekend cottage. They had moved into it and given up the London fiat altogether, partly at least, she suspected, because that was Steve's idea of what a successful author ought to do. However, she thought he was not going to feel like a successful author half as much in Stretton as he had in London. On the other hand, she supposed he might just start dashing up to London for the day to see his agent or have lunch with his publisher, leaving her behind in Stretton, and she thought on the whole she would like that.

1. What was Steve's attitude towards women who wrote love stories?

    A. He would have liked to earn as much money as they did.

    B. He was afraid of being compared unfavourably with them.

    C. He did not think he could write about the same subjects.

    D. He had a low opinion of the kind of books they wrote.

2. What did Helen have to be careful to hide?

    A. Her lack of interest in history.

    B. Her low opinion of her husband's writing.

    C. Her dislike of her husband's admirers.

    D. Her inability to understand his books.

3. What were Helen's feelings about the move from London to Stretton?

    A. She wanted to remain in the country.

    B. She had been unwilling to leave London.

    C. She thought it was time to return to London.

    D. She would have preferred a weekend house in the country.

4. Helen thought Steve might not be content in Stretton because _____

    A. he would not be able to write so well in the country.

    B. he would not feel so important in Stretton.

    C. his relationship with Helen was changing.

    D. he would not be lonely without all his London friends.

5. The passage as a whole suggests that Steve's novels were _____

    A. popular but unimportant.

    B. Serious works of literature.

    C. Admired for their historical truth.

    D. Written with women readers in mind.

Passage 10

Opinion polls are now beginning to show that, whoever is to blame and whatever happens from now on, high unemployment is probably here to stay. This means we shall have to make ways of sharing the available employment more widely.

But we need to go further. We must ask some primary questions about the future of work. Would we continue to treat employment as the norm? Would we not rather encourage many other ways for serf respecting people to work? Should we not create conditions in which many of us can work for ourselves, rather than for an employer? Should we not aim to revive the household and the neighborhood, as well as the factor and the office, as centers of production and work?

The industrial age has been the only period of human history during which most people's work has taken the form of jobs. The industrial age may now be coming to an end, and some of the changes in work patterns which it brought may have to be reversed. This seems a daunting thought. But, in fact, it could provide the prospect of a better future for work. Universal employment, as its history shows, has not meant economic freedom.

Employment became widespread when the enclosures of the 17th and 18th centuries made many people dependent on paid work by depriving them of the use of the land, and thus of the means to provide a living for themselves. Then the factory system destroyed the cottage industries and removed work from people's homes. Later, as transportation improved, first by rail and then by road, people commuted longer distances to their places of employment until, eventually, many people's work lost all connection with their home lives and the place in which they lived.

Meanwhile, employment put women at a disadvantage. In pre-industrial time, men and women had shared the productive work of the household and village community. Now it became a custom for the husband to go out to be paid through employment, leaving the unpaid work of the home and family to his wife. Tax and benefit regulations still assume this norm today and restrict more flexible sharing of work roles between the sexes.

It was not only women whose work status suffered. As employment became the dominant form of work, young people and old people were excluded—a problem now, as more teenagers become frustrated at school and more retired people want to live active lives.

All this may now have to change. The time has certainly come to switch some effort and resources away from the idealist goal of creating jobs for all to the urgent practical task of helping many people to manage without fun time jobs.

1. Research carried out in the recent opinion polls shows that _____

    A. available employment should be restricted to a small percentage of the population.

    B. new jobs must be created in order to rectify high unemployment figures.

    C. available employment must be more widely distributed among the unemployed.

    D. the nowadays high unemployment figures are a truth of life.

2. The arrival of the industrial age in our historical evolution meant that _____

    A. universal employment virtually guaranteed prosperity.

    B. economic freedom came within everyone's control.

    C. patterns of work were fundamentally changed.

    D. people's attitudes to work had to be reversed.

3. The enclosures of the 17th and 18th centuries meant that _____

    A. people were no longer legally entitled to own land.

    B. people were driven to look elsewhere for means of supporting themselves.

    C. people were not adequately compensated for the loss of their land.

    D. people were badly paid for the work they managed to find.

4. The effects of almost universal employment were overwhelming in that _____

    A. the household and village community disappeared completely.

    B. men now travelled enormous distances to their places of work.

    C. young and old people became superfluous components of society.

    D. the work status of those not in paid employment suffered.

5. The article concludes that _____

    A. the creation of jobs for all is an impossibility.

    B. our efforts and resources in terms of tackling unemployment are insufficient.

    C. people should begin supporting themselves by learning a practical skill.

    D. we should help those whose jobs are only part-time.

Passage 11

Watching shiatsu being performed on a friend of mine reminded me of a demonstration of the deep massage technique, "rolfing", in which the patient is kneaded and twisted with knuckles and elbows. Rolfing had been likened to torture, so when it was offered to me I made my excuses. Yet the shiatsu treatment, alarming though it looked, with the patient lying down as the operator prodded pressure points, was clearly not painful, apart from an occasionally twinge. Indeed, for most of the hour-long session, the patient was patently relaxed and enjoying it.

Shiatsu is a spin-off from acupresure, itself a spin-off from acupuncture. The traditional "meridians" (or channels of life energy.) are used, as are the traditional pints on these channels all over the body, but a thumb, knuckle, or even an elbow, is used instead of a needle.

In Japan, as in China, acupressure has long been a family first-aid affair, with parents teaching children and children in due course treating grandparents. But about 50 years ago, in Japan, shiatsu begin to acquire professional Status, and there are now thousands of full-time practitioners. The theory is still basically the same: that all of us have these channels along which ki, the life energy, flows; and that if one of these pressures, on the points indicated-ascertained either by pulse-taking, or by training, experience and trench—can start the energy moving again: the blockage will be removed and the symptoms will disappear.

Not that it is essential to accept the full oriental theory to accept shiatsu. That pain in one part of the body can sometimes be removed by pressure on another part has long been known in orthodox Western circles. So, for that matter, has the ability of acupuncture to relieve pain-though the acupuncture was of a different kind. But with the march of medical science, pressure points and acupuncture, British style, faded out; and now that they art, being restored to popularity, they are for the most part provided by medically unqualified practitioners.

To try to describe shiatsu is futile; it has to be experienced. But the aim is to relax mind and body together —in fact they are treated as one. If there is an occasional twinge, it is deemed to be necessary to break down a barrier; and patients often grope for words to express the feeling that the pain has in a way been pleasurable.

Although the aim is relaxation, paradoxically the effect may be arousal. Some people may feel in the mood for sleep; but for others, the removal of muscular and emotional tensions actually makes them feel pepped up. And they come back for more—either when they feel the need has arisen, or at regular intervals as a form of preventive therapy.

1. While observing a demonstration of shiatsu, the writer realized _____
    A. that the shiatsu treatment takes much longer than rolfing.
    B. that both shiatsu and miring could cause severe, discomfort.
    C. that the whole process could be most alarming.
    D. that the whole process could be a pleasant experience.
2. Shiatsu differs from acupuncture in that _____
    A. pressure is applied to different meridians all over the body.
    B. no pressure is applied to the traditional meridians of the body.
    C. pressure is applied to the meridians of the body using different methods.
    D. pressure is applied only to the thumb, knuckle and elbow areas of file body.
3. The theory behind shiatsu is that ailments can be cured by _____
    A. the removal of a blockage in one of the life-energy channels.
    B. the discovery of the number of life-energy channels in the body.
    C. teaching people to be able to diagnose their own treatment.
    D. encourage people to prevent a blockage occurring in a life-energy channel.
4. In the West, acupuncture _____
    A. has never been recognized as a serious medical treatment.
    B. has been totally ignored by Western medical circles.
    C. is now gaining popularity as an alternative medical treatment.
    D. is now becoming a popular study for qualified practitioner.
5. Although the aim of shiatsu is to relax the mind and body together _____
    A. the occasional twinge of pain often prevents dais from happening.

B. some people find that the experience makes them more tense.

C. some people experience renewed, vigor when their treatment is effective.

D. a compulsive desire to look for other forms of treatment often occurs.

Passage 12

World leaders met recently at United Nations headquarters in New York City to discuss the environmental issues raised at the Rio Earth Summit in 1992. The heads of state were supposed to decide what further steps should be taken to halt the decline of Earth's life-support systems. In fact this meeting had much the flavor of the original Earth Summit. To wit: empty, promises, hollow rhetoric, bickering between rich and poor, and irrelevant initiatives. Think U. S. Congress in slow motion.

Almost obscured by this torpor is the fact that there has been some remarkable progress over the past five years—real changes in the attitude of ordinary – people in the Third World toward family size and a dawning realization that environmental degradation and their own well-being are intimately, and inversely linked. Almost none of this, however, has anything to do with what the bureaucrats accomplished in Rio.

Or didn't accomplish. One item on the agenda at Rio, for example, was a renewed effort to save tropical forests. (A previous UN-sponsored initiative had fallen apart when it became clear that it actually hastened deforestation.) After Rio, a UN working group came up with more than 100 recommendations that have so far gone nowhere. One proposed forestry pact would do little more than immunize wood-exporting nations against trade sanctions.

An effort to draft an agreement on what to do about the climate changes caused by CO_2 and other greenhouse gases has fared even worse. Blocked by the Bush Administration from setting mandatory limits, the UN in 1992 called on nations to voluntarily reduce emissions to 1990 levels. Several years later, it's as if Rio had never happened. A new climate treaty is scheduled to be signed this December in Kyoto, Japan, but governments still cannot agree on limits. Meanwhile, the U. S. produces 7% more CO_2 than it did in 1990, and emissions in the developing world have risen even more sharply. No one would confuse the "Rio process" with progress.

While governments have dithered at a pace that could make drifting continents impatient, people have acted. Birth-rates are dropping faster than expected, not because of Rio but because poor people are deciding on their own to limit family size. Another positive development has been a growing environmental consciousness among the poor. From slum dwellers in Karachi, Pakistan, to colonists in Rondonia, Brazil, urban poor and rural peasants alike seem to realize that they pay the biggest price for pollution and deforestation. There is cause for hope as well in the growing recognition among business people that it is not in their long-term interest to fight environmental reforms. John Browne, chief executive of British Petroleum, boldly asserted in a major speech in May that the threat of climate change could no longer be ignored.

1. The writer's general attitude towards the world leaders meeting at the UN is _____

A. supportive.

B. impartial.

C. critical.

D. optimistic.

2. What does the author say about the ordinary-people in the Third World countries?

A. They are beginning to realize the importance of environmental protection.

B. They believe that many children are necessary for prosperity.

C. They are reluctant to accept advice from the government.

D. They think that earning a living is more important than nature conservation.

3. What did the UN call on nations to do about CO_2 and other greenhouse gases in 1992 _____

A. To sign a new climate treaty at Rio.

B. To draft an agreement among UN nations.

C. To force the United States to reduce its emissions.

D. To cut the release of CO_2 and other gases.

4. The word "deforestation" in paragraph 3 means _____

A. forest damage caused by pollution.

B. moving population from forest to cities.

C. the threat of climate change.

D. cutting large areas of tress.

5. Which of the following best summarizes the text?

A. As the UN hesitates, the poor take actions.

B. Progress in environmental protection has been made since the Rio Summit.

C. Climate changes can no longer be ignored.

D. The decline of earth's life-support systems has been halted.

Passage 13

In recent years, there has been a steady assault on salt from the doctors: salt is bad for you—regardless of your health. Politicians also got on board. "There is a direct relationship," US congressman Neal Smith noted, "between the amount of sodium a person consumes and heart disease, circulator disorders, stroke and even early death".

Frightening, if tree! But many doctors and medical researchers are now beginning to feel the salt scare has gone too far. "All this hue and cry about eating salt is unnecessary." Dr Dustan insists. "For most of us it probably doesn't make much difference how much salt we eat." Dustan's most recent short-term study of 150 people showed that those with normal blood pressure experienced no change at all when placed on an extremely low-salt diet, or later when, salt was reintroduced. Of the hypertensive subjects, however, half of those on the low-salt diet did experience a drop in blood pressure, which returned Io its previous level when salt was reintroduced.

"An adequate to somewhat excessive salt intake has probably saved many more lives than it has cost in the general population," notes Dr. John H. Laragh. "So a recommendation that the whole population should avoid salt makes no sense."

Medical experts agree that everyone should practice reasonable "moderation" in salt consumption. For the average person, a moderate amount might run from four to ten grams a day, or roughly 1/2 to 1/3 of a teaspoon. The equivalent of one to two grams of this salt allowance would come from the natural sodium in food. The rest would be added in processing, preparation or at the table.

Those with kidney, liver or heart problems may have to limit dietary salt, if their doctor advises. But even the very word "low salt" exponent, Dr. Arthur Hull Hayes, Jr. admits that "we do not know whether increased sodium consumption causes hypertension." In fact, there is glowing scientific evidence that other factors may be involved: deficiencies in calcium, potassium, perhaps magnesium; obesity (much more dangerous than sodium); genetic predisposition; stress.

"It is not your enemy," says Dr. Laragh. "salt is the No. 1 natural component of all human tissue. and the idea that you don't need it is wrong. Unless your doctor has proven that you have a salt-related health problem, there is no reason to give it up."

1. According to some doctors and politicians, the amount of salt consumed _____

    A. exhibits as an aggravating factor to people in poor health.

    B. cures diseases. such as stroke and circulator?

    C. correlates highly with some diseases.

    D. is irrelevant to people suffering from heart disease.

2. From Dr. Dustan's study we can inter that _____

    A. a low-salt diet may be prescribed for some people.

    B. the amount of salt intake has nothing to do with one's blood pressure.

    C. the reduction of salt intake can cure a hypertensive patient.

    D. an extremely low-salt diet makes no difference to anyone.

3. In the third paragraph, Dr. Laragh implies that _____

    A. people should not be afraid of taking excessive salt.

    B. doctors should not advise people to avoid sail.

    C. an adequate to excessive sail intake is recommended for people in disease.

    D. excessive salt intake has claimed victims in the general population.

4. The phrase "vocal ... exponent" (line 2 para. 5) most probably refers Io _____

    A. eloquent doctor.

    B. articulate opponent.

    C. loud speaker.

    D. strong advocate.

5. What is the main message of this text?

A. That the salt scare is not justified.

B. That the cause of hypertension is now understood.

C. That the moderate use of salt is recommended.

D. That salt consumption is to be promoted.

Passage 14

A scientist who does research in economic psychology and who wants to predict the way in which consumers will spend their money must study consumer behavior. He must obtain data both on resources of consumers and on the motives that tend to encourage or discourage money spending.

If an economist was asked which of three groups borrow most—people with rising incomes, stable incomes or declining income—he would probably answer: those with declining incomes. Actually, in the year 1947-1950, the answer was people with rising income. People with declining incomes were next and people with stable incomes borrowed the least. This shows us that traditional assumptions about earning and spending are not always reliable. Another traditional assumption is that if people who have money expect prices to go up, they will hasten to buy. If they expect prices to go down, they will postpone buying. But research surveys have shown that this is not always true. The expectations of price increases may not stimulate buying. One typical attitude was expressed by the wife of a mechanic in an interview at a time of rising prices. "In a few months," she said, "we will have to pay more for meat and milk, we will have less to spend on other things." Her family had been planning to buy a new car but they postponed this purchase. Furthermore, the rise in prices that has already taken place may be resented and buyer's resistance may be evoked. This is shown by the following typical comment: "I just don't pay these prices, they are too high."

The investigations mentioned above were carried out in America. Investigations conducted at the same time in Great Britain, however, yielded results more in agreement with traditional assumptions about saving and spending patterns. The condition most conductive to spending appears to be price stability. If prices have been stable and people consider that they are reasonable, they are likely to buy, thus, it appears that the Common business policy of maintaining stable prices is based on a correct understanding of consumer psychology.

1. According to the passage, if one wants to predict the way consumers will spend their money, he should _____

    A. rely on traditional assumptions about earning and spending.

    B. try to encourage or discourage consumers to spend money.

    C. carry out investigations on consumer money spending motives.

    D. do researches in consumer psychology in a lab.

2. According to the passage, research surveys have proved that _____

    A. price increases always stimulate people to hasten to buy things.

B. rising of prices may make people out of their purchase of certain things.

C. women are more sensitive to the rising in prices than men.

D. the expectations of price increases often make buyers feel angry.

3. The results of the investigation on consumer psychology carried out in America were _____ those of the investigations made at the same time in Great Britain.

   A. somewhat different from

   B. is exactly the same as

   C. much better than

   D. not as good as

4. From the results of the surveys, the writer of this article _____

   A. concludes that the saving and spending patterns in Great Britain are better than those in America.

   B. concludes the consumers always expect prices to remain stable.

   C. concludes that maintaining stable prices is a correct business policy.

   D. does not draw any conclusion.

5. Which of the following statement is always TRUE according to the surveys mentioned in the assage?

   A. Consumers will put off buying things if they expect prices to decrease.

   B. Consumers will spend their money quickly if they expect prices to increase.

   C. The price condition has an influence on consumer behavior.

   D. Traditional assumptions about earning and spending are reliable.

Passage 15

Travel is at its best a solitary enterprise: to see, to examine, to assess, you have to be alone and unencumbered. Other people can mislead you; they crowd your meandering impressions with their own; if they are companionable they obstruct your view, and if they are boring they corrupt the silence with non-sequiturs, shattering your concentration with "Oh, look, it's mining," and "You see a lot of trees here".

Traveling on your own can be terribly lonely (and it is not understood by Japanese who, coming across you smiling wistfully at an acre of Mexican butter cups tend to say things like "Where is the rest of your team?"). I think of evening in the hotel room in the strange city. My diary has been brought up to date; I hanker for company; what do I do? I don't know anyone here, so I go out and walk and discover the three streets of the town and rather envy the strolling couples and the people with children. The museums and churches are closed, and toward midnight the streets are empty. If I am mugged. I will have to apologize as politely as possible: "I am sorry. sir, but I have nothing valuable on my person." Is there a surer way of enraging a thief and driving him to violence?

It is hard to see clearly or to think straight in the company of other people. Not only do I feel serf-conscious, but the perceptions that are necessary to writing are difficult to manage when someone close by is thinking out loud. I am diverted, but it is discovery, not diversion, that I seek. What is required is the lucidity of loneliness to capture that vision, which, however banal, seems in my private mood to be special and worthy of interest. There is something in feeling object that quickens my mind and makes it intensely receptive to furtive might also be verified and refined; and in any case I had the satisfaction of finishing the business alone. Travel is not a vacation, and it is often the opposite of a rest. "Have a nice time."

People said to me at my send-off at South Station, Medford. It was not precisely what I had hoped for. I craved a little risk, some danger, an untoward event, a vivid discomfort, an experience of my own company, and in a modest way the romance of solitude. This I thought might be mine on that train to Limon.

1. Traveling companions are a disadvantage, according to the writer, because they _____
    A. give you the wrong impression about the journey.
    B. I distract you from your reading.
    C. intrude on your private observations.
    D. prevent you from saving what you think.

2. It has been assumed by Japanese that he _____
    A. belongs to a group of botanists.
    B. is excessively odd to travel alone.
    C. needs to be directed to his hotel.
    D. has wandered away from his pare.

3. His main concern in the evenings was to _____
    A. take some physical exercise.
    B. avoid being robbed in the street.
    C. overcome his loneliness.
    D. explore the sights of the city.

4. The writer regards his friends' farewell to him as _____
    A. inappropriate.
    B. unsympathetic.
    C. tactless.
    D. cynical.

5. We gather from the passage that his main purpose in traveling was to _____
    A. test his endurance.
    B. prove his self-sufficiency.
    C. experience adventure.
    D. respond to new experiences.

Passage 16

It can be shown in facts and figures that cycling is the cheapest, most convenient, and most environmentally desirable form of transport in towns, but such cold calculations do not mean much on a frosty winter morning. The real appeal of cycling is that it is so enjoyable. It has none of the difficulties and tensions of other ways of traveling so you are more cheerful after a ride, even through the rush hour.

The first thing a non-cyclist says to you is: "But isn't it terribly dangerous?" It would be foolish to deny the danger of sharing the road with motor vehicles and it must be admitted that there is an alarming number of accidents involving cyclists. However, although police records indicate that the ear driver is often to blame, the answer lies with the cyclist. It is possible to ride in such a way as to reduce risks to a minimum.

If you decide to join the thousands in Britain who are now returning to cycling as a cheap, satisfying form of transport your first problem will be trying to decide what bike to buy. Here are three simple rules for buying a bike:

1. Always buy the best you can afford. Of course there has to be a meeting point between what you would really like and economic reality, but aim as high as you can and you will get the benefit not only when you ride but also if you want to sell. Well-made bikes keep their value very well. And don't forget to include in your calculations the fact that you'll begin saving money on fares and petrol the minute you leave the shop.

2. Get the best frame, the main structure of the bicycle, for your money as you can. Cheap brakes, wheels or gears can easily be replaced by more expensive ones, but the frame sets the upper limit on any transformation. You should allow for the possibility that your cycling ambitions will grow with practice. When you begin, the four miles to work may be the most you ever dream of, but after a few months a Sunday ride into the country begins to look more and more desirable. The best thing is to buy a bike just a little bit better than you think you'll need, and then grow into it. Otherwise try to get a model that can be improved.

3. The fit is vital. Handlebars and seat height can be adjusted but you must get the right sized frame. On the whole it is best to get the largest size you can manage. Frame sizes are measured in inches and the usual adult range is from 21 inches to 25 inches, though extreme sizes outside those measurements can be found. Some people say if you take four inches off from your inside leg measurement you will end up with the right size of bike. The basic principle thought is that you should be able to stand with legs at either side of the crossbar (the bar that goes from the handlebars to the seat) with both feet comfortably flat on the ground.

1. As regards to road safety, the author thinks that _____

    A. people who say cycling is dangerous are foolish.

    B. driving is as dangerous as cycling.

C. cyclists can often avoid accidents by riding with caution.

D. cyclists are usually responsible for causing accident.

2. People were are buying their first bicycle are advised to _____

A. buy a cheap model to begin with.

B. get a bicycle which suits their current needs.

C. buy a, big a bicycle as they can afford.

D. spend as much money on a bicycle as they can.

3. After you have been cycling for a few months the author suggests that you will _____

A. want to ride only at weekends.

B. want to ride further than you first imagined.

C. find riding to work every, day boring.

D. find cycling in towns less dangerous.

4. The author says that the best way to ensure that a bike is the right size for you is to _____

A. alter the position of the handlebars and the seat.

B. measure the distance from the handlebars to the seat carefully.

C. take your leg measurements while sitting on the seat.

D. see if your feet rest firmly on the ground when you stand over the crossbar.

5. The author thinks that the main attraction of cycling is _____

A. the pleasure it gives people.

B. the benefits to people's health.

C. its comparative safety.

D. its relative comfort.

Passage 17

Few people doubt the fundamental importance of mother, in childrearing, but what do fathers do? Much of what they contribute is simply the result of being a second adult in the home. Bringing up children is demanding, stressful mid exhausting. Two adults can support and make up for each other's deficiencies and build on each other's strengths.

Fathers all so bring an array of unique qualities. Some are familiar: protector and role model. Teenage boys without fathers are notoriously prone to trouble. The pathway to adulthood for daughter is somewhat easier, but they must still learn from their fathers, in ways they cannot from their mothers, how to relate to men. They learn from their fathers about heterosexual trust, intimacy and difference. They learn to appreciate their own femininity from the one male who is most special in their lives. Most important, through loving and being loved by their fathers, they learn that they are love-worthy.

Current research gives much deeper—and more surprising—insight into the father's role in childrearing. One significantly overlooked dimension of fathering is play. From their children's birth through adolescence, fathers tend to emphasize play more than care-taking. The father's style of play is likely to be both physically stimulating and exciting. With older children it involves more teamwork, requiring competitive testing of physical and mental skills. It frequently resembles a teaching relationship: come on, let me show you how. Mothers play more at the child's level. They seem willing to let the child direct play.

Kids, at least in the early years, seem to prefer to play with daddy. In one study of 2-year-olds who were given a choice, more than two-thirds chose to play with their fathers.

The way fathers play has effects on everything from the management of emotions to intelligence and academic achievement. It is particularly important in promoting self-control. According to one expert, children who roughhouse with their fathers quickly learn that biting, kicking and other forms of physical violence are not acceptable. "They learn when to shut it down."

At play and in other realms, fathers tend to stress competition, challenge, initiative, risk-taking and independence. Mothers, as caretakers, stress emotional security and personal safety. On the playground fathers often try to get the children to swing ever higher, while mothers are cautious, worrying about an accident.

We know, too, that fathers' involvement seems to be linked to improved verbal and problem-solving skills and higher academic achievement. Several studies found that along with paternal strictness, the F amount of time fathers spent reading with them was a strong predictor of their daughters' verbal ability.

For sons the results have been equally striking. Studies uncovered a strong relationship between fathers' involvement and the mathematical abilities of their sons. Other studies found a relationship between paternal nurturing and boys' verbal intelligence.

1. The first paragraph points out that one of the advantages of a family with both parents is

   _____

   A. husband and wife can share housework.

   B. two adults are always better than one.

   C. the fundamental importance of mothers can be fully , recognized.

   D. husband and wife can compensate for each other's shortcomings.

2. According to paragraph 3, one significant difference between tile father's and mother's role in child-rearing is _____

   A. the style of play encouraged.

   B. the amount of time available.

   C. the strength of emotional ties.

   D. the emphasis of intellectual development.

3. Which of the following statements is TRUE?

   A. Mothers tend to stress personal safety less than fathers.

   B. Boys are likely to benefit more from their fathers' caring.

   C. Girls learn to read more quickly with the help of their fathers.

   D. Fathers tend to encourage creativeness and independence.

4. Studies investigating fathers' involvement in child-rearing show that _____

   A. this improves kids' mathematical and verbal abilities.

B. the more time spent with kids, the better they speak.

C. the more strict the fathers are, the cleverer the kids.

D. girls usually do better than boys academically.

5. The writer's main point in writing this article is _____

    A. to warn society of increasing social problems.

    B. to emphasize the father's role in the family.

    C. to discuss the responsibilities of fathers.

    D. to show sympathy for one-parent families.

Passage 18

Insurance is supposed to provide protection against financial rises, and while dying too soon is one major risk we face, another risk more and more people fear is outliving their money. As a result, a growing array of life insurance products make it possible to protect against both of those risks.

In many of today's life insurance products, MacDonald notes, "The death benefit portion really has become a commodity type product, so if someone is really concerned about the financial impact of dying young, then they can get a pretty, good deal by buying term insurance on a commodity basis—find the cheapest policy and buy it." But, he says, "The other side of the coin is that insurance companies have developed products that can be very creative, and very competitive to other alternatives, including investments. They can fill a very important role in any overall investment plan."

Variable and universal policies offer people choices in how much they want to put into their policies and how they want their funds invested. These funds can then be tapped later on to provide a lump sum for purchasing a retirement home or a stream of retirement income. Life insurance is an attractive investment vehicle, because the "inside buildup," the accumulation of funds, inside a policy structure, is not subject to taxes, in contrast to other personal investments.

However, MacDonald and others warn against using insurance policies purely as an investment.

While there are tax advantages, there are also the costs associated with the insurance coverage and if you don't need that coverage these can be expensive ways to invest.

Moreover, MacDonald notes that some companies are offering insurance that has a critical illness or long-term care benefit. These policies specify that if someone suffers a heart attack, for example, they will get 25% of the face amount of the insurance policy immediately rather than at death. Or if they must be confined to a nursing home, they will be able to use up to the face amount of the policy to pay the nursing home costs.

Amid the proliferation of insurance product, MacDonald says, "The positive side of it is there are better products they're cheaper and more flexible. The downside is that it's more complicated and easier to make a mistake. In the past, it was plain vanilla: everybody was selling the same product and everybody had to find an agent they liked. Now there has been significant changes in product structure and design, and benefits, and so it is worthwhile to shop around.

1. The purpose of insurance is to _____

    A. give you money whenever you need.

    B. keep you from financial risks.

    C. save money.

    D. outlive money.

2. What does the underlined word "they" in paragraph 2 refer to?

    A. creative and competitive insurance products.

    B. insurance companies.

    C. other alternatives.

    D. investments.

3. What advantage will there be if one buys life insurance instead of making other investments?

    A. He will have money to a retirement home.

    B. It will cost him nothing if he buys an life insurance.

    C. Profit he earns from insurance is tax-free.

    D. It is cheap to buy an life insurance.

4. What does MacDonald warn people when they intend to buy life insurance products?

    A. It is expensive to make investment on life insurance products.

    B. Some insurance has some specific terms.

    C. Some insurance companies will not provide satisfactory terms.

    D. People should not use insurance policies purely as an investment.

5. Which of the following statements is TRUE about insurance products?

    A. People have no choice when it comes to buying insurance products.

    B. There are so many choices in insurance products that people find it difficult to make a decision.

    C. Thee are no better and cheaper insurance products.

    D. It is better for people to have so many insurance products to choose.

Passage 19

Visitors to St Paul's Cathedral are sometimes astonished as they walk round the space under the dome to come upon a statue which would appear to be that of a retired gladiator meditating upon a wasted life. They are still more astonished when they see under it an inscription indicating that it represents the English writer, Samuel Johnson. The statue is by Bacon, but it is not one of his best works. The figure is, as often in eighteenth-century sculpture, clothed only in a loose robe which leaves arms, legs and one shoulder bare. But the strangeness for us is not one of costume only. If we know anything of Johnson, we know that he was constantly ill all through his life; and whether we know anything of him or not we are apt to think of a literary man as a delicate, weak, nervous sort of person. Nothing can be further from that than the muscular statue. And in this matter the statue is perfectly fight. And the fact which it reports is far from being unimportant. The body and the mind are inextricably interwoven in all of us, and certainly on Johnson's case the influence of the body was obvious and conspicuous. His melancholy, his constantly repeated conviction of the general unhappiness of human life, was certainly the result of his constitutional infirmities. On the other hand, his courage, and his entire indifference to pain, were partly due to his great bodily strengh. Perhaps the vein of rudeness, almost of fierceness, which sometimes showed itself in his conversation, was the natural temper of an invalid and suffering giant. That at any rate is what he was. He was the victim from childhood of a disease which resembled St Vitus's Dance. He never knew the natural joy of a free and vigorous use of his limbs; when he walked it was like the struggling walk of one in irons. All accounts agree that his strange gesticulations and contortations were painful for his friends to witness and attracted crowds of starers in the streets. But Reynolds says that he could sit still for his portrait to be taken, and that when his mind was engaged by a conversation the convulsions ceased. In any case, it is certain that neither this perpetual misery, nor his constant feat of losing his reason, nor his many grave attacks of illness, ever induced him to surrender the privileges that belonged to his physical strengh. He justly thought no character so disagreeable as that of a chronic invalid, and was determined not to be one himself. He had known what it was to live on four pence a day and scorned the life of sofa cushions and tea into which well-attended old gentlemen so easily slip.

1. We understand from the passage that most eighteenth-century sculpture was _____

    A. done by a man called Bacon.

    B. not very well made.

    C. loosely draped.

    D. left bare.

2. "The body and the mind are inextricably interwoven" means they _____

    A. have little effect on each other.

    B. are confused by all of us.

    C. interact with each other.

    D. are mixed up in all of us.

3. The author says Johnson found it very difficult to walk because _____

    A. he couldn't control his legs.

    B. he generally wore irons round his legs.

    C. people always stared at him.

    D. it hurt his friends to watch him.

4. Because Johnson was very strong physically he could _____

    A. expect to become insane.

    B. endure a lot of pain.

    C. claim certain benefits.

    D. experience great unhappiness.

5. According to the passage, Johnson had _____

    A. never had enough money to live on.

B. managed to live on tea only.

C. lived frugally in the past.

D. always lived in easy circumstances.

Passage 20

Recent research has claimed that an excess of positive ions in the air have an ill-effect on people's physical or psychological health. What are positive ions? Well, the air is full of ions, electrically charged particles. But sometimes this balance becomes disturbed and a larger proportion of positive ions are found. This happens naturally before thunderstorms, earthquakes or when winds such as the Mistral, Foehn, Hamsin or Sharav are blowing in certain countries. Or it can be caused by a build-up of static electricity indoors from carpets or clothing made of man-made fibers, or from TV sets, duplicators or computer display screens.

When a large number of positive ions are present in the air, many people experience unpleasant effects such as headaches, fatigue, irritability, and some particularly sensitive people suffer nausea or even mental disturbance. Animals are also found to be affected, particularly before earthquakes; snakes have been observed to come out of hibernation, rats to flee from their burrows; dogs howl and cats jump about unaccountably. This has led the US Geographical Survey to fund a network of volunteers to watch animals in an effort to foresee such disasters before they hit vulnerable areas such as California.

Conversely, when large numbers of negative ions are present, then people have a feeling of well being. Natural conditions that produce these large amounts are near the sea, close to waterfalls fountains, or in any place where water is sprayed, or forms a spray. This probably accounts for the beneficial effect of a holiday by the sea, or in the mountains with tumbling streams or waterfalls.

To increase the supply of negative ions indoors, some scientists recommend the use of ionizes: small portable machines which generate negative ions. They claim that ionizes not only clean and refresh the air but also improve the health of people sensitive to excess positive ions. Of course, there are the detractors, other scientists, who dismiss such claims and are skeptical about negative/positive ion research. Therefore people can only make up their own minds by observing the effects on themselves, or on others, of a negative rich or poor environment. After all, it is debatable whether depending on seismic readings to anticipate earthquake is more effective than watching the cat.

1. What effect does excessive positive ionization have on some people?

    A. They think they are insane.

    B. They feel rather bad-tempered.

    C. They become violently sick.

    D. They are too tired to do anything.

2. According to the passage, static electricity can be caused by _____

A. using home-made electric goods.

B. wearing clothes made of natural materials.

C. walking on artificial floor coverings.

D. copying TV programs on a computer.

3. By observing the behavior of animals, scientists may be able to _____

    A. prevent disasters.

    B. organize groups of people.

    C. predict earthquakes.

    D. control areas of California.

4. A high negative ion count is likely to be found _____

    A. near a pond with a water pump.

    B. close to a slow-flowing fiver.

    C. high in some barren mountains.

    D. by a rotating water sprinkler.

5. People should be able to come to a decision about ions in the air if the _____

    A. note their own reactions.

    B. move to a healthier area.

    C. observe domestic animals.

    D. watch how healthy people behave.

Passage 21

The man behind this notion, Jack Maple, is a dandy who affects dark glasses, homburgs and two-toe shoes; yet he has become something of a legend in America's police departments. For some years, starting in New York and moving on to high-crime spots such as New Orleans and Philadelphia, he and his business partner, John Linder have marketed a two-tier system for cutting crime.

First, police departments have to sort themselves out: root out corruption, streamline their bureaucracy, and make more contact with the public. Second, they have to adopt a computer system called Comstat which helps them to analyze statistics on all major crimes. These are constantly keyed into the computer, which then displays where and when the, have occurred on a color-coded map, enabling the police to monitor crime trends as they happen and to spot high-crime areas. In New York, Comstat's statistical maps are analyzed each week at a meeting of the city's police chief and precinct captains.

Maple and Linder("specialists in crime-reduction services") have no doubt that their system is a main contributor to the drop in crime. When they introduced it in New Orleans in January 1997, violent crime dropped by 22% in a year; when they merely started working informally with the police department in Newark, New Jersey, violent crime fell by 13%. Police departments are now lining up to pay as much as $ 50,000 a month for these two men to put them straight.

It is probable that all these new policies and bits of technical wizardry, added together, have made a big difference to crime. But there remain anomalies that cannot be explained, such as the fact that crime in Washington D. C. has fallen very fast, although the police department has been corrupt and hopeless and, in large "stretches of the city, neither police nor residents seem disposed to fight the criminals in their midst.

The larger reason for the fall in crime rates, many say, is a much less sophisticated one. It is a fact that crime rates have dropped as the imprisonment rate soared. In 1997 the national incarceration rate, at 645 per 100,000 people; was more than double the rate in 1985, and the number of inmates in city and country jails rose by 9.4%, almost double its annual average increase since 1990. Surely some criminologists argue, one set of figures is the cause of the other. It is precisely because more people are being sent to prison, they claim that crime rates are falling. A 1993 study by the National Academy of Sciences actually concluded that the tripling of the prison population between 1975 and 1989 had reduced violent crime by 10-15%.

Yet cause and effect may not be so obviously linked. To begin with, the sale and possession of drugs are at counted by file FBI in its crime index, which is limited to violent crimes and crimes against property. Yet drug offences account for more than a third of the recent increase in the number of those jailed; since 1980, the incarceration rate for drug arrests has increased by 100, aad although about three-quarters of those going to prison for drug offences have committed other crimes as well, there is not vet a crystal-clear connection between filling the jails with drug-pushers and a decline in the rate of violent crime. Again, though national figures are suggestive, local ones diverge: the places where crime has dropped most sharply (such as New York city) are not always the places where incarceration has risen fastest.

1. Jack Maple started his career in _____

　　A. Philadelphia.

　　B. Orleans.

　　C. New Orleans.

　　D. New York.

2. According to Jack Maple, to cut crime _____

　　A. the heads of police department should make more contact with the criminals.

　　B. the government should educate the residents more.

　　C. a computer system called Comstat should be adopted by the police.

　　D. the criminals should be severely punished.

3. In New York _____

　　A. violent crime dropped by 23% in one year.

　　B. police department pay as much as $50,000 for Jack Maple.

　　C. the crime rate is high.

　　D. Comstat's statistical maps are analyzed ever " week".

4. The meaning of the word "anomaly" in the second line of 4th paragraph is _____

　　A. something strange.

　　B. enjoyable things.

C. anomy.

D. comparison.

5. It can be inferred from the passage that _____

    A. the drop of crime rate is caused by Jack Maples's two-tier system.

    B. the drop of crime rate is caused by the increased imprisonment.

    C. it is difficult to identify the exact cause for the fall of crime rate.

    D. the increased imprisonment is not the reason for the fall of crime rate.

Passage 22

Statistically, each of these new changes in law-enforcement has made some difference to the picture. Yet it seems probably that the factors that have really brought the crime rates down have little to do with policemen or politicians, and more to do with cycles that are beyond their control.

The first of these is demographic. The fall in the crime rate has coincided with fall in the number of young men between the ages of 15 and 21, the peak age for criminal activity in any society, including America. In the same way, the rise in the crime rate that started in the early 1960s coincided with the teenage years of the baby-boomers. As the boomer generation matured, married, found jobs and shoulder mortgages, so the crime rate fell.

This encouraging trend was quickly overshadowed, starting in the mid-1980s, by a new swarm of teenagers caught up in a new sort of depravity: the craze for crack cocaine. Crack brought with it much higher levels of violence and, in particular, soaring rates of handgun murders by people less than 25 years old. Yet the terror became too much, and the young began to leave crack alone. Within a few years, at least in most big cities, the drug market had stabilized and settled, even moving indoors; the tuff-wars were over, and crack itself had become past. Studies of Brooklyn by Richard Curtis, of the John Jay College of Criminal Justice, show the clear connection; around 1992, many young bloods decided to drop the dangerous life of the street in favor of steady jobs. In direct consequence, the local crime rate fell .

Murder rates among Americans older than 25 had already been declining since 1980. Here, according to Alfred Blumstein, a professor of criminology at Carnegie-Mellon University, there may be even longer term social factors involved. In an age of easy divorce and more casual relationships, men and women are less likely to murder their partners: between 1976 and 1996, such murders fell by 40%. The decline in alcohol consumption, too, means that fewer bar-room brawls leave a litter of corpses on a Friday night.

It seems that changing social trends also sometimes lie behind the fall in property crime. Burglars tend not to steal television sets now because almost everyone has one; their value on the street has plummeted, At the same time, the fact that people stay in watching their sets, rather than going out, deters would be burglars. Extra garages are standard in the suburbs, to safeguard extra cars; credit cards mean that shoppers carry less cash in their pockets; people working from home, by means of computers, can keep a closer watch over their streets.

Lastly, people are going to greater lengths to protect themselves and their property than they did in the past. This is partly because of the huge fear of crime that preceded the present decline, and partly because even with recent increases in the number of policemen—the ratio of police to violent crimes reported is still wax below what it was in the 1960s.

1. This passage mainly concerns about _____
   A. the factors influencing the crime rate.
   B. the demographic causing the fall of crime rate.
   C. murder rate becoming lower.
   D. the effort of people to fight against crime.

2. In early 1970s the crime rate was _____
   A. the same as that in early 1960s.
   B. lower than that in early 1960s.
   C. higher than that in mid-1980s.
   D. the same as that in mid-1980s.

3. Murder rate among Americans older than 25 declined because _____
   A. they married and found jobs.
   B. they had to shoulder mortgage.
   C. they were in an age of easy divorce.
   D. they made great effort to protect themselves.

4. The word plummet in the 2nd line of the 5th paragraph means _____
   A. drop.
   B. disappear.
   C. enhance.
   D. stabilize.

5. Why do people make greater efforts to protect themselves?
   A. Because they fear the crime preceding the present decline.
   B. Because the policeman has become fewer.
   C. Because they were taught to do so.
   D. Because their extra garage are standard in the suburb.

Passage 23

Throughout history there have been many unusual taxes levied on such things as hats, beds, baths, marriages, and funerals. At one time England levied a tax on sunlight by collecting from every household with six or more windows. And according to legend, there was a Turkish ruler who collected a tax each time he dined with one of his subjects. Why? To pay for the wear and tear on his teeth!

Different kinds of taxes help to spread the tax burden. Anyone who pays a tax is said to "bear the burden" of the tax. The burden of a tax may fall more heavily on some persons than on others. That is why the three levels of government in this country, use several kinds of taxes. This spreads the burden of taxes among more-people. From the standpoint of their use, the most important taxes are income taxes, property taxes, sales taxes, and estate, inheritance, and gift taxes. Some are used by only one level of government: others by or even all three levels. Together these different taxes make up what is called our tax system.

Income taxes are the main source of federal revenues. The federal government gets more than three-fourths of its revenue from income taxes. As its name indicated, an income tax is a tax on earnings. Both individuals and business corporations pay a federal income tax.

The oldest tax in the United States today is the property tax. It provides most of the income for local governments. It provides at least a part of the income for all but a few states. It is not used by the federal government.

A sales tax is a tax levied on purchases. Most people living in the United States know about sales taxes since they are used in all but four states. Actually there are several kinds of sales taxes, but only three of them are important. They are general sales taxes, excise taxes, and import taxes.

Other three closely related taxes are estate, inheritance, and gift taxes. Everything a person owns, including both real and personal property, makes up his or her estate. When someone dies, ownership of his or her property or estate passes on to one or more individuals or organizations. Before the property is transferred, however, it is subject to an estate tax if its value exceeds a certain amount.

1. The reason that the Turkish ruler collected a dining tax is to pay for _____
   A. the inconvenience for him to put on and take off clothes.
   B. the damage that eating did to his teeth.
   C. his efforts to cut the focal into pieces.
   D. the decay of his teeth because of sugar.

2. The government levies different kinds of taxes so that _____
   A. the rich have to pay more and the poor less.
   B. a wider range of taxpayers can be included.
   C. each of three levels of government could get tax money.
   D. the burden of taxes falls evenly on everybody.

3. The federal government get most of their income from _____
   A. property tax.
   B. income tax.
   C. sales tax.
   D. estate tax.

4. How many states have import taxes in the U. S. A?
   A. 4.
   B. 50.
   C. 46.
   D. 54.

5. Which of the following statements is NOT true?

    A. Any form of property is subject to an estate tax when transferred:

    B. Property tax provides a part of income for local government.

    C. There are a few kinds of sales taxes.

    D. Individuals and corporations both pay income taxes.

Passage 24

The idea of a fish being able to produce electricity strong enough to light lamp bulbs—or even to run a small electric motor—is almost unbelievable, but several kinds of fish are able to do this. Even more strangely, this curious power has been acquired in different ways by fish belonging to very different families.

Perhaps the most known are the electric rays, or torpedoes, of which several kinds live in warm seas. They possess on each side of the head, behind the eyes, a large organ consisting of a number of hexagonal-shaped ceils rather like a honeycomb. The cells are filled with a jelly-like substance, and contain a series of flat electric plates. One side, the negative side, of each plate, is supplied with very fine nerves, connected with a main nerve coming form a special part of the brain. Current gets through from the upper, positive side of the organ downward to the negative, lower side. Generally it is necessary to touch the fish in two places, completing the circuit, in order to receive a shock.

The strength of this shock depends on the size of fish, but newly-born ones only about 5 centimeters across can be made to light the bulb of a pocket flashlight for a few moments, while a fully grown torpedo gives a shock capable of knocking a man down, and, if suitable wires are connected, will operate a small electric motor for several minutes.

Another famous example is the electric eel. This fish gives an even more powerful shock. The system is different from that of the torpedo in that the electric plates run-longitudinally and are supplied with nerves from the spinal cord. Consequently, the current passes along the fish from head to tail. The electric organs of these fish are really altered muscles and like all muscles are apt to tire, so they are not able to generate electricity for very long. People in some parts of South America who value the electric eel as food, take advantage of this fact by driving homes into the water against which the fish discharges their electricity. The horses are less affected than a man would be, and when the electric eels have exhausted themselves, they can be caught without danger.

The electric catfish of the Nile and of other African fresh waters has a different system again by which current passes over the whole body from the tail to the head. The shock given by this arrangement is not so strong as the other two, but is none the less unpleasant. The electric catfish is a slow, lazy fish, fond of gloomy places and grow to about 1 meter long: it is eaten by the Arabs in some areas.

The power of producing electricity may serve these fish both for defense and attack. If a large enemy attacks, the shock will drive it away; but it appears that the catfish and the electric eel use their current most often against smaller fish, stunning them so that they can easily be overpowered.

1. Which of the following can produce the strongest shock?

   A. The electric eel.

   B. The electric catfish.

   C. The newly-born electric torpedoes.

   D. The fully-grown electric ms'.

2. Why are horses used when people try to catch the electric eels?

   A. to frighten the eels.

   B. to exhaust the eels.

   C. to attract the eels.

   D. to stir the water.

3. The electric catfish has a different electric system in that _____

   A. current moves from the head to the tail.

   B. current moves from the tail to the head.

   C. current moves from the left to the right.

   D. current moves from the right to the left.

4. Which of the following statements is NOT true?

   A. Electric fish come from different families.

   B. One can get a shock by touching the electric rays in two places.

   C. The electric plates in the rays are connected with the spinal cord.

   D. The electric catfish and eels are edible.

5. The language of the passage is mostly _____

   A. descriptive.

   B. narrative.

   C. expositive.

   D. critic.

Passage 25

Among the possessions my mother brought home just after my grandmother died was a pile of love letters that had been kept in a biscuit tin.

As love letters go, they were really rather ordinary—mostly they dealt with details of meals and social encounters.

My grandfather was, after all, not given to flights of fancy.

But the black ink, written with precision on pieces of thin blue paper was a record of the early days of their courtship.

And, to my mind, my grandparents were transformed. They were no longer prey to illness, but became lovers and flirted at tennis parties.

Not many of us will leave a written record of our love affairs.

There will be no parcel tied with faded ribbon for my grandchildren to discover. Just the odd fervent answering machine message and notes held to the fridge door by small magnets are the sum of my romantic correspondence.

Passion is seldom transmitted these days on expensive writing paper. "I look back, and in every one point, every word and gesture, every letter, every silence, you have been entirely perfect to me. I would not change one word, one look," wrote the 19th century English poet Robert Browning to Elizabeth Barrett.

"And now listen to me in turn. You have touched me more profoundly than I thought even you could have touched me. My heart was full when you came here today. Henceforward I am yours for everything," she wrote back to him in one of 574 letters the pair exchanged over a 20 – month period.

Love letters probably come more easily to poets than they do to the rest of us.

It seems that these days we are unwilling to win the love of a spouse with words. Letter writing simply takes too long.

Why bother with stamps and post boxes when at the press of a button you can cut to the chase (get right to the point)?

Why struggle with complicated sentence structure when WT RU UP 2 (what are you up to) or FNCY MTING UP (do you fancy meeting up) will achieve the desired objective?

Most of us wouldn't know where to begin if we had to write a love letter. A guide to correct writing by a Briton named Thomas E. Hill, published in 1882, is enough to scare even the person most excited about writing.

Love letters, he said "should be written with the utmost regard for perfection. An ungrammatical expression, or word improperly spelled, may seriously interfere with the writer's prospect, by being turned to ridicule.

The death of the love letter is a real loss. Modern methods of communication are still undeveloped, hasty and lacking in romance; but, a letter has real substance. The writer has thought about the words and has struggled to express a particular quality of feeling. And letter writing is a sensual exchange.

Technology, with its cold logic and standard format, plays no part in a letter.

The paper has been pressed down upon by hand and pen, with handwriting that cannot be replicated. It has been touched and folded into the licked envelope.

A written correspondence lends intimacy to a relationship. The gap between posting and receipt heightens longing, delays gratification.

Above all, a love letter can be reread, pondered over, and kept in a tin box.

1. The title of the passage tells us that _____

    A. love letters are becoming increasingly popular among young people.

    B. love letters are preferred by old folks at present.

    C. love letters are gradually disappearing in our society.

D. love letters are no longer available nowadays.

2. What has the author's grandmother left her after she died?

    A. A large sum of money.

    B. A tin box full of biscuit.

    C. A book about how to write love letters.

    D. A pile of love letters written between the old couple.

3. What is the one thing that shows the romantic correspondence of modern people?

    A. A colorful parcel full of fervent words.

    B. An elegant envelop with passionate messages

    C. The fervent answering machine message.

    D. An electronic mail.

4. Why do people nowadays feel reluctant to write love letters?

    A. Because people have not learnt how to write love letters.

    B. Because it is too difficult to write love letters.

    C. Because letter writing is rather time consuming.

    D. Because letter writing is not fun enough.

5. What kind of communication channel is probably used when people write "WT RU UP 2"?

    A. A written form such as letters.

    B. An electronic mail through the computer and internet.

    C. A newspaper announcement.

    D. A public notice.

6. According to Thomas E. Hill, love letters should be written _____

    A. in a casual style.

    B. with the utmost regard for perfection.

    C. with ungrammatical expressions.

    D. with words improperly used.

7. Why does the author prefer letter writing?

    A. Because letter writing is a sensual exchange.

    B. Because letter writing saves much time.

    C. Because letter writing can help a person become clever.

    D. Because letter writing exercises one's mind and body.

8. In the opinion of the author, technology _____

    A. plays no role in letter writing.

    B. contributes a great deal to letter writing.

    C. plays an important part in people's lives.

    D. makes love letter writing more fun and romantic.

9. Love letters possess many advantages, one of which is _____

    A. that it is economical.

    B. that it can amuse people.

C. that it can help people solve their daily problems.

D. that it can be pondered over.

10. The attitude of the author towards love letters is _____ .

A. negative

B. positive

C. neutral

D. hard to say

Passage 26

Do you remember your pin number? I vividly remember what pin stands for—"Personal Identification Number," which means that "pin number" is redundant—but I can never keep in my memory bank the number that unlocks the key to my computer-crazed bank account. I am tempted to write the pin down and put it in a safe place, but my bank warns me never to do that.

The University of Chicago's Networking Service agrees: "Never write down a password." It warns and adds in a footnote: "If you do this, you should take extreme care not to lose the paper you have written it on. You should destroy the paper (e. g. tear it to shreds) once you have learned the password."

In the old days, I could safely hide my pin by writing it on the back of the label that hangs underneath my couch. That stern, official label used to say "Do Not Remove This Label"——but now, while it still proclaims "Under Penalty of Law," the newer couches have tags that read "This tag is not to be removed except by the Consumer Only," a clumsy formulation followed by some mumbo jumbo about flammability. That redundant "only" encourages furniture owners to yank the label off, and it means the back of the tag is no longer a safe hiding place on which to scribble PINs.

That has driven millions of us to the use of mnemonics. The min mnemonics is pronounced the same as the pin pneumonia—that is, not at all. A mnemonic, rooted in the Greek word for "mindful", is a mental string you tie around your brain in the form of rhyme or an association. For example, to create a four numeral pin, I took the word most closely associated with that acronym, needle, stuck need in the new-memory hippocampus region of my cerebral cortex, then picked out the numbers on my telephone pad that spelled out need: 6333.

"Auditors and consultants are prodding companies to require that employees pick tougher passwords," notes The Wall Street Journal, "and change them more frequently." That poses a linguistic problem.

The Yahoo security center advises that passwords should be "unique" (not used for another of my accounts), "difficult to guess" (at least seven characters long) and "made up of both lower and uppercase letters, numbers and symbols." "Bad passwords," in Yahoo's eyes, are complete words in any language; your own name or that of your spouse, child or pet spelled backwards; information about you easily obtained, like birthday, street address or license plate; or a sequence of numbers like 12345. In sum, if the code word is easy for you to remember, it's easier for a hacker to crack.

With all those words not to be used, what's left? "What people really do," says John R. Levine, co-author of Internet Privacy for Dummies, "is to pick the first thing that comes to mind." Several studies claim that the most popular password in the country is susan, which I can easily believe. This would be horrifying except that an awful lot of the stuff protected by passwords is barely worth protecting.

As a privacy nut, I consider every click of my keyboard worth protecting; does Levine have usable advice for paranoid dummies? "Think up a little phrase and use its initials, throwing in 4 in place of for and for are and $ for money and anything else that seems memorable. For example, mltw10# could be 'my laptop weighs 10 pounds'.

Too complicated? Language students are witnessing the emergence of a new form of coded communication, similar to Cockney rhyming slang(in which feet were "plates of meet"). In passwordage, however, we observe the crossing of the euphonic signage of license plates (the sporty 10 SNE1) with the ancient cognitive device of mnemonics—recollection by association. If you have found this page instructive, follow the prudent privacy advice of the University of Chicago: "Tear it to shreds."

1. The title of this passage means that _____
    A. password is important if you are a bank customer.
    B. password is rather difficult to create and remember.
    C. password can only be used by computer specialists.
    D. password should be changed frequently.

2. In this passage the author mainly discusses _____
    A. how to use password wisely.
    B. how to remember password by heart.
    C. how to invent password that can not be easily cracked by hackers.
    D. how to write password that can deceive others.

3. The author can't use his computer-crazed bank account because _____
    A. he has forgot the password.
    B. he has not obeyed the bank regulations.
    C. he has no money deposited in the bank.
    D. he has broken his computer.

4. According to the University of Chicago's Networking Services, if you write down a password on a piece of paper, you should _____
    A. keep the paper in your pocket.
    B. use the paper while others are not nearby.
    C. only show the paper to your close friends.
    D. remember the password and then destroy the paper.

5. The author used to hide and scribble his pins _____
    A. on his hands.
    B. in his notebook.
    C. on the back of the tag of the couch.

D. on the back of his textbook.

6. The fourth paragraph is primarily concerned with _____

    A. the way of memorizing password.

    B. the method of learning new words.

    C. the technique of creating strange words.

    D. the meaning of some complicated scientific terms.

7. The pronoun "them" in the second line of the fifth paragraph refers to _____ .

    A. companies

    B. passwords

    C. employees

    D. auditors

8. All of the following are code words which are easy for a hacker to crack except _____

    A. your birthday.

    B. you license plate.

    C. your own name.

    D. unique symbols, numbers and letters.

9. In the next to the last paragraph, Mr. Levine has provided useful suggestions mainly for you _____

    A. to construct a good password.

    B. to remember your password easily.

    C. to hide your password in a safe place.

    D. to tear your password paper to shreds.

10. In the last paragraph, the author has offered an example of _____

    A. a new password which is hard to remember.

    B. a complicated password which is easy to remember.

    C. a new form of coded communication.

    D. the instruction given by the University of Chicago.

Passage 27

    It takes a while, as you walk around the streets of Nantes, a city of half a million people on the banks of the Loire River, to realize just what it is that is odd. Then you get it: There are empty parking slots. That is highly unusual in big French towns, normally clogged with traffic crawling along ancient thoroughfares. But here, as one policeman said, "caroulait bien"—cars were rolling.

    Two decades of effort to make life more livable by dissuading people from driving into town has made Nantes a beacon for other European cities seeking to shake dependence on the automobile. "We are not anti-car," says Francois de Rugy, deputy mayor in charge of transport. "But we send people a lot of signals: If they come into town on buses, on foot, by train or by bike, we will help them. If they come in cars, we won't. "

The effects were clear recently during Mobility Week, a campaign sponsored by the European Union that prompted more than 1,000 towns across the Continent to test ways of making their streets, if not car-free, at least manageable. "That is an awfully difficult problem," acknowledged Joel Crawford, an author and leader of the "car free" movement picking up adherents all over Europe. "You can't take cars out of cities until there is some sort of alternative in place. But there are a lot of forces pointing in the direction of a major reduction in car use, like the rise in fuel prices, and concerns about global warming. "

Last week, proclaiming the slogan "In town, Without My Car! " hundreds of cities closed off whole chunks of their centers to all but essential traffic. Nantes closed just a few streets, preferring to focus on alternatives to driving so as to promote "Clever Commuting," the theme of this year's EU campaign. Volunteers pedaled rickshaws along the cobbled streets, charging passengers $1.2 an hour; bikes were available for free; and city workers encouraged children to walk to school along routes supervised by adults acting as Pied Pipers and picking up kids at arranged stops.

Some critics dismissed the idea as a gimmick. "We live in a society that is organized, like it or not, in such a way that we cannot do without cars," Christian Gerondeau, president of the French Federation of Auto Clubs, told French radio. "Stigmatizing the car is the wrong battle. " Authorities in Nantes, though, are trying to show that there might be another way.

The centerpiece of their efforts is a state-of-the-art tramway providing service to much of the town, and a network of free, multistory parking lots to encourage commuters to "park and ride. " Rene Vincendo, a retired hospital worker waiting at one such parking lot for his wife to return from the city center, is sold. "To go into town, this is brilliant," he says, "I never take my car in now. "

It is not cheap, though. Beyond the construction costs. City Hall subsidizes fares to the tune of 60 million euros ($72 million) a year, making passengers pay only 40 percent of operating costs.

That is the only way to draw people onto trams and buses, says de Rugy, since Nantes, like many European cities, is expanding, and commuters find themselves with ever-longer distances to travel. It's a chicken-and-egg problem, says John Adams, a professor of geography at University College in London. There is no longer room in European cities for cars to park, so drivers must live farther from work, and the traffic increases oblige urban planners to devote more room to roads and parking, which worsens urban sprawl. The danger, he warns, is that "the further you go down the route of car dependence, the harder it is to return, because so many shops, schools and other services are built beyond the reach of any finan- cially feasible public transport network. " This, adds de Rugy, means that "transport policy is only half the answer. Urban planners and transport authorities have to work hand in hand to ensure that services are provided close to transport links. "

The carrot-and-stick approach that Nantes has taken——cutting back on parking in the town center and making it expensive, while improving public transport—has not reduced the number of cars on the road. But it has "put a brake on the increase we would have seen otherwise" and that other European cities have seen, says Dominique Godineau, head of the city's "mobility department".

City Hall has other plans to keep up the pressure. Last week it launched a Web site to connect potential carpoolers. It has put out tenders for a car-sharing system that would allow city dwellers to rent a car for a few hours from curbside locations with the swipe of a magnetic card. The authorities are also encouraging big employers to match up to 15 percent of workers' monthly bus and tram passes.

1. The title of the passage suggests that _____

    A. people should not drive cars in cities.

    B. people are free to use cars inside cities.

    C. cars are the best means of transport for people in cities.

    D. cars are popular but expensive for people in cities.

2. The first paragraph mainly deals with _____

    A. the traffic problem in the city of Nantes.

    B. the location of the city of Nantes.

    C. the current traffic situation in Nantes.

    D. the population problem in Nantes.

3. According to the second paragraph, what happens if people come into town in cars instead of other means of transport such as buses or bikes?

    A. They will be punished severely by the police.

    B. They will not get any sort of assistance.

    C. They will have to pay a higher rate of tax.

    D. They will have difficulties in finding a parking lot.

4. What are some of the factors that lead to the reduction in car use?

    A. Cars become increasingly expensive to purchase.

    B. Cars are likely to cause traffic accidents.

    C. People like to do more exercise.

    D. People concern about global warming and fuel prices are rising.

5. What is the theme of this year's EU Mobility Week campaign?

    A. Free Driving.

    B. Driving Slowly.

    C. Clever Commuting.

    D. Clever Driving.

6. How do critics react to the car-free campaign?

    A. They entirely support the campaign.

    B. They are in favor of the cars.

    C. They tend to remain neutral.

    D. They are rather optimistic to the campaign.

7. What efforts do the authorities in Nantes plan to take?

    A. They plan to build a first class tramway providing service to much of the town.

    B. They intend to set up a network of free, multistory parking lots.

    C. They plan to build an underground system to ease the traffic problem.

  D. Both A and B.

8. How much will the City Hall subsidize fares a year?

  A. $ 40 million.

  B. $ 60 million.

  C. $ 72 million.

  D. $ 120 million.

9. The carrot-and-stick approach that Nantes has taken includes _____

  A. reducing parking in the town center.

  B. improving public transport.

  C. making parking in the town center expensive.

  D. All of the above.

10. The last paragraph primarily discusses_____

  A. various other means of reducing car use.

  B. the determination of the local government.

  C. the effects of the current strategies taken by City Hall.

  D. the potential problems of commuters who live far away from the city center.

Passage 28

The stories my father told to amuse his children of adventures in the Alps—but accidents only happened, he would explain, if you were so foolish as to disobey your guides—or of those long walks, after one of which, from Cambridge to London on a hot day, "I drank, I am sorry to say, rather more than was good for me." were told very briefly, but with a curious power to impress the scene. The things that he did not say were always there in the background. So, too, though he seldom told anecdotes, and his memory for facts was bad, when he described a person—and he had known many people, both famous and obscure—he would convey exactly what he thought of him in two or three words. And what he thought might be the opposite of what other people thought. He had a way of upsetting established reputations and disregarding conventional values that could be disconcerting, and sometimes perhaps wounding, though no one was more respectful of any feeling that seemed to him genuine. But when, suddenly opening his bright blue eyes and rousing himself from what had seemed complete abstraction, he gave his opinion, it was difficult to disregard it. It was a habit, especially when deafness made him unaware that this opinion could be heard, that had its inconveniences.

"I am the most easily bored of men," he wrote, truthfully as usual; and when, as was inevitable in a large family, some visitor threatened to stay not merely for tea but also for dinner, my father would express his anguish at first by twisting and untwisting a certain lock of hair. Then he would burst out, half to himself, half to the powers above, but quite audibly, "Why can't he go? Why can't he go?" Yet such is the charm of simplicity—and did he not say, also truthfully, that "bores are the salt of the earth?"—that the bores seldom went, or, if they did, forgave him and came again.

　　Too much, perhaps, has been said of his silence; too much stress had been laid upon his reserve. He loved clear thinking; he hated sentimental and gush; but this by no means meant that he was cold and unemotional, perpetually critical and condemnatory in daily life. On the contrary, it was his power of feeling strongly and of expressing his feeling with vigor that made him sometimes so alarming as a companion. A lady, for instance, complained of the wet summer that was spoiling her tour in Cornwell. But to my father, though he never called himself a democrat, the rain meant that the corn was being laid; some poor man was being ruined; and the energy with which he expressed his sympathy—not with the lady—left her discomfited. He had something of the same respect for farmers and fishermen that he had for climbers and explorers. So, too, he talked little of patriotism, but during the South African War—and all wars were hateful to him—he lay awake thinking that he heard the guns on the battlefield. Again, neither his reason nor his cold common sense helped to convince him that a child could be late for dinner without having been maimed or killed in an accident. The pictures that he would draw of old age and the bankruptcy court, of ruined men of letters who have to support large families in small houses at Wimbledon (he owned a very small house at Wimbledon), might have convinced those who complain of his understatements that hyperbole was well within his reach had he chosen.

　　In those last years, grown solitary and very deaf, he would sometimes call himself a failure as a writer; he had been "jack of all trades, and master of none". But whether he failed or succeeded as a writer, it is permissible of himself on the minds of his friends. The praise he would have valued most was Meredith's tribute after his death: "He was the one man to my knowledge worthy to have married your mother." And Lowell, when he called him "L. S., the most lovable of men," has best described the quality that makes him, after all these years, unforgettable.

1. What is special about the language in the text?

　　A. Many long and complex sentences are used.

　　B. The language is relatively easy to understand.

　　C. There are few new and difficult words in the text.

　　D. There are lots of comparisons and contrasts in the text.

2. What is the main idea of the first paragraph?

　　A. My father was an outstanding writer.

　　B. My father's opinion was usually novel.

　　C. My father was popular among his friends.

　　D. My father liked taking adventures in the risky mountains.

3. According to the first paragraph, how did my father describe a person he knew?

　　A. He would use a lot of descriptive adjectives and many vivid nouns.

　　B. He would use a few simple sentences and two or three complex ones.

　　C. He would use two or three exact words.

　　D. He would give us his title first and then his profession.

4. What is the main idea of the second paragraph?

A. My father was a boring person.

B. My father disliked guests who came for tea.

C. My father lived a simple life.

D. My father could not bear the bores.

5. What example(s) did the author use to describe her father's sympathy and concerns to others?

A. Some poor farmers were ruined because of the bad weather.

B. He kept thinking about the South African War.

C. He worried about the children who were late for dinner.

D. All of the above.

6. What can be inferred from the last sentence of paragraph 3?

A. My father usually preferred to use understatements to describe people or things, however, when he wrote about the poor, he put his feelings with vigor in his writings.

B. My father was a sentimental writer, so others often complained about him.

C. My father always used the technique of hyperbole in his writings.

D. My father was fond of writing something trivial in the society.

7. From the last paragraph, we may conclude that _____

A. The author's father was a failure in many ways.

B. The author's father was a good husband.

C. The friends of the author's father had a negative comment on him.

D. The author thought of her father as good for nothing.

8. How did the author evaluate her father?

A. She regarded her father as being a successful writer.

B. She believed that her father a complete failure in his life.

C. She thought her father learned many skills but not good at any of them.

D. She considered her father to be a stubborn character.

9. Why was the author's father unforgettable after many years of his death?

A. Because he was a great writer and influenced the succeeding generations a lot.

B. Because he liked to "call a spade a spade".

C. Because he wrote a great deal about the poor and the down trodden ones in society.

D. Because he was the most lovable of men.

10. What kind of writing style does this text belong to?

A. It is a narration with many details.

B. It is an exposition with multiple examples.

C. It is a vivid description of the character of a father.

D. It is an argumentation which focuses on how to become a good father.

Passage 29

China's successful launch of two taikonuats in its second manned space mission Wednesday tells the world a lot about how serious, formidable and well-prepared the Chinese space program is.

"You will again show that the Chinese people have the will, confidence and capability to mount scientific peaks ceaselessly," Chinese Premier Wen Jiabao told veteran fighter pilots Col. Fei Junlong and Col. Nie Haisheng after they blasted off from the Jiuquan Satellite Launch Center in Gansu province in China's desert northwest.

First, the Chinese are not going to sit on their laurels. They are entirely serious about developing their own space station and permanent base on the Moon and, indeed, look likely to have far more industrial and financial resources to do this in the foreseeable future than either the United States or Russia.

For while the Chinese waited for a full two years to follow up their first manned launch of taikonaut Col. Yang Liwei on Oct. 2, 2003, they were not content simply to repeat the exercise: They sent up a two man capsule rather than just another single-man one.

Second, two years is quite a long time, so the Chinese made clear that while their goals in space are ambitious, they are not going to needlessly risk taikonauts's lives or international embarrassment by pushing ahead too fast with their program.

Without access to any base closer to the equator like Cape Canaveral, Florida is for the United States, or France's launch base for its Ariane satellites in French Guyana, the Chinese limit their manned space launches from Gansu to either spring or fall, when the climate is temperate, and conditions are neither too hot nor too cold. They therefore allowed three previous windows of opportunities for a manned space mission go by before going ahead with this one.

Third, the Chinese are not in a rush because they do not have to be. They have no serious rivals for their expanding manned space program over the next decade or so.

The Chinese, of course, are watching closely what the United States and Russia are doing in space. While the Russian space program is on schedule, and looking good, even with Russia's booming oil revenues, there is no plan at the moment to spectacularly expand it. The Russians have only made clear that they are prepared to operate the International Space Station by themselves if the United States cannot or will not pull its own weight on it. Russia appears to have no plans to send its cosmonauts to the Moon by itself.

The U. S. manned space program is in far worse shape. NASA still plans to fly the remaining shuttle fleet on 19 missions over the next four years before retiring the three craft in 2010. But in reality no one knows when, or even if, the three remaining space shuttles will fly again following the concern about possible damage being caused to the Discovery on its most recent mission at the end of July, the first since the February 2003 immolation of the Challenger shuttle on reentry. And NASA's recently announced plan to send U. S. astronauts back to the Moon will have to wait for the successful development of man-rated missiles and space capsules to replace the shuttles. That is certainly not expected to happen before 2010 at the earliest and even if all goes well, the next U. S. manned mission to the Moon may have to wait until 2018, 46 years after U. S. astronauts last set foot on it.

Fourth, the Chinese are confident. Unlike most of Soviet launches through the Cold War, but like all U. S. manned space flights, they broadcast the launch of their Shenzhou-6 space craft Wednesday live on national state television. That augurs a great deal of confidence in the reliability of their technology.

Fifth, the two-year leap from a single manned space craft orbiting the earth for one day to a two-man mission that will stay up for five days is also revealing. It compares well with the similarly rapid evolution to two-manned space flight in the U. S. and Soviet space programs in the early 1960s.

The United States, indeed, went from orbiting its first astronauts around the earth, Col. John Glenn, the second American in space after Alan B. Shepard, Jr. in 1962, to orbiting the moon only six-and-half years later at the end of 1968. If the Chinese can develop their booster rockets reliably over the next six or seven years, there is no reason why they could not become the second nation in history to send men around the Moon by 2011 or 2012. Their current big Shenzhou spacecraft certainly has the size to carry the necessary air and provisions. And orbiting the Moon is a far less complex and risky undertaking than having a spacecraft land upon it and then take off again.

Finally, the Chinese are methodical as well as patient and determined. They have already announced what the next major stepping-stone in their space program will be. Sun Laiyan, head of the China National Space Administration has said it will be a space walk by a taikonaut in 2007. If all continues to go well, one should not bet against them.

1. The title of the passage suggests that _____

    A. China's space program is successful.

    B. China has exceeded US and Russia in its space program.

    C. China lags behind US and Russia in its space program.

    D. There is much room for improvement in China's space program.

2. The tone of the passage is _____

    A. indifferent and cold.

    B. admiring and inspiring.

    C. negative and hospitable.

    D. neutral and without bias.

3. What kind of spirit did the successful launch of the manned spacecraft Shenzhou VI show to the world about the Chinese people?

    A. They are industrious and diligent.

    B. They are warm-hearted and friendly.

    C. They are confident and capable.

    D. They are fond of taking risks.

4. What is the plan of the Chinese space program in the future?

    A. The Chinese plan to fly to the planet Mars.

B. The Chinese intend to explore other planets except the Moon.

C. The Chinese want to build a space station and permanent base on the Moon.

D. The Chinese are going to colonize on the Moon.

5. What is one fact that can indicate that the Chinese were not content simply to repeat the exercise in the space program?

A. Their first manned space craft was smaller than the second one.

B. Their rockets were more powerful than before.

C. Their taikonauts were more intelligent than the previous ones.

D. They launched a two-man capsule instead of just another one-man capsule.

6. Why do the Chinese scientists plan to launch their manned space craft either in spring or fall?

A. Because taikonauts usually feel better physically and mentally in these seasons.

B. Because the climate is temperate and conditions are neither too hot nor too cold.

C. Because it is the best time of the year for TV to broadcast live the launch of the space craft.

D. Because audience usually has enough free time during such seasons to watch closely the launch of the space craft.

7. What is the current situation of the Russian space program?

A. The Russians plan to expand its space program.

B. The Russians will send its cosmonauts to the Moon.

C. The Russian space program is on schedule.

D. The Russians can not make progress in its space program without the help of the Americans.

8. What is the present situation of the US manned space program?

A. The US manned space program is in far worse shape compared with that of China and Russia.

B. The US manned space program is going smoothly though there are some setbacks.

C. NASA plans to send US astronauts back to the Moon in the next couple of years.

D. NASA intends to explore planet Mars with manned capsule within the next decade.

9. What evidence does the author use to show that the Chinese scientists are confident?

A. They invited all correspondents both at home and abroad to the launch site.

B. They asked some VIPs to be present.

C. They looked happy and cheerful.

D. They broadcast the launch of the space craft Shenzhou VI live on CCTV 1.

10. What is the next major stepping-stone in the Chinese space program?

A. It will be a space craft which will be sent up to orbit the Moon.

B. It will be a space vehicle which is scheduled to land on the surface of the Moon.

C. It will be a space craft with an animal such as a dog launched to do scientific experiments.

D. It will be a space walk by a taikonaut in the year 2007 just two years after Shenzhou VI.

Passage 30

Graduates of Stanford University, on behalf of all members of the Stanford family, I congratulate and commend you. You also have my deep thanks for the contributions you have made to our community of scholars during your time at Stanford.

I would like to reflect for a few minutes on a phrase that has been repeated several times since this ceremony begun. As each group of graduates was presented to me, I responded by conferring your degrees and admitting you to the "rights, responsibilities and privileges" that are associated with a degree granted by this university.

You have worked extraordinarily hard to earn this degree and accomplished much in your time here, and you certainly deserve this day of celebration.

But at Stanford, we believe the rights and privileges of an education also bring a responsibility to make good use of your knowledge, to change the world for the better and to help ensure that succeeding generations have the same opportunities you have had here at Stanford.

In recent years, I have made it a Commencement tradition to talk about alumni who made good use of their knowledge, who demonstrated great personal vision and who took their responsibilities as educated citizens very seriously. This year, I want to talk about someone who, like our Commencement speaker, was a visionary with a Stanford connection, but not an alumnus. This person died 100 years ago, but the mark that Jane Stanford left on this university remains indelible.

Jane Lathrop was born in Albany, New York. The daughter of a successful merchant, who established the Albany Orphan Asylum, learned at an early age the importance of service to others.

After courtship and a simple announcement in the local paper, she married Leland Stanford in Albany in 1850. After a few years in Wisconsin, they eventually made their way to California to join Leland's brothers.

Their only child, Leland Jr. , was born after 18 years of marriage. Jane was 39; Leland was 44. They doted on their son and encouraged young Leland's curiosity in other cultures, as well as his interests in history, mathematics and engineering. Tragically, he contracted typhoid fever during a trip to Europe and died before his 16th birthday.

In their brief grief, Jane and Leland Stanford committed themselves to "educating other people's children" and dedicated their wealth to establish this university. Many ridiculed their decision, but it was neither folly nor egotism. The Stanfords believed that, despite their grief, they still had much to be thankful for and that it was their duty to share their wealth.

Nearly 500 students, men and women, attended the opening day ceremonies in 1891. Sen. Stanford asked his wife to address them. She agreed, but when the time came, she was overcome by the emotion of the day. Six days later, she sent President David Starr Jordan a copy of the remarks she was unable to read. To those first Stanford students, she had written:

Our hearts have been more deeply interested in this work than you can conceive. It was born in sorrow but has now become a great joy ... I desire to impress upon the minds of each one ... male and female, that we have at heart ... I think you will resolve to go forth from these classrooms determined in the future to be leaders with high aims and standards ... I think we both feel a personal and individual interest in each one of you ... It seems to me you have become a part of our lives ...

The new university was everything she had hoped, but it was not long before Jane Stanford was dealt another terrible blow. Sen. Stanford died in his sleep on June 21, 1893.

The university was just two years old. It was managed as though it was part of Leland Stanford's estate; when the estate went into probate, the assets were frozen. No one expected the university to remain open. But Jane Stanford was a strong-willed woman. After two weeks of reflection, she declared that Stanford University would not close its doors.

She took control. University expenses were cut. After the probate court set aside an allowance for her, she slashed her own expenses. She released most of her personal staff and took only a small amount for her needs; the rest she channeled to the university to meet its expenses. Then she learned that the federal government was suing the estate for loans made to the Central Pacific Railroad. The Supreme Court eventually rejected the government's claims, and in 1898, the estate was released from probate. Jane Stanford had guided the university through five very long and tough years, and by her tenacity and willingness to sacrifice she had ensured that Stanford University would endure for generations to come.

In 1904, a year before her death, she turned control of the university over to its trustees, with the following message:

Through all these years I have kept a mental picture before me. I could see a hundred years ahead when all the present trials were forgotten, and all of the present active parties gone, and nothing remaining but the institution. I could see beyond all this the children's children coming here from the East, the West, the North and the South.

It is not over-reaching to say that our graduates here today are the Stanfords' "children's children's children." You represent the fruition of this bold vision, the vindication of a risky investment fueled by a deep belief that there are fewer higher purposes than the pursuit of learning in the service of a greater good. That is the legacy you inherit as you prepare to leave the university—a remarkable story of personal vision and deep commitment, of dedication and service to the highest purposes—everything we know today to be the Stanford spirit.

Stanford is committed to keeping the spirit envisioned by Jane and Leland alive, and instilling it in the generations of students who pass this way. And so, I hope that you leave this campus with a strong reservoir of the Stanford spirit, a reservoir that will grow over the years. I hope this spirit inspires you as you make your contributions to the world, and I hope it brings you back often to this special place where the Stanford spirit was born in you.

Thank you and congratulations!

1. What does the title of the passage suggest?

A. Education should be available to everyone.

B. Education is indispensable in the poor countries.

C. Rights of education are to benefit the society.

D. Rights of education are to release people from heavy manual work.

2. What style of language is used in this text?

A. It is a description about present day education in the US.

B. It is a narrative about the personal education experience.

C. It is an argumentation over the rights of private institutions.

D. It is a public speech delivered at the commencement ceremony of a university.

3. According to the author, what is the responsibility of graduates from Stanford?

A. They should appreciate the professors who have taught him during his school days.

B. They should make some contributions to the world by using his knowledge.

C. They ought to donate some money to the university.

D. They ought to keep a written record of his academic performance.

4. Who was the subject for President John Hennessy's talk at this year's ceremony?

A. Alumni from Stanford University.

B. Distinguished scholars from Stanford University.

C. A strong-willed lady named Jane Stanford.

D. A wealthy merchant named Leland Stanford.

5. What happened to Jane and Leland after their only child died?

A. They decided to set up a university.

B. They moved to live in California.

C. They adopted another child.

D. They became seriously ill.

6. Why did not Jane Stanford make a speech in the opening day ceremony of the university?

A. Because she was too old and weak to walk there.

B. Because she suddenly became sick physically.

C. Because she was overcome by the emotion of the day.

D. Because her husband insisted on doing it by himself.

7. What was the second blow to Jane Stanford?

A. The university was faced with financial problem.

B. Senior Stanford, Jane's husband died in his sleep.

C. The federal government confiscated all her property.

D. She suffered from heart attack.

8. What measures did Jane Stanford take after the death of her husband?

A. She cut the university expenses as well as her own ones.

B. She became the president and hired a lot of personal staff for her.

C. She fired some professors and used the money to build another beautiful house for her.

D. She reduced the number of students enrolled by the university and increased the tuition fees.

9. What was the dream of Jane Stanford?

A. She wanted the American government to support private institutions.

B. She wished the Stanford to become a leading university in the US.

C. She hoped all the new graduates from the Stanford could find a better job with fat salary.

D. She pictured lots of children from different parts to receive their education in Stanford.

10. According to the author, what is the Stanford spirit?

A. Study hard and make progress everyday.

B. No pains, no gains.

C. The pursuit of learning for one's own interest and benefits.

D. The pursuit of learning in the service of a greater good and a deep commitment of dedication and service to the highest purposes.

Part 2

Basic Skills Needed for Listening
听力基础必备

According to the information provided by ETS (Educational Testing Service), which is responsible for making and administering the TOEFL test, the listening section is designed to measure the candidates' ability to understand spoken English. Candidates are expected to demonstrate their capability of comprehending auditory skills, namely, conversations and talks in English. Since students will be exposed to such kind of English when they go abroad to study in the English speaking country, it is necessary for them to have a fairly good command of spoken English before they put their feet on the foreign soil. Experience shows that an effective way of developing the listening skill is through the provision of carefully selected practice material. In this part, you are offered with ample conversations both short ones as well as the longer ones, and sufficient talks or lectures. The objective of providing such listening materials is to assist you to improve your listening comprehension ability step by step so that you will be well prepared for the more challenging tasks in the iBT TOEFL that you intend to take in the near future.

根据 ETS(负责托福考试的制作和管理)所提供的信息, 听力测试部分主要的目的是在于考查考生对听力的理解能力。考生将展示他们在听力技能上的能力, 也就是说用英语对话和交谈。基于考生们将来会去官方语为英语国家用到这种语言, 所以在去说英语的国家学习之前能对口语有一个好的掌握是很必要的。以往的经验告诉我们,最有效的提高听力技能的办法就是通过精心挑选的听力练习进行训练。在这里,我们提供了大量的长对话和短对话,以及足够的谈话和讲座。提供这些听力材料的主要目的就是为了使您的听力得到一步步地提高。也为不久的更具挑战性的 iBT TOFEL 考试打下坚实的基础。

Section A
Short Conversations

Directions: In this part, you will hear 150 short conversations between two people. After each conversation, You'll hear a question about what has been said. The conversations and questions will not be repeated. Listen carefully and decide which of the four choices is the best answer to each question you've heard.

1. A. He needs the woman to drive him somewhere.
   B. He wants to sell the car to the woman.
   C. He has to bring the car in for repairs.
   D. He is satisfied with the car.
2. A. He has been helping Tom with his studies.
   B. The woman is being unfair about Tom.
   C. Tom should consider quitting the track team.
   D. Tom did better than expected in his first year on the team.
3. A. She often spends time in the sun.
   B. The sun has already gone down.
   C. Too much sun makes her dizzy.
   D. Her skin is sensitive to the sun.
4. A. They don't enjoy swimming.
   B. They won't go swimming in the lake today.
   C. They don't know how to swim.
   D. They'll swim in the lake tomorrow.
5. A. The style of sweater she is wearing is very common.
   B. The man saw Jane wearing the sweater.
   C. She wore the sweater for the first time yesterday.
   D. She usually doesn't borrow clothes from Jane.
6. A. The man should look into buying a new car.
   B. The car looks better than it used to.
   C. The man should fly to Florida.
   D. The man should get his car checked.
7. A. She is on a special diet.
   B. She doesn't like to walk to the cafeteria.
   C. She thinks the cafeteria is too expensive.
   D. She doesn't eat lunch anymore.
8. A. Keep looking for his wallet.
   B. Report the theft of the wallet right away.

C. Put his wallet in his jacket pocket.

D. Be more careful with his wallet.

9. A. To tell him they are busy.

B. To cancel an appointment.

C. To invite him to go to a film.

D. To ask him a question about homework.

10. A. She wants to exercise before she runs.

B. It's too hot to go running.

C. Her jogging suit isn't warm enough.

D. She already went jogging.

11. A. She appreciates the man's help.

B. Her presentation was somewhat long.

C. She needed more time to prepare.

D. She worked hard on her presentation.

12. A. It's just past ten o'clock.

B. There's no time to talk.

C. She needs a little more time.

D. She has more than ten cents.

13. A. He wants a glass of water.

B. He won't do as the woman asks.

C. He can't wait any longer.

D. He's looking for the waiter.

14. A. Bob has been married for a long time.

B. The woman should go to California.

C. He plans to go to the wedding.

D. He hasn't been to California for a long time.

15. A. He wants to know which scarf the woman chose.

B. He wants to know what color the jacket is.

C. He thinks he selected a nice scarf.

D. He thinks any color would go well with the jacket.

16. A. She'll find the reference books for the man.

B. The paper is already long enough.

C. The information may be inaccurate.

D. The man's ideas are good enough to be published.

17. A. He has trouble remembering when things happen.

B. He usually forgets to meet people for appointments.

C. He doesn't like to go out on dates.

D. He doesn't want to reveal Thomas' birth date.

18. A. Down jackets are now on sale.

B. She can't wait for winter to arrive.

C. It's hard to know how heavy a jacket to buy.

D. She needs a warm jacket.

19. A. She's only known Becky a short time.

    B. She saw Becky recently.

    C. She and Becky usually go to the market together.

    D. Becky has been away for a week.

20. A. She does a lot of part-time work in museums.

    B. She isn't really interested in art museums.

    C. Her artwork is displayed in a museum.

    D. She has a large art collection.

21. A. The man shouldn't have invited her roommate to the meeting.

    B. Her roommate was unable to attend the meeting.

    C. Her roommate is unreliable about delivering messages.

    D. She forgot about the time change.

22. A. She thinks Mary is too critical.

    B. She doesn't know how to react.

    C. She thinks the man is too sensitive.

    D. She wants to know what the man thinks.

23. A. He'll attend both the concert and the party.

    B. He'll change his plans at once.

    C. He has saved a place for Janet.

    D. He regrets that he can't go to the party.

24. A. He has to work late tonight.

    B. He'd rather go at another time.

    C. He's already seen the show.

    D. It'll be hard to get to the auditorium on time.

25. A. Bill has found an acting job.

    B. Bill was at his last job a long time.

    C. Bill's new position as the boss is challenging.

    D. Bill's behavior could cause him to lose his job.

26. A. The woman's roommate went to get it.

    B. It was sent to the woman's roommate by mistake.

    C. The woman picked it up at the post office.

    D. The postal service delivered it to the woman's house.

27. A. Nothing can help Debra pass the exam.

    B. Debra doesn't need to study at all.

    C. Being well rested will help Debra on the exam.

    D. Debra should get some fresh air in the morning.

28. A. He's growing very quickly.

    B. He's the tallest of three boys.

    C. He can jump high.

    D. He has to leave today at three.

29. A. Now he understands the system.

    B. He has no use for technology.

    C. He has to do some calculations.

    D. He doesn't know how to operate the computer.

30. A. Discuss the situation with the person in charge of the dormitory.

    B. Ask her roommate not to make so much noise.

    C. Go to bed after midnight.

    D. Send a letter to the residents.

31. A. Read the operation manual.

    B. Try the buttons one by one.

    C. Ask the shop assistant for advice.

    D. Make the machine run slowly.

32. A. The woman found the mail-box empty.

    B. The man is waiting for some important mail.

    C. The man has just sent out his application.

    D. The woman will write h postcard to her daughter.

33. A. To do whatever the committee asks him to do.

    B. To make decisions in agreement with the committee.

    C. To run the committee his way.

    D. To make himself the committee chairman.

34. A. Someone has taken away her luggage.

    B. Her flight is 50 minutes late.

    C. Her luggage has been delayed.

    D. She can't find the man she's been waiting for.

35. A. She doesn't have a fax machine.

    B. She may quit her present job soon.

    C. She is tired of her present job.

    D. Her phone number has changed.

36. A. The man should buy a watch in a jewelry store.

    B. The jewelry store doesn't have a good selection of watches.

    C. The man has been looking at poorly made watches.

    D. The watches in the jewelry store are even more expensive.

37. A. Move to a cheaper apartment.

    B. Find a person to share their apartment.

    C. Hire a new worker.

D. Write an accurate description of a friend.

38. A. Buy an Italian cookbook.

B. Go to an Italian restaurant.

C. Take a night flight to Italy, instead.

D. Cook some Italian dishes on Saturday.

39. A. His paycheck is late.

B. The book bag is too expensive.

C. He can't lend the woman any money.

D. The woman doesn't need a new book bag.

40. A. Sit further back.

B. Sit closer together.

C. Find their reserved seats.

D. Find seats closer to the screen.

41. A. She is away for a few days.

B. She recently hurt herself.

C. She tore her skirt on a hook.

D. She seldom stops studying.

42. A. She's looking forward to her history class.

B. She's surprised how long her reading assignment is.

C. She thinks the book is too expensive.

D. She's late for her history class.

43. A. Start writing letters.

B. Mail her letters immediately.

C. Stop thinking about her exams.

D. Study instead of writing letters.

44. A. The woman should return his tape player by Friday.

B. The woman should buy him a new tape player.

C. By Friday he should be able to borrow a tape player.

D. He can't wait until Friday for his tape player.

45. A. Wait until the sale is over.

B. Watch for the ad on television.

C. Return his suit to Conrad's.

D. Buy a new suit.

46. A. He makes a lot of money.

B. He has just been left some money.

C. He doesn't believe three hundred dollars is enough.

D. He can't afford to spend that much.

47. A. He knows what is wrong with the watch.

B. The woman doesn't need to buy another battery.

C. The woman should get a new watch.

D. The jewelry store can probably repair the woman's watch.

48. A. He has another meeting to attend on that day.

    B. He's available either day.

    C. He can't attend a two-day conference.

    D. Not everybody will go to the same meeting.

49. A. Go to the beach with her friends.

    B. Postpone her meeting with Professor Jones.

    C. See Professor Jones after class.

    D. Give a speech in Professor Jones's class.

50. A. She isn't a very good student.

    B. She hasn't gotten her grades yet.

    C. She shouldn't worry about her grades.

    D. She doesn't like to talk about grades.

51. A. Spend more time working on calculus problems.

    B. Talk to an advisor about dropping the course.

    C. Work on the assignment with a classmate.

    D. Ask the graduate assistant for help.

52. A. Go home to get a book.

    B. Return a book to the library.

    C. Pick up a book at the library for the woman.

    D. Ask the librarian for help in finding a book.

53. A. The woman could use his metric ruler.

    B. He'll finish taking the measurements for the woman.

    C. The woman's ruler is better than his.

    D. He's faster at making the conversions than the woman.

54. A. She wants the man to attend the tournament with her.

    B. The tournament begins next week.

    C. The man should check with his doctor again.

    D. She hopes the man will be able to play in the tournament.

55. A. The advisor has already approved the man's class schedule.

    B. The man should make an appointment to see his advisor.

    C. The man should change his courses schedule.

    D. The man should sign the document before leaving.

56. A. She didn't teach class today.

    B. She noticed that the students didn't do their homework.

    C. She usually assigns homework.

    D. She usually talks quietly.

57. A. It started to rain when she was at the beach.

B. She'd like the man to go to the beach with her.

C. The forecast calls for more rain tomorrow.

D. She won't go to the beach tomorrow if it rains.

58. A. She disagrees with the man.

B. She doesn't enjoy long speeches.

C. She hadn't known how long the speech would be.

D. She doesn't have a strong opinion about the speaker.

59. A. He makes more money than the woman.

B. He's satisfied with his job.

C. He has trouble finding a job.

D. He doesn't like working outdoors.

60. A. He has already finished his report.

B. He hasn't chosen a topic for his report.

C. The woman's report is already long enough.

D. The woman will have time to finish her report.

61. A. The classes have improved his health.

B. His new glasses fit better than the old ones.

C. He's thinking of taking exercises classes.

D. He's unhappy about his life.

62. A. She also found the book difficult.

B. She has learned a lot about names.

C. She doesn't remember the title of the novel.

D. She read a different book.

63. A. They'll have to go to a later show.

B. The people in line all have tickets.

C. She doesn't want to go to the second show.

D. They won't have to wait much longer.

64. A. If it's too late for her to drop the course.

B. If she sympathizes with him.

C. If she apologized for what she did.

D. If she regrets taking the course.

65. A. She'll be traveling during the winter break.

B. She'll be working during vacation.

C. She's looking forward to going home.

D. She wants to hire another research assistant.

66. A. She'll speak to Larry about the problem.

B. Larry has apologized to his roommate.

C. Larry should find a new roommate.

D. Larry's roommate may be partly responsible for the problem.

67. A. The man should take his vacation somewhere else.

B. She doesn't know when her semester ends.

C. She hasn't called the travel agent yet.

D. The man may have to reschedule his trip.

68. A. She didn't work hard enough on it.

B. It wasn't as good as she thought.

C. Her professor was pleased with it.

D. It was written according to the professor's guidelines.

69. A. Go to the ballet later in the year.

B. Take ballet lessons with his sister.

C. Get a schedule of future performances.

D. Get a ticket from his sister.

70. A. Her hotel is located far from the conference center.

B. She didn't want to stay at the Gordon.

C. The man should consider moving to a different hotel.

D. She isn't sure how to get to the conference center.

71. A. Few readers agreed with his ideas.

B. Very few people have read his article.

C. He doesn't expect the article to be published.

D. The woman doesn't fully understand the article.

72. A. He'll go with the woman to the next hockey game.

B. He missed the hockey game because he was ill.

C. He forgot about the hockey game.

D. He doesn't like to go to hockey games.

73. A. Karen can drive the man to the airport on Tuesday.

B. Karen can attend the meeting on Tuesday.

C. Karen had to change her plans at the last minute.

D. Karen is returning from a trip on Tuesday.

74. A. Call her after five.

B. Make calls from her phone.

C. Go to the meeting with her.

D. Fix her phone.

75. A. Look for more information for their financial plan.

B. Ask for more time to finish their financial plan.

C. Finish their financial plan with the material available to them.

D. Turn in their financial plan late.

76. A. He probably calls his brothers frequently.

B. He should call his brothers more often.

C. He does a lot of traveling.

D. He's saving money to visit his brothers.

77. A. The battery is not correctly positioned.

B. She doesn't know how the calculator works.

C. The calculator needs a new battery.

D. The man should enter the numbers in a different order.

78. A. They can get a guidebook in Montreal.

B. It might not be necessary to buy a guidebook.

C. He doesn't mind the cost of a guidebook.

D. It's no use trying to study on a trip.

79. A. Being hungry.

B. Having a big lunch.

C. The weather.

D. Cooking.

80. A. Tom's apartment probably costs more than the man's.

B. The man's place is becoming more expensive.

C. Her apartment is better than the man's.

D. She wants to see Tom's new apartment.

81. A. Drop out of the play.

B. Switch parts with another actor.

C. Be patient about learning his part.

D. Have his lines memorized by tomorrow.

82. A. She agrees with the man.

B. The man missed the last study session.

C. She didn't understand the last chemistry class.

D. The man should be more serious about his studies.

83. A. He can't meet the woman at the engineering building.

B. He can't give the woman a ride.

C. He has already passed the engineering building.

D. He'll meet the woman after his appointment.

84. A. He'll give the quiz at a later time.

B. The quiz will be very short.

C. The quiz won't be ready until Thursday.

D. He'll score the quiz quickly.

85. A. Take the medicine as she was directed to do.

B. Schedule another appointment with her doctor.

C. Stop taking the medicine.

D. Rest her back for a few days.

86. A. Decide which movie to see.

B. Order his food quickly.

C. Go to a later movie.

D. Go to a different restaurant.

87. A. She doesn't like to watch basketball.

B. She would like the man to accompany her to the game.

C. She doesn't have a television.

D. She'll sell the man her ticket.

88. A. She needs to find a new place to live.

B. She spends a lot of time in the library.

C. She prefers to study at home.

D. She needs to return some books to the library.

89. A. Spend more time outdoors.

B. Take short naps during the day.

C. Try to get to bed earlier.

D. Stay indoors until he feels better.

90. A. Sharpen the man's pencil.

B. Give the man a new sheet of paper.

C. Show the man a drawing technique.

D. Ask the model to move his arm.

91. A. She doesn't like to write letters.

B. She is happy to be here with her friends.

C. She likes to mail her letters herself.

D. She's written a lot of letters recently.

92. A. She teaches high school.

B. She wants more ice in her glass.

C. She never misses class.

D. She thinks cold weather is nice.

93. A. The woman should ask someone else for help.

B. He wonders if the woman hears a noise.

C. They can work together the next day.

D. He didn't hear her question.

94. A. John is too at away to hear.

B. John is out of money.

C. John hasn't left yet.

D. John doesn't hear well.

95. A. The guests aren't thirsty.

B. Water isn't appropriate for guests.

C. The guests don't want to be served water.

D. There isn't enough water.

96. A. Lend the man some money.

B. Take the man to the bank.

C. Ask the man when he'll be paid.

D. Ask the man to write her a check.

97. A. She forgot to call the man.

   B. Her answering machine is broken.

   C. She didn't get the man's messages.

   D. She couldn't remember the man's phone number.

98. A. He received permission to carry on an extra bag.

   B. He doesn't know the woman ahead of him.

   C. lie's carrying someone else's suitcase.

   D. He'd like some help at the baggage counter.

99. A. Travel into the city on another day.

   B. Pick up her medicine beore they leave.

   C. Avoid driving after taking her medicine.

   D. Wait to take her medicine until after their trip.

100. A. The air will be cleaner if they go to a different city.

   B. It'll soon be too late to control the pollution.

   C. Society will not pay attention to the new laws.

   D. The situation will improve when changes are made.

101. A. He didn't have time to look for his jacket.

   B. He misunderstood the weather report.

   C. He didn't know it would be cold.

   D. He forgot to bring his jacket.

102. A. Attend a conference with her.

   B. Mail her the paper after the deadline.

   C. Submit a handwritten draft of the paper.

   D. Complete the course without submitting the paper.

103. A. He saw Mary earlier.

   B. Someone else saw Mary.

   C. He can't help the woman.

   D. Mary asked for directions to the office.

104. A. She fell asleep before the program ended.

   B. She especially enjoyed the end of the program.

   C. She missed the beginning of the program.

   D. She wishes she had gone to sleep earlier.

105. A. He doesn't like to take pills.

   B. He may not be able to wake up.

   C. He may feel better soon.

   D. He may want to take the pills without food.

106. A. He is playing tennis tomorrow.

    B. Someone else has borrowed his racket.

    C. His racket is not useable.

    D. The woman should buy a new tennis racket.

107. A. The shirt is clean.

    B. The shirt was not expensive.

    C. The man should try to get his money back.

    D. The shirt needs to be washed again.

108. A. She's willing to help the man.

    B. She's sorry that she injured the man.

    C. She'd like the man to repeat what he said.

    D. She wants to know what happened to the man.

109. A. He tried to call the woman.

    B. He was too busy to call the woman.

    C. He didn't know he was supposed to call the woman.

    D. He spoke to the woman on the phone last night.

110. A. She's annoyed by the man.

    B. She's like a sandwich.

    C. She has already eaten.

    D. She doesn't want anything to eat now.

111. A. She's pleased they were invited.

    B. Susan gave them the wrong directions.

    C. They'll probably be late for dinner.

    D. Susan's house is probably nearby.

112. A. Buy some orange juice for the woman.

    B. Borrow some money from the woman.

    C. Drive the woman to the store.

    D. Pay back money the woman lent him.

113. A. She hasn't worn the dress in a long time.

    B. She doesn't like the dress very much.

    C. She intends to give the dress to her sister.

    D. She doesn't remember where her sister bought the dress.

114. A. She never cleans the apartment.

    B. She's doing a report with her roommate.

    C. She's too busy to clean the apartment.

    D. She doesn't like sharing an apartment.

115. A. He'll try to finish the novel tonight.

    B. He liked the novel very much.

    C. He doesn't remember where he put the novel.

D. He's looking forward to the next literature assignment.

116. A. He doesn't like to wake up early in the morning.

B. The woman seems unusually sad.

C. There's no special reason for his good mood.

D. He wasn't in a good mood when he woke up.

117. A. Get a ride to the station with the woman.

B. Take the woman to the station.

C. Borrow the woman's car to go to the station.

D. Drive his car instead of taking the train.

118. A. Review the assignment by himself.

B. Wait a few minutes before trying to phone John again.

C. Ask one of John's housemates about the assignment.

D. Go over to John's house.

119. A. He won't vote for the woman.

B. He may also run for class president.

C. The woman already asked him for his vote.

D. The woman should ask his roommate to vote for her.

120. A. She isn't sure that the author's ideas would work.

B. The author isn't an expert in economics.

C. She has a better theory about the economy.

D. The author spends too much time arguing about details.

121. A. The bookstore is rarely crowded.

B. She's bought all her textbooks for this semester.

C. Many students have used books to sell.

D. Last semester's books cost her several hundred dollars.

122. A. The graph belongs in the center of the page.

B. She can't discuss the problem until later.

C. She's only finished half of the document.

D. They should look for another graph immediately.

123. A. He's supposed to go to the meeting.

B. He wants the woman to give George the message.

C. He doesn't know why George can't attend the meeting.

D. He forgot to deliver a message.

124. A. End his conversation quickly.

B. Make several calls for the woman.

C. Take the phone off the hook.

D. Write down his phone number.

125. A. Where to meet Sally.

B. Why Sally wants to meet them.

C. The location of the park.

D. The time of the meeting.

126. A. Fill out an application form.

B. Apply for a different position.

C. File the papers in the cabinet.

D. Show her the advertisement from the newspaper.

127. A. Go with her to the airport.

B. Talk to her for a short time.

C. Find out when the plane is leaving.

D. Make the phone call now.

128. A. He can give the woman directions to Chicago.

B. He can drive the woman to Chicago.

C. He can get a map for the woman.

D. He can take the woman to the bookstore.

129. A. He didn't show his paintings at the exhibit.

B. He didn't see the paintings.

C. He doesn't understand Ted's art.

D. The exhibit was canceled.

130. A. She has canceled her trip to Iowa.

B. The snowstorm is getting weaker.

C. The man's information isn't accurate.

D. They also may get a lot of snow.

131. A. She needs more time to get ready for the dinner.

B. She thought the dinner was at another time.

C. She forgot about the plans she made for dinner.

D. She won't be able to come to dinner.

132. A. Take the class this semester.

B. Get permission to take the class.

C. Take the class over again.

D. Register for the class next semester.

133. A. He doesn't like his new eyeglass frames.

B. He hasn't had a haircut.

C. He got his eyeglasses a long time ago.

D. Several people have asked him about his new eyeglass frames.

134. A. The grades have been calculated correctly.

B. The woman will get the grade she deserves.

C. The woman received one of the highest grades.

D. The woman's grade can't be changed.

135. A. She left the lecture for a few minutes.

B. She was reading during the lecture.

C. She may have fallen asleep.

D. She misunderstood the speaker's last points.

136. A. The woman does not remember her brother's address.

B. The letters were probably lost in the mail.

C. The woman will soon get used to college life.

D. The woman's brother probably hasn't had time to write.

137. A. The man ordered his favorite flavor for the woman.

B. The woman doesn't have a favorite flavor.

C. The man didn't like the new flavor.

D. The woman has tested the new flavor.

138. A. He started to work in a paint shop.

B. He hasn't started looking for an apartment.

C. He had an appointment with a painter today.

D. He isn't on schedule with his paintings.

139. A. The woman's health has improved.

B. He does not have enough energy to exercise.

C. By themselves diets are not useful.

D. Diets can be harmful.

140. A. His neighbors don't need his help.

B. His neighbors aren't very sociable.

C. His neighbors intend to go on vacation.

D. He's too busy to meet his neighbors.

141. A. He's disappointed with his interview.

B. He had to cancel his interview.

C. He doesn't want to discuss the interview now.

D. He shouldn't have applied for the job.

142. A. Have a cookie.

B. Make cookies with the woman.

C. Give the woman a cookie.

D. Take a cookie for his roommate.

143. A. He felt better an hour ago.

B. His headache should be gone in an hour.

C. He forgot to take the medicine for his headache.

D. His head still hurts.

144. A. She hasn't spoken to her friend in a long time.

B. She intends to visit her friend in Texas.

C. She sometimes travels abroad for her job.

D. Her friend has never been to Texas before.

145. A. Meet at the bus stop.

B. Finish their candy bars.

C. Get off the bus at the next stop.

D. Meet in front of the rest rooms.

146. A. He won't be able to repair the briefcase.

B. The repair shop is closed until Tuesday.

C. The woman should buy a smaller briefcase.

D. The briefcase will be ready before Tuesday.

147. A. Find out how much work will be required for the class.

B. Take another class instead of creative writing.

C. Ask his advisor about the instructor in the Wednesday class.

D. Sign up for the Wednesday class.

148. A. He'll take his friends to Florida.

B. He's not sure what he'll do.

C. He planned his trip a long time ago.

D. He'd rather not travel during spring break.

149. A. He thinks clothing prices will decrease even further.

B. He's going to go shopping soon.

C. He didn't know that stores were-having sales now.

D. He wants to see what the woman bought.

150. A. She is glad the man waited for her.

B. She'd like to reschedule the meeting.

C. She wasn't very late for the meeting.

D. She's sorry that she missed the meeting.

Section B
Longer Conversations and Lectures

Directions: In this part, you are going to hear some lectures and longer conversations. Each lecture or conversation is followed by some questions. Below each question, there are four options marked A, B, C, and D. Listen carefully and choose the best answer to each question.

Lecture 1

1. What does the speaker mainly talk about?

A. Education during the Civil War

B. Post-Civil War developments in higher education

C. Current trends in technological education

D. Benefits for women in state universities

2. How many major educational changes does the speaker discuss?

    A. Two.

    B. Three.

    C. Ten.

    D. One hundred.

3. How many foreign students have studied in the United States since 1945.

    A. 150 thousand.

    B. 115 thousand.

    C. Over one million.

    D. Over ten million.

4. Which university took the lead in providing graduate study for the students?

    A. Vassar.

    B. Wellesley.

    C. Smith.

    D. Harvard and John Hopkins Universities.

5. What can you infer about the education for women in the United States before the Civil War?

    A. It was well established.

    B. It was the same as that available to men.

    C. It was only available in the northern states.

    D. It was not highly developed.

Lecture 2

1. Whom does the speaker address?

    A. College students.

    B. Graduate students.

    C. International students.

    D. High school students.

2. What does the speaker mainly talk about?

    A. Students' social activities on campus.

    B. The experience of a foreign student.

    C. How to find a residence hall.

    D. The advantages and the disadvantages of living on and off campus.

3. Which place would a student most likely choose if he wants to have easy access to campus facilities?

    A. A residence hall.

    B. A motel.

    C. A hotel.

    D. The house of a host family.

4. Which of the following is NOT an advantage of living on campus?

    A. Enjoying time with peers.

    B. Having much privacy.

C. Cheap food.

D. Maximum interaction with various students.

5. What is the disadvantage of living off campus?

    A. Experiencing real world life.

    B. Sharing a room with others.

    C. Having few books to read.

    D. Wasting time in transportation.

Lecture 3

1. Who is the speaker?

    A. A visitor to the park.

    B. A presidential campaign worker.

    C. A park service employee.

    D. A tour guide from a travel agency.

2. According to the speaker, who originated the idea of the public park?

    A. Several explorers.

    B. Representatives of Congress.

    C. President Grant.

    D. A group of animal lovers.

3. What does the speaker say about Yellowstone National Park?

    A It was the first national park in the world.

    B. It was the first region explored by pioneers.

    C. It is not accessible to everyone.

    D. It is not managed by the National Park Service.

4. How many parks are there in the US National Park System?

    A. More than 3,600.

    B. More than 360.

    C. More than 300.

    D. More than 80.

5. According to the speaker, which of the following is NOT a duty of a park ranger?

    A. To guide nature walks.

    B. To offer guided tours.

    C. To offer campfire talks.

    D. To train other staff members.

Lecture 4

1. In which course does this talk probably take place?

    A. United States History.

    B. Famous Short Story riters.

    C. Survey of American Literature.

    D. The Great American Novel.

2. What subject had the student just finished studying?

    A. Edgar Allan Poe.

    B. American poets.

    C. American novelists.

    D. Short story writers.

3. According to the speaker, what kind of life did Poe have?

    A. Short.

    B. Symbolic.

    C. Tragic.

    D. Fulfilled.

4. Which of the following is NOT a characteristic of his work?

    A. Symbolism.

    B. Impressionism.

    C. Eerie tone.

    D. Humor.

5. What should the students do to prepare for the next class?

    A. Read about Poe's life.

    B. Prepare for a discussion of a short story.

    C. Study the American novelist.

    D. Write an analysis of one of the stories.

Lecture 5

1. What is the SAT?

    A. The most widely used graduate school admissions test in the US.

    B. An admissions test for non-native English speakers.

    C. The most widely used college admissions test in the US.

    D. A test used to judge if a person is qualified in his later career.

2. What is the purpose of the SAT?

    A. To help college officials identify which students would be successful in college.

    B. To help graduate school officials identify the students' thinking ability.

    C. To let parents know the IQ of their children.

    D. To let employers know the English proficiency of their employees.

3. How is the new SAT to be different from the former one?

    A. The new SAT focuses on a student's calculating skills.

    B. The new SAT emphasizes a student's speaking ability.

    C. The new SAT better tests a student's reasoning and thinking skills.

    D. The new SAT underlines a student's memorizing ability.

4. Which of the following is NOT true about the change of the SAT?

    A. Analogy questions will be replaced with questions that better show the students'

       reading ability.

B. Higher level mathematics questions will be added.

C. A writing test will be added.

D. Listening comprehension questions will be put at the beginning of the test.

5. Why did the president of the University of California call on his school to stop using the SAT as an entrance requirement?

A. The skills it tests are not taught in high school.

B. The results of the test do not show if students are prepared to attend college.

C. On the SAT, too much attention is paid to students' reading ability.

D. Both A and B.

Lecture 6

1. Which of the following is the most common tax?

A. Luxury tax.

B. Property tax.

C. Income tax.

D. Sales tax.

2. "The income tax is usually graduated. " What does the sentence mean?

A. The tax percentage increases as a family's income increases.

B. The tax percentage increases as a family's salaries increase.

C. The tax percentage decreases as a family's expenses increase.

D. The tax percentage increases as a family's property increases.

3. What is the amount of property tax based on?

A. How long the family owns the property.

B. The property's value.

C. The owner's income.

D. The property's value and the owner's income.

4. What is the revenue from sales tax used for?

A. Public schools.

B. Public safety.

C. Roads, parks and benefits for the poor.

D. All of the above.

5. Where does the revenue from income tax go?

A. To the state government.

B. To the federal government.

C. To the local government.

D. To the community.

Lecture 7

1. How many tons of iron are produced per year for steel mills in America?

A. 200,000 tons.   B. 1. 2 million tons.

C. 75 million tons.   D. 1,290 million tons.

84

2. What is the second major natural resources in America?

    A. Copper.   B. Silver.

    C. Iron.   D. Coal.

3. What is most of the coal used to do?

    A. To produce electricity.

    B. To manufacture plastics.

    C. To supply chemical industries.

    D. To heat homes and buildings.

4. How many barrels of petroleum are produced in America per year?

    A. 1. 2 million barrels.

    B. 1,290 million barrels.

    C. 1,977 million barrels.

    D. 2,700 million barrels.

5. What is the percentage of natural gas and manufactured gas in the total power of America?

    A. One quarter.   B. One third.

    C. One half.   D. Three quarters.

Lecture 8

1. How did the emperors plan the city and arrange the residential areas?

    A. According to the etiquette systems of the Zhou Dynasty.

    B. According to the etiquette systems of the Ming Dynasty .

    C. According to the social status of the residents.

    D. According to what they liked.

2. Who lived near the palace to the east and west?

    A. Artists.

    B. Poor people.

    C. Laborers.

    D. Imperial kinsmen and aristocrats.

3. Where were simple and crude hutongs mostly located?

    A. Very near the palace.

    B. In the Forbidden City.

    C. Far to the north and south of the palace.

    D. Far to the east and west of the palace.

4. What do you know about the ordinary people's quadrangles?

    A. They were small in size but beautifully built.

    B. They were simply built with small gates and low houses.

    C. They had beautifully painted big gates but small windows.

    D. The roof beams were beautifully carved and painted.

5. What is the percentage of the houses along hutongs in the urban district of Beijing today?

    A. 1/3.   B. 1/2.

C. 1/4.   D. 2/3.

Lecture 9

1. According to FBI Director Muller, what is the main responsibility of the FBI?

    A. To protect the United States from terrorist attacks.

    B. To investigate threats from other countries.

    C. To employ more people skilled in languages.

    D. To appoint more people to intelligence positions.

2. Why does the Justice Department reorganize "the FBI"?

    A. The FBI has failed to collect information about religious organizations.

    B. The FBI headquarters lacks skilled agents.

    C. More hands are greatly needed in gathering information about terrorist attacks.

    D. The FBI has been criticized for its actions in relation to the Sep. 11th terrorist attacks.

3. How many more agents does the FBI plan to hire?

    A. 11,500.   B. 900.

    C. 500.   D. 1,900.

4. What kind of people does the FBI plan to hire?

    A. People whose major is information technology.

    B. People who studied foreign languages in college.

    C. People skilled in computer technology, science and languages.

    D. People skilled in gathering and studying intelligence information.

5. What do some civil rights groups say about the new rules of the FBI?

    A. The new rules interfere with traditional American rights.

    B. The new rules have threatened the safety of American Muslims.

    C. The new rules will bring efficiency to the FBI.

    D. Under the new rules, political dissenters will be expelled from the US.

Lecture 10

1. Where was George Washington's home located?

    A. In Massachusetts.

    B. In Washington, D. C.

    C In Virginia.

    D. In Alabama.

2. What are David Milarch and his son?

    A. Environmentalists.

    B. Mount Vernon workers.

    C. Mount Vernon officials.

    D. Tree experts.

3. Where does David Milarch plan to clone the thirteen oldest trees?

    A. In tree nurseries in Massachusetts.

    B. In tree nurseries in Alabama and Oregon.

C. At Mount Vernon.

D. In Arnold Arboretum at Harvard University.

4. Which of the following is NOT true about cloning trees?

    A. Grafting is the name of the process used to copy trees.

    B. Grafting has existed for a very short time.

    C. The T-bud technique often is used to clone trees.

    D. Grafting technique has been used for thousands of years.

5. Why are the old trees at Mount Vernon important?

    A. Many of them died of environmental pollution.

    B. They are on the verge of extinction.

    C. They existed when George Washington was alive.

    D. They were planted by George Washington himself.

Longer Conversation 1

1. According to the professor, if a student wants to find a best college, what is the first thing he should
    do?

    A. Ask himself some important questions.

    B. Ask a good professor for help.

    C. Ask his parents for help.

    D. Ask his friends for help.

2. What kind of college is NOT mentioned as one for a student to choose?

    A. Large university.

    B. Large private university.

    C. Junior college.

    D. Technical college.

3. How many ways are mentioned for a student to pay for tuition?

    A. Two.

    B. Three.

    C. Four.

    D. Five.

4. When it comes to the choice of majors, what kind of school should a student apply to?

    A. A school that has hot majors.

    B. A school that has literature majors.

    C. A school that has business majors.

    D. A school that has a wide range of majors.

5. Which school of the following is the best choice for a student?

    A. A school that has good college representatives.

    B. A school that has characteristics that are important to him.

    C. A school that has a beautiful campus.

    D. A school that costs less.

Longer Conversation 2

1. Why did the women talk to the professor?

    A. She wants him to recommend books.

    B. She wants to reply to graduate schools.

    C. She wants to take an advanced course.

    D. She wants him to give her a good grade.

2. What is the professor's first reply to the woman's request?

    A. He does not intend to offer the course.

    B. He does not think the course will interest her.

    C. He never accepts undergraduates in his course.

    D. He thinks the course will be too difficult for her.

3. What does the woman say to persuade the professor to help her?

    A. She is unusually well prepared.

    B. She wants to take an easy course.

    C. She needs additional credits in the subject.

    D. She wants to read a book in this field.

4. What does the woman say about the geology course she had already taken?

    A. She had a hard time keeping up.

    B. She found it much too easy.

    C. She didn't think she was qualified.

    D. She wasn't satisfied with her grade.

5. What does the professor promise to do?

    A. Pick out some books for her.

    B. Tutor her himself.

    C. Let her enroll in an easier course.

    D. Ask another professor for his opinion.

Longer Conversation 3

1. Why did the man suggest that the woman read the book?

    A. The professor had written it.

    B. It is the kajor text for the course.

    C. It contains new sociological evidence.

    D. The students from last year liked it.

2. Why doesn't the woman buy the book?

    A. She doesn't really need it.

    B. She will borrow it from the library.

    C. She doesn't want a used copy.

    D. She doesn't have enough money.

3. Why did the woman have problems getting the book from the library?

    A. It wasn't published recently.

B. It is in great demand.

C. It was sold out already.

D. It isnt owned by the library.

4. What will the man ask Henry to do?

 A. To lend the book to the woman.

 B. To sell the book to the woman.

 C. To coach the woman for the course.

 D. To read the book with the woman.

5. How did the woman react to Jim's idea?

 A. She wonders if she can afford it.

 B. She doesn't want to bother Jim's roommates.

 C. She thinks it wouldn't work.

 D. She thinks it's a good one.

Longer Conversation 4

1. Where do you suppose the above converstaion took place?

 A. In the classroom.

 B. In the library.

 C. In the restaurant.

 D. In the drugstore.

2. When will the man probably see the woman again?

 A. Tomorrow.

 B. Next week.

 C. Next month.

 D. Next Saturday.

3. Who do you think the woman speaker is?

 A. A librarian.

 B. A student.

 C. A teacher.

 D. A waitress.

4. What seems to be the matter with the woman speaker's title?

 A. It's too narrow.

 B. It's too broad.

 C. It's too heavy.

 D. It's too trifle.

5. What did the man promise to do for the woman next time they meet?

 A. To help her out.

 B. To look at her tough draft of the term paper.

 C. To correct the mistakes.

 D. To select a better topic.

Longer converstion 5

1. What is the woman probably working on?

    A. B. A.

    B. M. A.

    C. Ph. D.

    D. Postdoctoral.

2. What is the requirement for her degree?

    A. She needs 36 credits.

    B. She'll have to get 15 credits each from the English and the Education Departments.

    C. She can write a thesis.

    D. She can take 2 more selected courese.

3. What is NOT true according to this talk?

    A. She should take American Literature.

    B. Her English is not so good as he expected.

    C. She's had English Literature.

    D. She must take American Prose and Fiction.

4. How many hours must a full-time student have one semester?

    A. More than 20.

    B. About 12.

    C. No less than 12.

    D. 12 at most.

5. What conclusion may be drawn from the talk?

    A. She's been in the United States before.

    B. She'd like to go fast in her studies.

    C. She'll also take exams on audited courses.

    D. She would rather take fewer classes than fail any.

Longer converstion 6

1. What is the conversation mainly about?

    A. Why must the man take a science course?

    B. Which science teachers are the best?

    C. Which science course should the man take?

    D. Which science courses has he woman taken?

2. Why is the man going to take a science course?

    A. He's thinking of becoming a science major.

    B. He wants to study medicine after he graduates.

    C. His parents insist that he take one.

    D. The school requires it for graduation.

3. Why isn't the man going to take astronomy?

    A. He has heard the teacher is poor.

B. It won't fit in his schedule.

C. He did badly in it in high school.

D. The labs are too time-consuming.

4. What is the man's objection to take biology?

A. It requires too much math for him.

B. It is too hard for nonscience majors.

C. Cutting up animals makes him feel ill.

D. The labs meet at the same time as his drama course.

5. What course has the woman not taken?

A. Astronomy.

B. Physics.

C. Chemistry.

D. Biology.

Longer converstion 7

1. What are these people talking about?

A. How the man is doing at his studies.

B. The way time passes.

C. The town they live in.

D. The things they like to do.

2. Why is the woman surprised at what the man says?

A. He doesn't remember when they moved.

B. He has done so much in two years.

C. He has already studied for four years.

D. He still doesn't know the town very well.

3. What does the man say about the passage of time?

A. It always goes too fast.

B. It always goes too slowly.

C. It seems slower when one has too much to do.

D. It seems slower when one has little to do.

4. How does the woman feel?

A. She is bored by her work.

B. She has too much to do.

C. She is studying too hard.

D. She doesn't like the town.

5. What will the man and the woman do in the future?

A. Open a biochemical laboratory.

B. Continue their education.

C. Refinish the furniture.

D. Teach biochemistry.

Longer converstion 8

1. Where was the old Ghost Town located?

    A. Close to Denver.

    B. Near the Grand Canyon.

    C. Near Virginia City.

    D. Close to Indian Falls.

2. What was the result of Jimmy's sickness?

    A. They had to stay in Denver two days.

    B. They missed seeing the Grand Canyon.

    C. They started out on the wrong highway.

    D. Thay almost didn't see Indian Falls.

3. Which highway did the family take from Denver?

    A. Highway 40.

    B. Highway 14.

    C. Highway 90.

    D. Highway 19.

4. What occurred in Phoenix, Arizona?

    A. John was prevented from going fishing.

    B. Jimmy got sick from eating too many grapes.

    C. They stayed with the wife's cousin.

    D. They had some trouble with their automobile.

5. Which of these statements is correct?

    A. They visited all the places they wanted to see.

    B. They had a good time despite some difficulties.

    C. They came back from their trip quite refreshed.

    D. They had their car repaired when they got home.

Longer converstion 9

1. What is the woman interestd in seeing?

    A. An exhibit of paintings.

    B. A Broadway play.

    C. A modern dance production.

    D. An opera.

2. Who gave New York its nickname?

    A. Artists.

    B. Tour guides.

    C. Grocers.

    D. Musicians.

3. When did New York get its nickname?

    A. The late seventeenth century.

B. The early eighteenth century.

C. The late nineteenth century.

D. The early twentieth century.

4. What does the word "apple" in the phrase "the big apple" mean?

A. An instrument.

B. A city.

C. A theater.

D. A concert.

5. How does the woman describe New York?

A. Interesting.

B. Huge.

C. Popular.

D. Old.

Longer converstion 10

1. What is the subject of this conversation?

A. San Francisco.

B. Forest Fires.

C. Redwood trees.

D. Survival skills.

2. Where can the tallest trees be found?

A. In Muir Woods.

B. Near Los Angeles.

C. In San Francisco.

D. Along the northern California coast.

3. Why do so many tourists visit Muirwoods, rather than other redwood forests?

A. It has no admission fee.

B. It is near San Francisco.

C. It has a good view of the coast.

D. It can be seen in one hour.

4. Approximately what is the oldest documented age for a redwood tree?

A. 350 years.

B. 400 years.

C. 800 years.

D. Over 2,000 years.

5. What has contributed most to the redwoods survival?

A. Absence of natural enemies.

B. Resistant bark and damp climate.

C. Coastal isolation.

D. Cool weather and daily fog.

Part 3

Basic Skills Needed for Writing
写作基础必备

Generally speaking, there are five skills in English. Namely they are listening, speaking, reading, writing and translation/interpretation. In TOEFL test four skills are tested by ETS, and writing is one of them. Like speaking, writing is a kind of productive skill in which candidates are expected to generate output. Therefore, the amount of the output and the quality of the output produced by candidates are of great importance. In order to produce an effective and sufficient writing output, it is imperative for candidates to lay a solid foundation on basic writing skills such as paragraph writing before they attempt to undertake the more complicated one like summary writing and essay writing.

In the following you will learn how to write coherent and unified paragraphs and essays as well as summary through a systematic way.

一般说来,英语有五大技能,即听、说、读、写、译。在托福考试里这几项都是需要经过 ETS 测试的,如同口语部分一样,写作测试部分是一种输出型技能,主要考查考生们的写作能力。因此,考生们写出文章的质和量就显得非常重要。为了使考生写出质量高和量足的文章,在尝试较难的写作,诸如概要、短文之前,基础写作技巧(如,段落写作)打下一个坚实的基础是十分重要的。

在以下面的部分,你将会通过一个系统的方法学会如何写出连贯流畅的段落和文章以及概要。

Section A
Paragraph Writing

An essay is made up of several paragraphs. First study paragraph form and struction. Then study essay form and structure.

(一) Topic Sentences

The topic sentence states the topic and a controlling idea concerning that topic. Look at the following example.

People give many reasons for owning a car.

The topic of the sentence is "owning a car". The controlling idea is "reasons". All the supporting ideas in the paragraph should be "reasons for owning a car".

The following phrases, or ones similar to these, can be used in your topic sentence to express the controlling idea:

The reasons for

The causes of (the effects of)

The steps for (the procedure for)

The advantages of (the disadvatnages of)

The ways to (the methods of)

The different sections (parts, kinds, types) of

The charactristics (traits, qualities) of

The problems of

The precautions for

The changes to

Exercise 1. Looking at topic sentences

Write a topic sentene for each of the following topics. Use one of the phrases above or one of your own for your controlling idea.

Example: catching colds

People can avoid catching a cold by taking certain precautions.

This topic sentence includes the topic "catching colds" and the controlling idea "taking precautions".

1. large cars _____

2. living in a remote area _____

3. studying abroad _____

4. accidents _____

5. airports _____

6. absenteeism _____

7. taking exams _____

8. computers _____

9. rice _____

10. camping _____

Exercise 2. Checking topic sentences

Your topic sentence should tell the person who is reading your paragraph what the paragraph is about. Read the following prargraph and decide whether the topic sentence is stong or weak. (The topic is underlined.)

Basebal is a popular sport in the United States. There are two teams of nine players each. Players on one team take turns batting, and the other team tries to put the batters out. The batter hits the ball and then tries to run around the bases and get "home" safely. The other team tries to put the batter out by catching the ball before it hits the ground, throwing the ball to the base before the batter gets there, or by tagging the batter with the ball. The batter can stop at any one of the three bases if it is impossible to make it "home".

The topic sentence in the paragraph is weak because it tells us that "baseball is a popular sport', but the rest of the paragraph tells us how baseball is played. A strong topic sentence would tell us, the readers, that the paragraph is going to describe how baseball is played. Here is a strong topic sentence.

Baseball, a popular game in the United states, is played in the following way.

Now the reader knows that the paragraph will describe how baseball is played instead of where it is played, or who plays it, or why it is popular.

Read the following paragraphs. The topic sentences are underlined. If the topic sentence is weak, rewtire it in the space provided.

1. <u>Even though the procedures followed to enroll in an American university vary according to each university, some steps are the same.</u> First, you should contact the registration office of the university you want to attend to get the necessary forms and information concerning that particular university's entrance requirements. The you must follow the steps outlined in their response. You will probably have to send copies of your high school diploma, get letters of recommendation, and write an essay on why you want to study there. You may have to achieve a cetain score on the TOEFL test and have your scores forwarded to that university. Finally, you will have to contact the American Embassy to start the procedures to obtain a student visa.

_____

_____

2. <u>I like to go to the beach whenever I have the opportunity.</u> I start the day by enjoying a refrshing swim. Then I walk along the beach and collect shells. Later you'll find me relaxing in the warm sunshine and making sand castles. The I sleep for a while before I open the basket of food and drinks that I always pack to take.

_____

_____

3. <u>Many students cannot afford a car.</u> The city bus service usually passes the university, so those students can get to class on the bus. Many universities have a special shuttle bus that is provided for student transportation. Some students like to ride to class on bicycles. This is good exercise. Also, it is easier to find a space to leave a bicycle than to find a parking space for a car on a crowded university campus. Those students who live close to campus or on campus can enjoy a leisurely walk to their classes.

_____

_____

Exercise 3. Writing topic sentences

The following paragraphs consist of supporting ideas. Read each paragraph and ask yourself what is being discussed or described (the topic) and how the topic is approached (the controlling idea). Then write a topic sentence for each paragraph.

1. _____

_____

Pictures or posters on the wall make a dormitory room feel more like home. A rug on the floor beside the bed is a nice addition to an otherwise cold hard floor. Besides textbooks, favorite books from home on the bookshelf and a photograph or two of the family on the desk also add a comforting touch to the impersonal dormitory room.

2. _____

_____

_____

The white pages of an American telephone book give the phone number of residences. The blue pages contain the numbers of government offices, and the yellow pages have advertisements and business numbers. There are maps as well as indexes at the back of the book. The telephone books of larger cities may provide separate books for different sections of the city, while those of small towns may have room to include the numbers from several towns all in one book.

3. _____

_____

_____

First, the fast-food restaurant is good for people who must have a quick bite because of a busy schedule. Second, the food is inexpensive yet tasy. A person can eat an enjoyable meal out and stay within a limited budget. Finally, the food is usually consistent. For example, a cheeseburger from a well-known fast-food restaurant looks and tastes about the same no matter where in the world it is purchased. Consequently, buyers know exactly what they are getting.

(二) Supporting Ideas

Your topic sentence tells the reader what the paragraph will be about. The ideas stated in the rest of the paragraph should all refer to the given topic and the controlling idea. Look at the following example.

There are many ways to eat peanut butter. You can spread it on a slice of bread like butter, or you can make it into a sandwich with jam. Peanut can be a major ingredient of very tasty cookies as weel as cakes and candies. It is delicious in ice cream. Peanut butter was invented by George Washington Carver. My favorite way to eat peanut butter is to lick it off a spoon.

Our topic sentence tells the reader that we are discussing peanut butter. The controlling idea is "way of eating it". All of the sentences should be about ways of eating peanut butter. Are they? No. The sentence "peanut butter was invented by George Washington Carver" does not refer to ways of eating peanut butter.

Exercise 4. Checking supporting ideas

Look at the following outlines. Circle the letter of the idea that does not support the topic.

1. Ways to get rid of hiccups _____ .

    A. breathe into a paper bag

    B. hold your breath to the count of 10

    C. have someone frighten you

    D. make an appointment with your doctor

2. Steps for planning a trip _____ .

    A. purchasing a map

    B. working late

    C. making an itinerary

    D. reserving a ticket

3. Reasons for car accidents _____ .

   A. fast driving

   B. drinking and driving

   C. not following traffic regulations

   D. giving signals

4. Advantages of small apartments _____ .

   A. good school facilitie

   B. easy to clean

   C. cheaper to furnish

   D. relatively inexpensive

5. Chararacteristics of a good restaurant _____ ,

   A. efficient waiters

   B. tasty food

   C. jacket and tie required

   D. pleasant atmosphere

Exercise 5. Checking paragraphs for supporting ideas

Read these paragraphs and cross out the one idea that doesn't support the topic sentence.

1. Working at a part-time job while studying at a university has many advantages. If students can get a job in their area of study, they are gaining valuable experience and putting their knowledge to use immediately. The extra money they can earn will be useful for meeting tuition fees and enjoying university activities. Also, they will have the personal satisfaction of having contributed to their own education. Students who need extra money can hold down a full-time temporary job during their summer vacation.

2. Hobbies are important for many reasons. First, a hobby can be educational. For example, if the hobby is stamp collecting, the person can learn about the countries of the world and even some of their history. Second, engaging in the hobby can lead to meeting other people with the same interests. A person can also meet other people by going to parties. Third, a person's free time is being used in a positive way. The person has no time to be bored or get into mischief while engaged in the hobby. Finally, some hobbies can lead to a future job. A person who enjoys a hobby-related job is more satisfied with life.

3. There are several features of spoken English that make it difficult for me to understand. First, many words are not pronounced as they are spelled, so when I learn new words through reading, I sometimes don't understand them when they are spoken. Second, native speakers contrac words and phrases. "What are you doing?" becomes "Whacha doin?" In my opinion, people should wrie clearly. Third, native speakers have a wide range of accents. A British accent is very different from a Texas one. Fourth, there are lots of idioms and slang experssions. These expressions also differ depending on the area a speaker is from. Finally, there are sounds that don't exist in my language that do eist in English and vice versa. These sounds are difficult for me to distinguish.

Exercise 6. Writing supporting ideas

Use the topic sentencs that you wrote for Exercise 1. Outline four supporting ideas.

Example: catching colds

Topic sentece: People can aviod catching a cold by taking certain prcautions.

Supporting ideas: A. avoid people with colds

B. get plenty of sleep

C. eat nutritious food

D. take vitamin C

1. Topic sentece _____
    Supporting ideas A. _____
    B. _____
    C. _____
    D. _____

2. Topic sentence _____
    Supporting ideas A. _____
    B. _____
    C. _____
    D. _____

3. Topic sentence _____
    Supporting ideas A. _____
    B. _____
    C. _____
    D. _____

4. Topic sentence _____
    Supporting ideas A _____
    B. _____
    C. _____
    D. _____

5. Topic sentence _____
    Supporting ideas A _____
    B. _____
    C. _____
    D. _____

6. Topic sentence _____
    Supporting ideas A _____
    B. _____
    C. _____
    D. _____

7. Topic sentence _____
    Supporting ideas A _____

B. _____

C. _____

D. _____

8. Topic sentence _____

   Supporting ideas A _____

B. _____

C. _____

D. _____

9. Topic sentence _____

   Supporting ideas A _____

B. _____

C. _____

D. _____

10. Topic sentence _____

   Supporting ideas A _____

B. _____

C. _____

D. _____

Exercise 7. Writing supporting ideas in a paragraph

On your own paper, write out the paragraphs you outlined in Exercise 6 by expanding your supporting ideas into complete sentences.

Example: Catching Colds

People can avoid catching a cold by taking certain precautions. Perhaps the most important precaution is to avoid people who already have cold so that you are not exposed to cold germs. You should also get plenty of sleep so that you are not exposed to cold germs. You should also get plenty of sleep so that your resistance is strong. Eating nutritious food will ensure that you have the vitamins that can help fight cold germs. Finally, you could try vitamin C supplements, which may help prevent your catching a cold.

Extended practice: Use the sample outlines in the Answer Key for Exercise 6 to practice writing more paragraphs.

(三) Practice with details

To make a more fully developed paragraph, you need to add details to your supporting ideas. Your ideas can be facts, examples, personal experiences, or descriptions.

Look at this topic sentence:

The Smithsonian Institution is worth visiting for a number of reasons.

The topic is "the Smithsonian Institution," and the controlling idea is "reasons for a visit".

Look at the following supporting ideas and details:

Supporting idea 1.

The Smithsonian Institution is composed of various museums that offer something for everyone.

Details-facts:

These museums consist of the National Museum of History and Technology, the National Aeronautics and space Museum, the National Collection of Fine Arts, the National Museum of Natural History, and several others.

Supporting idea 2.

A person can do more than just look at the exhibits.

Details-example:

For example, in the insect zoo at the National Museum of National History, anyone who so desires can handle some of the exhibits.

Supporting idea 3.

The museums provide unforgettable experiences.

Details-personal experience:

In climbing through Skylab at the National Aeronautics and Space Museum, I was able to imagine what it would be like to be an astronaut in space.

Supporting idea 4.

Movies shown at regular intervals aid in building an appreciation of our world.

Details-description:

In the National Aeronautics and Space Museum, there is a theater which has a large screen. When the movie is shown, it gives the illusion that the viewer is in the movie itself, either floating above the earth in a hot-air balloon or hang gliding over cliffs.

On your own paper, write out the paragraphs you outlined in Exercise 6 by expending your sapporting ideas into complete sentences.

Exercise 8. Adding details

Write one sentence that adds a detail to each of the following ideas. Use facts, examples, personal experiences or descriptions.

1. The capital city of our country is Bejing.

_____

2. My favorite pastime is reading.

_____

3. The videocassette player may make movie theaters obsolete.

_____

4. It is very important for me to pass the TOEFL test.

_____

5. A long vacation at the beach is a nice way to relax.

_____

6. Habits such as smoking are hard to break.

_____

7. Many bad traffic acidents could be prevented.

8. Modern architecture has its critics as well as its admirers.

_____

9. The city was built on an ancient site.

_____

10. The suburban mall has taken away a lot of business from cith centers.

_____

Exercise 9. Adding details to paragraphs

Many paragraphs can be made better by adding details. Read the following paragraph.

Although seat belts have been shown to save lives, people give a number of reasons for not using them. First, many people think they are a nuisance. Second, many people are crazy. Third, some people don't believe they will have an accident. Finally, some people are afraid the seat belt will trap them in their car. All of these reasons seem inadequate, since statistics show that wearing seat belts saves lives and prevents serious injuries.

The pragraph can be improved. Read the following questions.

A. Why don't people like seat belts?

B. In what way are people lazy?

C. Why do people think they won't have an accident?

D. Under what circumstances might people get trapped?

Asking and answering these kinds of questions will help strengthen the paragraph. Now read the paragraph with details. Notice how adding the answers to these questions has improved it.

Although seat belts have been shown to save lives, people give a number of reasons for not using them. First many people think they are a nuisance. They say the belt is unconfortable and inhibits freedom of movement. Second, many people are lazy. For them it is too much trouble to put on and adjust a seat belt, especially if they are only going a short distance. Third, some people don't believe they will have an accident because they are careful and experienced drivers. They think they will be able to resond quickly to avoid a crash. Finally, some people are afraid the seat belt will trap them in their cars. If they have an accident, they might not be able to get out of a car that is burning, or they might be unconscious and another person won't be able to get them out. All of these reasons seem inadequate, since statistics show that wearing seat belts saves lives and prevents serious injuries.

On your own paper, rewrite the following . "weak" paragraphs by answering the questions and using those answers within the paragraph.

1. When you plant a tree, you are helping your environment in many ways. Your tree will provide a home and food for other creatures. It will hold the soil in place. It will provide shade in the summer. You can watch it grow and someday show your children or even grandchildren the tree you planted.

A. What kind of home would the tree provide?

B. What kind of food would the tree provide?

C. What kind of creatures might use the tree?

D. Why is holding the soil in place important?

E. Why is shade important?

2. Airplanes and helicopters can be used to save people's lives. Helicopters can be used for rescuring people in trouble. Planes can transport food and supplies when disasters strike. Both types of aircraft can transport people to hospitals in emergencies. Helicopters and airplanes can be used to provide medical servies to people who live in remote areas.

A. In What situations do people need rescuring by helicopters?

B. What kinds of disasters might happen?

C. What kinds of emergencies may require transporting people to hospitals?

D. How can helicopters and airplanes be used to provide medical services to people in remote areas?

3. Studying in another country is advantageous in many ways. A student is exposed to a new culture. Sometimes he or she can learn a new language. Students can often have learning experiences not available in their own countries. A student may get the opportunity to study at a university where a leading expert in his or her field may be teaching.

A. How can exposure to a new culture be an advantage?

B. How can learning a new language be an advantage?

C. What kinds of experiences might a student have?

D. What are the benefits of studying under a leading expert?

Exercise 10. Further practice in adding details to paragraphs

The following paragraphs are weak. They could be improved by adding details. On your own paper, write your own questions. Then make the pragraph stronger by inserting the answers to your questions.

1. Even though airplanes are fast and comfortable, I prefer to travel by car. When traveling by car, I can look at the scenery. Also, I can stop along the road. Sometimes I meet interesting people from the area I am traveling through. I can carry as much luggage as I want, and I don't worry about missing flights.

2. Wild animals should no be kept in captivity for many reasons. First, animals are often kept in poor and inhumane conditions. In addition, many suffer poor health from lack of exercie and indicate frustration and stree theough their neurotic behavior. Also, some animals will not breed in captivity. Those animals that mate often do so with a related animal such as a sister or brother. In conclusion, money spent in the upkeep of zoos would be better spent in protecting natural habitats.

3. Good teachers should have the following qualities. First, they must know the material that they are teaching very well. Second, they should be able to explain their knowledge. Third, they must be patient and understanding. Last, they must be able to make the subject interesting to the students.

（四） Organizing and writing pragraphs

Brainstorming means thinking of and writing down ideas concerning a topic. Ask yourself questions such as "who?" "what?" "where?" "when?" "why?" and "how"? to get ideas about your topic. Write down any idea that comes into your head. Later you can go through your list and pick the ideas you want to write about. You will have to do this quickly when you write the TOEFL essay. Practice first with simple topics, as in the following example:

Example

Topic: TV

Ideas

1. a TV set	16. public announcement
2. programs	17. news
3. sports	18. broadcaster
4. black-and-white	19. technology
5. color	20. commercials
6. directors	21. private and public
7. major studios	22. movies
8. cartoons	23. actors and actresses
9. schedules	24. camera operators
10. sound effects	25. soap operas
11. makeup	26. satellites
12. education	27. scriptwriters
13. entertainment	28. weather
14. violence	29. censorship
15. cable	30. documentaries

After you have listed your ideas, group the related ideas together. In the following example about the topic "TV".

A. marks the ideas concerning programming

B. marks the ideas concerning technology

C. marks the ideas concerning people, and

D. marks the ideas concerning informative programs

Notice that not all ideas have been used. Aslo, some ideas may fit into two categories.

Example:

A. programs, sports, cartoons, sceduls, education, entertainment, violence, news, commercials, movies, soap operas, weather, censorship, documentaries

B. a TV set, black-and-white, color, sound effects, makeup cable, technology, satellites

C. directors, broadcaster, actors and actresses, camera operators scriptwriters

D. education, news, weather, documentaries

Each group of the related ideas above can be made into a pragraph. A topic sentence is needed to introduce the paragraph.

Look at the following topic sentences which cover the related ideas concerning TV.

Example:

A. A large variety of programs can be seen on TV today.

B. Modern technology plays an important part in today's TV broadcasting.

C. Many highly trained and skilled people are involved in making and present the programs we watch.

D. The main purpose of many programs on TV is to bring the viewer up to date on important world or regional events.

Now take out a piece of paper and write as many ideas as you can about the topic "Cars". Then write topic sentences for your related ideas concerning "Cars".

After you have finished them, the next thing for you to do is to write an outline to put your ideas in order. You may want to leave some of the ideas out or add more.

Example:

1. A large variety of programs can be seen on TV today_____.

   A. sports

   B. news

   C. children's programs

   D. educational programs

   E. movies

   F. soap operas

2. Modern technology plays an important part in today's TV broadcasting_____.

   A. satellites

   B. TV sets

   C. Special effects

3. Many highly trained and skilled people are involved in making and presenting the programs we watch_____.

   A. directors

   B. actors and actresses

   C. camera operators

   D. costume designers

   E. hair stylistists and makeup artists

   F. special effects experts.

4. The main purpose of many programs on TV is to bring the viewer up to date on important world or regional events_____.

   A. news

   B. public announcements

   C. weather

Once you have done the outline, the following step is to add details to your outline. As you do this, you may decide to revise your outline in some way.

Example:

A large variety of programs can be seen on TV today.

   A. sports

      1. variety such as footbal, basketbal

      2. day of week and time of day when shown

    3. Olympic games

B. News

    1. local

    2. national

    3. international

C. children's programs

    1. educational

    2. cartoons

D. educational programs

    1. children

    2. university home study

    3. documentaries

E. movies

    1. movies made for TV

    2. films shown on TV

    3. old movies

F. soap operas

    1. variety

    2. time shown

Now add details to all of your outlines from Exercise 6.

Exercise 11. Brainstorming

For each of the following topics, write at least 12 ideas. Then combine related ideas and make an outline. Do not spend more than five minutes on any topic.

1. books

2. education

3. space exploration

4. travel

5. holidays

Brainstorming for questions

Read the following questions.

1. What things need to be considered before taking a long trip?

2. What are some of the advantages of large cars?

3. What factors should a student take into consideration when Choosing a university?

4. What are some problems a person has to deal with when living with a roommate?

5. What are some of the disadvantages of having a job and being a student at the same thime?

Use the steps described in brainstorming part to write about the preceding five questions. First, brainstorm ideas about each question. Next, combine related ideas and write topic sentences. Then organize your ideas into an outline and add details. Your outlines do not have to be very elaborate. Don't spend more than eight minutes on each question. Look at the following example first.

Example:

What are some of the programs a working mother faces?

1. child care

2. sick children

3. exhaustion

4. raising children

5. worry and anxiety

6. housework after job

7. cost of trnasportation

8. child-care expenses

9. getting time off

10. staying late at work

We will now group the related ideas together. Note that C = children, EE = extra expenses, PP = physical problems, and WP = world-related problems.

C: child care, sick chidren, raising children

EE: cost of transportation, child-care expenses

PP: exhaustion, worry and anxiety

WP: housework after job, getting time off, staying late at work

(一) The major problems a working mother faces concern her children.

    A. child care

        1. finding a related person to be at home with the child

        2. finding a day-care center where the child can go

    B. sick children

        1. special arrangements

        2. mother must skip work

    C. raising children

        1. who's teaching mother's values

        2. how smaller children attend activities after school

(二) Even though a mother is frequently forced into working for economic reasons, she soon

        discovers that there are added expenses.

    A. child-care expenses

    B. cost of transportation

        1. to work

        2. to day care

    C. clothes to work in

(三) A working mother sometimes suffer physically.

    A. exhaustion

    B. worry and anxiety

        1. children's safety

    2. being a good parent

C. extra work

    1. housework after job

    2. chid care after job

（四）Women who have chidren sometimes face problems at work that don't affect other working women.

    A. can't stay late

        1. must pick up chid

        2. must check up on child

    B. needs extra time off

        1. care for newborns

        2. has ill child

        3. must attend school meetings

Exercise 12. Writing paragraphs

Write paragraphs for the topics you outlined in Exercise 11.

Sample:

The major problems a working mother faces concern her children. She must either find a reliable person who will be loving toward the children or a good day-care center where the children can go. If a child gets sick, the mother must make special arrangements for the child to be cared for at home, or she must stay home from work. While at work, the mother may worry about her children. She may wonder if they are safe, if they are learning the values she wants them to have, and if her absence is hurting them emotionally. She may also regret not being able to take them to after-school activities or participate in family activities with them.

Section B
Essay Writing

The parts of an essay are much like the parts of a paragraph. The essay begins with an introductory paragraph which tells the reader what the essay is about, just as the topic sentence tells the reader what the paragraph is about. The body of the essay is made up of paragraphs that support the introduction, and the concluding paragraph completes the essay.

Study the following model essay.

Question

Some people believe that a mother should not work. Others argue against this. Consider the problems that a working mother faces. Do you believe a mother should work? Support your opinion.

Essay

Nowadays it is very common for mothers to work outside the home. Whether a woman should stay at home or join the work force is debated by many people. Some argue that the family, especially small children, may be neglected. The fact is, however, that many women need to work because of economic reasons or want to work to maintain a career. I believe that every mother has the right to work, and the decision to work should be one that a woman makes on her own. But first she should carefully consider the many problems that affect mothers who work. (Introductory paragraph)

The major problems a working mother faces concern her children. She must either find a reliable person who will be loving toward the children or a good day-care center where the children can go. If a child gets sick, the mother must make special arrangements for the child to be cared for at home, or she must stay home from work. While at work, the mother may worry about her children. She may wonder if they are safe, if they are learning the values she wants them to have, and if her absence is hurting them emotionally. She may also regret not being able to take them to after-school activities with them. (Supporting/developmental paragraph I)

Even though a mother is frequently forced into working for economic reasons, she soon discovers that there are added expenses. Her biggest expense is child care. Another expense is transportation. This may include purchasing and maintaining a car. Yet another expense is clothing, such as uniform or stylish suits to maintain a professional appearance. Finally, if her company does not have a subsidized cafeteria, she will have to pay for food in restaurants. (Supporting/developmental paragraph II)

After a mother takes into account all of the above problems and perhaps other problems unique to her situation, she must decide if a job is worth it. I believe that even though she faces major obstacles, these obstacles are not insurmountable. Many mothers do work and manage a family very successfully. In conclusion, it is a woman's right to make this choice, and only the woman herself should decide this matter. (Conclusion)

Analysis

1. Introductory paragraph

Notice that the essay has an introductory paragraph which states the general topic "working mothers". It restates the information in the question about people being in disagreement. It states the opinion that every mother has the right to work and that the decision to work should be a mother's choice. It then tells the reader that the essay will focus on a controlling idea—the problems that a woman must first consider before making this decision. The sentence containing the controlling idea of an essay is called the thesis statement. The thesis statement is usually the last sentence of the introductory paragraph.

2. Second paragraph

The second paragraph in this essay is the first paragraph of the body of the essay. It is called the first developmental paragraph. It supports the controlling idea of problems that was identified in the introduction. The topic sentence(the first sentence) of this paragraph states the idea of "problems concerning chidren". All the sentences in this paragraph describe either a problem concerning chidren or a detail explaining a problem concerning children.

3. Third paragraph

The third paragraph, or second developmental paragraph, in this essay also supports the controlling idea of problems that was identified in the introduction. The topic sentence of this paragraph states the idea of "problem of added expenses". All the sentences in this paragraph describe either an added expense or a detail explaining the added expense.

4. Conclusion

The last paragraph in this essay is the conclusion. The conlusion restates the topic of working mothers. Again, the controlling idea of prolems which face a working mother is repeated. Also, the opinion that it should be a woman's choice is restated. All of these restatements are in different words. The last statement is the concluding statement. It completes the essay.

1. Introduction

To write an introduction for an essay that answers a question, follow these procedures. First, introduce the topic in general. Then narrow the topic down to focus more on the question. Restate the question in your own words and in statement form. The concluding statement of the introduction is the thesis statement and indicates the controlling idea of the essay. Study the following question and the introduction.

Question

Living in an apartment instead of a university dormitory has advantages and disadvantages. Discuss some of the advantages and disadvantages of apartment living and then defend your preference.

Introduction

When a person decides to enter a university away from home, he or she must also consider living accommodations. Although most universities offer student dormitories, students frequently opt to live in an apartment. While there are many advantages to apartment, there are also many disadvantages. Before a student decides to live in an apartment, all the aspects of that kind of accommodation should be reviewed.

(1)The first sentence introduces the general topic of university living accommodations.

When a person decides to enter a university away from home, he or she must also consider living accomodations.

(2)The second sentence narrows the topic down to apartment living.

Although most university offer student dormitories, students frequently opt to live in an apartment.

(3)The third sentence restates the specific question.

While there are many advantages to apartment living, there are also many disadvantages.

(4)The fourth sentence is the thesis statement. It gives the controlling idea of the essay.

Before a student decided to live in an apartment, all the aspects of that kind of accommodation should be reviewed.

Exercise 13. Rewriting introductions

The following student-written introductory paragraphs are weak. Some of them don't state the problem. Some don't include a thesis statement. Others try to put into the introduction all the information that will be discussed in the body or developmental paragraphs of the essay.

Rewrtie these essay introductions using the procedures stated above.

(1)Question: In your opinion, what is the most dangerous threat the world faces today? Discuss some reasons for its existence. Give some possible ways of preventing its occurence.

Weak introduction: War is the most dangerous threat. Everyone in the world fears it. We must try to avoid it.

(2)Question: Modern technology has brought about changes in the roles of men and women. Discuss some of these changes. Do you think these changes have been beneficial?

Weak introduction: There are more changes in the roles of men and women due to technological development in recent times than in the past. This has changed our society.

(3) Question: Advances in technology and science have solved many problems. However, they have also created new problems. Discuss some of the new problems caused by technological advancement and give your opinon on how they should be dealt with.

Weak introduction: Nowadays, we have many great advantages in our society which came from technology and science. For that reason, we must protect our lives by taking care of the dangerous problems advanced technolgy has caused.

2. Developmental paragraph

The body of the essay should consist of at least two developmental paragraphs. Each developmental paragraph should have a topic sentence that supports the controlling idea mentioned in the thesis statement of the introduction. All the ideas in each paragraph should support their topic sentence.

Study the following developmental paragraphs of the essay about apartmental living.

Living in an apartment has many advantages. First, students can choose to live in a quiet neighborhood. A quiet neighborhood is conducive to studying. Away from the distractions of campus life, students can be more serious about their studies. Second, apartment life allows students to be more independent. For example, they can cook whatever they want to eat and have their meals whenever they want them. Third, students can often find apartments that are cheaper than the fee for room and board in a dormitory.

However, living in an apartment also has disadvantages. Being away from campus life can make students feel isolated. Another disadvantage is that apartments close to campus are usually expensive, and those farther away are not within walking distance. Therefore, transportation must be considered. Finally, students who live in apartments must cook their own meals, shop for food, perhaps carry their laundry to a laundromat, and clean their entire apartment-not just their room.

The first developmental paragraph in the body of the essay addresses the question of advantages. The second developmental paragraph addresses the question of disadvantages. Both paragraphs consider aspects of apartment living, which is the controlling idea or the thesis statement.

Now write the developmental paragraphs for the introductions that you rewrote in Exercise 13.

Exercise 14. Comparing and contrasting

When answering an essay question, you may need to compare and contrast some information. Look at the following question.

Question: Both living in an apartment and living in a university dormitory have advantages and disadvantages. Compare these two kinds of living accommodations and defend your preference.

To campare and contrast, you may want to use some of the following words and phrases.

Words used for comparing:

alike, like	identical	equivalent
similar, similarities	also	resembles
just as	likewise	corresponds to

the same	comparable to	by the same token

Words used for contrasting:

unlike	more than, less than, fewer than
different, difference	is different from, differs from
in contrast	worse, better
whereas	conversely
but	on the other hand

To brainstorm for a developmental paragraph that compares and contrasts, list the ideas that are similar and those that are different.

Similarities	Differences
(1)places to live	(1)kitchen facilities
(2)may need to share	(2)space
(3)housing rules	(3)privacy
(4)rent	

There are two ways you can approach writing this essay:

(1)You can discuss both apartment and dormitory similarities in one developmental paragraph and bother apartment and dormitory differences in the second developmental paragraph.

(2)You can discuss only apartments in one paragraph and only dormotories in the other paragraph.

Study the following developmental paragraph on the question concerning apartments and dormitories.

Apartments and dormitories are similar in several ways. First, they are both living accommodations which provide a student with a place to sleep, wash, and keep belongings. They are also alike in that they require living with or near another person. An apartment is usually in a building that houses other people as well. Frequently the person renting the apartment has a roommate to share the expenses. Similarly, in a dormitory, there are many rooms, and students either share rooms or live next door to each other. Another similarity is that both apartments and dormitories have certain rules by which people must abide.

This paragraph uses the first type of development and discusses similarities. Write the second developmental pragraph and discuss the differences between apartments and dormitories. You can use the list of differences on this page as a guide.

Write two developmental paragraphs on this essay question using the second type of development. Discuss only apartments in one paragraph and only dormitories in the other paragraph.

3. Conclusion

So far you have practised writing the introduction(which restates the problem and states the controlling idea) and writing the body(which discusses the problem). To end the essay, you need to write a concluding paragraph.

For the essay question, your concluding paragraph will:

(1)Restate the thesis statement.

(2)Restate the topic sentences from the developmental paragraphs.

(3)State your opinion or preference, make a prediction, or give a solution.

(4)Conclude with a statement that sums up the essay.

Look at the essay question in Exercise 13 again and read the following conclusion.

Conclusion

Even though there are many advantages to apartment living, I would prefer to live in the university dormotory for the following reasons. First, I will be new at the university and meeting people will be easier in a dormitory setting. Second, I won't have to worry about purchasing and cooking food or cleaning up afterwards. Consequently, I will have more time for my studies. Finally, I will be within walking distance of my classes and the university library. In conclusion, living on campus is more advantageous for me than living in an apartment.

Notice that this conclusion restates the topic gives a personal preference. The writer lists the reasons for the preference and concludes with a summary statement.

Exercise 15. Rewriting conclusions

The following student-written conclusions go with the essays you began writing in Exercise 13. These conclusions are weak. Some do not give a solution, prediction, reason, or opinion. Others have a topic sentence but do not support it.

Rewrite the following concluding paragraphs so that they are stronger. Do they apply to your introduction and developmental paragraphs? If not, modify them. You will then have three complete essays.

(1) In summary, there must be a solution to any threat in the world, but a possible solution to this problem is difficult to find. Indeed, there is one possible solution, and that is all people must become pacifists, but it is doubtful that will happen.

(2) To summarize, technological development has given us a new and better lifestyle, and I hope that it will remain so.

(3) For these problems we must find a solution. They can destroy our lives by killing us and making our lives boring. Our lives depend on progress, so we cannot stop it. But at the same time, we cannot kill ourselves by avoiding finding a solution.

Checklist for essay writing

Read the following checklist. You will not have time to rewrite your essay during the test. Therefore, keep this list in mind as you write your outline and essay.

(1) Is there an introductory paragraph?

(2) Does the introductory paragraph restate the question?

(3) Does the introductory paragraph have a thesis statement (a controlling idea)?

(4) Does each paragraph have a clear topic sentence?

(5) Do the topic sentences of the developmental paragraphs support the thsis statement?

(6) Do the ideas in each developmental paragraph support the topic sentence of the paragraph?

(7) Are the details (examples, facts, descriptions, personal experiences) clear?

(8) Is there a concluding paragraph?

(9) Does the concluding paragraph give (A) an opinion, preference, prediction, or solution and (B) reasons?

(10) Does the essay end with a concluding statement?

(11) Does the essay answer all parts of of question?

(12) Have the grammar and spelling been corrected? (Incorrect grammar, spelling, punctuation, and word usage count against you if those errors lead to a lack of clarity. Your essay will be clearer if you correct as many of these errors as you can find in the limited time that you have.)

Answering essay questions

Now that you have studied all the parts of an essay and a checklist for analyzing essays, review the steps used for writing essays that answer essay questions.

Step 1 Read the question carefully

Ask yourself questions. (What is the question about? What is it asking me to do?) Underline and number the key parts of the question. For example, Question Violent TV programs have been blamed for causing crime rates to rise in many cities. But many people do not agree that violence is related to TV viewing. Discuss the possible reasons for both opinions. Give your opinion as to whether or not violent TV programs should be taken off the air. The question is about TV violence. It asks me to:

1. Discuss reasons for both opinions:
    (1). opinion that TV violence is bad
    (2). opinion that TV violence is acceptable
2. Give my own opinion.

Step 2 Brainstorm

In eight minutes or less, write down your ideas, group them into related ideas, and write a thesis statement and a modified outline. Compare the following complete outline and modified outline.

1. Example of a complete outline

    (1) Introduction

        A. state general topic

        B. restate question

        C. give thesis statement-reasons for both sides

    (2) Body

        1) crime related to violent TV programs

            ① children imitate what they see

                A. learn unacceptable values

                B. copy behavior

            ② heroes are frequently violent

            ③ given ideas for crimes

        2) crime not related to violent TV programs

            ① crime related to social pressures

                A. unemployment

                B. homelessness

            ② aggressive feelings vicariously released

            ③ parental guidance more influential

            ④ frequently bad consequences of violence shown

    (3) Conclusion

1) my opinion

   ① shouldn't be censored

     A. people enjoy it

     B. change station

     C. turning if off

   ② censorship questions

     A. who decides?

     B. what else may they censor?

     C. concluding statement

2. Example of modified outline

   T. S. (thesis statement) reasons for supporting both

   1) why crime related to TV

     imitate

     violent heroes

     given ideas

   2) why crime not related to TV

     social pressures-joblessness, homeleness

     rids aggression

     parental influence

     bad consequences

     conclude with opinion

     no censor-enjoyment, change, or turn off

     censor-who decides what

   C. S. (concluding statement) needed evidence

Step 3 Check if the topic sentences will support the thesis statement

According to the preceding outlines, the thesis statement will introduce the essay with reasons for both sides of the question.

Topic sentence 1. indicates that the paragraph will discuss one side of the question—— "Reasons crime is related to TV". This sentence supports the thesis statement.

Topic sentence 2. indicates that the paragraph will discuss the other side of the question—— "Reasons crime is not related to TV". This sentence supports the thesis statement.

Step 4 Check if all supporting ideas related to the topic

According to the preceding outlines, the first topic sentence will discuss "Reasons crime is related to TV". The supporting ideas-imitate what is seen, heroes sometimes violent, and give ideas for crimes-support the argument that TV and crime are related.

The second topic sentence will discuss "Reasons crime is not related to TV". The supporting ideas-social pressures, rids aggression, parental influence, and bad consequences-support the argument that TV and crime are not related.

Step 5 Add more details if necessary

Step 6 Put ideas in a logical order if necessary

Step 7 Write the introduction

Keep in mind the checklist for essay writing. You will not have time to rewrite your essay, so be certain your introduction is clear.

The crime rate in many cities is rising alarmingly. Some people have the idea that violent TV programs are the cause of real crime. However, many others disagree that TV violence can be blamed for this rise. Both sides of the questions of whether TV may or may not be to blame are supported by good reasons.

Step 8 Write the body

Keep in mind the checklist for essay writing. You will not have time to rewrite your essay, so be certain the paragraphs support the thesis statement.

Those who believe that violent TV programs cause crime give many reasons. First, many viewers are children who have not formed a strong understanding of right and wrong. They imitate what they see. If a person on TV gets what he or she wants by stealing it, a child may copy this behavior. Thus, the child has learned unacceptable values. Second, many heroes in today's programs achieve their goals by violent means. Unfortunately, viewers might use similar means to achieve their objectives. Finally, people get ideas about how to commit crimes from watching TV.

Other people argue that violent programs have no relation to the rise in crime rates. First, they claim that social factors, such as unemployment and homelessness, are to blame. Second, some argue that watching violence on TV is an acceptable way to reduce aggressive feelings. In other words, people may become less aggressive through viewing criminal and violent scenes. Third, even though children learn by imitation, their parents are the most influential models. Finally, the villains are usually punished for their crimes.

Step 9 Write the conclusion

Keep in mind the checklist for essay writing. You will not have time to rewrite your essay, so be certain your conclusion completes the essay.

Whether or not violent programs are a factor in the rising crime rate, I am against their removal for the following reasons. First, some people enjoy them, and those who don't can change channels or turn their TVs off. Second, I disagree with other people deciding what I should watch. If violent programs can be censored, perhaps other programs which may be important for our well-being will also be censored. In conclusion, even though I am not fond of violent programs, I am against their removal until conclusive evidence proves that viewing violence creates violence.

Step 10 Read over the essay

Make any minor corrections in spelling and grammar that will make your essay clearer. Remember, you will not have time to make major changes.

Section C
Summary Writing

Most of the compositions you write are based on your personal experiences and opinions. However, one important kind of composition is based on your reading. It is the summary of an article giving information taken from several sources.

In almost any of your classes, including the iBT TOEFL, you may be asked to read an article in a magazine, an encyclopedia, or a book, and write a summary of it. Your problem is to give in a brief composition the main points in the article. To do this, you must read carefully and write a summary in your own words, being careful not to omit important information or to add any ideas of your own.

In preparing a summary, you should proceed in four steps, some of which overlap.

1. Read the article carefully.

It is wise to read the article at least twice. The first time, you may skim it quickly to note the overall organization and to identify the major ideas. Pay special attention to any subtitles, because they indicate the important points made in the article.

The second time, you should read the article more carefully. Read the introductory paragraph slowly and thoughtfully, since the whole idea of the article is usually expressed there in a general way. As you read the body of the article, noting subtitles, pay special attention to the first and last sentences in each paragraph; the topic sentences and "clincher" sentences are usually found in these positions. Also, watch for signaling words and phrases (like another factor, a major reason) that indicate key supporting points. Finally, read the last paragraph carefully; it often sums up the major points of the article.

2. Take notes in your own words, using your own abbreviations.

At the top of the page or card on which you are taking notes, record the facts about the article as follows: author(last name first); title in quotation marks; name of magazine or encyclopedia, underlined; date of magazine(volume of encyclopedia); page numbers. If the article is anonymous, begin with the title. For example:

Magazine Krutch, Joseph Wood, "Men, Apes, and Termites," Saturday Review, Sept. 21, 1963, P22.

Encyclopidia Grey, Francis Temple, "Capital Punishment," Encyclopdia Britannica, Vol. 4, P809.

Book Hamilton, Edith, "The Quest of the Golden Fleece," Mythology, P117.

Having recorded the facts about the article, you proceed to read and take notes on its contents. You will find it to your advantage to force yourself to used your own words in taking notes. You should do very little copying. If you find phrases or lines that will be useful as a direct quotation in your summary, copy the exact words accurately and enclose them in quotation marks. Remember, however, that the summary is to be in your own words, not a series of sentences copied from the article.

You will find it useful to use abbreviations in your note-taking. Be sure, however, that the abbreviations you use are clear so that you will understand them later.

The notes you take should consist of only the main ideas or the most important pieces of information in the article. You should omit examples, anecdotes, minor details, and digressions. Stick to the essentials. You are not rewriting the article; you are summarizing it.

3. Write the summary, making it one fourth to one third the length of the article.

Put aside the article, and use your notes in writing the summary. If you have jotted down the pincipal ideas in the order in which the article presented them, you need only write out these ideas in sentence form, following your notes. In writing the summary, pretend that you are the author of the article, summarizing what your article said. Don't begin with "This article is about . . . " or "In this article, Mr. White says . . . " Begin directly, "Capital punishment, which is the death penalty for crime, has existed as long as there have been laws and courts . . . . " It is very important that you do not leave out any important ideas and that you do not add any that are not in the article.

4. Compare your summary with the article.

If the article is still available, skim it rapidly, comparing your summary with it. Is the summary complete and accurate? Does it follow the order of the original? Finally, is your summary free of grammatical and mechanical errors?

You will find two summaries of the following article on meteors. Read the article and the summaries that follow the article. One summary is acceptable, while the other is rather poor.

Meteors and Meteorites

On September 1, 1962, above Covington, West Virgina, and then again on September 5, over Clarksburg, West Virginia, great fireballs struck down through the atmosphere. The sky was ablaze with their bursting fragments, and sonic booms rattled dishes, furniture, and windows. Nespaper advertisements asked for eye-witness accounts to help plot the paths of these fireballs so they might be traced to the spots where they fell.

An amazing number of meteors hit the earthat which time they become meteoritesin a 24-hour period, yet no one has ever been killed by one as far as is known. Only one human injury has been defintely recorded when, on November 30, 1954, "stars fell on Alabama" . A small, stony meteoritic fragment weighing about 9 pounds crashed through the roof of a house in Sylacauga, Alabama, where Mrs. E. H. Hodges was resting on a sofa after lunch. The fragment ricocheted off a radio and struck her on the upper thigh, causing a slight bruise.

Called meteoroids in space, meteors as they penetrate the earth's atmosphere, and meteorites if they strike, very few of these stony, stony-iron, or iron bodies are ever recovered. For the most part, they land in the oceans, at the poles, or in such sparsely inhabited regions as forests and deserts. The bright but transitory streaks they make in the sky, which give them the name shooting stars, are due to friction with the atmosphere. The streaks are usually described as white, and sometimes as greenish, reddish, or yellowish. Very large and brilliant meteors ar callled fireballs, and when, rarely, these fireballs explode, they may be known as bodies. The term meteoroid, or meteoric body, is reserved for any small object in space, smaller than an asteroid and considerably larger than an atom or molecule, before it enters the earth's atmosphere, which only a very small proportion of them ever do. Meteoroids in space are nonluminous and thus not detectable by optical telescopes, but eventually some may be picked up by radar telescopes. Because of the threat to space probes ans ships, meteoroid-detection satellites with 50-foot wings are being launched to measure the probable extent of meteoroid penetration to which spacecraft on long flights may be exposed.

Here is the hostory of one meteorite that fell in Alberta, Canada, just a few years ago and was observed in some detail. It entered the earth's atmosphere at 1: 06 a. m. , Mountain Standard Time, on March 4, 1960. It was an evening meteor, entered the atmosphere at a velocity close to 8 miles a second (29, 000 miles an hours), and detonated when about 20 miles above the surface. Fragments from the explosion were discovered across an ellipse-shaped area about 3. 3 miles long by 2 miles wide, near Bruderheim, 30 miles northwest of Edmonton, Alberta. The flash of the detonation was visible for some 200 miles, and the noise audible over an area of 2,000 square miles (the equivalent of a square 450 miles on a side) . Many fragments were subsequently recovered. Some were picked up on thesnow over which they had bounded and rebounded, and farmers plowed up others that spring. The fragments had not had time to disintegrate, as many do. Some 188 sizable chuncks were collected, weighing a total of 670 pounds. The Bruderheim meteorite was a chondrite, one type of stony meteorite, gray in color, with a low iron content.

It has been estimated that about 24 million visible meteors pass through the atmosphere of the entire earth in 24 hours. Observations with telescopes up to the 10th visual magnitude indicate that 8 billion meteors must plunge into the earth's atmosphere a day. Added to this are the much more numerous micrometeorites, objects with a diameter of less than a millimeter, and the cosmic debris or dust.

Among the over 1, 500 meteorites actually recovered, the stony type predominates, with over 900; then come the irons with about 550; and, finally, the very scare stony-irons, of with only 67 are known. Of the total number of meteorites recovered, 680 were picked up or located after atually being observed falling. A greater number, 860, were discovered and identified merely by their characteristics.

Meteoroids are travelling at many miles a second when they dash into the earth's atmosphere, but meeting the resistance of the gases high in the atmosphere begins to slow them down. Their great energy of motion must be dissipated, and by the time they have reached a height of 75 to 50 miles they are glowing in the sky because of the heat that has been produced. They become white-hot and their surfaces molton, streaming back from the direction of their travel, with drops flaming off and sometimes exploding or fragmenting and forming a number of wakes or trains in the sky. They lose fluid and vapors to the atmosphere in the process known as ablation, by which heat is rapidly cariied away. The same ablation effects have been used to advantages in the design of spacecraft or missile cones, which must re-enter the atmosphere with as little destruction as possible. The intense heat produced by the friction of their passage through the air must run off or be shucked off, as it were, with the molton nose-cone material.

As they pass through the atmosphere the alrger meteors produce lound booms, the result of shock waves formed by their supersonic speed of entry. Few meteors are large enough to survive the atmosphere. Those that reach the earth's surface have been so slowed down that they have lost most of their surface heat, have formed what is called a fusion crust on their surfaces, and are barely warm, or may even be cold. They cannot possibly start fires, as one might assume. The Hoba iron meteorite of southwest Africa probably weighed 100 tons when it fell, and a number of others weighing from 10 to 30 tons are known.

Meteorites of over 100 tons will probably never be found, since their impact would be so explosive that they would be entirely vaporized or fragmented. Meteors fraters constitute the sole evidence that such massive bodies have fallen from the sky.

The place of origin of meteorites, particularly the stones, and the paths and times taken to reach the earth, are up in the air, both literally and figuratively. The theories now current hold that the meteorites came from the breakup of an original planet-sized body, occupying the space between Mars and Jupiter, from a number of bodies the size of the moon, from comets, or perhaps from a variety of smaller asteroidal or planetesimal bodies.

——From *Pictorial Guide to the Planets* by Joseph H. Jackson

An acceptable summary

Meteors are pieces of stone and iron from space that enter the earth's atmosphere. Those that land on the earth are called meteorites. Although a great many meteors do strike the earth, they are only a small proportion of those that enter the atmosphere. As far as is known, no one has ever been killed by a meteor, and there is only one known instnace of anyone's being struck by one.

About 24 million visible meteors go through the atmosphere every 25 hours. From telescope observation, however, astronomers estimate that 8 billion actually enter the atmosphere daily.

Stone meteorites are the most common kind; iron are about half as common as stone; meteorites that are a combination of stone and iron are very rare.

Entering the atmosphere at a speed of many miles a second, meteors are slowed down and, at a height of 75 to 50 miles, become white hot from the heat generated by friction with the atmosphere. Pieces of their molten surface by fly off, carrying away heat and forming a tail. Those meteorites large enough to get through the atmosphere are so cooled by the time they reach the earth that there is no danger of their starting fires. The largest known meteorite probaly weighed 100 tons; larger than 100 tons would be so vaporized or fragmented on landing that nothing would be left of it.

Although no one really knows the origin of meteors, astronomers think they come from the breakup of a planet or some smaller bodies in space.

A poor summary

This article says that an amazing number of meteors hit the earthat which time they become meteoritesin a 24-hour period, yet no one has ever been killed by one as far as is known. An Alabama, Mrs. E. H. Hodges of Sylacauga, was struck on the thigh by a 9-pound metor that came through the roof of her house after lunch one day.

Called meteoroids in space, meteors as they penetrate the atmosphere, and meteorites if they strike, very few of thesestony, stony-iron, or iron bodies are ever recovered. Because of their appearance, they are called shooting stars.

A meteorite exploded over Alberta, Canada, in 1960 about 20 miles above the ground. The flash was visible 200 miles away. Some 188 sizable chunks of meteorite were collected, weighing 670 pounds.

While about 24 million visible meteors pass through the atmosphere in 24 hours, astronomers with telescopes estimate that 8 billion must plunge into the earth's atmosphere a day.

Meteors glow in the sky because they are white hot as a result of friction produced when they hit the earth's atmosphere. They travel eight miles a second. By the time a meteor reaches the earth, it is so cooled off it can't start a fire.

Comments: This paper violates much of what is essential to a good summary. It begins incorrectly with, "This article says . . . . " Half of the summary consists of sentences copied word-for-word. The writer was so much interested in the examples in the original article—Mrs. Hodges and the Alberta incident— that he had little space for the main ideas the article expresses. The summary omits mention of the size of meteors and ignores the probable origin of metors.

Exercise: Read the following article, carefully talking notes on the most important ideas. Then write a summary based upon your notes. After you have written it, check your work by answering the questions in the first paragraph under rule 4.

A professor who's spent thirty years gathering tall tornado tales says tornadoes are "pretty much like people".

"They have their likes and dislikes, whims and ambitions, their impulses good and bad," says Dr. Howard C. Key, North Texas State University English professor.

From folklore he has gathered, Dr. Key made this analysis of tornadoes' personalities:

1. Tornadoes are partial to infants. Dr. Key has collected thirty-two stories about miraculous preservation of infants. One tornado in southeastern Kansas about fifty years ago gathered a six-week-old baby out of its cadle and deposited him unscathed but plastered with mud in a haystack a mile away.

2. They like flowers. Houses and furniture have been scattered over many acres, but a vase of roses will be left undisturbed on the living room table. Dr. Key has this story from Arkansas, Oklahoma, Texas, and Louisiana.

3. Twisters don't care for chickens. One storm picked thrity chickens absolutely clean and left them bolt upright, but dead, on their perches. Another popped a rooster into a jug, leaving only its head sticking out.

4. Tornadoes are musically inclined. Dr. Key gave this account of Colonel William Porter, who was carried away in an 1893 twister at Cisco.

"He found that instead of running toward the back room as he intended, he was waving his arms and legs somewhere in mid-air. Seconds later he slammed into some object that felt like a wire fence. Then he heard music and decided he was either dead or dying. "

"It was their new player piano, the kind that had to be pumped with foot pedals. The suction of the storm had somehow started it going and it was appropriately playing "Nearer My God to Thee. " Both Mr. Porter and the piano were lodged in a pecan tree 50 yards away. Neither was much damaged. "

5. Tornadoes can be accommodating. One lady in a farm town had written her sister in Ponca City, Oklahoma, 35 miles away. The letter was lying stamped and addressed on the dinning room table and disappeared when the storm struck. The letter fell uncanceled in Ponca City in the yard of a neighbor only a block away from its intended address.

6. Tornadoes like to show off. An east-bound Northern Pacific locomotive was uncoupled from its freight cars by a twister, which set it down full steam ahead on a parallel track headed west. Tornadoes in East Texas and Arkansas forty years ago whipped together the branches of a 60-foot cottonwood tree and

dropped a cast-iron wagon wheel over it the way you would put a ring on your finger.

"The worst mistake tornadoes have ever made was to venture into New England in 1954," Dr. Key said. "Up until that time tornadoes had been running wild all over the rest of the United States and people had been accepting them—like measles."

"But not New Englanders. They immediately set up a public howl and demanded that Congress do something. So now, through special appropriations to the U. S. weather Bureau, the awful eye of science has been turned upon these murderous intruders. And justice is about to be done."

Dr. Key is apparently optimistic about the results. He doesn't own a storm cellar.

——From *Tornado Record Shows Humanlike Ambitions* by Dr. Howard C. Key

Section D
TOEFL Writing Topic Bank

In the actual iBT TOEFL test, there are two writing tasks for candidates to accomplish. The first one is a summary which is comparatively short and relatively easy for most candidates, while the second is the essay writing which is pretty hard. In order to better your score in the writing section, it is rather essential for you to do lots of practice as one saying goes "Practice makes perfect". The following 185 writing topics are selected from the TOEFL Writing Topic Bank. They are exactly the writing topics which you are asked to do during the near future TOEFL test. Therefore, you need to get familiar with these topics before you take the TOEFL test. If you have neither adequate time nor ability to write on every topic listed below, it is suggested that you do try to write on some topics while write the outline for the rest of the topics in advance. Ample experience shows that it pays you to do so.

Writing Topic List

1. People attend college or university for many different reasons(for example, new experiences, career preparation, increased knowledge). Why, do you think people attend college or university? Use specific reasons and examples to support your answer.

2. Do you agree or disagree with the following statement?
   Parents are the best teachers. Use specific reasons and examples to support your answer.

3. Nowadays, food has become easier to prepare. Has this change improved the way people live? Use specific reasons and examples to support your answer.

4. It has been said, "Not everything that is learned is contained in books." Compare and contrast knowledge gained from experience with knowledge gained from books. In your opinion, which source is more important? Why? Use specific reasons and examples to support your answer.

5. A company has announced that it wishes to build a large factory near your community. Discuss the advantages and disadvantages of this new influence on your community. Do you support or oppose the factory? Explain your position.

6. If you could change one important thing about your hometown, what would you change? Use reasons and specific examples to support your answer.

7. How do movies or television influence people's behavior? Use reasons and specific examples to

support your answer.

8. Do you agree or disagree with the following statement?

Television has destroyed communication among friends and family.

Use specific reasons and examples to support your opinion.

9. Some people prefer to live in a small town. Others prefer to live in a big city.

Which place would you prefer to live in? Use specific reasons and details tosupport your answer.

10. When people succeed, it is because of hard work. Luck has nothing to do with success. Do you

agree or disagree with the quotation above?

Use specific reasons and examples to explain your position.

11. Do you agree or disagree with the following statement?

Universities should give the same amount of money to their students' sports activities as they give

to their university libraries.

Use specific reasons and examples to support your opinion.

12. Many people visit museums when they travel to new places. Why do you think people visit

museums? Use specific reasons and examples to support your answer.

13. Some people prefer to eat at food stands or restaurants. Other people prefer to prepare and eat

food at home. Which do you prefer? Use specific reasons and examples to support your answer.

14. Some people believe that university students should be required to attend classes. Others believe

that going to classes should be optional for students. Which point of view do you agree with? Use

specific reasons and details to explain your ansxver.

15. Neighbors are the people who live near us. In your opinion, what are the qualities of a good

neighbor? Use specific details and examples in your answer.

16. It has recently been announced that a new restaurant may be built in your neighborhood. Do you

support or oppose this plan? Why? Use specific reasons and details to support your answer.

17. Some people think that they can learn better by themselves than with a teacher. Others think that

it is always better to have a teacher. Which do you prefer? Use specific reasons to develop your

essay.

18. What are some important qualities of a good supervisor (boss)? Use specific details and examples

to explain why these qualities are important.

19. Should governments spend more money on improving roads and highways, or should governments

spend more money on improving public transportation(buses, trains, subways)? Why? Use spe-

cific reasons and details to develop your essay.

20. It is better for children to grow up in the countwside than in a big city. Do you agree or disagree?

Use specific reasons and examples to develop your essay.

21. In general, people are living longer now. Discuss the causes of this phenomenon. Use specific

reasons and details to develop your essay.

22. We all work or will work in our jobs with many different kinds of people. In your opinion, what

are some important characteristics of a co-worker (someone you work closely with)? Use reasons

and specific examples to explain why these characteristics are important.

23. In some countries, teenagers have jobs while they are still students. Do you think this is a good idea? Support your opinion by using specific reasons and details.

24. A person you know is planning to move to your town or city. What do you think this person would like and dislike about living in your town or city? Why? Use specific reasons and details to develop your essay.

25. It has recently been announced that a large shopping center may be built in your neighborhood. Do you support or oppose this plan? Why? Use specific reasons and details to support your answer.

26. It has recently been announced that a new movie theater may be built in your neighborhood. Do you support or oppose this plan? Why? Use specific reasons and details to support your answer.

27. Do you agree or disagree with the following statement?

People should sometimes do things that they do not enjoy doing.

Use specific reasons and examples to support your answer.

28. Do you agree or disagree with the following statement?

Television, newspapers, magazines, and other media pay too much attention to the personal lives of famous people such as public figures and celebrities. Use specific reasons and details to explain your opinion.

29. Some people believe that the Earth is being harmed(damaged) by human activity. Others feel that human activity makes the Earth a better place to live. What is your opinion? Use specific reasons and examples to support your answer.

30. It has recently been announced that a new high school may be built in your community. Do you support or oppose this plan? Why? Use specific reasons and details in your answer.

31. Some people spend their entire lives in one place. Others move a number of times throughout their lives, looking for a better job, house, community; or even climate. Which do you prefer: staying in one place or moving in search of another place? Use reasons and specific examples to support your opinion.

32. Is it better to enjoy your money when you earn it or is it better to save your money for some time in the future? Use specific reasons and examples to support your opinion.

33. You have received a gift of money. The money is enough to buy either a piece of jewelry you like or tickets to a concert you want to attend. Which would you buy? Use specific reasons and details to support your answer.

34. Businesses should hire employees for their entire lives. Do you agree or disagree? Use specific reasons and examples to support your answer.

35. Do you agree or disagree with the following statement?

Attending a live performance (for example, a play, concert, or sporting event) is more enjoyable than watching the same event on television. Use specific reasons and examples to support your opinion.

36. Choose one of the following transportation vehicles and explain why you think it has changed people's lives.

A. automobiles   B. bicycles   C. airplanes

Use specific reasons and examples to support your answer.

37. Do you agree or disagree that progress is always good? Use specific reasons and examples to support your answer.

38. Learning about the past has no value for those of us living in the present. Do you agree or disagree? Use specific reasons and examples to support your answer.

39. Do you agree or disagree with the following statement?

    With the help of technology, students nowadays can learn more information and learn it more quickly. Use specific reasons and examples to support your answer.

40. The expression "Never, never give up" means to keep trying and never stop working for your goals. Do you agree or disagree with this statement? Use specific reasons and examples to support your answer.

41. Some people think that human needs for farmland, housing, and industry are more important than saving land for endangered animals. Do you agree or disagree with this point of view? Why or why not? Use specific reasons and examples to support your answer.

42. What is a very important skill a person should learn in order to be successful in the world today? Choose one skill and use specific reasons and examples to support your choice.

43. Why do you think some people are attracted to dangerous sports or other dangerous activities? Use specific reasons and examples to support your answer.

44. Some people like to travel with a companion. Other people prefer to travel alone. Which do you prefer? Use specific reasons and examples to support your choice.

45. Some people prefer to get up early in the morning and start the day's work. Others prefer to get up later in the day and work until late at night. Which do you prefer? Use specific reasons and examples to support your choice.

46. What are the important qualities of a good son or daughter? Have these qualities changed or remained the same over time in your culture? Use specific reasons and examples to support your answer.

47. Some people prefer to work for a large company. Others prefer to work for a small company. Which would you prefer? Use specific reasons and details to support your choice.

48. People work because they need money to live. What are some other reasons that people work? Discuss one or more of these reasons. Use specific examples and details to support your answer.

49. Do you agree or disagree with the following statement?

    Face-to-face communication is better than other types of communication, such as letters, e-mail, or telephone calls.

    Use specific reasons and details to support your answer.

50. Some people like to do only what they aleady do well. Other people prefer to try new things and take risks. Which do you prefer? Use specific reasons and examples to support your choice.

51. Some people believe that success in life comes from taking risks or chances. Others believe that success results from careful planning. In your opinion, what does success come from? Use

specific reasons and examples to support your answer.

52. What change would make your hometown more appealing to people your age?

    Use specific reasons and examples to support your opinion.

53. Do you agree or disagree with the following statement?

    The most important aspect of a job is the money a person earns.

    Use specific reasons and examples to support your answer.

54. Do you agree or disagree with the following statement?

    One should never judge a person by "external appearances".

    Use specific reasons and details to support your answer.

55. Do you agree or disagree with the following statement?

    A person should never make an important decision alone.

    Use specific reasons and examples to support your answer.

56. A company is going to give some money either to support the arts or to protect the environment. Which do you think the company should choose? Use specific reasons and examples to support your answer.

57. Some movies are serious, designed to make the audience think. Other movies are designed primarily, to amuse and entertain. Which type of movie do you prefer?

    Use specific reasons and examples to support your answer.

58. Do you agree or disagree with the following statement?

    Businesses should do anything they can to make a profit.

    Use specific reasons and examples to support your position.

59. Some people are always in a hurry to go places and get things done. Other people prefer to take their time and live life at a slower pace. Which do you prefer? Use specific reasons and examples to support your answer.

60. Do you agree or disagree with the following statement?

    Games are as important for adults as they are for children.

    Use specific reasons and examples to support your answer.

61. Do you agree or disagree with the following statement?

    Parents or other adult relatives should make important decisions for their older (15-to 18-year-old) teenage children.

    Use specific reasons and examples to support your opinion.

62. What do you want most in a friend—someone who is intelligent, someone who has a sense of humor, or someone who is reliable? Which one of these characteristics is most important to you?

    Use reasons and specific examples to explain your choice.

63. Do you agree or disagree with the following statement?

    Most experiences in our lives that seemed difficult at the time become valuable lessons for the future.

    Use reasons and specific examples to support your answer.

64. Some people prefer to work for themselves or own a business. Others prefer to work for an em-

ployer. Would you rather be self-employed, work for someone else, or own a business? Use specific reasons to explain your choice.

65. Should a city try to preserve its old, historic buildings or destroy them and replace them with modern buildings? Use specific reasons and exampies to support your opinion.

66. Do you agree or disagree with the following statement?

Classmates are a more important influence than parents on a child's success in school.

Use specific reasons and examples to support your answer.

67. If you were an employer, which kind of worker would you prefer to hire: an inexperienced worker at a lower salary, or an experienced worker at a higher salary? Use specific reasons and details to support your answer.

68. Many teachers assign homework to students every day. Do you think that daily homework is necessary for students? Use specific reasons and details to support your answer.

69. If you could study a subject that you have never had the opportunity to study, what would you choose? Explain your choice, using specific reasons and details.

70. Some people think that the automobile has improved modern life. Others think that the automobile has caused serious problems. What is your opinion? Use specific reasons and examples to support your answer.

71. Which would you choose: a high-paying job with long hours that would give you little time with family and friends or a lower-paying job with shorter hours that would give you more time with family and friends? Explain your choice, using specific reasons and details.

72. Do you agree or disagree with the following statement?

Grades (marks) encourage students to learn.

Use specific reasons and examples to support your opinion.

73. Some people say that computers have made life easier and more convenient.

Other people say that computers have made life more complex and stressful.

What is your opinion? Use specific reasons and examples to support your answer.

74. Do you agree or disagree with the following statement?

The best way to travel is in a group led by a tour guide.

Use specific reasons and examples to support your answer.

75. Some universities require students to take classes in many subjects. Other universities require students to specialize in one subject which is better? Use specific reasons and examples to support your answer.

76. Do you agree or disagree with the following statement?

Children should begin learning a foreign language as soon as they start school. Use specific reasons and examples to support your position.

77. Do you agree or disagree with the following statement?

Boys and girls should attend separate schools.

Use specific reasons and examples to support your answer.

78. Is it more important to be able to work with a group of people on a team or to work indepen-

dently? Use reasons and specific examples to support your answer.

79. Your city has decided to build a statue or monument to honor a famous person in your country. Whom would you choose? Use reasons and specific examples to support your choice.

80. Describe a custom from your country, that you would like people from other countries to adopt. Explain your choice, using specific reasons and examples.

81. Do you agree or disagree with tile following statement?

Technology has made the world a better place to live.

Use specific reasons and examples to support your opinion.

82. Do you agree or disagree with the following statement?

Advertising can tell you a lot about a country.

Use specific reasons and examples to support your answer.

83. Do you agree or disagree with the following statement?

Modern technology is creating a single world culture.

Use specific reasons and examples to support your opinion.

84. Some people say that the Internet provides people with a lot of valuable information. Others think access to so much information creates problems. Which view do you agree with? Use specific reasons and examples to support your opinion.

85. A foreign visitor has only one day to spend in your country. Where should this visitor go on that day? Why? Use specific reasons and details to support your choice.

86. If you could go back to some time and place in the past, when and where would you go? Why? Use specific reasons and details to support your choice.

87. What discovery in the last 100 years has been most beneficial for people in your country? Use specific reasons and examples to support your choice.

88. Do you agree or disagree with the following statement?

Telephones and e-mail have made communication between people less personal.

Use specific reasons and examples to support your opinion.

89. If you could travel back in time to meet a famous person from history, what person would you like to meet? Use specific reasons and examples to support your choice.

90. If you could meet a famous entertainer or athlete, who would that be, and why?

Use specific reasons and examples to support your choice.

91. If you could ask a famous person one question, what would you ask? Why? Use specific reasons and details to support your answer.

92. Some people prefer to live in places that have the same weather or climate all year long. Others like to live in areas where the weather changes several times a year. Which do you prefer? Use specific reasons and examples to support your choice.

93. Many students have to live with roommates while going to school or university.

What are some of the important qualities of a good roommate? Use specific reasons and examples to explain why these qualities are important.

94. Do you agree or disagree with the following statement?

Dancing plays an important role in a culture.

Use specific reasons and examples to support your answer.

95. Some people think governments should spend as much money as possible exploring outer space (for example, traveling to the moon and to other planets). Other people disagree and think governments should spend this money on our basic needs on Earth. Which of these two opinions do you agree with? Use specific reasons and details to support your answer.

96. People have different ways of escaping the stress and difficulties of modern life. Some read; some exercise; others work in their gardens. What do you think are the best ways of reducing stress? Use specific details and examples in your answer.

97. Do you agree or disagree with the following statement?

Teachers should be paid according to how much their students learn.

Give specific reasons and examples to support your opinion.

98. If you were asked to send one thing representing your country to an international exhibition, what would you choose? Why? Use specific reasons and details to explain your choice.

99. You have been told that dormitory rooms at your university must be shared by two students. Would you rather have the university assign a student to share a room with you, or would you rather choose your own roommate? Use specific reasons and details to explain your answer.

100. Some people think that governments should spend as much money as possible on developing or buying computer technology. Other people disagree and think that this money should be spent on more basic needs. Which one of these opinions do you agree with? Use specific reasons and details to support your answer.

101. Some people like doing work by hand. Others prefer using machines. Which do you prefer? Use specific reasons and examples to support your answer.

102. Schools should ask students to evaluate their teachers. Do you agree or disagree? Use specific reasons and examples to support your answer.

103. In your opinion, what is the most important characteristic (for example, honesty, intelligence, a sense of humor) that a person can have to be successful in life? Use specific reasons and examples from your experience to explain your answer.

104. It is generally agreed that society benefits from the work of its members. Compare the contributions of artists to society with the contributions of scientists to society. Which type of contribution do you think is valued more by your society? Give specific reasons to support your answer.

105. Students at universities often have a choice of places to live. They may choose to live in university dormitories, or they may choose to live in apartments in the community. Compare the advantages of living in university housing with the advantages of living in an apartment in the community. Where would you prefer to live? Give reasons for your preference.

106. You need to travel from your home to a place 40 miles (64 kilometers) away. Compare the different kinds of transportation you could use. Tell which method of travel you would choose. Give specific reasons for your choice.

107. Some people believe that a college or university education should be available to all students. Others believe that higher education should be available only to good students. Discuss these views. Which view do you agree with? Explain why.

108. Some people believe that the best way of learning about life is by listening to the advice of family and friends. Other people believe that the best way of learning about life is through personal experience. Compare the advantages of these two different ways of learning about life. Which do you think is preferable? Use specific examples to support your preference.

109. When people move to another country: some of them decide to follow the customs of the new country. Others prefer to keep their own customs. Compare these two choices. Which one do you prefer? Support your answer with specific details.

110. Some people prefer to spend most of their time alone. Others like to be with friends most of the time. Do you prefer to spend your time alone or with friends? Use specific reasons to support your answer.

111. Some people prefer to spend time with one or two close friends. Others choose to spend time with a large number of friends. Compare the advantages of each choice. Which of these two ways of spending time do you prefer? Use specific reasons to support your answer.

112. Some people think that children should begin their formal education at a very early age and should spend most of their time on school studies. Others believe that young children should spend most of their time playing. Compare these two views. Which view do you agree with? Why?

113. The government has announced that it plans to build a new university. Some people think that your community would be a good place to locate the university. Compare the advantages and disadvantages of establishing a new university in your community. Use specific details in your discussion.

114. Some people think that the family is the most important influence on young adults. Other people think that friends are the most important influence on young adults. Which view do you agree with? Use examples to support your position.

115. Some people prefer to plan activities for their free time very carefully. Others choose not to make any plans at all for their free time. Compare the benefits of planning free-time activities with the benefits of not making plans. Which do you prefer—planning or not planning for your leisure time? Use specific reasons and examples to explain your choice.

116. People learn in different ways. Some people learn by doing things; other people learn by reading about things; others learn by listening to people talk about things. Which of these methods of learning is best for you? Use specific examples to support your choice.

117. Some people choose friends who are different from themselves. Others choose friends who are similar to themselves. Compare the advantages of having friends who are different from you with the advantages of having friends who are similar to you. Which kind of friend do you prefer for yourself? Why?

118. Some people enjoy change, and they look forward to new experiences. Others like their lives to

stay the same, and they do not change their usual habits. Compare these two approaches to life. Which approach do you prefer? Explain why.

119. Do you agree or disagree with the following statement?

People behave differently when they wear different clothes.

Do you agree that different clothes influence the way people behave? Use specific examples to support your answer.

120. Decisions can be made quickly, or they can be made after careful thought. Do you agree or disagree with the following statement?

121. The decisions that people make quickly are always wrong.

Use reasons and specific examples to support your opinion.

122. Some people trust their first impressions about a person's character because they believe these judgments are generally correct. Other people do not judge a person's character quickly because they believe first impressions are often wrong. Compare these two attitudes. Which attitude do you agree with? Support your choice with specific examples.

123. Do you agree or disagree with the following statement?

People are never satisfied with what they have; they always want something more or something different.

Use specific reasons to support your answer.

124. Do you agree or disagree with the following statement?

People should read only those books that are about real events, real people, and established facts.

Use specific reasons and details to support your opinion.

125. Do you agree or disagree with the following statement?

It is more important for students to study history and literature than it is for them to study science and mathematics.

Use specific reasons and examples to support your opinion.

126. Do you agree or disagree with the following statement?

All students should be required to study art and music in secondary school.

Use specific reasons to support your answer.

127. Do you agree or disagree with the following statement?

There is nothing that young people can teach older people.

Use specific reasons and examples to support your position.

128. Do you agree or disagree with the following statement?

Reading fiction (such as novels and short stories) is more enjoyable than watching movies.

Use specific reasons and examples to explain your position.

129. Some people say that physical exercise should be a required part of every school day. Other people believe that students should spend the whole school day on academic studies. Which opinion do you agree with? Use specific reasons and idetails to support your answer.

130. A university plans to develop a new research center in your country: Some people want a center

for business research. Other people want a center for research in agriculture (farming). Which of these two kinds of research centers do you recommend for your country? Use specific reasons in your recommendation.

131. Some young children spend a great amount of their time participating in sports. Discuss the advantages and disadvantages of this. Use specific reasons and examples to support your answer.

132. Do you agree or disagree with the following statement?

Only people who earn a lot of money are successful.

Use specific reasons and examples to support your answer.

133. If you could invent something new, what product would you develop? Use specific details to explain why this invention is needed.

134. Do you agree or disagree with the following statement?

A person's childhood years (the time from birth to twelve years of age) are the most important years of a person's life.

Use specific reasons and examples to support your answer.

135. Do you agree or disagree with the following statement?

Children should be required to help with household tasks as soon as they are able to do so.

Use specific reasons and examples to support your answer.

136. Some high schools require all students to wear school uniforms. Other high schools permit students to decide what to wear to school. Which of these two school policies do you think is better? Use specific reasons and examples to support your opinion.

137. Do you agree or disagree with the following statement?

Playing a game is fun only when you win.

Use specific reasons and examples to support your answer.

138. Do you agree or disagree with the following statement?

High schools should allow students to study the courses that students want to study.

Use specific reasons and examples to support your opinion.

139. Do you agree or disagree with the following statement?

It is better to be a member of a group than to be the leader of a group.

Use specific reasons and examples to support your answer.

140. What do you consider to be the most important room in a house? Why is this room more important to you than any other room? Use specific reasons and examples to support your opinion.

141. Some items (such as clothes or furniture) can be made by hand or by machine. Which do you prefer —items made by hand or items made by machine? Use reasons and specific examples to explain your choice.

142. If you could make one important change in a school that you attended, what change would you make? Use reasons and specific examples to support your answer.

143. A gift (such as a camera, a soccer ball, or an animal) can contribute to a child's development. What gift would you give to help a child develop? Why? Use reasons and specific examples to

support your choice.

144. Some people believe that students should be given one long vacation each year. Others believe that students should have several short vacations throughout the year. Which viewpoint do you agree with? Use specific reasons and examples to support your choice.

145. Would you prefer to live in a traditional house or in a modern apartment building? Use specific reasons and details to support your choice.

146. Some people say that advertising encourages us to buy things we really do not need. Others say that advertisements tell us about new products that may improve our lives. Which viewpoint do you agree with? Use specific reasons and examples to support your answer.

147. Some people prefer to spend their free time outdoors. Other people prefer to spend their leisure time indoors. Would you prefer to be outside, or would you prefer to be inside for your leisure activities? Use specific reasons and examples to explain your choice.

148. Your school has received a gift of money. What do you think is the best way for your school to spend this money? Use specific reasons and details to support your choice.

149. Do you agree or disagree with the following statement?

Playing games teaches us about life.

Use specific reasons and examples to support your answer.

150. Imagine that you have received some land to use as you wish. How would you use this land? Use specific details to explain your answer.

151. Do you agree or disagree with the following statement?

Watching television is bad for children.

Use specific details and examples to support your answer.

152. What is the most important animal in your country? Why is the animal important? Use reasons and specific details to explain your answer.

153. Many parts of the world are losing important natural resources, such as forests, animals, or clean water. Choose one resource that is disappearing and explain why it needs to be saved. Use specific reasons and examples to support your opinion.

154. Do you agree or disagree with the following statement?

A zoo has no useful purpose.

Use specific reasons and examples to explain your answer.

155. In some countries, people are no longer allowed to smoke in many public places and office buildings. Do you think this is a good rule or a bad rule? Use specific reasons and details to support your position.

156. Plants can provide food, shelter, clothing, or medicine. What is one kind of plant that is important to you or the people in your country? Use specific reasons and details to explain your choice.

157. You have the opportunity to visit a foreign country for two weeks. Which country would you like to visit? Use specific reasons and ctetails to explain iyour choice.

158. In the future, students may have the choice of studying at home by using technology such as

computers or television or of studying at traditional schools. Which would you prefer? Use reasons and specific details to explain your choice.

159. When famous people such as actors, athletes and rock stars give their opinions, many people listen. Do you think we should pay attention to these opinions? Use specific reasons and examples to support your answer.

160. The twentieth century saw great changes. In your opinion, what is one change that should be remembered about the twentieh century? Use specific reasons and details to explain your choice.

161. When people need to complain about a product or poor service, some prefer to complain in writing and others prefer to complain in person. Which way do you prefer? Use specific reasons and examples to support your answer.

162. People remember special gifts or presents that they have received. Why? Use specific reasons and examples to support your answer.

163. Some famous athletes and entertainers earn millions of dollars every year. Do you think these people deserve such high salaries? Use specific reasons and examples to support your opinion.

164. Is the ability to read and write more important today than in the past? Why or why not? Use specific reasons and examples to support your answer.

165. People do many different things to stay healthy. What do you do for good health? Use specific reasons and examples to support your answer.

166. You have decided to give several hours of your time each month to improve the community where you live. What is one thing you will do to improve your community? Why? Use specific reasons and details to explain your choice.

167. People recognize a difference between children and adults. What events (experiences or ceremonies) make a person an adult? Use specific reasons and examples to explain your answer.

168. Your school has enough money to purchase either computers for students or books for the library. Which should your school choose to buy—computers or books? Use specific reasons and examples to support your recommendation.

169. Many students choose to attend schools or universities outside their home countries. Why do some students study abroad? Use specific reasons and details to explain your answer.

170. People listen to music for different reasons and at different times. Why is music important to many people? Use specific reasons and examples to support your choice.

171. Groups or organizations are an important part of some people's lives. Why are groups or organizations important to people? Use specific reasons and examples to explain your answer.

172. Imagine that you are preparing for a trip. You plan to be away from your home for a year. In addition to clothing and personal care items, you can take one additional thing. What would you take and why? Use specific reasons and details to support your choice.

173. When students move to a new school, they sometimes face problems. How can schools help these students with their problems? Use specific reasons and examples to explain your answer.

174. It is sometimes said that borrowing money from a friend can harm or damage the friendship. Do

you agree? Why or why not? Use reasons and specific examples to explain your answer.

175. Every generation of people is different in important ways. How is your generation different from your parents' generation? Use specific reasons and examples to explain your answer.

176. Some students like classes where teachers lecture (do all of the talking) in class.

Other students prefer classes where the students do some of the talking. Which type of class do you prefer? Give specific reasons and details to support your choice.

177. Holidays honor people or events. If you could create a new holiday, what person or event would it honor and how would you want people to celebrate it? Use specific reasons and details to support your answer:

178. A friend of yours has received some money and plans to use all of it either to go on vacation or to buy a car Your friend has asked you for advice. Compare your friend's two choices and explain which one you think your friend should choose. Use specific reasons and details to support your choice.

179. The twenty-first century has begun. What changes do you think this new century will bring? Use examples and details in your answer.

180. What are some of the qualities of a good parent? Use specific details and examples to explain your answer.

181. Movies are popular all over the world. Explain why movies are so popular. Use reasons and specific examples to support your answer.

182. In your country, is there more need for land to be left in its natural condition or is there more need for land to be developed for housing and industry? Use specific reasons and examples to support your answer.

183. Many people have a close relationship with their pets. These people treat their birds, cats, or other animals like members of their family. In your opinion, are such relationships good? Why or why not? Use specific reasons and examples to support your answer.

184. Films can tell us a lot about the country in which they were made. What have you learned about a country from watching its movies. Use specific examples and details to support your response.

185. Some students prefer to study alone. Others prefer to study with a group of students. Which do you prefer? Use specific reasons and examples to support your answer.

186. You have enough money to purchase either a house or a business. Which would you choose to buy? Give specific reasons to explain your choice.

Part 4

Basic Skills Needed for Speaking
口语基础必备

Unlike reading and listening which are receptive skill, speaking belongs to productive skill. In other words, speaking is a kind of activity which is involved with the production of material orally. To be more specific, speakers on both sides are expected to generate information on certain topics such as weather, health or education, to name only a few. Speaking is a sort of active activity in which people must participate actively. They are supposed to air their views on a particular subject. In the iBT TOEFL test, candidates are encouraged to describe a person or event they are familiar with or experienced before or talk on a given topic conerning current affair or academic matters.

In order to help candidates improve their performance in the speaking section of the iBT TOEFL test, it is necessary for them to lay a good foundation on some basic skills in speaking. In the following, you are provided with an opportunity to practice your ability to speak in Englsih. There are three sections. Section A is situational dialogs which are designed to assist you to better your interactive ability in various situations. Section B is guided conversations which are made to help you improve your ability to express your opinion on certain topics. Section C is a description which is designed to teach you how to give a word picture of somebody or something. For each section there are a variety of exercises designed to offer you a chance to practice your oral English. You are suggested to do all kinds of these exercises since they are quite conducive to the result of your near future TOEFL test.

阅读和听力是接受型技能,而口语为产出型技能。也就是说,口语是一种需要口头交流的活动。更具体地说,谈话者需要根据特定话题例如天气、健康或教育等等进行互相沟通交流信息。口语交流是一项需要每个人都积极参与的开放型活动。他们将会一起分享在一个特定话题上的意见看法。在新托福考试中,要求考生口述一个熟悉的人、事以前的经历,或是谈论一下热点话题或学术问题。

为了使考生在新托福中的口语部分中发挥得更好,在口语基本技巧中打一个坚实的基础是很必要的。在以下的部分,您将有机会练习您的口语能力。这里有3个部分。A部分是为提高您在各个多变情况下应变能力的情景对话,B部分是为表达您的观点的指导型对话。C部分是描写篇告诉您如何用文字来描述人或事物。每一部分都会有大量练习,提高您的口语能力。建议你做完全部提供的练习,因为它们与正式托福考试都比较类似。

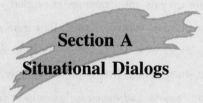

Section A
Situational Dialogs

1. Greetings and introductions

How to greet somebody or introduce someone is of great importance in communication, since this is the starting point from which the real communication begins. Look at the following expressions people usually use in greeting and introducing someone.

How do you do? How are you? Hello!

You are (Mr. Smith), aren't you?

We've met before.

Nice to see you again.

Excuse me, are you (Mr. Smith)?

I'm (Wang Nan). I'm (a student) from Xi'an International Studies University.

My name is (Zhang Hua).

I'm very pleased to meet you.

So glad to meet you.

I have been looking forward to meeting you.

Welcome to Beijing.

May I introduce (Mr. Brown)?

Have you met (Mr. Brown)?

Do you know (Susan)?

I'd like you to meet (Miss Li).

This is (Mrs Brown).

Examples:

Dialog 1.

Bob   : Hello Marion, how are you?

Marion: I'm very well, thanks. How are you?

Bob   : Fine, thanks. May I introduce Roger Morley? Roger, this is Marion Povey?

Roger : How do you do?

Marion: How do you do? Please to meet you.

Roger : I met your sister at a meeting in Bristol, a month or two ago. How is she?

Marion: Oh, she is fine, thanks. Yes, she told me she'd met you.

Roger : Do give her may regards when you see her, won't you?

Marion: Yes, I will. Thank you.

Dialog 2.

Wang Hai   : Exercise me, my name is Wang Hai. I'm from the China Travel Service.

Marry Green: Oh, good. I'm very delighted to meet you. My name's Mary Green from New York.

Wang Hai   : How do you do? Welcome to China.

Marry Green: Thank you.

Practice:

Introduce yourself and introduce others to someone.

1. You are in your institute with a classmate. By chance you meet an American student (Bob) in the corridor. Approach him, introduce yourself and your classmate.

2. You take a student from Australia, who is studying Chinese at your university, to your home town to meet your parents. Introduce the foreign student to your parents who are able to speak and understand Englsih.

3. You go to the railway station with the Chairman of the Students' Union, to meet an American instructor, Jane greenwood, who is travelling around China and who will give some talks at your university. Approach her, introduce yourself, and introduce the Chairman of the Students's Union to this instructor.

4. You see a stranger in your office all by himself/herslef, but in fact you know the person, though not well. What do you say?

137

2. Asking for information

The following are some of the expressions commonly used in this aspect.

Exercise me, could you tell me. . . ?

Could you tell me how to . . . ?

Do you know . . . ?

What happens if . . .

Where / When / How do I . . . ?

Examples:

Dialog 1.

A: Exercise me, could you tell me where Buckingham Palace is, please?

B: Certainly, madam. Go round Trafalgar Square. Second left and up the wall. It's at the end.

A: Do you know how far it is?

B: Oh, about a mile.

Dialog 2.

A: Can you tell me how much a sightseeing tour costs, please?

B: Certainly, a half-day-trip is $ 6.

A: And when does the boat leave?

B: There are departures at 10 a. m. and 2 p. m. every day.

A: Is it necessary to book in advance?

B: Well, the boats are always popular on fine days.

A: And what happens if the weather's bad?

B: Well, if it's really rough, of course, we cancel the trip.

A: What's the weather going to be like next Saturday?

B: I'm afraid I really don't know. Why not take a chance!

Practice:

1. You have to send a telegram to your hometown. Ask the way to the post office.

2. Now you are in the post office. Tell the clerk what you want and ask him to tell you what to do.

3. You have finished your telegram, and you take it to the clerk. Ask him how much it will cost and how long it will take to be delivered.

3. Making a request

The commonly used ways of making a request are these:

(1) To ask someone to do something for you:

① Asking for a small service:

Would you. . . ? / Could you . . . ? / Would you mind doing . . . ?

② Asking someone to do something rather bothersome:

I wonder if you would . . . ? / Could I bother you to . . . ?

Would you do me a favour?

(2) Asking someone for permission to do something:

May I . . . ? / Would you mind if I (did) . . . ? / I'd like to . . . if . . .

(3) Asking someone for something:

Could you ... ? / May I ... ?

Examples:

Dialog 1.

A: Could you lend me a hand, sir? I can't close the suitcase.

B: Of course.

A: Would you just sit on it while I fasten the locks? There, that's fine, thanks a lot.

B: No trouble, any time.

Dialog 2.

A: Would you drop in at the post office on your way home and send off this book for me?

B: Sure, I'll be glad to.

A: Thanks a lot.

Dialog 3.

A: May I use your dictionary?

B: Certainly. Here you are.

A: Thank you. I just want to look up a few words.

B: There's no hurry. Take your time. I'm not using it now.

A: Thanks.

B: You're welcome.

Practice:

1. Ask someone to do the following things for you:

   A. to turn on the light

   B. to hand you the newspaper

   C. to get some hot water for you

   D. to see Mr. Smith off at the station tomorrow morning

2. Ask a friend to do you a favor:

   A. You want him to drop in at Li Lin's house on his way home and give him his package.

   B. You want to borrow his bicycle for a few days while he's away.

3. Ask someone's permission to do the following things:

   A. to read the text aloud

   B. to use his telephone

   C. to keep his book for a few days

   D. to cut a few pictures out of his old magazine

4. Complaints and apologies

The following are some of the frequently used patterns:

There seems to have been a mistake. I wanted ...

I say, ...

I'm sorry to say that ...

Look here.

I'm terribly / really / so sorry, but . . .

I do apologize.

I can assure you it won't happen again.

Examples:

Dialog 1.

A: I say, waiter, this soup is cold.

B: I'm sorry, sir. I'll change it for you. What kind of soup was it?

A: Cucumber.

B: Ah, I see, sir. Actually it's iced cucumber soup.

A: Oh dear, my mistake. I'm afraid I didn't realize . I am sorry.

B: That's quite all right, sir.

Dialog 2.

A: I'm afraid I have a complaintment to make.

B: Please take a seat.

A: I'm sorry to say the bill you sent me was incorrect.

B: Incorrect, madam? That's very strange.

A: Yes, I know, and what's more, this isn't the first time.

B: Really madam? I find that very hard to believe.

A: Look, it's happened five or six times in the last three months. It really isn't good enough.

B: Ah, well, I must apologize, madam. It's the new computer.

A: Well, don't you think it's about time you got it working properly?

B: I agree entirely. I'm awfully sorry about it. I assure you it won't happen again.

Practice:

1. You receive a bill which is much higher than it should be. You ring the manager of the shop to complain. What do you say?

2. You had the engine of your car repaired last week. It's making the same noise as before. You send it back to the garage. What do you say to the mechanic?

3. Apologize for the lost theatre tickets your friend asked you to look after.

4. You didn't post the letter your friend asked you to.

5. You knocked one of your colleagues' beautiful vase off the table.

6. You promised to telephone your classmate, but you didn't.

5. Compliments and congratulations

Here are some widely used expressions:

You look very nice.

That's a very attractive / pretty / smart . . .

That suits you very well.

Congratulations!

How marvellous!

That's great news.

I'm glad to hear that.

You're a very good . . .

You were terrific.

How clever of you to . . .

That's marvellous . . .

That was a really delicious meal.

That smells wonderful.

Aah . . . superb!

Examples:

Dialog 1.

A: You do look smart in that dress.

B: Do you really think so?

A: Yes, the color suits you very well. It brings out the blue in your eyes.

B: Thank you. How nice of you to say so!

Dialog 2.

A: Well, my dear. I thought you were marvellous. Congratulations!

B: Oh it was nothing really.

A: Oh, come on. It was a very fine job. And you yourself. You looked wonderful.

B: Thank you very much.

A: And you look fantastic in that Indian dress.

B: Do you really think so? I bought it especially for the conference.

A: Did you? I say, what are you doing this evening?

B: I'm going to a concert with my husband. He's coming to pick me up.

A: Oh, by the way. I don't think I quite agree with your theory of population control . . .

Practice:

1. Your friend says "I make my own wine. You must try a glass." To your surprise the wine is quite delicious. What do you say?

2. You find your boyfriend/girlfriend has had his/her hair styled in a very modern way, and is wearing an extremely smart outfit. What do you say?

3. Two young friends of yours, Robert and Anne, are looking very pleased with themselves, but a little shy. Robert says "I've just asked anne to marry me, and she's said yes! " What do you say?

6. Persuasion and advice

The following are some of the most frequently used expressions:

Why don't you . . . ?

I think you should . . .

My advice would be to . . .

I'm sure you ought to . . .

If I were you, I'd . . .

Don't you think it would be better if . . .

If you did that, then you'd be able to . . .

If you don't do it, you won't be able to . . .

Examples:

Dialog 1.

A: You must take some rest. You've been working much too hard.

B: But how can I? The deadline is Friday.

A: Come on, couldn't you take the afternoon off?

B: Well, if you really think so.

A: I really think you should. We can manage without you.

Dialog 2.

A: Why don't you get a decent job for a change?

B: But I like my job.

A: Look, digging gardens is not a job for a university graduate.

B: But the money's not too bad and there's plenty of fresh air.

A: If I were you, I'd go on some other kind of course—teaching, accountancy? Anything but that. It's so boring.

B: Come on, you really must think of the future. Why don't you just write a few application forms?

A: I'll tell you what. I'd really like to be a doctor.

B: Well, you should think very seriously about that. It means a lot of study, and then working all sorts of hours.

A: Yes, maybe. But the idea appeals to me.

B: Well then, you ought to get more information about it as soon as possible.

Practice:

1. You are in New York. You are on the telephone to your head office in Chicago. You try to persuade them to let you stay for another week.

2. Your daughter tells you she is getting married. Advise her about her position and persuade her to think hard about what seems to you to be a sudden decision.

3. Your colleague phones you for some advice. He sounds depressed and over-worked. What do you say to him?

4. You have invited an American friend to visit you in your country, but he's decided to travel in another place. Try to make him change his mind.

5. You have got tickets for a dance. At the last moment your girlfriend rings up and says she has a headache and can't come. What do you say?

7. Disagreeing and agreeing

Practice the following sentence patterns that are used for disagreeing and agreeing.

I don't agree with you on . . . (at all).

I'm not really sure about that.

I'm afraid I disagree with you on . . .

I don't think so.

You must be joking!

There's no evidence for that. (Disgreeing strongly and impolitely)

Oh, that's ridiculous! (Disgreeing strongly and impolitely)

Nonsense! rubbish! (Disgreeing strongly and impolitely)

I don't believe that at all.

You don't know what you are talking about.

Your're completely wrong about that.

Yes, that's how I feel.

Yes, I entirely agree with you.

Yes, that's exactly my opinion.

Examples:

Dialog 1.

A: What do you think about TV?

B: I think it's the worse invention of the 20th century.

A: Do you? Why?

B: Well, in my opinion, it wastes people's time and it stops conversation.

A: I'm afraid I really don't agree with you. There are some good educational programes on TV, and lots of entertainment such as filmns, plays, ...

B: In my opinion, TV is boring.

A: Oh no, that's not true, not all of it is boring. I really enjoy television and it's probably one of the best inventions of the 20th century.

Dialog 2.

A: What did you think about the film we went to see last night?

B: Well, I was a bit disappointed. I didn't really enjoy it at all.

A: In my opinion, it was the best film I've seen all year.

B: Oh, you don't really mean that, do you?

A: Yes, I do ...

B: I'm afraid I don't agree with you at all.

A: Why?

B: Well, the acting was terrible, and there was no story to it. I was so bored.

A: You're the first person I have met who hasn't enjoyed it.

B: In fact, I thought the music was so bad. I nearly left!

A: I can't understand. How did you feel about the main actor?

B: Well, he was quite good, I suppose.

A: That's exactly how I felt! I'm glad we agree on something.

Practice:

1. Work with your friend. Agree or disagree about the following sujects.

A. The Chinese National Games

B. The city of Xi'an

C. Pandas

2. Respond to these statements:

A. A kilo of iron is obviously heavier than a kilo of feathers.

B. Everyone knows that women are far too emotional to be good doctors.

C. The Chinese footbal team is the best in the world.

8. Positive feelings—delight

Remember the following expressions that indicate a feeling of delight.

Oh, how wonderful! /marvellous!

I'm absolutely fascinated/thrilled!

See? I told you you'd be very pleased.

Good! I never thought you'd care!

How can I thank you? (It must have cost you a fortune!)

Examples:

Dialog 1.

A: I saw the scarf and it reminded me of you. Aren't the color and pattern to your taste?

B: Good John, I never thought you'd pay attention to things like this. My appreciation and gratitude!

Dialog 2.

A: I've got a little surprise for you.

B: For me? What is it?

A: A good ring.

B: Oh, John, you shouldn't have. It must have cost you a lot of money.

Dialog 3.

A: Here's a leather handbag for you.

B: Oh, I'm absolutely trilled! I just can't believe it, so exquisitely made.

A: I'm glad you like it.

Practice:

Imagine you receive the following things as presents. Show your delight and appreciation in various ways.

1. a beautiful skirt

2. a jewellery box

3. a stereo cassette player

4. a set of tapes of your favorite singer

9. Negative feeling-worry, disappointment, depression

Look at the following patterns:

(1) How to show worry:

I am concerned/nervous/terrified about (the exam).

I am frightened/terrified of (the exam).

She is petrified/out of her mind with worry.

(2) How to express disappointment:

He was disappointed/dissatisfied with (his job).

He found (this job) disappointing/unsatisfactory.

He was tired of/sick of/fed up with (doing it every day).

(The film) wasn't up to much good. /could have been better. /wasn't worth watching. /wasn't as good as (the film last week).

I don't think much of the film.

(3) How to express feelings of depression:

Things are getting me down a bit.

I'm just a bit fed up, /a bit depressed/feeling a bit low, that's all.

Example:

A: I dread the coming exam. If only I could have time to preview my lessons.

B: What was the matter with you?

A: My mother was ill, I had to attend to her. And I was worried about her operation.

B: I'm sorry to hear that. Has she recovered now?

A: Yes, she's well now. And I find myself nearly out of my mind with the exams.

B: When are they?

A: Only two weeks away. I'm really nervous about them. I've lost my appetite and I can't sleep well.

B: It's no use worrying like this.

A: But, you know, if I don't pass them, I don't know what I'll do.

B: Very simple, take them next year.

A: That means I'll graduate one year late. My mother would be greetly disappointed.

B: I'm sure she'll understand. You'd worry yourself sick if you keep up this very nervous state.

A: Yes, I've already been suffering from symptoms of a bad cold.

B: My advice is that you'd better take it easy.

Practice:

1. You have lost your handbag/briefcase. You are extremely worried because it contains money, train/plane tickets, identification papers, letters, etc. How to express your worry?

2. You are worried about your little brother, who hasn't come home from school yet. It's late, very dark, and is raining very hard. What do you say?

3. You have just started a new job and aren't enjoying it at all. What do you say?

10. Offering help

Please remember the following sentence patterns. They are often used by people when they offer help to others and the corresponding responses when people receive help from others.

1. Offers

Would you like me to (get a ticket for you)?

Can I (get a ticket) for you?

I could (buy the ticket for you)if you want.

Could I (show you the way to the post office)?

May I get you (something to drink)?

Shall I help you to (look after your little brother)?

I can (go with you) if you like.

What can I do for you?

Is there anything I can do for you?

I'm going to (Beijing). Is there anything you'd like me to do for you?

If there's anything I can do for you, do please tell me.

2. Responses

Many thanks.

Thanks a lot.

Oh, thank you! (Oh, thanks.)

Thank you very much.

Oh, would you?

Thank you, I'd appreciate it (if you would).

Thank you, if it isn't too much trouble/bother.

Wouldn't that be too much bother?

Please don't bother; it isn't necessary. Thank you all the same.

I can do it by myself. But thank you just the same.

I'd very much like you to (help me with my English), but right now I have to (attend a meeting).

Thank you just the same.

Examples:

Dialog 1.

Wang: Oh, what's wrong with my bike?

Zhang: Let me see. Ah, you've got a flat tyre.

Wang: Oh, that's too bad. Is there a place nearby where I can get it repaired?

Zhang: Yes, but you'll probably have to wait at least a couple of hours.

Wang: What shall I do? I have to go to the hospital to see my friend.

Zhang: Why don't you ride my bike there first while I get yours repaired?

Wang: That's very kind of you. Thank you very much.

Zhang: You're welcome. Please say hello to him for me. See you.

Wang: See you.

Dialog 2.

Li Ming:　　　　Good morning, Professor Wu.

Professor Wu: Hello, Li Ming. Are you getting on well with your spoken English these days?

Li Ming:　　　　I'm afraid not. But I've been trying to speak English as much as possible even though I find it difficult.

Professor Wu: You have made great progress recently. But you still have a long way to go. Stick to it, and you're sure to succeed. By the way, I have a lot of English tapes in my office.

You can borrow some if you like.

Li Ming:　　　Thank you. I'd like to. Would you help me choose some?

Professor Wu: All right.

Practice:

1. You and Mr. Smith watch a film at the cinema. After the film, you ask Mr. Smith whether he needs a taxi.

2. A new play is on this evening. You offer a ticket to your roommate.

3. It's Sunday. You want to help your mother to cook.

4. You offer help to an old lady crossing the street.

11. Invitations

Here are some of the most frequently used expressions when people extend an invitation and give replies:

1. Extending an invitation:

Would you like to come for dinner this evening?

I wonder if you'd like to /care to . . . ?

I was wondering if you felt like going to a concert with me?

Do you feel like going . . . ?

How about going . . . ?

Would you like something to drink?

If you're not doing anything important Friday night, we'd like you to come to a party at our place.

2. Replies:

A. How to accept an invitation and ask for further details:

　　How nice!

　　Yes, I'd love to.

　　Yes, I'd like to very much. What time?

　　Why, yes. That would be very nice.

　　Thank you. That would be very nice of you.

　　Yes, that sounds like a good idea. Where exactly?

　　That sounds nice/lovely/marvellous. When exactly?

B. How to refuse an invitation and suggest an alternative:

　　I'd really like to, but I can't, I'm afraid. What another night?

　　It's nice of you to ask, but I don't think I can. Can you make it another time/day?

　　I'd love to, but I'm not able to, thanks all the time.

　　I'm afraid (Friday's) a bit difficult. But another day perhaps.

　　No, (tomorrow's) impossible, I'm afraid.

　　Unfortunately, I can't come on (Friday). Is there any other time/ day that would suit you?

C. How to turn down an invitation with excuse:

　　I can't, I'm afraid. I really must do some work tonight. / I don't feel like it tonight. / I'm really too busy at the moment. / I've already arranged to go somewhere else.

Examples:

Dialog 1.

A: Do you feel like going to a football match next weekend?

B: That sounds like a good idea, but where is it exactly?

A: It's in the center of the town, in the new stadium.

B: That sounds marvellous. But when?

A: On Saturday afternnon, I think, 3 o'clock.

B: What a pity. I'm afraid Saturday afternoon's a bit difficult. What about another day?

A: I think they are playing on Saturday night too. Is that all right?

B: Yes, fine. I look forward to it.

Dialog 2.

A: I was wondering if you felt like going sightseeing on Sunday.

B: Unfortuntely, I can't on Sunday. Can you make it another day?

A: What about Tuesday?

B: Oh, no. Tuesday's impossible, I'm afraid. I really must do some work then; I have an oral exam on Wednesday. But another time perhaps.

A: Okay, perhaps the following weekend. Let's wait and see.

Practice:

Make up dialogs using the situations below. Accept or refuse the invitation politely, give an excuse for refusing, suggest an alternative day/time.

1. go cycling on Sunday

2. help me move into my new flat

3. go away for the day on May 1st

4. invite your classmate to attend a concert

5. invite your friend to a new film, but he is too busy

6. invite your foreign teacher to your evening party

12. Hobbies and habits

Look at the following expressions concerning hobbies and habit.

1. Asking about other's hobby/hobbies

Do you have a hobby?

What's your hobby?

Do you have any special interests other than your job?

What do you usually do in your spare time?

Could you please tell me your favourite recreational activities?

Do you have other pastimes besides (playing tennis)?

2. Telling others your own hobby:

My hobby is collecting stamps.

I prefer chess as a hobby.

I find gardening very interesting.

I like to get my mind off my work by listening to music or watching TV.

3. Telling about advantages and disadvantages of a hobby:

It's fun to collect sea shells.

The value does not lie in what you collect but in the process of collecting it.

I find fishing very relaxing.

I find travelling enriching.

It pays off to spend some money on photography.

Travelling is very interesting but very expensive.

The problem with photography is that it is too expensive.

The trouble with collecting stamps is that it is too time-consuming.

I don't find fishing agreeable because it requires a lot of patience.

4. Getting into and out of a habit:

I don't know how I fell into this habit.

I wonder whether I can break myself of the habit.

You'd better get out of the habit of staying late.

Are you still in the habit of getting up late?

I used to have the habit of reading in bed, but I have got out of it.

Examples:

Dialog 1.

A: I have run out of film. I must buy a roll of Kodak.

B: This way, please. Now I know what your hobby is.

A: What?

B: Taking pictures.

A: Not only pictures, but also slides. My hobby is photography in all its aspects.

B: It's expensive, isn't it?

A: Yes, it is. Since hobbies cost a lot, others almost nothing. A hobby is something we do in our
    spare time for the fun of it. The pleasure it gives us is important, not the money it costs.

B: Do you develop the film and makes prints yourself?

A: I did many years ago with black and white photos.

B: It's a very time-consuming process, isn't it?

A: Yes, it is.

B: Here we are. Let's leave our bikes over there.

Dialog 2.

A: Do you have other pastimes beside stamp collecting?

B: Yes, fishing.

A: That's very popular, too. Everytime I pass this lake, I see many people sitting there with a rod in
    hand, but I've never seen anyone catch anything.

B: Maybe its because you lack the patience.

A: I would break my rod if I sat about for hours getting nothing.

B: Wouldn't you hope that you were just about to land a giant fish?

A: No, my mind doesn't work like that.

B: Oh, look at that man's pole. It's bent like a bow. There must be a huge fish on the end of the line. Let's go over and have a look.

A: Go ahead. I'll wait here and take a few shots.

Practice:

Make up dialogs according to the following situations:

1. You are chatting with someone who is very fond of travelling to different parts of the world.

2. Two stamp collectors are commenting on the advantages of stamp collecting.

3. A Chinese student and an American students are talking about popular habits.

4. Ask your friend about his hobbies and talk about them with your friend.

5. You are very keen on pop music. Talk about it with a singer from Hongkong.

13. Uncertainty

In the following you will see a variety of ways to express uncertainty.

1. How to express not knowing what to do, when to do, how to do, why to do, etc.

I'm not sure about/certain about the way of doing ...

I suppose it could be ...

Perhaps I might ...

It looks as if I might ...

Perhaps it's better to ...

It seems I'd better to ...

I wonder if I might ...

2. How to express uncertainties/bewilderment about the instruction given.

I am puzzled/ am baffled/ got confused by (his instructions).

I don't know/ can't understand what (he's) talking about.

3. How to express the speaker's uncertainty when he tries to explain further but find he can't do it.

As he tried to explain further, (Tim) got confused (mixed up).

4. How to express uncertainties in identifying, distinguishing something or someone.

I can't tell when the meeting was held. / Which boy is older, Jack or Jim. / Why he is absent from class.

5. How to express uncertainties in seeing and hearing something or someone.

I can't make out who is speaking in the room. / what is there on the floor.

Examples:

Dialog 1.

A: What did you do last Monday?

B: Last Monday? Let me see ... I suppose I got up early, as it was a Monday.

A: Weren't you suffering from a cold?

B: Ah, yes. I had a cold, but was it Monday? I'm not at all certain about that.

A: Do you remember going to work on a crowded bus?

B: Of course, I do. The scene of packed buses always remains fresh in my mind, but it's hard to say whether I experienced that last Monday.

A: Don't tell me that your memory is so short.

B: But you got me all confused by asking me so many questions.

Dialog 2.

A: I've received a birthday card signed "from Amelia". I have no idea who she is.

B: I suggest that you recall her by first going over your covsins, then your classmates, then your friends, the people you've met at your aunt's and uncles's.

A: That's a good idea! I suppose she could be one of my second cousins, but I am not at all sure that the name is "Amelia".

B: And your schoolmates, old and new.

A: Yes, it looks a bit like I'd have better chance here, as I have so many.

B: Any idea that this "Amelia" is one of them?

A: Mm ... no! I wonder if she might be someone I've met at my uncles' or aunts'.

B: It's quite possible, as you have so many aunts and uncles.

A: Mm ... My head is swimming. I give up!

Practice:

1. You try to recall what happened last Sunday.

2. You received a New Year card signed "from Mary". You have no idea who she is.

3. You were told that some young man called on you. The description given was very general. You try to make out who he is.

4. You and your friend are talking about a picture of the famous Nanjing Lu of Shanghai City. You try to identify the exact location.

Section B
Guided Conversations

1. Express one's opinion

In this part, you are provided with some topics which are likely to arouse arguments. Remember people of different ages, of different occupations and of different social status may have totally different opinions on the same topic. For instance:

Topic: Do you agree with the idea "Eating at restaurant is a waste of money?"

The groups of people who may participate in the discussion are chefs, rich people and ordinary people. These people will address the topic from their own perspectives.

Chef: I'm afraid I can't agree on this statement. On the contrary, I think eating at a restaurant is a kind of enjoyment. Because people can taste many different delicious foods that are usually not available at home. And also, people can relax themselves and enjoy being served. So, spending money in the restaurant is really worthwhile.

Rich man: In my opinion, eating at a restaurant is convenient and enjoyable. Why on earth should we take the trouble to do cooking ourselves while so many palatable foods are available at restaurants? Money should serve our needs first.

Ordinary man: I think this statement is reasonable. While we can cook ourselves, why should we spend money eating outside at the restaurant? Since we are still not very rich, we should save money as much as we can, and we should spend money on something more important such as children's education.

Imagine you are the people of different groups, try to air your own views on the following subjects.

1. The government is planning to buid a new international airport next to a small quiet village. All the people who take part in the discussion live in the village.

   The groups are old people/young people/estate agents/town council.

2. Should loud pop music be banned from radio sets, and should radio sets be banned from public places?

   The groups are old people/young people/record producers/teachers.

3. The Town Council has been given one million yuan. Should the money be used to build a school or an art gallery?

   The groups are parents/teachers/school children/artists.

4. "Advertisements are full of lies." What's your opinion?

   The groups are customers/factory producers/traders.

5. Should the Olympic Games become a meeting of professional athletes?

   The groups are althletes/spectators/sports organizers/sports goods manufacturers.

6. Should people in power (politicians and business people) retire at 60?

   The groups are politicians/businessmen/students/journalists.

7. Children should go to single-sex schools, wear uniforms and stay at school until they are sixteen.

   The groups are school teachers/school chidren/parents/children's clothing manufacturers.

8. Should journalists be prevented from writing about the private lives of famous people?

   The groups are newspaper editors/newspaper readers/film stars/publicity agents.

9. The local council has decided to knock down th oldest building in the town and build some shops and offices. What do you think?

   The groups are supermarket directors/shoppers/Town Council/environmentalists.

10. Some countries have compulsory military service. Others like Great Brtain don't. Should all young people do military serivce?

    The groups are colonels/politicians/students/parents of teenagers.

11. Travelling is a useful experience for children and adults alike. The best way to travel is by train.

    The groups are parents/school students/school teachers.

12. Work at home is usually less interesting, and therefore less important. What do you think of this statement?

    The groups are husbands/wives/young people.

13. Have we learnt enough about other planets, or should we spend more money on space research?

    The groups are presidential advisors/spacemen/tax-payers/environmentalists.

14. "Smoking and drinking should be forbidden by law in every country".

The groups are men/doctors/nonsmokers/old people.

15. Should examinations be banned so as to relieve students from severe pressures?

The groups are students/teachers/parents/educators.

2. Questions for short answers

Here are 50 questions. For each question, you have about 30 seconds to prepare and 60 seconds to talk.

1. In what kind of jobs do you think you would learn most about society? Why?

2. When people talk about their children, what kind of things do they usually say?

3. "Young people should lead their own lives and not worry about their parents." What do you think of this statement?

4. Do you think there is really a generation gap? If yes, what are the main differences between old people and young people?

5. What's the best way to save money in your opinion?

6. Which month of the year do you find most expensive? Why?

7. "Fathers spend too little time with their children." What is your opinion on this issue?

8. What kind of people do you prefer to make friends with, rich, interesting, successful or useful?

9. What are the major traditional Chinese festivals? Talk about how people in your part of the country celebrate these festivals.

10. How do you get to work? Talk about the advantages and disadvantages of the different means of transportation in modern cities.

11. Do you agree that modern life isn't at all enjoyable? Why or why not?

12. What would you do to help someone who is feeling homesick?

13. Do you think children today have more time to play than you when you were a kid?

14. What are the possible difficulties when you go on a long journey?

15. Describe any great personal effort you have made to give up a bad habit.

16. Is it bad to watch films about crime? Why or why not?

17. Some people are very interested in the private lives of great men. What's your opinion of it?

18. Say how you "make ends meet".

19. Suppose someone asked you for advice about choosing a job. What would you tell him or her?

20. Give an account of any wedding you have been to recently.

21. What advice would you give on how to bring up a child to become a healthy happy adult?

22. The most capable people are not always the best paid. What do you think of this statement?

23. Decribe some of the photos you like in your photo album.

24. Talk about some of the demands which society makes on us.

25. Describe any dreams you can remember vividly.

26. "Too much money is spent on the wrong things in society." What's your view?

27. "We must all work hard and play hard." What do you think?

28. Talk about the prices of goods in the shops and the rising cost of living.

29. Do you ever read books or magazines written for children? Why or why not?

30. "Money isn't the most important thing in a job." What do you think of this statement?

31. What kind of countryside do you like most, forest, woodland or open countryside? Why?

32. Would you like to teach your own langauge to foreign students? How would you do it?

33. What do you like and dislike about a small shop?

34. Why do you think many immigrants go back to their native places after two or three years?

35. What's your favorite kind of entertainment?

36. What do you think are the important factors for one's success in life?

37. What is the use of knowing a foreign language in China now?

38. Would you rather live in town or in the countryside? Why?

39. Is it better to live a busy life or a leisure one?

40. "Medical care should be free." Do you agree to this statement? Give your reasons.

41. Do you think students need long holidays? Are your holidays long enough for you?

42. How would you excuse yourself if you want to get away from someone who keeps talking to you?

43. "There is no point in making plans for anything. You never know what may happen tomorrow." Give your own comment on this remark.

44. How often do you go to the cinema? Do you enjoy watching movies? What kind of movies do you like most?

45. "All children should start a foreign language in primary school." What do you think?

46. Would you like to be a teacher? Why or why not?

47. Can you name a famous singer/actor/player? Say something about him or her.

48. Can you suggest why hospitals tend to keep people waiting?

49. Talk about situations you can think of in which a person finds it difficult to keep the conversation going.

50. Do you like going to parties? If yes, what kinds of partis do you prefer, and why? If not, why not?

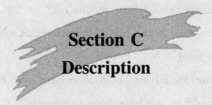

Section C
Description

In the speaking section of the iBT TOEFL test, candidates are asked to describe a person or an object or a place. Therefore, it is naturally important for you to know how to describe them so that you will be well prepared before you actually take the test.

First and formost. What is description? Description is a word-picture of persons, places, objects and emotions by using a careful selection of details to make an impression on the listener or reader. Look at the following example:

My Bedroom

My bedroom is very cozy. It is a small room with thick carpeting and light blue walls. Below the north window is my double bed covered with an imitation leopard skin bedspread. To the left of the bed against the wall is a walnut nightstand with a reading lamp, a clock, and a radio. At the foot of the bed is a wooden stand holding my portable black-white TV and stereo. In all four corners of the room my speakers are mounted just below the ceiling. Behind the wooden stand and in front of the closet are three red bean bag chairs that are sagging from years of use. On the east and west walls are posters of rock groups, and a family of stuffed moneys sits on the north and south window ledges. My room is small and cluttered and has that "lived-in" feeling I like.

In the model above, the speaker organizes the details in a sequential order. Beginning with a topic sentence stating that the bedroom is a "cozy" place to live in, he describes the objects in the room, moving from the largest, the bed, to the smallest, a family of stuffed monkeys. All the details help support the topic sentence "My bedroom is very cozy. "

There are two approaches to description: one is called objective, the other, subjective(or impressionistic). In objective decription, the writer may use details that describe factual information about the subject. Ther is no emotion or opinion in objective detail. In contrast, in subjective description, the speaker uses details that express the personal opinion on the subject. The details do not have to be based on factual information.

Note the differences between the following two descriptions of a tall, thin boy: the objective speaker sticks to the facts by saying.

"The eighteen-year-old boy was 61 and weighed 125 pounds. "

Whereas the subjective speaker gives an impressionistic description,

"The young boy was as tall and scrawny as a birth tree in winter. "

According to the purpose, a speaker may use either subjective or objective way of description. For example, a speaker will describe a scentific experiment or a business transaction in straight factual detail. However, he may use subjective approach to convey a particular attitude toward his subject. In academic area, it is the objective approach that usually functions.

1. Description of a person

In describing a person, we can give many details about his or her physical appearance and behavior. We can describe a person's appearance in many ways. We can tell about the person's style of clothing, manner of walking, color and style of hair, facial appearance, body shape, and expression. We can also describe the person's way of talking. When we are describing a person, we are the painter with words, so we want our description to be vivid and coherent-logically arranged so that the readers can have a clear picture in their minds of the person we are describing.

Read the following description and see if you can get a good image of the person being described.

Mary has long black hair that falls down to her shoulders and surrounds her diamond-shaped face, which is usually suntanned. She has dark brown eyebrows over her blue eyes, which are rather large. Her nose is straight, and on the left side of the bottom of her nose, by her nostril, is a small mole. She has a small mouth, with lips that are usually covered with light pink lipstick. Her teeth are straight and white.

This decription is coherent and the picture is clear. We can get a good picture of Mary in our mind's eye. But the description is not fully satisfying. We can not see the speaker's attitude about Mary's appearance. Is the girl attractive or plain? Does she have a regal appearance or does she look rather ordinary? This is merely a descritiopn of physical appearance but conveys no emotion or feeling, since there is no controlling idea here. If we improve the description by adding a sentence like "Mary is as beautiful as any Hollywood star", the description might be better. In addition, the picture the speaker has painted with words is rather vague since there are a lot of descriptive details he has not included. As a result, his picture is not vivid. Let us see how this description can be improved.

Mary is as beautiful as any Hollywood star. Her thick, wavy, long black hair gracefully falls down to her shoulders and surrounds her exquisite, diamond-shaped face. A golden suntan usually highlights her smooth, clear complexion. Her slightly arched chestnut brown eyebrows draw attention to her deep blue eye, which remind me of a lake on a stormy day. Her eyes are large, but not too large, with thick eyelashes. Her nose is straight and neither too long nor too short. A small black mole on the left side of her mouth that looks delicate and feminine. Her lips are rather thin; her light pink lipstick adds another touch of beauty. When she smiles, which is often, her well-formed and even, white teeth brighten up her whole face. There is nothing but extraordinary beauty in the face of Mary.

Now we can tell what the attitude is about the girl's appearance. The description has a strong controlling idea—beautiful—appearance and has much more decriptive details than the first version.

In describing a person's physical appearance, it is not necessary to describe every detail about the person's appearance. Sometimes it is better to focus on one or two outstanding features that convey something about the person's character which distinguish the person from others. And we should select those details that help support the main idea of the description and omit those impertinent ones. In this way, we can create an image which is not only vivid but also affecting.

However, in describing a person, it is far from enough to merely give details of the person's appearance. We should try to reveal the person's character, thoughts, and feelings. We may also describe the person's behavior and manner. We can describe what the person does and says or how the person behaves to others.

2. Description of a place

If you are asked to describe a limited interior, such as a classroom or a dormitory or a very broad area, such as the continent of Asia or the solar system, what should you describe first and how should you proceed your development? Spatial development is especially suited to te subject matter dealing with spaces. The decription must be organized so that the reader can vividly imagine the scene being described; so you must make the location of the object being described very clear. Here the spatial order is essential in organization.

The arrangement of the details in your description depends on your subject and purpose. But generally speaking, there are four main types of spatial organization:

A. from left to right or from right to left

B. from top to bottom or from bottom to top

C. from near to far or from far to near

D. clockwise or counter-clockwise

You can employ one of the ways to organize the details in spatial description. But, no matter what kind of order is being used, it is better to stick to one direction or one way all the way down. Do not shift it now and again. Look at the following description. The speaker used a far to near movement to describe a scene in a library.

While standing in front of the information desk in the library, I saw some students using the files in the reference room some distance away. About fifteen feet away from me, an old lady wearing large red hat put on her glasses. She was studying a rare book in one of the locked display cases. Much closer to me, two students were quietly but seriously talking about a book.

Let's look at another example and see which way of organiztion the speaker used in his decription.

My Living Room

My key snaps open the lock on the thick wooden door, and I feel a warm rush of air as I walk into the cozy living room. The whole room is done in soft blues and greens. There is a thick heavy blue rug that runs from wall to wall. On one side of the room is a big padded green armchair. The arms look like they want to pull you in and hold you. Next to the chair is the televison, which is turned on at a quiet level and gives off the muted sounds of voices and laughter, while colors flirk across the screen. On the other side of the room is a royal-blue couch so soft and deep that it looks like an invitation to take a nap. The whole back wall, except for the entrance to the kitchen, is made of brick and features a fireplace. The orange coals of the fire send a warm glow into the room and give off quiet crackles and pops sizzling in vegetable oil, and the footsteps of my mother as she prepares out dinner. I'm glad to be home.

The speaker in this description used a near to far way of organization.

3. Decription of an object

To describe an object we have to depend on our senses because we need to mention its size, shape, color, texture, taste, and smell. It is also necessary to tell how it is used if it is useful, and what part it plays in a person's life if it is in some way related to him. But emphasis should be placed on only one aspect of the object, probably its most important characteristic. Look at the following example.

A Rug

A thick, reddish-brown shap rug is laid wall to wall across the living-room floor. The long, curled fibers of the shag seem to whisper as you walk through them in bare feet, and when you squeeze your toes into the deep covering, the soft fibers push back at you with a spongy resiliency.

This is a very vivid description of a rug that covers the living room floor. The speaker used sensory details. For instance, sight thick, reddish-brown shap rug; laid wall to wall; walk through them in your bare feet; squeeze your toes into the deep covering; push back, hearing (whisper) and touch (bare feet, soft fibers, spongy resiliency).

In addition to the spatial order, description can also be approached by using chronological order. In other word, the information can be organized in time order. For example, the following describes the process of man's improving the travel speed.

Man has learnt to travel faster and faster throughout history. When the wheel was invented over a thousand years ago, man learned that it was possible to travel faster on wheels than on foot. With the invention of the steam engine about two hundred years ago, man began to travel at what was called "dangerous" speeds of between 20 to 30 miles an hour. The gasoline engine that were used between 1900 developed speeds up to 60 miles an hour. In the late 1920s, propeller airplanes began to fly at speeds of more than 100 miles an hour. About twenty years ago, man began to travel in commercial jet planes at speeds above 500 miles an hour.

By using the transitional expression as "over a thousand years ago", "about two hundred years ago", "between 1900 and 1920", "In the late 1920s", and "About twenty years ago", the speaker indicates clearly the order in which the events actually take place.

Practice:

1. Describe the arrangement of your classroom.

2. Describe a person you are familiar with (a friend, a classmate, a teacher, a colleague, a person in your family, etc.)

3. Describe a phtograph.

4. Describe your favorite restaurant or store in your city.

5. Describe a place where you can go and relax.

6. Describe the work you are now doing.

7. Describe a person who has impressed you most or influenced you greatly in your life.

8. Describe your hometown or a place you have been before.

9. Describe an interesting book you have read before.

10. Describe a film you have recently seen.

11. Describe the subject you are now studying.

12. Describe your university campus.

13. Describe the future life you will have when living and studying abroad.

14. Describe a sports event you have particiapted in.

15. Describe the development of the computer.

Chapter Three

Analysis of iBT TOEFL Questions and Practical Techniques
新托福考题分析应试技巧

In chapter two, you have learnt and practiced systematically to build up your skills which are essential for four areas in the iBT TOEFL test. You are now ready academically and mentally for the iBT TOEFL test.

In order to perform well in the new test, it is necessary for us to analyze the nature of the four sections in the iBT TOEFL, and sum up a few practical skills which will enable you to achieve a satisfactory score in the upcoming test.

在第二章里，我们已经学习并且对新托福考试技巧做了一系列系统的练习，它们是考试的四个部分的关键所在。你现在无论在知识上或思想上肯定都做好了准备。

为了在新托福考试中出色发挥，分析 iBT 托福四个部分是很有必要的，再总结一些应试技巧以便在考试中能取得一个满意的分数。

Part 1

iBT TOEFL Reading
新托福阅读

TOEFL iBT Reading questions are designed to measure basic information skills, inferencing skills, and reading to learn skills, There are 10 question types. They can be summed up in the following:

Basic information and Inferencing questions (11 to 13 questions per sets)

1. Factual Information questions (3 to 6 questions per set)

2. Negative Factual Information questions (0 to 2 questions per set)

3. Inference questions (0 to 2 questions per set)

4. Rhetorical Purpose questions (0 to 2 questions per set)

5. Vocabulary questions (3 to 5 questions per set)

6. Reference questions (0 to 2 questions per set)

7. Sentence Simplification questions (0 to 1 question per set)

8. Insert Text question (0 to 1 question per set)

Reading to Learn questions（1 per set）

9. Prose Summary

10. Filling a Table

The following sections will explain each of these question types one by one. You'll find out how to recognize each type, and you'll see examples of each type with explanations. You'll also find hints that can help you answer each TOEFL Reading Question type.

托福阅读理解的问题分为 10 类,分别是:

1. 事实信息题(3－6 题)

2. 否定事实信息题(0－2 题)

3. 推理题(0－2 题)

4. 修辞题(0－2 题)

5. 词汇题(3－5 题)

6. 指代题(0－2 题)

7. 句子简化题(0－1 题)

8. 文本插入题(0－1 题)

9. 摘要题

10. 填表题

下面将分别讲解这 10 类问题,你将学会怎样辨认各类问题,同时你会找到回答各类问题的提示。

Type 1: Factual Information Questions

These questions ask you to identify factual information that is explicitly stated in the passage. Factual Information questions can focus on facts, details, definitions, or other information presented by the author. They ask you to identify specific information that is typically mentioned only in part of the passage. They generally do not ask about general themes that the passage as a whole discusses. Often the relevant information is in one or two sentences.

第一类 事实信息

这类题型要求你辨识文章中清楚陈述的事实。事实信息题基本集中在事实、细节、定义或其他信息。在答这些题时要求你对文章中某一部分提到的细节进行辨认。一般不要求你辨认文章大意。通常情况下,相关信息就在一两句中。

How to Recognize Factual Information Questions

如何辨认事实信息题

Factual information questions are often phrased in one of these ways:

事实信息题的问法如下:

1. According to the paragraph, which of the following is true of X?

2. The author's description of X mentions which of the following?

3. According to the paragraph, X occurred because. . .

4. According to the paragraph, X did Y because. . .

5. According to the paragraph, why did X do Y?

6. The author's description of X mentions which of the following?

Hints for Factual Information Questions

1. You may need to refer back to the passage in order to know what exactly is said about the subject of the question. Since the question may be about a detail, you may not recall the detail from your first reading of the passage.

2. Eliminate choices that present information that is contradicted in the passage.

3. Do not select an answer just because it is mentioned in the passage. Your choice should answer the specific question that was asked.

||| 提 醒 |||

1. 您需要重新回顾文章，了解问题的出处。因为问题有可能问的是一个细节，所以就没有必要把整篇文章读完。

2. 排除与文章内容相矛盾的选项。

3. 不要只因为一个答案在文章中被提到就草率地选择它。你所作出的选择必须能够回答具体的问题。

Example

Passage Excerpt: "... Sculptures must, for example, be stable, which requires standing of the properties of mass, weight distribution, and stress. Paintings must have rigid stretchers so that the canvas will be taut, and the paint must not deteriorate, crack, or discolor. These are problems that must be overcome by the artist because they tend to intrude upon his or her conception of the work. For example, in the early Italian Renaissance, bronze statues of horses with a raised foreleg usually had a cannonball under that hoof. This was done because the cannonball was needed to support the weight of the leg. In other words, the demands of the laws of physics, not the sculptor's aesthetic intentions, placed the ball there. That this device was a necessary structural compromise is clear from the fact that the cannonball quickly disappeared when sculptors learned how to strengthen the internal structure of a statue with iron braces (iron being much stronger than bronze) ... "

According to paragraph 2, sculptors in the Italian Renaissance stopped using cannonballs in bronze statues of horses because

A. They began using a material that made the statues weigh less.

B. They found a way to strengthen the statues internally.

C. The aesthetic tastes of the public had changed over time.

D. The cannonballs added too much weight to the statues.

Explanation

The question tells you to look for the answer in paragraph 2. You do not need to skim the entire passage to find the relevant information.

Choice A says that sculptors stopped putting cannonballs under the raised legs of horses in statues because they learned how to make the statue weigh less and not require support for the leg. The passage does not mention making the statues weigh less; it says that sculptors learned a better way to support the weight. Choice C says that the change occurred only because people's taste changed, meaning that the cannonballs were never structurally necessary. That directly contradicts the passage.

Choice D says that the cannonballs weakened the structure of the statues. This choice also contradicts the passage. Choice B correctly identifies the reason the passage gives for the change: sculptors developed a way to strengthen the statue from the inside, making the cannonballs physically unnecessary.

Type 2: Negative Factual Information Questions

These questions ask you to verify what information is true and what information is NOT true or not included in the passage based on information that is explicitly stated in the passage. To answer this kind of question, first locate the relevant information in the passage. Then verify that three of the four answer choices are true and that the remaining choice is false. Remember, for this type of question, the correct answer is the one that is NOT true.

第二类 否定事实信息

这些问题要求你根据文章中所提供的信息来判断选项的真实与否，或选项的内容在文章中有无陈述。回答这类问题，首先就要紧扣文章信息。然后辨认其中三个选项正确，剩下的那个错误。一定记住，这里要选择的是不对的选项。

How to Recognize Negative Factual Information Questions
怎样辨认否定事实信息题

You can recognize negative fact items because either the word "NOT" or "EXCEPT" appears in the question in capital letters. For example:

您可从问题中是否存在大写字母"NOT" or "EXCEPT"来区别此类问题：

1. According to the passage, which of the following is NOT true of X?

2. The author's description of X mentions all of the following EXCEPT.

Hints for Negative Factual Information Questions

1. Usually a Negative Factual Information question requires you to check more of the passage than a Factual Information question. The three choices that are mentioned in the passage may be spread across a paragraph or several paragraphs.

2. In Negative Factual Information questions, the correct answer either directly contradicts one or more statements in the passage or is not mentioned in the passage at all.

3. After you finish a Negative Factual Information Question, check your answer to make sure you have accurately understood the task.

1. 通常此类问题要求你查阅的段落多于事实信息题。其中三个选项的分布很有可能是跨越一段甚至多个段落。

2. 在此类问题中，正确的选项既可以是与文章直接矛盾的论述又可以是在文章中完全没有被提到过的信息。

3. 在做完此类问题后，对答案进行检查。

Example

Passage Exerpt: " The United States in the 1800's was full of practical, hardworking people who did not consider the arts—from theater to painting—useful occupations. In addition, the public's attitude that European art was better than American art both discouraged and infuriated American artists. In the early 1900's there was a strong feeling among artists that the United States was long overdue in developing art that did not reproduce European traditions. Everybody agreed that the heart and soul of the new country should be reflected in its art. But opinions differed about what this art would be like and how it would develop".

According to paragraph 1, all of the following were true of American art in the late 1800's and early 1900's EXCEPT:

A. Most Americans thought art was unimportant.

B. American art generally copied European styles and traditions.

C. Most Americans considered American art inferior to European art.

D. American art was very popular with European audiences.

Explanation

Sometimes in Negative Factual Information questions, it is necessary to check the entire passage in order to make sure that your choice is not mentioned. However, in this example, the question is limited to one paragraph, so your answer should be based just on the information in that paragraph. Choice A is a restatement of the first sentence in the paragraph: since most Americans did not think that the arts were useful occupations, they considered them unimportant. Choice B makes the same point as the third sentence: "... the United States was long overdue in developing art that did not reproduce European traditions" means that up to this point in history, American art did reproduce European traditions. Choice C is a restatement of the second sentence in the paragraph: American artists were frustrated because of "the public's attitude that European art was better than American art " Choice D is not mentioned anywhere in the paragraph. Because you are asked to identify the choice that is NOT mentioned in the passage or that contradicts the passage, the correct answer is choice D.

Type 3: Inference Questions

These questions measure your ability to comprehend an argument or an idea that is strongly implied but not explicitly stated in the text. For example, if an effect is cited in the passage, an Inference question might ask about its cause. If a comparison is made, an Inference question might ask for the basis of the comparison. You should think about not only the explicit meaning of the authors words, but the logical implications of those words.

第三类 推理

此类问题是衡量你对理解辩论或概念中暗示到但并非具体陈述部分的能力。例如,如果文章中陈述了一件事的结果,那么此类问题或许会问到它的原因。如果有比较,此类问题或许会问到比较的根据。您不仅应该考虑到文章的字面意思,还应想到这些词的引申义。

How to Recognize Inference Questions

如何辨认推理题

Inference questions will usually include the word infer, suggest, or imply. For instance:

推理题通常会包括 infer, suggest, or imply,例如:

1. Which of the following can be inferred about X?

2. The author of the passage implies that X...

3. Which of the following can be inferred from paragraph 1 about X?

Hints for Inference Questions

1. Make sure your answer does not contradict the main idea of the passage.

2. Don't choose an answer just because it seems important or true. The correct answer must be inferable from the passage.

3. You should be able to defend your choice by pointing to explicitly stated information in the passage that leads to the inference you have selected.

|| 提醒 ||

1. 确认你的答案与文章大意不矛盾。

2. 不要选择一个看起来重要或正确的答案。正确的答案一定是从文章中推理出来的。

3. 你所选择的推理选项必须以文章中明确陈述的信息为依据。

Example

Passage Excerpt: "...The nineteenth century brought with it a burst of new discoveries and inventions that revolutionized the candle industry and made lighting available to all. In the early-to-mid-nineteenth century, a process was developed to refine tallow (fat from animals) with alkali and sulfuric acid. The result was a product called stearin. Stearin is harder and burns longer than unrefined tallow. This breakthrough meant that it was possible to make tallow candles that would not produce the usual smoke and rancid odor. Stearins were also derived from palm oils, so vegetable waxes as well as animal fats could be used to make candles..."

Which of the following can be inferred from paragraph 1 about candles before the nine-teenth century?

A. They did not smoke when they were burned.

B. They produced a pleasant odor as they burned.

C. They were not available to all.

D. They contained sulfuric acid.

Explanation

In the first sentence from the excerpt the author says that "new discoveries and inventions" made "lighting available to all". The only kind of lighting discussed in the passage is candles. If the new discoveries were important because they made candles available to all, we can infer that before the discoveries, candles were not available to everyone. Therefore, choice C is an inference about candles we can make from the passage.

Choices A and B can be eliminated because they explicitly contradict the passage ("the usual smoke" and "rancid odor").

Choice D can be eliminated because sulfuric acid was first used to make stearin in the nineteenth century, not before the nineteenth century.

Type 4: Rhetorical Purpose Questions

Rhetoric is the art of speaking or writing effectively. In Factual Information questions you are asked what information an author has presented. In Rhetorical Purpose questions you are asked why the author has presented a particular piece of information in a particular place or manner. Rhetorical Purpose questions ask you to show that you understand the rhetorical function of a statement or paragraph as it relates to the rest of the passage.

Sometimes you will be asked to identify how one paragraph relates to another. For instance, the second paragraph may give examples to support a statement in the first paragraph. The answer choices may be expressed in general terms, (for example, "a theory is explained and then illustrated") or in terms that are specific to the passage. ("The author explains the categories of adaptation to deserts by mammals and then gives an example.")

A Rhetorical Purpose question may also ask why the author mentions a particular piece of information (Example: Why does the author mention "the ability to grasp a pencil"? Correct answer: It is an example of a motor skill developed by children at 10 to 11 months of age) or why the author quotes a certain person.

第四类 修辞

修辞是一种说话和写作的艺术体现。在事实信息题中，你被问文章中提到什么信息。在此类问题中，会问您为什么作者在一个特定场景下提到的特定信息。此类问题将会展现您对理解修辞功能在句子或段落上如何体现的能力。

How to Recognize Rhetorical Purpose Questions

如何辨别修辞题

These are examples of the way Rhetorical Purpose questions are typically worded:

下面为此类问题的通常问法:

1. The author discusses X in paragraph 2 in order to...

2. Why does the author mention X?

3. The author uses X as an example of..

Hints for Rhetorical Purpose Questions

1. Know the definitions of these words or phrases, which are often used to describe different kinds of rhetorical purposes: "definition," "example," "to illustrate," "to explain," "to contrast," "to refute," "to note," "to criticize," "function of."

2. Rhetorical Purpose questions usually do not ask about the overall organization of the reading passage. Instead, they typically focus on the logical links between sentences and paragraphs.

‖ 提 醒 ‖

1. 了解这些经常被用来形容不同修辞单词或词组的定义:"example," "to illustrate," "to explain," "to contrast," "to refute," "to note," "to criticize," "function of"

2. 此类问题通常不会对文章总体进行提问。所以,它通常会问到句子或段落互相之间的逻辑联系。

Example

Passage Excerpt: "... Sensitivity to physical laws is thus an important consideration for the maker of applied-art objects. It is often taken for granted that this is also true for the maker of fine-art objects. This assumption misses a significant difference between the two disciplines. Fine-art objects are not constrained by the laws of physics in the same way that applied-art objects are. Because their primary purpose is not functional, they are only limited in terms of the materials used to make them. Sculptures must, for example, be stable, which requires an understanding of the properties of mass, weight distribution, and stress. Paintings must have rigid stretchers so that the canvas will be taut, and the paint must not deteriorate, crack, or discolor. These are problems that must be overcome by the artist because they tend to intrude upon his or her conception of the work. For example, in the early Italian Renaissance, bronze statues of horses with a raised foreleg usually had a cannonball under that hoof. This was done because the cannonball was needed to support the weight of the leg..."

Why does the author discuss the bronze statues of horses created by artists in the early Italian Renaissance?

A. To provide an example of a problem related to the laws of physics that a fine artist must overcome

B. To argue that fine artists are unconcerned with the laws of physics.

C. To contrast the relative sophistication of modern artists in solving problems related to the laws of physics.

D. To note an exceptional piece of art constructed without the aid of technology.

Explanation

You should note that the sentence that first mentions "bronze statues of horses" begins "For example..." The author is giving an example of something he has introduced earlier in the paragraph. The paragraph overall contrasts how the constraints of physical laws affect the fine arts differently from applied arts or crafts. The fine artist is not concerned with making an object that is useful, so he or she is less constrained than the applied artist. However, because even a fine-arts object is made of some material, the artist must take into account the physical properties of the material. In the passage, the author uses the example of the bronze statues of horses to discuss how artists had to include some support for the raised foreleg of the horse because of the physical properties of the bronze. So the correct answer is choice A.

Type 5: Vocabulary

These questions ask you to identify the meanings of individual words and phrases as they are used in the reading passage (a word might have more than one meaning, but in the reading passage, only one of those meanings is relevant.) Vocabulary is chosen as it actually occurs in the passage. There is no "list of words" that must be tested. Usually a word or phrase is chosen to be tested as a vocabulary item because understanding that word or phrase is important to understanding a large or important part of the passage. On the iBT TOEFL, words in the passage that are unusual, technical, or have special meaning in the context of the topic are defined for you. If you click on the word in the passage, a definition will appear in a box. In this book, words of this type are defined at the end of the passage. Naturally, words that are tested as vocabulary questions are not defined for you.

第五类　单词

此类问题要求您对文章中的单词或短语意思进行辨认(一个单词或许会有很多意思,但在文章中,只会用到一种意思)。单词会在文章中出现,没有备考词汇表。通常被考单词是对理解段落甚至文章大意都有关系的词。如果你点中一个单词,将会显示出该词的定义。在本书里,此类单词的定义会出现在文章末尾。通常被考单词的定义不会被列出。

How to Recognize Vocabulary Questions

如何辨认单词题

Vocabulary questions are usually easy to identify. You will see one word or phrase highlighted in the passage. You are then asked a question like this:

此类问题通常很好辨认。你将会看到一个文章中划线的单词或短语。问法如下:

The word X in the passage is closest in meaning to...

In the case of a phrase, the question might be: ...

In stating X, the author means that...

Hints for Vocabulary Questions

1. Remember that the question is not just asking the meaning of a word; it is asking for the meaning as it is used in the passage. Do not just choose an answer just because it can be a correct meaning of the word; understand which meaning the author is using in the passage.

2. Reread the sentence in the passage, substituting the word or phrase you have chosen. Confirm that the sentence still makes sense in the context of the whole passage.

‖ 提 醒 ‖

1. 一定记住此类问题并非考察单词的本意，而是在文章中的意思。不要选择一个仅仅解释正确的选项，要理解单词在文中的具体含义。

2. 重读此句，把您所选择的意思带入句子中。确定此句依然通顺，符合文章逻辑。

Examples

Passage Excerpt: "in the animal world the task of moving about is fulfilled in many ways. For some animals locomotion is accomplished by changes in body shape..."

The word "locomotion" in the passage is closest in meaning to _____ .

A. evolution   B. movement

C. survival   D. escape

Explanation

Locomotion means "the ability to move from place to place." In this example, it is a way of restating the phrase "the task of moving" in the preceding sentence. So the correct answer is choice B.

Passage Excerpt: "Some poisonous snake bites need to be treated immediately or the victim will suffer paralysis..."

In stating that the victim will "suffer paralysis" the author means that the victim will _____ .

A. lose the ability to move   B. become unconscious

C. undergo shock   D. feel great pain

Explanation

In this example, both the words tested from the passage and the possible answers are phrases. Paralysis means "the inability to move," so if the poison from a snake bite causes someone to "suffer paralysis," that person will "lose the ability to move" The correct answer is choice A.

Type 6: Reference Questions

These questions ask you to identify referential relationships between the words in the passage. Often, the relationship is between a pronoun and its antecedent (the word to which the pronoun refers). Sometimes other kinds of grammatical reference are tested (like which or this).

第六类 指代题

此类问题会要求你辨认文章中单词之间关系。一般说来,会问指示代词和被指代名词。某些情况下语法性指代(像 which 或 this)也会考到。

How to Recognize Reference Questions

如何辨认指代题

Reference questions look similar to vocabulary questions. In the passage, one word or phrase is highlighted. Usually the word is a pronoun. Then you are asked:

指代题与单词题较为相似。文章中,会有一个单词或短语被提问。那个单词通常是指示代词。问法如下:

The word "X" in the passage refers to

The four answer choices will be words or phrases from the passage. Only one choice is the word to which the highlighted word refers.

Hintss for Reference Questions

1. If the reference question is about a pronoun, make sure your answer is the same number (singular or plural) and case (first person, second person, third person) as the highlighted pronoun.

2. Substitute your choice for the highlighted word or words in the sentence. Does it violate any grammar rules? Does it make sense?

提醒

1. 如果问题是关于一个指示代词,保证你的答案为形式相同或一致(单数或复数)和人称(第一人称,第二人称或第三人称)。

2. 同样地,把选项带入原句中。有没有违背语法规则? 说的通顺吗?

Examples

Passage Excerpt: "... These laws are universal in their application, regardless of cultural beliefs, geography, or climate. If pots have no bottoms or have large openings in their sides, they could hardly be considered containers in any traditional sense. Since the laws of physics, not some arbitrary decision, have determined the general form of applied-art objects, they follow basic patterns, so much so that functional forms can vary only within certain limits ...

The word "they" in the passage refers to _____ .

A. applied-art objects　　　　　B. the laws of physics

C. containers　　　　　　　　　D. the sides of pots

Explanation

This is an example of a simple pronoun-referent item. The highlighted word they refers to the phrase "applied-art objects," which immediately precedes it, so choice A is the correct answer.

Often the grammatical referent for a pronoun will be separated from the pronoun. It may be located in a preceding clause or even in the preceding sentence.

Passage Excerpt: "... The first weekly newspaper in the colonies was the Boston Gazette, established in 1719, the same year that marked the appearance of Philadelphia's first newspaper, the American Mercury, where the young Benjamin Franklin worked. By 1760 Boston had 4 newspapers and 5 other printing establishments; Philadelphia, 2 newspapers and 3 other presses; and New York, 3 newspapers. The distribution, if not the sale, of newspapers was assisted by the establishment of a postal service in 1710, which had a network of some 65 offices by 1770, serving all 13 colonies ..."

The word "which" in the passage refers to _____.

A. distribution   B. sale

C. newspaper   D. postal service

Explanation

In this example, the highlighted word is a relative pronoun, the grammatical subject of the relative clause "which had a network of some 65 offices" The relative clause is describing the postal service, so choice D is the correct answer.

Passage Excerpt: "... Roots anchor the plant in one of two ways or sometimes by a combination of the two. The first is by occupying a large volume of shallow soil around the plant's base with a fibrous root system, one consisting of many thin, profusely branched roots. Since these kinds of roots grow relatively close to the soil surface, they effectively control soil erosion. Grass roots are especially well suited to this purpuse. Fibrous roots capture water as it begins to percolate into the ground and so must draw their mineral supplies from the surface soil before the nutrients are leached to lower levels..."

The phrase "this purpose" in the passage refers to _____.

A. combining two root systems   B. feeding the plant

C. preventing soil erosion   D. leaching nutrients

Explanation

In the example, the highlighted words are a phrase containing a demonstrative article (this) and a noun (purpose). Because a fibrous root system can keep soft in place, it can be used to stop erosion, and grass roots are a fibrous root system. The sentence could be reworded as "Grass roots are especially well suited to preventing soil erosion," so choice C is the correct answer.

Type 7: Sentence Simplification Questions

In this type of question you are asked to choose a sentence that has the same essential meaning as a sentence that occurs in the passage. Not every reading set includes a Sentence Simplification question. There is never more than one in a set.

第七类 句子简化题

在此类问题中，要求选择一个与文章中标出句子意思相同的选项。并不是每套阅读题都会有此类问题，每套题中最多就一道。

How to Recognize Sentence Simplification Questions

如何辨别句子简化词题

Sentence Simplification questions always look the same. A single sentence in the passage is highlighted. You are then asked：

这类问题看起来都一样，在文章中一个简单句被划线。问法如下：

Which of the following best expresses the essential information in the highlighted sentence? Incorrect answer choices change the meaning in important ways or leave out essential information.

Hints for Sentence Simplification Questions

1. Make sure you understand both ways a choice can be incorrect.

2. It contradicts something in the highlighted sentence.

3. It leaves out something important from the highlighted sentence.

4. Make sure your answer does not contradict the main argument of the paragraph in which the sentence occurs, or the passage as a whole.

提 醒

1. 确定通过二种方式判断一个选项不正确。

2. 它与被划线的句子在某些地方矛盾。

3. 它与划线句子相比，选项中有重要信息丢失。

4. 保证你的答案与文章中句子出现部分或文章的大意不矛盾。

Example

Passag Excerpt: "... Although we now tend to refer to the various crafts according to the materials used to construct them—clay, glass, wood, fiber, and metal—it was once common to think of crafts in terms of function, which led to their being known as the "applied arts". Approaching crafts from the point of view of function, we can divide them into simple categories: containers, shelters, and supports. There is no way around the fact that containers, shelters, and supports must be functional. The applied arts are thus bound by the laws of physics, which pertain to both the materials used in their making and the substances and things to be contained, supported, and sheltered. These laws are universal in their application, regardless of cultural beliefs, geography, or climate. If a pot has no bottom or has large openings in its sides, it could hardly be considered a container in any traditional sense. Since the laws of physics, not some arbitrary decision, have determined the general form of applied-art objects, they follow basic patterns, so much so that functional forms can vary only within certain limits. Buildings without roofs, for example, are unusual because they depart from the norm. However, not all functional objects are exactly alike; that is why we recognize a Shang Dynasty vase as being different from an Inca vase. What varies is not the basic form but the incidental details that do not obstruct the object's primary function. . . "

Which of the following best expresses the essential information in the highlighted sentence? Incorrect answer choices change the meaning in important ways or leave out essential information.

A. Functional applied-art objects cannot vary much from the basic patterns determined by the laws of physics.

B. The function of applied-art objects is determined by basic patterns in the laws of physics.

C. Since functional applied-art objects vary only within certain limits, arbitrary decisions cannot have determined their general form.

D. The general form of applied-art objects is limited by some arbitrary decision that is not determined by the laws of physics.

Explanation

It is important to note that the question says that incorrect answers change the original meaning of the sentence or leave out essential information. In this example, choice D changes the meaning of the sentence to its opposite; it says that the form of functional objects is arbitrary, when the highlighted sentence says that the forms of functional objects are never arbitrary. Choice B also changes the meaning. It says that the functions of applied-art objects are determined by physical laws. The highlighted sentence says that the form of the object is determined by physical laws but the function is determined by people, choice C leaves out an important idea from the high lighted sentence. Like the highlighted sentence, it says that the form of functional objects is not arbitrary, but it does not say that it is physical laws that determine basic form. Only choice A makes the same point as the highlighted sentence and includes all the essential meaning.

Type 8: Insert Text Questions

In this type of question, you are given a new sentence and are asked where in the passage it would best fit. you need to understand the logic of the passage, as well as the grammatical connections (like pronoun reference) between sentences. Not every set includes an Insert Text question. There is never more than one in a set.

第八类 插入文本题

在此类问题中，会给你有一个新的句子，需要判断它适合放置于文章中的哪个部分，所以你必须了解文章的逻辑以及句与句间的语法关联。不是每套阅读题都会有此类问题，每套不超过一道。

How to Recognize Insert Text Questions

如何辨别插入文本题

In the passage you will see four black squares. The squares are located at the beginnings or ends of sentences. Sometimes all four squares appear in one paragraph sometimes they are spread across the end of one paragraph and the beginning of another. You are then asked this question:

在文章中您将会看到四个黑色方块，这些方块会在句首或句尾出现。有时这些方块会在同一句中出现,有时它会出现在一段末尾和另一段开头。

Look at the four squares ■ that indicate where the following sentence could be added to the passage.

You will see a sentence in bold.

Where would the sentence best fit?

Your job is to click on one of the squares and insert the sentence in the text.

Hints for Insert Text Questions

1. Try the sentence in each of the places indicated by the squares. You can place and replace the sentence as many times as you want.

2. Look at both the structure of the sentence you are inserting and the logic. Pay special attention to logical connecting words; they can provide important information about where the sentence should be placed.

3. Frequently used connecting words:

    On the other hand

    For example

    On the contrary

    Similarly

    In coutrast

    Further, or Furthermore

    Therefore

    In other words

    As a result

    Finally

4. Make sure that the inserted sentence connects logically to both the sentence before it and the sentence after it.

||提 醒||

1. 把句子依次放入每个方块处,替换句子,反复推敲。

2. 注意你所放入句子的结构和逻辑,尤其是更要注意词语的逻辑联系。它们通常会对句子的放置位置起到很大帮助。

3. 使用频率高的关联词:另一方面,比如,相反,同样的,相对的,更加,因此,换句话说,结果,终于。

4. 保证被替换的句子在前后两句中的逻辑意思通顺连贯。

Example

Passage Excerpt with Example Square: "Scholars offer three related but different opinions bout this puzzle." ■One opinion is that the paintings were a record of the seasonal migrations made by herds. ■

Because some paintings were made directly over others, obliterating them, it is probable that a painting's value ended with the migration it pictured. ■ Unfortunately, this explanation fails to explain the hidden locations, unless the migrations were celebrated with secret ceremonies. "■

Look at the four squares ■ that indicate where the following sentence could be added to the passage.

All three of them have strengths and weaknesses, but none adequately answers all of the questions the paintings present.

Where would the sentence best fit?

A. Scholars offer three related but different opinions about this puzzle. All three of them have strengths and weaknesses, but none adequately answers all of the questions the paintings present. One opinion is that the paintings were a record of the seasonal migrations made by herds. ■ Because some paintings were made directly over others, obliterating them, it is probable that a painting's value ended with the migration it pictured. ■ Unfortunately, this explanation fails to explain the hidden locations, unless the migrations were celebrated with secret ceremonies. ■

B. Scholars offer three related but different opinions about this puzzle. ■ One opinion is that the paintings were a record of the seasonal migrations made by herds. All three of them have strengths and weaknesses, but none adequately answers all of the questions the paintings present. Because some paintings were made directly over others, obliterating them it is probable that a painting's value ended with the migration it pictured. ■ Unfortunately, this explanation fails to explain the hidden locations, unless the migrations were celebrated with secret ceremonies. ■

C. Scholars offer three related but different opinions about this puzzie. ■ One opinion is that the paintings were a record of the seasonal migrations made by herds. ■ Because some paintings were made directly over others, obliterating them, it is probable that a painting's value ended with the migration it pictured. All three of them have strengths and weaknesses, but none adequately answers all of the questions the paintings present. Unfortunately, this explanation fails to explain the hidden locations, unless the migrations were celebrated with secret ceremonies. ■

D. Scholars offer three related but different opinions about this puzzle. ■ One opinion is that the paintings were a record of the seasonal migrations made by herds. ■ Because some paintings were made directly over others, obliterating them, it is probable that a painting's value ended with the migration it pictured. ■ Unfortunately, this explanation fails to explain the hidden locations, unless the migrations were celebrated with secret ceremonies. All three of them have strengths and weaknesses, but none adequately answers all of the questions the paintings present.

Explanation

In this example, choice A is the correct answer. The new sentence makes sense only if it occurs in the first position, after the first sentence. In that place, "All three of them" refers back to "three related but different opinions." The information in the sentence is a commentary on all three of the "opinions"; the opinions are related, but none is a complete explanation. Logically, this evaluation of all three opinions must come either as an introduction to the three opinions, or as a conclusion about all three. Only the introductory position is available, because the paragraph does not include all three opinions.

Reading to Learn questions

Reading to Learn items are a new question category that is being introduced in the TOEFL iBT test. There are two types of Reading to Learn questions: "Prose Summary" and "Fill in a Table". Reading to Learn questions will require you to do more than the Basic Information questions. As you have seen, the Basic Information questions focus on your ability to understand or locate specific points in a passage at the sentence level. The Reading to Learn questions will also involve.

1. recognizing the organization and purpose of the passage

2. organizing the information in the passage into a mental framework

3. distinguishing major from minor ideas and essential from nonessential information

4. understanding rhetorical functions such as cause-effect relationships, compare-contrast relationships, arguments, and the like.

In other words, these questions will require you to demonstrate an understanding of the passage as a whole, not just specific information within it.

Reading to Learn questions require you to show that you are able not only to comprehend individual points, but also to place the major ideas and supporting information from the passage into an organizational framework or structure such as a prose summary or a table. By answering correctly, you will demonstrate that you can recognize the major points of a text, how and why the text has been organized, and the nature of the relationships within the text. Having an organized mental representation of a text is critical to learning because it allows you to remember important information from the text and apply it in new situations. If you have such a mental framework, you should be able to reconstruct the major ideas and supporting information from the text. By doing so, you will demonstrate a global understanding of the text as a whole. On the iBT TOEFL, each reading passage will have one Reading to Learn item. It will be either a Prose Summary or a Fill in a Table item, never both.

Type 9: Prose Summary Questions

These items measure your ability to understand and recognize the major ideas and the relative importance of information in a passage. You will be asked to select the major ideas in the passage by distinguishing them from minor ideas or ideas that are not in the passage. The correct answer choice will synthesize major ideas in the passage. Because the correct answer represents a synthesis of ideas, it will not match any particular sentence from the passage. To select the correct answer, you will need to create a mental framework to organize and remember major ideas and other important information. Understanding the relative importance of information in a passage is critical to this ability.

In a Prose Summary question, you will be given six answer choices and asked to pick the three that express the most important ideas in the passage. Unlike the Basic Information questions, each of which is worth just one point, a Prose Summary question can be worth either one or two points depending on how many correct answers you choose. If you choose no correct answers or just one correct answer, you will earn no points. If you choose two correct answers, you will earn one point. If you choose all three correct answers, you will earn two points. The order in which you choose your answers does not matter for scoring purposes.

第九类 摘要题

这类题型测试你理解和认识文章大意和各信息间关系重要性的能力。它要求通过排除次要意思或其他干扰选项来选出文章大意。正确选项需体现文章的整体意思,它不会重复文章中任何句子的意思。做这种题,您需要在头脑中构建一个框架去组织和记忆这些大意和其他重要信息。对于关联信息的重要性的了解是提高这一能力的关键所在。

Example

Because the Prose Summary question asks you to show an understanding of the different parts of the passage it is necessary to read the entire passage. Parts of the following passage have already been used to illustrate other question types.

Applied Arts and Fine Arts

Although we now tend to refer to the various crafts according to the materials used to construct them—clay, glass, wood, fiber, and metal. It was once common to think of crafts in terms of function, which led to their being known as the "applied arts". Approaching crafts from the point of view of function, we can divide them into simple categories: containers, shelters, and supports. There is no way around the fact that containers, shelters, and supports must be functional. The applied arts are thus bound by the laws of physics, which pertain to both the materials used in their making and the substances and things to be contained, supported, and sheltered. These laws are universal in their application, regardless of cultural beliefs, geography, or climate. If a pot has no bottom or has large openings in its sides, it could hardly be considered a container in any traditional sense. Since the laws of physics, not some arbitrary decision, have determined the general form of applied-art objects, they follow basic patterns, so much so that functional forms can vary only within certain limits. Buildings without roofs, for example, are unusual because they depart from the norm. However, not all functional objects are exactly alike; that is why we recognize a Shang Dynasty vase as being different from an Inca vase. What varies is not the basic form but the incidental details that do not obstruct the object's primary function.

Sensitivity to physical laws is thus an important consideration for the maker of applied-art objects. It is often taken for granted that this is also true for the maker of fine-art objects. This assumption misses a significant difference between the two disciplines. Fine-art objects are not constrained by the laws of physics in the same way that applied-art objects are. Because their primary purpose is not functional, they are only limited in terms of the materials used to make them. Sculptures must, for example, be stable, which requires an understanding of the properties of mass, weight distribution, and stress. Paintings must have rigid stretchers so that the canvas will be taut, and the paint must not deteriorate, crack, or discolor. These are problems that must be overcome by the artist because they tend to intrude upon his or her conception of the work. For example, in the early Italian Renaissance, bronze statues of horses with a raised foreleg usually had a cannonball under that hoof. This was done because the cannonball was needed to support the weight of the leg. In other words, the demands of the laws of physics, not the sculptor's aesthetic intentions, placed the ball there. That this device was a necessary structural compromise is clear from the fact that the cannonball quickly disappeared when sculptors learned how to strengthen the internal structure of a statue with iron braces (iron being much stronger than bronze).

Even though the fine arts in the twentieth century often treat materials in new ways, the basic difference in attitude of artists in relation to their materials in the fine arts and the applied arts remains relatively constant. It would therefore not be too great an exaggeration to say that practitioners of the fine arts work to overcome the limitations of their materials, whereas those engaged in the applied arts work in concert with their materials.

An introductory sentencefor a brief summary of the passage is provided below. Complete the summary by selecting there answer choices that express the most important ideas in the passage. Some sentences do not belong in the summary because they express ideas that are not presented in the passage or are minor ideas in the passage. This question is worth 2 points.

This passage discusses fundamental differences between applied-art objects and fine-art objects.

Answer Choices

1. The fine arts are only affected by the laws of physics because of the limitations of the materials that are used.

2. Applied-art objects are bound by the laws of physics in two ways: by the materials used to make them, and the punction they are to serve.

3. Crafts are known as "applied arts" because it used to be common to think of them in terms of their function.

4. In the fine arts, artists must work to overcome the limitations of their materials, but in the applied arts, artists work in concert with their materials.

5. Making fine-art objects stable requires an understanding of the properties of mass, weight, distribution, ard stress.

6. In the twentieth century, artists working in the fine arts often treat materials in new ways whereas applied arts specialists continue to think of crafts in terms of function.

Explanation

Correct Choices:

Choice 2: Applied-art objects are bound by the laws of physics in two ways: by the materials used to make them, and the function they are to serve.

Explanation: This answer is correct because it represents the major theme of the first paragraph. It is a broad statement of a general, overriding fact. The paragraph then provides support for that general statement with several specific examples of how the laws of physics apply to all applied-art objects. The examples are presented in over five or six sentences.

Choice 4: In the fine arts, artists must work to overcome the limitations of their materials, but in the applied arts, artists work in concert with their materials.

Explanation: This answer is correct because it summarizes the basic compare-contrast relationship of the entire passage. Although the last sentence of the passage is nearly identical to this answer choice, the able reader with a well developed mental framework of the passage will recognize that this is not a minor, discrete point. Like the first correct answer choice, this is a broad, general statement, in this case about both applied and fine arts. The first two paragraphs of the passage are devoted to providing support for this statement with numerous examples throughout the passage.

Choice 6: In the twentieth century, artists working in the fine arts often treat materials in new ways whereas applied arts specialists continue to think of crafts in terms of function.

Explanation: This answer is also correct in that it is a general statement about the ongoing and fundamental distinction between applied arts and fine arts. Like the previous correct answer choice it is nearly identical to a sentence in the passag(the first sentence of the last paragraph). It reaffirms that the distinctions discussed and illustrated in the first two paragraphs are real and that the evidence presented about them is sound.

Incorrect Choices:

Choice 1: The fine arts are only affected by the laws of physics because of the limitations of the materials that are used.

Explanation: This answer is incorrect because it is a minor point mentioned in sentence 4 of paragraph 2. The statement is true, but it is made only to support the broader theme (of the second correct answer choice above) about the differences between the two forms of art. Thus, it is used as an example in support of a major idea and is not itself one of the major themes in the passage.

Choice 3: Crafts are known as "applied arts" because it used to be common to think of them in terms of their function.

Explanation: This choice is not correct because it is a minor point. It is mentioned as part of the passage's first, introductory sentence and then is never developed further. It is a true statement from the text, but is merely stated once without further elaboration.

Choice 5: Making fine-art objects stable requires an understanding of the properties of mass, weight, distribution, and stress.

Explanation: This answer choice is also a minor point and is therefore not correct. Like the other incorrect choices, it is true and mentioned in the passage (in paragraph 2, sentence 5). However, it too is raised only as an example. Much like the first incorrect answer choice, it is presented as an example of how fine artists are constrained by physics and is not itself a major theme in the passage.

Type 10: Fill in a Table Questions

In this kind of item, you will be given a partially completed classification table based on information in the passage. Your job is to complete the table by clicking on correct answer choices and dragging them to their correct locations in the table.

Fill in a Table items measure your ability to conceptualize and organize major ideas and other important information from across the passage and then to place them in appropriate categories. This means that you must first recognize and identify the major points from the passage, and then place those points in their proper context.

Just as for Prose Summary questions, the able reader will create a mental framework to organize and remember major ideas and other important information.

Doing so requires the ability to understand rhetorical functions such as cause-effect relationships, compare-contrast relationships, arguments, and the like.

When building your mental framework, keep in mind that the major ideas in the passage are the ones you would include if you were making a fairly high-level outline of the passage. The correct answer choices are usually ideas that would be included in a slightly more detailed outline. Minor details and examples are generally not included in such an outline because they are used only to support the more important, higher-level themes. The distinction between major ideas/important information and less important information can also be thought of as a distinction between essential and nonessential information.

Passages used with Fill in a Table items have more than one focus of development in that they include more than one point of view or perspective. Typical passages have the following types of organization: compare/contrast, problem/solution, cause/effect, alternative arguments (such as theories, hypotheses), and the like.

Correct answers represent major ideas and important supporting information in the passage. Generally these answers will not match specific phrases in the passage. They are more likely to be abstract concepts based on passage information or paraphrases of passage information. Correct answers will be easy to confirm by able readers who can remember or easily locate relevant text information.

Incorrect answers may include information about the topic that is not mentioned in the passage or that is not directly relevant to the classification categories in the table. They may also be obviously incorrect generalizations or conclusions based on what is stated in the passage. Be aware that incorrect answers may include words and phrases that match or resemble words or phrases in the passage.

第十类　填表题

在此类问题中,会有一个根据文章内容并且经过分类的表格。您需要做的是选出正确的选项然后把表格补充完整。

填表题测试的是对文章大意和其他重要信息概念化以及组织的能力。把需要的内容在不同段落找出来后填入恰当的地方。这意味着您首先要了解和辨别文章要点,然后把它们归到表格中。

就像文本插入题一样,这里也需要您构造一个框架去组织和记忆文章大意和其他相关重要信息。

要做到这些就需要理解逻辑、修辞功能,例如因果关系,比较对比关系,辩论等等。

当您构建框架时,尤其是要构建比较复杂的轮廓,在头脑中要始终保持对文章要点的记忆。正确选项的答案通常会包括在一个相对比较细致的轮廓中,不太重要的细节一般不会包括其中。因为它们是为了支持那些重要的主题而存在的。重要信息大意和次重要信息大意的区别也同样是本质和非本质信息的区别。

那些用于填表的段落可能会包含多方面的信息。典型的段落会有以下类型结构:比较/对比,问题/办法,原因/结果,其他论点(比如理论,假设)等等。

正确答案可以代表文章大意和重要支持信息。一般说来,这些答案不会重复文章中的短语。它们通常是通过文章大意而总结出来的比较抽象的概念。能够记忆细节或轻松锁定相关文章信息的读者将会很快确定正确答案。

不正确的答案会包括一些文章中没有提到或不直接相关的信息。需要注意的是,那些不正确的选项或许会跟文章中提到的某些短语或词组的意思类似。

Table Rules

Tables can have 2 or 3 columns/rows containing bullets representing either 5 or 7 correct answer choices. So there are four possible types of tables, as follow:

Type 1: 2 - column/row table with 5 correct answer choices

Type 2: 3 - column/row table with 5 correct answer choices

Type 3: 2 - column/row table with 7 correct answer choices

Type 4: 3 - column/row table with 7 correct answer choices

There will always be more options than correct answer choices. Some answer choices will not be used.

An answer choice can be used only once in the table. If an answer choice applies to more than one category, or to no category in a table, a row or column labeled "both" or "neither" will be available in the table for placement of that answer choice.

Scoring

To earn points, you must not only select correct answer choices, but also organize them correctly in the table. You may receive partial credit, depending upon how many correct answers you choose.

For tables with 5 correct answers (both type 1 and type 2), you can earn up to a total of 3 points, depending on how many correct answers you select and correctly place. For 0, 1, or 2 correct answers you will receive no credit. For 3 correct answers you will receive 1 point; for 4 correct answers you will receive 2 points; and for all 5 correct answers you will receive the entire 3 points.

For tables with 7 correct answers (both type 3 and type 4), you can earn up to a total of 4 points, depending on how many correct answers you select and correctly place. For 0, 1, 2, or 3 correct answers you will receive no credit. For 4 correct answers you will receive 1 point; for 5 correct answers you will receive 2 points; for 6 correct answers you will receive 3 points, and for all 7 correct answers you will receive the entire 4 points.

得分情况

不是仅仅选出正确答案的选项就会得分,同时,必须把它们在表格中组织好。或许会得到一部分的分数,这就要根据您到底选对多少个选项而定了。

有5个答案的表格,总分为3分。这会根据您选对答案的数目以及放入的位置而定。没有或有1,2个正确选项不得分,3个正确选项得1分,4个正确选项得2分,5个都正确为满分3分。

有7个答案的表格,总分为4分。同样根据您选对答案的数目以及放入的位置而定。没有或有1,2或3个正确答案不得分,4个正确选项得1分,5个正确选项得2分,6个正确选项得3分,7个都正确那就是满分4分。

Example

(Note: The passage used for this example is the same one that was used above for the Prose Summary example question.)

Directions: Complete the table below to summarize information about the two types of art discussed in the passage. Match the appropriate statements to the types of art with which they are associated. This question is worth 3 points.

TYPES OF ART	STATEMENTS
The Applied Arts	Select 3
A	
B	
C	
The Fine Arts	Select 2
A	
B	

Statements

An object's purpose is primarily aesthetic.

Objects serve a functional purpose.

The incidental details of objects do not vary.

Artists work to overcome the limitations of their materials.

The basic form of objects varies little across cultures.

Artists work in concert with their materials.

An object's place of origin is difficult to determine.

Drag your answer choices to the spaces where they belong. To review the passage, click on View Text

Correctly Completed Table

Directions: Complete the table below to summarize information about the two types of art discussed in the passage. Match the appropriate statements to the types of art with which they are associated.

This question is worth 3 points.

TYPES OF ART	STATEMENTS
The Applied Arts	Select 3
	A. Objects serve a functional Purpose.
	B. The basic form of objects varies little across cultures.
	C. Artists work in concert with their materials.
The Fine Arts	Select 2
	A. An object's purpose is primarily aesthetic.
	B. Artists work to overcome the limitations of their materials.

Explanation

Correct Choices:

Choice 1: An object's purpose is primarily aesthetic. (Fine Arts)

Explanation: This is an example of a correct answer that requires you to identify an abstract concept based on text information and paraphrases of text information. In paragraph 2, sentence 5, the passage states that the primary purpose of Fine Art is not function. Then, in paragraph 2, sentence 11, the passage mentions a situation in which a sculptor had to sacrifice an aesthetic purpose due to the laws of physics. Putting these statements together, the reader can infer that fine artists, such as sculptors, are primarily concerned with aesthetics.

Choice 2: Objects serve a functional purpose. (Applied Arts)

Explanation: This is stated more directly than the previous correct answer. Paragraph 1, sentences 1, 2, and 3 make it clear how important function is in the applied arts. At the same time, paragraph 2 states that Fine Arts are not concerned with function, so the only correct place for this statement is in the Applied Arts category.

Choice 4: Artists work to overcome the limitations of their materials. (Fine Arts)

Explanation: This is stated explicitly in the last paragraph of the passage. In that paragraph, it is made clear that this applies only to practitioners of the fine arts.

Choice 5: The basic form of objects varies little across cultures. (Applied Arts)

Explanation: In paragraph 1, sentence 5, the passage states that certain laws of physics are universal. Then in sentence 7, that idea is further developed with the statement that functional forms can vary only within limits. From these two sentences, you can conclude that because of the laws of physics and the need for functionality, the basic forms of applied art objects will vary little across cultures.

Choice 6: Artists work in concert with their materials. (Applied Arts)

Explanation: This is stated explicitly in the last paragraph of the passage. In that paragraph, it is made clear that this applies only to practitioners of the applied arts.

Incorrect Choices:

Choice 3: The incidental details of objects do not vary.

Explanation: This idea is explicitly refuted by the last sentence of paragraph 1 in reference to the applied arts. That sentence (referring only to applied arts) states that the incidental details of such objects do vary, so this answer cannot be placed in the applied arts category. This subject is not discussed at all in reference to fine art objects, so it cannot he correctly placed in that category either.

Choice 7: An object's place of origin is difficult to determine.

Explanation: This answer choice is implicitly refuted in reference to applied arts in the next to last sentence of paragraph 1. That sentence notes that both Shang Dynasty and Inca vases are identifiable as such based upon differences in detail. By inference, then, it seems that it is not difficult to determine an applied-art object's place of origin. Like the previous incorrect answer, this idea is not discussed at all in reference to fine art objects, so it cannot be correctly placed in that category either.

Improving Your Performance on iBT TOEFL

Reading Questions

The best way to improve reading skills is to read frequently and to read many different types of texts in various subject areas (sciences, social sciences, arts, business, and so on). The Internet is one of the best resources for this, and of course books, magazines, and journals are very helpful as well. Make sure to read regularly texts that are academic in style, the kind that are used in university courses.

Here are some suggestions for ways to build skills for the three reading purposes covered by iBT TOEFL.

1. Reading to find information

 (1) Scan passages to find and highlight key facts (dates, numbers, terms) and information.

 (2) Practice this frequently to increase reading rate and fluency.

2. Reading for basic comprehension

 (1) Increase your vocabulary knowledge, perhaps by using flashcards.

 (2) Rather than carefully reading each word and each sentence, practice skimming a passage quickly to get a general impression of the main idea.

 (3) Build up your ability to skim quickly and to identify the major points.

 (4) After skimming a passage, read it again more carefully and write down the main idea, major points, and important facts.

 (5) Choose some unfamiliar words in a passage and guess the meaning from the context (surrounding sentences).

 (6) Select all the pronouns (he, him, they, them, etc) and identify which nouns they refer to in a passage.

 (7) Practice making inferences and drawing conclusions based on what is implied in the passage as a whole.

3. Reading to learn

 (1) Identify the passage type (e. g. classification, cause/effect, compare/contrast, problem/solution, description, narration, and so on.)

 (2) Do the following to organize the information in the passage:

  ① Create an outline of the passage to distinguish between major and minor points.

  ② If the passage categorizes information, create a chart and place the information in appropriate categories. (Remember: On the iBT TOEFL test, you do not have to create such a chart. Instead, a chart with possible answer choices is provided for you, and you must fill in the chart with the correct choices.) Practicing this skill will help you think about categorizing information and be able to do so with ease.

  ③ If the passage describes the order of a process or is a narration, create an out- line of the steps in the process or narration.

 (3) Create a summary of the passage using the charts and outlines.

 (4) Paraphrase individual sentences in a passage, and then progress to paraphrasing an entire paragraph.

Note: The iBT TOEFL Reading section measures the ability to recognize paraphrases. The ability to paraphrase is also important for the integrated tasks in the Writing and Speaking sections of the test.

提高 iBT 托福阅读能力

 1. 读取信息

 (1)浏览文章并找出标记部分的关键事实(如日期,数字,术语)和相关信息。

 (2)反复练习来提高阅读速率。

2. 基本理解

(1)可以用小卡片的方法扩大词汇量。

(2)与其选择一词一句的读,不如练习泛读每篇文章,了解大意。

(3)提高您快速浏览和辨别要点的能力。

(4)快速浏览过一篇文章后,再仔细读一遍并写下文章大意,文中要点及重要事实。

(5)选择一些较难的单词然后通过上下文猜测这些单词在文章中的意思。

(6)选出所有的人称代词(他,他们等等)并且弄清每一个词在文章中都指的什么。

(7)练习通过全文来作出推理判断,根据文章的隐含内容下定论。

3. 阅读学习

(1)辨别文章类型(例如分类,因果,对比,描写,叙述等等)。

(2)按照以下的做法找出文中信息。

①提炼文章轮廓来区分重点和次重点。

②如果文章为归类信息,那么列表并把相关信息填入适当的表格中 (注意: 在托福 iBT 考试中您无需制作这样一个表格。它会提供给您一个表格和相关答案选项,您只需在表格中填入正确选项)。这项练习技巧可以有效的您对信息进行归类并渐渐对这类问题从容应答。

③如果文章为顺序描述或叙述,找出描述或叙述顺序的每一步,形成文章轮廓。

(3)用表格和文章轮廓提炼出文章总结。

(4)对文章中个别句子进行改写,进而改写出整段含义。

注意:托福 iBT 考试阅读部分考查改写的能力,它同样对写作和口语部分起到重要作用。

Part 2
iBT TOEFL Listening
新托福听力

一. iBT TOEFL Listening Materials

There are two types of Listening materials on the iBT TOEFL, conversations and lectures. Both are based on the actual speech that is used in North American colleges and universities.

Each lecture or conversation is four to six minutes long and, as far as possible, represents authentic academic language. For example, a professor giving a lecture may digress somewhat from the main topic, interactions between students and the Professor can be extensive, and explanations of content can be elaborate. Features of oral language such as false starts, misspeaks with self-corrections, and repetitions are included. The speakers who record the texts are encouraged to use their own speech patterns(e. g., pauses, hesitations), as long as they preserve the content of the text. You should take notes during the lectures and conversations. This material is not meant to challenge your memory.

一、听力材料

新托福考试中一般有两种听力材料——对话和讲座。两类材料都是以北美大学校园中的实际讲座为模板。

每个讲座或对话会有4~6分钟，都是代表真实学术性语言。例如，有时教授在讲座会偶尔离题。学生和教授间的交流可以多种多样，内容的解释会是详尽全面的。在口头交流中，说错话及自我更正，重复等等也会被包含在内。我们鼓励采用原版演讲的形式(例如有停顿，犹豫延迟)。在听的过程中，我们建议适当做笔记，这部分材料重点不在于考察您的记忆力。

CONVERSATIONS

There are two types of conversations in TOEFL:

1. office encounters

2. service encounters

These conversations are typical of those that occur on North American university campuses. Office hours are interactions that take place in a professor's office. The content may be academic or related to course requirements. For example, in an office conversation a student could request an extension on a due date (nonacademic content), or a student could ask for clarification about the content of lecture (academic content). Service encounters are interactions that take place on an university campus and have noncademic content. Examples include inquiring about a payment for housing or registering for class. Each conversation is followed by five questions.

对话

托福考试中一般有两类对话：

1. 办公场景

2. 服务场景

听力材料所选取的这些对话都是典型的北美大学校园里场景。办公对话是大多发生在教授办公室的场景，其内容一般与学术或课程要求有关。例如，在办公场景中有可能是一个学生要求延长原定日期(非学术内容)，或者是一个学生要求教师对讲座内容进一步阐明(学术内容)，服务场景通常是发生在大学校园中的事情，并无学术内容，例如要求支付房费或登记入校上课。每个对话后会有5个问题。

LECTURES

Lectures in iBT TOEFL represent the kind of language used when teachers teach in a classroom. The lecture excerpt may be just a teacher speaking, a student asking the teacher a question, or the teacher asking the students a question and calling on one student for a response. Each lecture is approximately 5 minutes in length and is followed by six questions.

The content of the lectures reflects the content that is presented in introductory-level academic settings. Lecture topics cover a broad range of subjects. You will not be expected to have any prior knowledge of the subject matter. All the information you need to answer the questions will be contained in the Listening passage. The lists below are provided to give you an idea of the topics that typically appear in the Listening section. In general these topics are divided into four major categories:

1. Arts

2. Life Science

3. Physical Science

4. Social Science

讲座

新托福中的讲座部分用到的语言环境是老师在教学过程中的场景，例如老师讲话，学生提问，或者是教师问问题时并要求一名学生自答等等。每个讲座大约会有5分钟并配有6道问题。

讲座的内容反映了大学中初级阶段的场景，讲座的话题涵盖了方方面面。你将不需要在做题前了解相关信息，所需要的全部信息会在听的段落中找到。以下是听力部分经常/一般会出现的话题：

1. 艺术

2. 生命科学

3. 自然科学

4. 社会科学

Arts lectures may be on topics such as:

1. Architecture

2. Industrial design/art

3. City planning

4. Crafts: weaving, knitting, fabrics, furniture, carving, mosaics, ceramics, etc.; folk and tribal art

5. Cave/rock art

6. Music and music history

7. Photography

8. Literature and authors

9. Books, newspapers, magazines, journals

Life Science lectures may be on topics such as:

1. Extinction of or conservation efforts for animals and plants

2. Fish and other aquatic organisms

3. Bacteria and other one-celled organisms

4. Viruses

5. Medical techniques

6. Public health

7. Physiology of sensory organs

8. Biochemistry

9. Animal behavior, e.g. migration, food foraging, defensive behavior

10. Habitats and the adaptation of animals and plants to them

11. Nutrition and its impact on the body

12. Animal communication

Physical Science lectures may be on topics such as:

1. Weather and atmosphere

2. Oceanography

3. Glaciers, glacial landforms, ice ages

4. Deserts and other extreme environments

5. Pollution, alternative energy, environmental policy

6. Other planets' atmospheres

7. Astronomy and cosmology

8. Properties of light, optics

9. Properties of sound

10. Electromagnetic radiation

11. Particle physics

12. Technology of TV, radio, radar

13. Math

14. Chemistry of inorganic things

15. Computer science

16. Seismology (plate structure, earthquakes, tectonics, continental drift, structure of volcanoes)

Social Science lectures may be on topics such as:

1. Anthropology of non-industrialized civilizations

2. Early writing systems

3. Historical linguistics

4. Business, management

5. TV/radio as mass communication

6. Social behavior of groups, community dynamics, communal behavior

7. Child development

8. Education

9. Modern history (including the history of urbanization and industrialization and their economic and social effects)

二、iBT TOEFL Listening Questions

Most of the iBT TOEFL Listening questions that follow the lectures and conversations are traditional multiple-choice questions with four answer choices and a single correct answer. There are, however, some other types of questions:

1. Multiple-choice questions with more than one answer (for example, two answers out of four or more choices)

2. Questions that require you to put in order events or steps in a process

3. Questions that require you to match objects or text to categories in a table At least one of the questions following most lectures and conversations will be a replay question. In replay questions you will hear a portion of the lecture or conversation again. You will then be asked a multiple-choice question about what you have just heard.

There are eight types of questions in the Listening section. These types are divided into three categories as follows:

Basic Comprehension Questions

1. Gist-Content

2. Gist-Purpose

3. Detail

Pragmatic Understanding Questions

4. Understanding the Function of What Is Said

5. Understanding the Speaker's Attitude

Connecting Information Questions

6. Understanding Organization

7. Connecting Content

8. Making Inferences

The following sections will explain each of these question types one by one. You'll find out how to recognize each type, and you'll see examples of each type with explanations. You'll also find hintss that can help you answer each TOEFL Listening question type.

二、新托福听力问题

新托福听力问题通常会采用多项选择的形式即四选一的方式。但是,问题有时也会有以下种类:

1. 多选题有时会有一个以上的答案(例如,两个答案和四个或多个选项)

2. 事件按事情的进行顺序排序题

3. 事件按相应空格的填表题

在多个问题中,只有一个问题为应答题。在这类问题中,您将重新听到对话或讲座中的一部分,然后回答一道多选题。

听力部分共有八种类型的题目。这八种类型又分为以下三种:

基本理解题

1. 中心意思 – 内容

2. 中心意思 – 目的

3. 细节

语用理解题

4. 理解谈话功能

5. 理解谈话人态度

相关信息题

6. 理解联系材料

7. 联系内容

8. 做出推理

以下会对上面所讲述的内容分别解释。有很多例子教会你如何辨别每种听力材料的类型。同时提供例题供参考。

(一)BASIC COMPREHENSION QUESTIONS 基础理解题

Basic comprehension of the listening passage is tested in three ways: with Gist-Content, Gist-Purpose, and Detail questions.

Type 1: Gist-Content Questions

Understanding the gist of a lecture or conversation means understanding the general topic or main idea. The gist of the lecture or conversation may be expressed explicitly or implicitly. Questions that test understanding the gist may require you to gener-alize or synlhesize information in what you hear.

第 1 类　中心意思——内容题

了解听力材料的中心意思就等于已掌握了它的大意。一段材料的中心意思或许会详尽说明。你必须对所听到的材料进行总结归纳。

How to Recognize Gist-Content Questions

如何识别中心意思——内容题

Gist-Content questions are typically phrased as follows:

1. What problem does the man have?

2. What are the speakers mainly discussing?

3. What is the main topic of the lecture?

4. What is the lecture mainly about?

5. What aspect of X does the professor mainly discuss?

Hints for Gist-Content Questions

1. Gist-Content questions ask about the overall content of the listening. Eliminate choices that refer to only small portions of the listening passage.

2. Use your notes. Decide what overall theme ties the details in your notes together.

Choose the answer that comes closest to describing this overall theme.

‖ 提 醒 ‖

1. 此类问题主要会问到听力全文的意思。排除只包含听力材料一部分内容的选项。

2. 利用所作的笔记做题,判断选项中哪个主题包括所有细节,并选择最接近主题的那个选项。

Example：

Excerpt from a longer listening passage:

Professor

. . . So the Earth's surface is made up of these huge segments, these tectonic plates. And these plates move, right? But how can, uh, motion of plates, do you think, influence climate on the Earth? Again, all of you probably read this section in the book, I hope, but, uh, uh, how—how can just motion of the plates impact the climate?

. . . when a plate moves, if there's landmass on the plate, then the landmass moves too, okay? That's why continents shift their positions, because the plates they're on move. So as a landmass moves away from the equator, its climate would get colder. So, right now we have a continent the landmass Antarctica—

that's on a pole.

So that's dramatically influencing the climate in Antarctica. Urn, there was a time when most of the landmasses were closer to a pole; they weren't so close to the Equator. Uh, maybe million years ago Antarctica was attached to the South American continent, oh and Africa was attached too and the three of them began moving away from the equator together.

... in the Himalayas. That was where two continental plates collided. Two continents on separate plates. Um, when this, uh, Indian, uh, uh, plate collided with the Asian plate, it wasn't until then that we created the Himalayas. When we did that, then we started creating the type of cold climate that we see there now. Wasn't there until this area was uplifted.

So again, that's something else that plate tectonics plays a critical role in. Now these processes are relatively slow; the, uh, Himalayas are still rising, but on the order of millimeters per year. So they're not dramatically influencing climate on your — the time scale of your lifetime. But over the last few thousands of — tens of thousands of years, uh — hundreds of thousands of years-yes, they've dramatically influenced it.

Uh, another important thing — number three — on how plate tectonics have influenced climate is how they've influenced — we talked about how changing landmasses can affect atmospheric circulation patterns, but if you alter where the landmasses are connected, it can impact oceanic, uh, uh, uh, circulation patterns.

... Urn, so, uh, these other processes, if — if we were to disconnect North and South America right through the middle, say, through Panama that would dramatically influence climate in North and South America — probably the whole globe. So suddenly now as the two continents gradually move apart, you can have different circulation patterns in the ocean between the two. So, uh, that might cause a dramatic change in climate if that were to happen, just as we've had happen here in Antarctica to separate, uh, from South America.

What is the main topic of the talk?

A. The differences in climate that occur in different countries.

B. How movement of the earth's plates can affect climate.

C. Why the ocean has less affect on climate than previously thought.

D. The history of the climate of the region where the college is located Explanation.

Choice B is the answer that best represents the main topic of the passage. The professor uses Antarctica and the Himalayas as examples to make his general point that climate is affected by plate tectonics, the movement of Earth's plates.

Note that for Gist-Content questions the correct answer and the incorrect choices can sometimes be worded more abstractly.

Example

The following Gist-Content question refers to the same lecture:

What is the main topic of the talk?

A. A climate experiment and its results.

B. A geologic process and its effect.

C. How a theory was disproved.

D. How land movement is measured.

Explanation

Once again, the correct answer is choice B. Even though the wording is very different, it basically says the same thing as choice B in the previous example: A geologic process （movement of the earth's plates）has an effect（changes in climate）.

Type 2: Gist-Purpose Questions

Some gist questions focus on the purpose of the conversation rather than on the content. This type of question will more likely occur with conversations, but Gist Purpose questions may also occasionally be found with lectures.

第 2 类　中心意思——目的题

此类题多集中考查对话的目的而不是对话本身。这种问题与对话比较相似,但同样在讲座中也会出现。

How to Recognize Gist-Purpose Questions

如何辨别中心意思——目的题

Gist-Purpose questions are typically phrased as follows:

1. Why does the student visit the professor?

2. Why does the student visit the registrar's office?

3. Why did the professor ask to see the student?

4. Why does the professor explain X?

Hints for Gist-Purpose Questions

1. Listen for the unifying theme of the conversation. For example, during a professor's office hours, a student asks the professor for help with a paper on *Glaciers*. Their conversation includes facts about *Glaciers*, but the unifying theme of the conversation is that the student needs help writing his paper. In this conversation the speakers are not attempting to convey a main idea about *Glaciers*.

2. In Service Encounter conversations, the student is often trying to solve a problem. Understanding what the student's problem is and how it will be solved will help you answer the Gist-Purpose question.

提 醒

1. 分清对话的主要思想。例如,一个学生要求教授辅导关于一篇《冰山》的文章。他们的谈话一定会有冰山出现,但主要的意思是学生希望教授能在撰写文章上给予帮助。在这个对话中,谈话人的主题并非是冰山。

2. 在服务情景中,学生会尝试着解决问题。了解学生要解决的问题以及解决的方法,这样更好的帮助回答相关问题。

Example

Narrator

Listen to a conversation between a professor and a student.

Student: I was hoping you could look over my notecards for my presentation just to see what you think of it.

Professor: Okay, so refresh my memory: what's your presentation about?

Student: Two models of decision making . . .

Professor: Oh, yes—the classical and the administrative model.

Student: Yeah, that's it.

Professor: And what's the point of your talk?

Student: I'm gonna talk about the advantages and disadvantages of both models.

Professor: But what's the point of your talk? Are you going to say that one's better than the other?

Student: Well I think the administrative model's definitely more realistic. But I don't think it's complete. It's kind of a tool. ., a tool to see what can go wrong.

Professor: Okay, so what's the point of your talk? What are you trying to convince me to believe?

Student: Well, uh the classical model—you shouldn't use it by itself. A lot of companies just try to follow the classical model, but they should really use both models together.

Professor: Okay, good. So let me take a look at your notes here. . . Oh typed notes . . . Wow you've got a lot packed in here. Are you sure you're going to be able to follow this during your talk?

Student: Oh, sure that's why I typed them, because otherwise . . . well my handwriting's not very clear.

Why does the student visit the professor?

A. To get some notecards for his presentation.

B. To show her some examples of common errors in research.

C. To review the notes for his presentation with her.

D. To ask for help in finding a topic for his presentation Explanation.

While much of the conversation is concerned with the content of the man's presentation, the best answer to the question "Why does the man visit the professor?" is choice C: To review the notes for his presentation with her.

Type 3: Detail Questions

Detail questions require you to understand and remember explicit details or facts from a lecture or conversation. These details are typically related, directly or indictly, to the gist of the text, by providing elaboration, examples, or other support. In some cases where there is a long digression that is not clearly related to the main idea, you may be asked about some details of the digression.

第3类 细节题

这类问题需要对细节和事实作清楚地记忆。这些细节通常都通过一些解释或支持的观点与中心思想有着相应的联系。在某些对话中可能会有大部分话离题,那么需要弄清其中的一些细节。

How to Recognize Detail Questions

如何辨别细节题

Detail questions are typically phrased as follows:

1. According to the professor, what is one way that X can affect Y?

2. What are X?

3. What resulted from the invention of the X?

4. According to the professor, what is the main problem with the X theory?

Hints for Detail Questions

1. Refer to your notes as you answer. Remember, you will not be asked about minor points. Your notes should contain the major details from the conversation or lecture.

2. Do not choose an answer only because it contains some of the words that were used in the conversation or lecture. Incorrect responses will often contain words and phrases from the listening.

3. If you are unsure of the correct response, decide which one of the choices is most consistent with the main idea of the conversation or lecture.

|| 提 醒 ||

1. 记住在答题时参考笔记。因为问题不会问次重点,所以笔记中必须涵盖主要细节。
2. 不要选择那些包含在对话中的只字片语的选项,那些往往是错误的。
3. 如果您对答案不确定,那么就选择与原文大意最符合的选项。

Examples

Professor

Uh, other things that glaciers can do is, uh, as they retreat, instead of depositing some till, uh, scraped up soil, in the area, they might leave a big ice block and it breaks off and as the ice block melts it leaves a depression which can become a lake. These are called kettle lakes. These are very critical ecosystems in this region, um because uh uh they support some unique biological diversity, these kettle lakes do.

The Great Lakes are like this, they were left over from the Pleist — from the Pleistocene glaciers, uh, the Great Lakes used to be a lot bigger as the glaciers were retreating, some of the lakes were as much as a hundred feet higher in elevation. The beach of a former higher stage of Lake Erie was about fifty miles away from where the beach — the current beach of Lake Erie is right now. So I just wanted to tell you a little bit more about glaciers and some positive things uh that we get from climate change, like the ecosystems that develop in these kettle lakes, and how we can look at them in an environmental perspective. . .

What are kettle lakes?

A. Lakes that form in the center of a volcano.

B. Lakes that have been damaged by the greenhouse effect.

C. Lakes formed by unusually large amounts of precipitation.

D. Lakes formed when pieces of glaciers melt.

How did the glaciers affect the Great Lakes?

A. They made the Great lakes smaller.

B. They made the Great Lakes deeper.

C. They reduced the biodiversity of the Great Lakes.

D. They widened the beaches around the Great Lakes.

Explanation

The answer to the first question is found in the beginning of the lecture when the professor explains what a kettle lake is. Remember that new terminology is often tested in Detail questions. The answer to the second question is found later in the lecture where the professor says, "... the Great Lakes used to be a lot bigger as the glaciers were retreating..."

(二)PRAGMATIC UNDERSTANDING QUESTIONS

Pragmatic Understanding questions test understanding of certain features of spoken English that go beyond basic comprehension. Generally speaking, these types of questions test how well you understand the function of an utterance or the stance that the speaker expresses. In most instances, Pragmatic Understanding questions will test parts of the conversation or lecture where a speaker's purpose or stance is not expressed directly. In these cases, what is directly stated — the surface expression — will not be an exact match of the speaker's function or purpose.

What people say is often intended to be understood on a level that lies beyond or beneath the surface expression. To use an often-cited example, the sentence "It sure is cold in here" can be understood literally as a statement of fact about the temperature of a room. But suppose the speaker is, say, a guest in your home, who is also shivering and glancing at an open window. In that case, what your guest may really mean is that he wants you to close the open window. In this example, the function of the speaker's statement — getting you to close the window — lies beneath the surface expression. Other functions that often lie beneath surface expression include directing, recommending, complaining, accepting, agreeing, narrating, questioning, and so on.

Understanding meaning within the context of an entire lecture or conversation is critical in instances where the speaker's stance is involved. Is a given statement intended to be taken as fact or opinion? How certain is the speaker of the information she is reporting? Is the speaker conveying certain feelings or attitudes about some person or thing or event? As above, these feelings or attitudes may lie beneath the surface expression. Thus they can easily go unrecognized or be misunderstood by non-native speakers.

Pragmatic Understanding questions typically involve a replay of a small portion of the listening passage in order to focus your attention on the relevant portion of the spoken text. Two question types test pragmatic understanding: Understanding the Function of What Is Said questions and Understanding the Speaker's Attitude questions.

Type 4: Understanding the Function of What Is Said Questions

The first type of Pragmatic Understanding question tests whether you can understand the function of what is said. This question type often involves replaying a portion of the listening passage.

第 4 类　理解谈话功能

第一类语用理解题主要测试是否能够了解谈话的功能。此类问题通常涉及到听力部分材料的重放。

How to Recognize Understanding the Function of What Is Said Questions

如何辨别理解谈话功能题

Understanding the Function of What Is Said questions are typically phrased as follows:

1. What does the professor imply when he says this: （replay）

2. What can be inferred from the professor's response to the student? （replay）

3. What is the purpose of the woman's response? （replay）

4. Why does the student say this: （replay）

Hint for Understanding the Function of What Is Said Questions

Remember that the function of what is said may not match what the speaker directly states. In the following example, a secretary asks a student if he knows where the housing office is. She is not, however, doing this to get information about the housing office's location.

注意谈话的用语功能往往和谈话人的字面意思不相符。例如，一位秘书问某个学生住房办在哪里,然而她并非真正想知道住房办的位置。

Example

Excerpt from a conversation between a male student and a female housing office secretary. They are discussing his dorm fees.

Narrator

Listen again to a part of the conversation. Then answer the question.

Student: Okay. I'll just pay with a credit card. [use] And where do I do that at?

Secretary: At, um, the housing office.

Student: Housing office, all right.

Secretary: Do you know where they are?

Narrator

What is the woman trying to find out from the man?

A. Where the housing office is?

B. Approximately how far away the housing office is?

C. Whether she needs to tell him where the housing office is?

D. Whether he has been to the housing office already?

Explanation

The pragmatic function of the woman's question is to ask the man whether or not he needs to be told the location of the housing office. The best answer for this question is choice C.

Type 5: Understanding the Speaker's Attitude Questions

The second type of Pragmatic Understanding question tests whether you understand a speaker's attitude or opinion. You may be asked a question about the speaker's feelings, likes and dislikes, or reason for anxiety or amusement. Also included in this category are questions about a speaker's degree of certainty: Is the speaker referencing a source or giving a personal opinion? Are the facts presented generally accepted or are they disputed?

第 5 类 理解谈话人态度

这部分题在于考查您对谈话人的态度和观点是否了解。或许题目会问您说话人的感受,喜欢什么或不喜欢什么,或是焦虑或兴奋的原因。同样这类问题也会问到谈话人肯定的程度:谈话人是就事论事还是在发表个人意见? 谈论中的事实是普遍接受的还是仍有争论?

How to Recognize Understanding the Speaker's Attitude Questions?

如何辨别理解谈话人态度题?

Understanding the Speaker's Attitude questions are typically phrased as follows:

1. What can be inferred about the student?

2. What is the professor's attitude toward X?

3. What is the professor's opinion of X?

4. What can be inferred about the student when she says this: (replay)

5. What does the woman mean when she says this: (replay)

Hint for Understanding the Speaker's Attitude Questions

Learn to pay attention to the speaker's tone of voice. Does the speaker sound apologetic? Confused? Enthusiastic? The speaker's tone can help you answer this kind of question.

提 醒

学会理解谈话人的语音、语调。谈话人是否透露出抱歉、迷惑、热情?通常谈话人的语调会帮助您回答此类问题。

Example

Excerpt from a conversation between a male student and his female advisor. In this part of a longer conversation, they are discussing the student's job.

Advisor: Well, good. So, bookstore isn't working out?

Student: Oh, bookstore's working out fine. I just I — this pays almost double what the bookstore does.

Advisor: Oh wow!

Student: Yeah. Plus credit.

Advisor: Plus credit.

Student: And it's more hours, which . . . The bookstore's — I mean it's a decent job's all. Everybody I work
with. . . that part's great; it's just. . . I mean I'm shelving books and kind of hanging out and not
doing much else. . ., if it weren't for the people, it'd be totally boring.

Narrator:

What is the student's attitude toward the people he currently works with ?

A. He finds them boring.

B. He likes them.

C. He is annoyed by them.

D. He does not have much in common with them.

Explanation

In this example it may be easy to confuse the student's attitude toward his job with his attitude toward the people he works with. The correct answer is choice B. The student is bored with the job, not the people he works with.

(三)CONNECTING INFORMATION QUESTIONS

Connecting Information questions require you to make connections between or among pieces of information in the text. Your ability to integrate information from different parts of the listening passage, to make inferences, to draw conclusions, to form generalizations, and to make predictions is tested. To choose the right answer, you will need to be able to identify and explain relationships among ideas and details in a text. These relationships may be explicit or implicit.

There are three types of Connecting Information questions.

Type 6: Understanding Organization Questions

In Understanding Organization questions you may be asked about the overall organization of the listening passage, or you may be asked about the relationship between two portions of the listening passage. Here are two examples:

1. How does the professor organize the information that she presents to the class?

In the order in which the events occurred.

2. How does the professor clarify the points he makes about Mexico?

By comparing Mexico to a neighboring country

The first of these questions asks about the overall organization of information, testing understanding of connections throughout the whole listening passage. The second asks about a portion of the passaee, testing understanding of the relationship between two different ideas.

Some Understanding Organization questions may ask you to identify or recognize how one statement functions with respect to surrounding text. Functions may include indicating or signaling a topic shift, connecting a main topic to a subtopic, providing an introduction or a conclusion, giving an example, starting a digression, or even making a joke.

第 6 类　理解联系材料题

此种类型的问题着重在于考查对听力全文的理解，也或者会问到听力材料中部分之间的关系。这里有两个例子：

1. 教授是怎样组织她上课的信息的——利用事情发生的顺序。

2. 教授是怎样阐述他对墨西哥的看法的——把墨西哥和一个邻国作比较。

第一个问题问的是关于全文的信息，测试对听力整个材料的理解。第二个问题问的是部分材料，测试材料各部分之间的关系。

某些问题或许会要求识别一句话在文章中的作用，也许会体现主题转移，涵盖次主题或提供一个介绍或结论，举例子，甚至一个玩笑。

Narrator:

Listen again to a statement made by the professor. Then answer the question.

Professor: "There's this committee I'm on . . . The name of the thing and it's probably, well, you don't have to take notes about this , um, the name of the thing is academic standards."

Narrator:

Why does the professor tell the students that they do not have to take notes?

A. The information is in their books.

B. The information may not be accurate.

C. She is going to tell a personal story.

D. They already know what she is going to talk about.

The listening text preceding the replayed statement is about how bureaucracies work. What follows the replayed statement is a personal story about bureaucracies. The key lies in recognizing that the portion of the lecture following the replayed statement is a personal story. The correct answer is choice C. With the replayed statement the professor indicates to the class that what she is about to say does not have the same status as what she was talking about previously.

How to Recognize Understanding Organization Questions?

如何辨别理解联系材料题？

Understanding Organization questions are typically phrased as follows:

1. How does the professor organize the information about X that he presents to the class?

2. How is the discussion organized?

3. Why does the professor discuss X?

4. Why does the professor mention X?

Hints for Understanding Organization Questions

Questions that ask about the overall organization of the passage are more likely to be found after lectures than after conversations. Refer to your notes to answer these questions. It may not have been apparent from the start that the professor organized the information (for example) chronologically, or from least to most complex, or in some other way.

Pay attention to comparisons made by the professor. In the following example the professor is discussing the structure of plants. He uses steel and the steel girders in a new building to make a point. When the professor mentions something that is seemingly off-topic, you should ask yourself what point the professor is making.

‖ 提醒 ‖

这种类型题目通常在讲座中比较容易出现,在回答问题时要参考笔记。教授讲座的组织方式(比如按年月顺序,或是从简到繁,或其他方式)从一开始并非显而易见。

特别注意教授所提到的对比部分。在以下的例子中教授正在谈论植物的结构,他用盖房子的钢材和钢梁为例来说明一个观点。当教授似乎跑题时,您应该问问自己教授想要说什么。

Examples

Professor:

So, we have reproductive parts—the seeds, the fruit-walls —we have leaf parts, but the great majority of plant fibers come from vasculature within the stem. ., fibers that occur in stem material. And what we do is consider these fibers [1st start]—basically they're what are called bast fibers. Now basically bast fibers are parts of the plant that the plant uses to maintain vertical structure.

Think about it this way: what's the first thing you see when you see a building being built. . .uh what's the first thing they put up? besides the foundation of course? The metal-work, right? They put all those steel girders up there, the framework. OK, well, think of [1st start] — bast fibers basically constitute the structural framework to support the stem of the plant. OK? So as the plant grows, it basically builds a girder system within that plant, like steel, so to speak.

So Suppose you cut across the stem of one of these plants, take a look at how the bast fibers are arranged, so you're looking at a cross-section . . . you'll see that the fibers run vertically side-by-side. Up and down next to each other forming a kind of tube, which is significant . . . 'cause, which is physically stronger a solid rod or a tube-physics tells you that. What's essentially happening—well, the plant is forming a structural ring of these bast fibers all around the stem, and that shape allows for structural rigidity, but also allows for bending and motion.

Why does the professor talk about steel?

A. To identify the substance that has replaced fiber products.

B. To explain a method for separating fibers from a plant.

C. To compare the chemical structure of fibers to metals.

D. To illustrate the function of fibers in a plant's stem.

Why does the professor mention a tube?

A. To explain how some fibers are arranged in a plant.

B. To show how plants carry water to growing fibers.

C. To describe an experiment involving plant fibers.

D. To explain why some plant stems cannot bend.

Explanation

The lecture is about plants and plant fibers, not steel girders. The professor mentions steel girders only to compare them to the structural framework of fibers in a plant.

The best answer to the first question is choice D. Likewise, the second question also concerns the professor's attempts to help the students visualize a plant's structure.

The best answer to the second question is choice A.

Type 7: Connecting Content Questions

Connecting Content questions measure your understanding of the relationships among ideas in a text. These relationships may be explicitly stated, or you may have to infer them from the words you hear.

The questions may ask you to organize information in a different way from the way it was presented in the listening passage. You might be asked to identify comparisons, cause and effect, or contradiction and agreement. You may also be asked to classify items in categories, identify a sequence of events or steps in a process, or specify relationships among objects along some dimension.

第7类 联系内容题

此种类型的题目考查了解整个文章各个概念之间关系的能力。这些关系或许会详细说明,也或许需要借助参考相应的单词。

此类问题或许会要求你对原文的信息用其他方式进行总结,或许会要求进行辨别对比,辨识因果关系,矛盾与一致。也可能会要求把信息按表格归类,辨别一系列事件或事情的进程等等。

Example

Narrator:

What type of symmetry do these animals have? Place a checkmark in the correct box.

	Asymmetry	Radial Symmetry	Bilateral Symmetry
Earthworm			√
Human			√
Sponge	√		
Sea Anemone	√	√	

In this question you are asked to present information in a different format from that in which it was presented in a lecture.

Other Connecting Content questions will require you to make inferences about the relationships among things mentioned in the listening passage. You may have to predict an outcome, draw a logical conclusion, extrapolate some additional information, infer a cause-and-effect relationship, or specify some particular sequence of events.

How to Recognize Connecting Content Questions

如何辨别联系内容题

Connecting Content questions are typically phrased as follows:

1. What is the likely outcome of doing procedure X before procedure Y ?

2. What can be inferred about X?

3. What does the professor imply about X?

Hint for Connecting Content Questions

Questions that require you to fill in a chart or table or put events in order fall into this category. As you listen to the lectures on the CD accompanying this study guide, pay attention to the way you format your notes. Clearly identifying terms and their definitions as well as steps in a process will help you answer questions of this type.

提 醒

这类问题要求填表或对相关事件排序并填入表格。在听讲座的同时，注意记笔记的方式。清楚地区分术语和它们定义以及事情的进程会很好地帮助你回答此类问题。

Example

Professor:

OK, Neptune and its moons. Neptune has several moons, but there's only. ., we'll probably only worry about two of them, the two fairly interesting ones. The first one's Triton. So you have this little struggle with the word Titan which is the big moon of Saturn and the name Triton which is the big moon of Neptune. Triton it's it's the only large moon in the solar system to go backwards, to go around its what we call its parent planet, in this case Neptune, the wrong way. OK? Every other large moon orbits the parent planet in the same counterclockwise direction . . . same as most of the other bodies in the solar system. But this moon. ., the reverse direction, which is perfectly OK as far as the laws of gravity are concerned. But it indicates some sort of peculiar event in the early solar system that gave this moon a motion in contrast to the general spin of the raw material that it was formed from.

The other moon orbiting Neptune that I want to talk about is Nereid [ER ee ihd]. Nereid is, Nereid has the most eccentric orbit, the most lopsided elliptical type orbit for a large moon in the solar system. The others tend more like circular orbits.

. . . Does it mean that the planets Pluto and Neptune might have been related somehow in the past and then drifted slowly into their present orbits. If Pluto . . . did Pluto ever belong to the Neptune system? Do Neptune's moons represent Pluto type bodies that have been captured by Neptune? Was some sort of. . . was Pluto the object that disrupted the Neptune system at some point in the past?

It's really hard to prove any of those things. But now we're starting to appreciate that there's a few junior Plutos out there. Not big enough to really call a planet, but large enough that they're significant in history of the early solar system. So we'll come back to those when we talk about comets and other small bodies in the fringes of the outer solar system.

What does the professor imply about the orbits of Triton and Nereid?

A. They used to be closer together.

B. They might provide evidence of an undiscovered planet.

C. They might reverse directions in the future.

D. They might have been changed by some unusual event.

Explanation

In Connecting Content questions you will have to use information from more than one place in the listening passage. In this example, the professor describes the orbits of Triton and Nereid. In both cases he refers to events in the early solar system that might have changed or disrupted their orbits. The best answer for this question is choice D, "They might have been changed by some unusual event."

Type 8: Making Inferences Questions

The final type of connecting information question is Making Inferences questions. In this kind of question you usually have to reach a conclusion based on facts presented in the listening passage.

第8类 推理题

在这种类型题中,您通常需要根据听力材料提供的信息对全文行得出结论。

How to Recognize Making Inferences Questions?

如何辨别做推理题?

Making Inferences questions are typically phrased as follows:

1. What does the professor imply about X?

2. What will the student probably do next?

3. What can be inferred about X?

4. What does the professor imply when he says this: (replay)

Hint for Making Inferences Questions

In some cases, answering this kind of question correctly means adding up details from the passage to reach a conclusion. In other cases, the professor may imply something without directly stating it. In most cases the answer you choose will use vocabulary not found in the listening passage.

一般说来，做对这种问题就相当于对原文添加一些细节来作出结论。某些时候，教授会做出一些暗示。多数情况下，您所选择的答案的单词不会在听力文章中出现。

Example

Professor:

Dada is often considered under the broader category of Fantasy. It's one of the early directions in the Fantasy style. The term "Dada" itself is a nonsense word — it has no meaning..., and where the word originated isn't known. The "philosophy" behind the "Dada" movement was to create works that conveyed the concept of absurdity — the artwork was meant to shock the public by presenting the ridiculous absurd concepts. Dada artists rejected reason — or rational thought. They did not believe that rational thought would help solve social problems...

... When he turned to Dada, he quit painting and devoted himself to making a type of sculpture he referred to as a "ready-made" ... probaly because they were constructed of readily available objects... At the time, many people reacted to Dadaism by saying that the works were not art at all and in fact, that's exactly how Duchamp and others conceived of it — as a form of "NON-art"... or ANTI-art.

Duchamp also took a reproduction of DaVinci's famous painting, the Mona Lisa, and he drew a mustache and goatee on the subject's face. Treating this masterpiece with such disrespect was another way. Duchamp was challenging the established cultural standards of his day.

What does the professor imply about the philosophy of the Dada movement?

 A. It was not taken seriously by most artists.

 B. It varied from one country to another.

 C. It challenged people's concept of what art is.

 D. It was based on a realistic style of art.

Explanation

Note the highlighted portions of the listening passage. You can see that Dadaism was meant to challenge the public's conception of what art was meant to be. The best answer to the question is choice C.

(四)BASIC STRATEGIES FOR THE iBT TOEFL LISTENING SECTION

1. Take notes while you listen. Only the major points will be tested, so do not try to write down every detail. After testing, notes are collected and shredded before you leave the test center.

2. When listening to a lecture, pay attention to the new words or concepts introduced by the professor. These will often be tested.

3. When listening to a lecture, pay attention to the way the lecture is structured and the way the ideas in the lecture are connected.

4. Listening questions must be answered in order. Once you mark an answer, you cannot go back and change it.

5. Choose the best answer. The computer will ask you to confirm your choice. After clicking yes, you

automatically go on to the next question.

How to Sharpen Your Listening Skills

Listening is one of the most important skills necessary for success on iBT TOEFL and in academics in general. The ability to listen and understand is tested in three out of four sections of iBT TOEFL.

The best way to improve your listening skills is to listen frequently to many different types of material in various subject areas (sciences, social sciences, arts, business, etc.). Of course, watching movies and TV and listening to radio is an excellent way to practice listening. Audio tapes and CDs of talks are available in libraries and bookstores; those with transcripts of the listening material are particularly helpful. The Internet is also a great resource for listening material.

Here are some ways you can strengthen skills for the three listening purposes tested on the iBT TOEFL.

Listening for Basic Comprehension

1. Increase your vocabulary knowledge, perhaps by using flashcards.

2. Focus on the content and flow of material. Do not be distracted by the speaker's style and delivery.

3. Anticipate what the speaker is going to say as a way to stay focused.

4. Stay active by asking yourself questions (e. g., What main idea is the professer communicating?)

5. Copy the words "main idea," "major points," and "important details" on different lines of paper. Listen carefully and write these things down while listening. Listen again until all important points and details are written down.

6. Listen to a portion of a lecture or talk and write a brief summary of important points. Gradually increase the amount you listen to and summarize. Note — Summarizing skills are not tested in the Listening section, but they are useful for the integrated tasks in the Writing and Speaking sections.

Listening for Pragmatic Understanding

1. Think about what each speaker hopes to accomplish; that is, what is the purpose of the speech or conversation? Is the speaker apologizing, complaining, making suggestions?

2. Notice the way each speaker talks. Is the level of language formal or casual? How certain does each speaker sound? Is the speaker's voice calm or emotional? What does the speaker's tone of voice tell you?

3. Notice the degree of certainty of the speaker. How sure is the speaker about the information? Does the speaker's tone of voice indicate something about his or her degree of certainty?

4. Listen for changes in topic or side comments in which the speaker briefly moves away from the main topic and then returns (digressions).

5. Watch television or movie comedies and pay attention to stress and intonation patterns used to convey meaning.

Listening to Connect Ideas

1. Think about how the lecture is organized. Listen for the signal words that indicate the introduction, major steps or ideas, examples, and the conclusion or summary.

2. Identify the relationships between ideas in the information being discussed.

   Possible relationships include: cause-and-effect, compare-and-contrast, steps in a process.

3. Listen for words that show connections and relationships between ideas.

4. When you listen to recorded material, stop the recording at various points and try to predict what information or idea will be expressed next.

5. Create an outline of the information discussed while listening or after listening.

如何提高听力技巧

听力是新托福考试中较为重要的一项。在托福考试中,三部分都涉及到听力和理解。

最好的提高听力的方法当然就是经常性的利用各种各样的材料进行听力练习 (如科学,社会科学,艺术,商务等等)。当然,看英文电视、电影,听广播也是练习听力不错的选择。在图书馆或书店会提供对话的录音带和 CD,尤其是那些有听力原文的材料更加有帮助。同样,网络也是一个很大的资源库。

这里介绍一些强化听力技巧的方法,希望会对你有所帮助。

基本理解:

1. 可以利用小卡片来扩大您的词汇量。

2. 注意把重心放在材料的内容上。

3. 把自己融入对话当中,进行想象。

4. 积极的不断问自己问题(例如,教授谈话的大意是什么)。

5. 把听到材料的中心,主要思想和要点细节逐一记下。

6. 在听力练习中培养作笔记和总结的能力。它们虽然在听力部分不是重点,但却对写作和口语部分有很大帮助。

语用理解:

1. 学会弄清楚谈话人想要表达什么,即谈话目的。谈话人是道歉,抱怨或是在建议什么?

2. 注意谈话人谈话的方式, 是随意还是比较正式? 语气有多肯定? 谈话人的声音是冷静还是激动的?他/她的音调又是怎样的?

3. 注意谈话人语气的肯定程度。他/她对一件事有多肯定?他/她的语音语调是否暗示了其肯定程度?

4. 还应注意谈话人切换话题时的变化和反面信息。

5. 在看电视,电影时多注意语音语调是怎样传递其意思的。

相关信息:

1. 想想讲座是怎样组织的。注意抓听其中用来暗示简介,文章大意,例子或是结论性的标志词语。

2. 注意辨别文章中各个要点之间的关系。关系可能包括: 因果关系,对比关系等等。

3. 关注表示连接要点之间的关系词。

4. 当您听录音材料时,可以试着在听过很多东西之后猜猜下面该说什么了。

5. 在听的同时把信息有条理的在头脑中串联起来,像做作文的提纲一样。

Part 3
iBT TOEFL Speaking
新托福口语

一 . Introduction to the Speaking Section

The iBT TOEFL Speaking section is designed to evaluate the English speaking proficiency of students like you whose native language is not English but who want to pursue undergraduate or graduate study in an English-speaking context. Like all the other sections of the iBT TOEFL, the Speaking section is delivered via computer.

In the Speaking section you will be asked to speak on a variety of topics that draw on personal experience, campus-based situations, and academic-type content material. There are six questions. The first two questions are called Independent Speaking Tasks because they require you to draw entirely on your own ideas, opinions, and experiences, when responding. The other four questions are Integrated Speaking Tasks. In these tasks you will listen to a conversation or to an excerpt from a lecture, eact a passage and then listen to a brief discussion or lecture excerpt, before you are asked the question. These questions are called Integrated Tasks because they require that you integrate your English-language skills—listening and speaking, or listening, reading, and speaking. In responding to these questions, you will be asked to base your spoken response on the listening passage or on both the listening passage and the reading passage together.

Speaking section takes approximately 20 minutes. Response time allowed for each section ranges from 45 to 60 seconds. For Speaking questions that involve listening, you will hear short spoken passages or conversations on headphones. For Speaking questions that involve reading, you will read short written passages on your computer screen. You can take notes throughout the Speaking section and use your notes when responding to the Speaking questions. For each of the six questions, you will be given a short time to prepare a response. You will answer each of the questions by speaking into a microphone. Your spoken responses will be recorded and sent to a scoring center, and they will be scored by experienced raters. Your responses will be scored holistically. This means that the rater will listen for various features in your response and assign a single score based on the overall skill you display in your answer. Although the scoring criteria vary somewhat depending on the question, the raters will generally be listening for the following features in your answer:

1. Delivery: How clear your speech is. Good responses are those in which the speech is fluid and clear, with good pronunciation, natural pacing, and natural-sounding intonation patterns.

2. Language Use: How effectively you use grammar and vocabulary to convey your ideas. Raters will be looking to see how well you can control both basic and more complex language structures and use appropriate vocabulary.

3. Topic Development: How fully you answer the question and how coherently you present your ideas. Good responses generally use all or most of the time allotted, and the relationship between ideas and

the progression from one idea to the next is clear and easy to follow.

It is important to note that raters do not expect your response to be perfect, and high scoring responses may contain occasional errors and minor lapses in any of the hree areas described above.

一. 口语考试部分简介

新托福口语测试部分是检查和评估希望出国留学深造的考生们的英语口语掌握运用程度的。像新托福考试的其他部分一样,口语考试部分同样利用计算机进行。

在口语考试这部分,你将会被问到很多种类的问题。例如,个人经历,学校环境或者是学术内容的东西,总共会有六个问题。前二个问题称为独立问题,因为完全要依据你自己的意见、观点或是经历来回答。其他四个问题为综合问题。在回答这类问题前,你会听到对话或是讲座的片断,然后会听到简短的讨论,之所以被称为综合问题的原因是, 这类问题是要求综合你的英语语言运用技巧: 听和说或是听、读和说。在回答时,需根据听力原文,或听力和阅读的原文。

口语部分大约会有20分钟时间, 每部分的作答时间基本在45 – 60秒之间。口语问题同样有听的部分, 你将会从耳机中听到短文章或对话。同样, 也有阅读的部分,你需要在电脑上读一小段文章。你可以在此过程中作笔记以便很好地回答后面问题。每个问题之后, 都会给您时间来准备回答。你将通过麦克风来回答所有的问题。你的作答将会被录下来并且送到考试评分中心,然后给出分数。你的得分将是公正的,因为评分员会根据你的表现情况来判分。评分员评分依据:

1. 表达:您回答的清晰度。好的回答一般都是清晰流畅的,会有自然的语音语调。

2. 语言运用能力: 您怎样有效地利用语法和词汇来组织你所要表达的信息。评分员会关注你如何熟练地掌握以上技巧甚至是运用更难的语言结构和用词。

3. 话题发挥:怎样全面地应答问题并完整表达意思。通常,好的回答在语言过度时都会显得清晰易懂。

需要提醒的是,评分员并不会要求你回答必须完美,得高分者很有可能也会在这些方面出现常见错误,所以,无需太紧张。

二. Speaking Question Types

INDEPENDENT: QUESTIONS 1 AND 2

Question 1

For this task, you will be asked to speak about a person, place, object, or event that is familiar to you. You will be given 45 seconds for your response. The topics for this question will vary, but you will always be asked to base your response on personal experience or a familiar topic. You might, for example, be asked about a place you like to visit, an important event in your life, a person who influenced you, or an activity that you enjoy.

This question will always ask you both to describe something (for example, an important event, a favorite activity, an influential person) and to give reasons—to explain why the event was important, why the activity is one of your favorites, how the person influenced you, etc. Be sure to respond to all parts of the question. Your response should include specific details and／or examples because they will make your description informative and your reasons comprehensible.

After you are presented with the question, you will have 15 seconds to prepare an answer. You may want to jot down a few brief notes about what you will want to say, but you should not try to write out a full and complete answer. There will not be enough time for you to do that, and raters want to know how well you can speak in response to a question, not how well you can read aloud from something you have written. If you do jot down notes during the preparation time, you should not rely on them too much in giving your answer.

The question will be read aloud by a narrator and will remain on the screen throughout the time you are giving your response.

二．口语问题类型

独立题：问题 1 和问题 2

问题 1

这部分会要求你谈论一下你熟悉的人、场所或事物，有 45 秒的回答时间。这些话题多种多样，但回答要根据个人经历和熟悉的话题展开。例如，有可能会被问到想去的一个地方，人生要事，一个对你影响深远的人或是你所钟爱的其他活动。

这些问题总是首先让你进行描述（难忘的事，喜爱的活动，对你影响深远的人），接着陈述原因（为什么事情难忘，为什么喜爱这项活动，那个人是怎样影响你的等等）。确保你的回答全面化，回答中应该包含有一些细节和事例，也可以使回答更加完整易懂。

每道题问完后，会有 15 秒钟准备时间。你可以对您所要回答的内容作简要笔记，但无须记下全部内容。而且也没有那么多时间来让你把答案写下来，更重要的是这部分重在考察运用口语回答问题的能力，而不是照着念的能力。

问题会由专人大声读出，在回答问题的过程中，问题也会同样出现在屏幕上。

Example

The following example shows how a question of this type will appear on your computer screen.

1. Choose a teacher you admire and explain why you admire him or her. Please include specific examples and details in your explanation.

Preparation Time: 15 Sedonds

Response Time: 45 Seconds

You will be told when to begin to prepare your response and when to begin Speaking. After the question is read, a "Preparation Time" clock will appear below the question and begin to count down from 15 seconds（00: 00: 15）. At the end of 15 seconds you will hear a short beep. After the beep, the clock will change to read "Response Time" and will begin to count down from 45 seconds（00: 00: 45）. When the response time has ended, recording will stop and a new screen will appear alerting you that the response time has ended.

To answer a question like the one above, you would probably begin by briefly identifying the teacher you are going to speak about — not necessarily by name, of course, but by giving just enough relevant information so that someone listening to response can make sense of your explanation. For example, what subject did the teacher teach? How old were you when you had him or her as a teacher? After briefly describing the teacher in whatever way is useful, you could then proceed to explain what it was about the teacher that made you admire him or her. Perhaps it was something specific that he or she did If so, you should describe what the teacher did and provide details that illustrate why the action was admirable. Maybe the teacher displayed a special personal quality or had a special character trait. If so, you would want to describe it and give details that provide evidence of it — occasions when you noticed it, the effect it had on you, and so forth. There are many, many ways to answer this question, and of course there is no "right" or "wrong" answer. The important thing, if you were to receive this particular question, is that you communicate enough information about the person to help the rater understand why you find that person admirable.

Question 2

In this second Independent Speaking Task, you will be presented with two possible actions, situations, or opinions. Then you will be asked to say which of the actions or situations you think is preferable or which opinion you think is more justified and then explain your choice by providing reasons and details. As with question l, you will have 45 seconds to give your response.

Topics for this question include everyday issues of general interest to a student. You may be asked, for example, whether you think it is better to study at home or at the library, or whether you think students should take courses from a wide variety of fields or else focus on a single subject area, or whether first-year college students should be required to live in the dormitory or be allowed to live off campus in apartments of their own. You could also be presented with two opposing opinions about a familiar topic — for example, about whether or not television has been a benefit for humanity — and you would then be asked which of the two opinions you agree with.

This question will always ask you to state what your choice or preference or opinion is and to explain why — in other words, to support your answer with reasons, explanations, details, and/or examples. It is important that you respond to all parts of the question, and that you are clear about what your opinion is and give reasons that will communicate why you have made the choice you did. It does not matter which of the two actions, situations, or opinions you choose, and, as with Question 1, there is no "right" or "wrong" answer. Your response will be rated not on which of the alternatives you choose but rather on how well you explain your choice by supporting it with reasons and details.

Like Question l, this question will appear on your computer screen and be read aloud at the same time by the narrator, and you will be given 15 seconds to prepare an answer. You should use this time to think about what you want to say, organize your thoughts, and jot down some notes if you feel this will be helpful. But remember, you should not try to write out a full answer — just a few words or phrases that may help remind you of the direction you want to take in giving your response.

问题2

在这部分中,会提供一些可能的动作,场景或观点。将会问到那些动作或场景你觉得更喜欢,或者哪个观点更公正,然后说出原因。同样,有45秒时间回答问题。

这部分话题包括学生生活有关事情。有可能会被问到,例如:你觉得学生在家还是在图书馆学习好，你觉得学生应该修各个方面的课程还是专心在一门课程上，你觉得大学一年级的新生是在住校还是可以允许他们在外面的公寓里住等等。同时，也会问一个在同一话题上不同观点的问题。例如，你觉得电视机是否对我们有益——将会问你支持哪种观点。

这些问题总会问道你的选择、意见观点和看法来解释为什么——也就是说，用原因、解释、细节以及举例来支持你的答案。回答问题的方方面面是很重要的，这样以来，你也就对你所要陈述的观点和原因会更加清楚明白。你选择什么没有关系，就像问题 1 一样，这里没有"对"或者"错"。你所选择的不是重点，关键在于如何利用好的事例和充分的原因来支持你的选择。

像问题 1 一样，问题 2 同样会由专人读出并一直出现在显示屏上，也会有 15 秒钟的准备时间。在这期间，您必须尽快的想好想要说的内容，组织好语言，调整好思路，适当时候记下笔记来帮助回答。但同样记住，记笔记时不要记下全部内容。

Example

The following example shows how a question of this type will appear on your computer screen.

2. Some students study for classes individually. Others study in groups. Which method of studying do you think is better for students and why.

Preparation Time: 15 Seconds

Response Time: 45 Seconds

After you hear the question, you will be told when to begin to prepare your response and when to begin speaking. As with question 1, a "Preparation Time" clock will appear below the question and begin to count down from 15 seconds (00: 00: 15). At the end of 15 seconds you will hear a short beep. After the beep, the clock will change to read "Response Time" and will begin to count down from 45 seconds (00: 00: 45). When the response time has ended, recording will stop and a new screen will appear alerting you that the response time has ended.

In answering a question like this one, it is important that you begin by clearly stating what your opinion is: do you think it is better for students to study for classes individually or do you think it is better for them to study in groups? If you do not begin by stating your opinion, it may be difficult for someone listening to your response to understand your reasons for holding that opinion. As for the reasons you give in support of your opinion, they can vary widely and may be based on your own experience and observations. For example, if the position you take is that it is better for students to study alone, you might say that when students meet to study in groups, they often waste time discussing matters that have nothing to do with their class work. You might continue this explanation by contrasting the inefficiency of studying in a group with the kind of productivity a student can achieve when studying alone. If you have personal experiences that help illustrate your point, you might want to include them in your explanation. If so, you should be clear about how they illustrate your point. Or perhaps you want to take the opposite position, that it is better for students to study in groups. In that case, you would explain the advantages of group study and the disadvantages of studying alone. Perhaps you think that the more capable students can help the less capable students when students study together. Or perhaps you have found that students who study in groups often share each other's lecture notes and this way they can make sure everyone understands all the material that has been covered in a course. There are any number of good reasons for either choice. In fact, it may be your opinion that in some cases it is better to study in groups and in other cases it is better to study alone. If that is the opinion you would like to express, you should explain — with reasons, examples, and/or specific details — why group study is better in some cases and individual study is better in others. Here again, there is no "right" or "wrong" answer to a question like this. The important thing is to clearly communicate to the person who will be listening to your response what your opinion is and explain the reasons you have for holding it.

INTEGRATED LISTENING/READING/SPEAKING: QUESTIONS 3 AND 4

Question 3

Question 3 is the first of the four Integrated Tasks in the Speaking section. For this question, you will read a short reading passage on your computer screen about a topic of campus-related interest. You will then listen to two people (or in some cases, one person) discussing that topic and expressing an opinion about the topic from the reading. Then you will be asked a question based on what you have read and what you have heard. You will have 60 seconds to speak your response. The general areas from which these topics are typically drawn include university policies, rules or procedures; university plans; campus facilities or quality of life on campus. The topics are designed to be accessible to all test takers and will be presented to you in a way that does not require that you have prior firsthand experience of college or university life in North America.

The reading passage could take various forms. For example, it could be a bulletin from the administration of a university regarding a new parking rule, or a letter to the editor of a campus newspaper responding to a new university policy restricting the use of radios in dormitory rooms, or an article from the campus newspaper discussing a proposal to build a new football stadium. In addition to describing the proposal, the reading passage will usually present two reasons either for or against the proposal. The reading passage is brief, usually between 75 and 100 words long. You will be given sufficient time to read the passage.

In the dialogue (or monologue) that will be played after you have read the reading passage, you will hear one or two speakers—usually students—speaking about the same article (or letter or announcement) that you have just read. If there are two speakers, one of them will have a strong opinion about the the proposed change— either in favor of it or against it—and will give reasons to support that opinion. The discussion is brief and typically lasts between 60 and 80 seconds.

After you have read the passage and then listened to the discussion, you will be asked a question about what you have read and heard. For example, there may be a reading passage that describes plans to make a new university rule and a conversation in which a professor and a student are discussing the rule. If in the conversation the student thinks the new rule is a bad idea, you would be asked to state what the student's opinion is and to explain the reasons the student gives for holding that opinion using information from both the reading and the listening.

This task tests your ability to integrate information from two sources—the reading passage and the listening—and to summarize some aspect of what you have heard. The reading passage provides the context that allows you to understand what the speakers are talking about. The speakers will generally refer to the reading pasage only indirectly. Therefore, as you read the reading passage, you should pay attention to a number of things: the description of the proposal (what has been proposed, planned, changed, etc.), and the reasons that are given for or against the proposal. This will help you understand what it is that the two speakers are discussing as you listen to their conversation.

In some cases, a speaker will object to the position taken in the reading and will give information that challenges the reasons offered in the reading for that position. In other cases, a speaker will agree with the position from the reading and will give information that supports those reasons. It is therefore important, as you listen to the discussion, to determine the speaker's opinions toward the proposal and to understand the relationship between what the speakers say and what you have learned from the reading passage.

To answer question 3, it is important to understand not only what the question asks you to do, but also what the question does not ask you to do. This type of Integrated Speaking task does not ask for your own opinion; rather, it asks you to state the opinion of one of the speakers and to summarize the speaker's reasons for having that opinion.

You will be given between 40 and 45 seconds to read the passage, depending on its length, after which you will listen to the discussion. Then you will be given 30 seconds to prepare your answer and 60 seconds to respond. As with all the other questions, you may take notes while reading, listening, and preparing your answer, and you may refer to your notes while answering the question.

问题3

第3个问题是4个综合题中的第1道题。这时,你需要根据显示屏上的内容读一段与校园内容有关系的小段落,之后,你将会听到1-2个人对于刚才问题的一些态度和观点。最后,将根据听到和读过的内容,问一个相关的问题,有60秒钟回答时间。这些问题将会围绕校园制度条例,学校计划,校园设施或校内生活质量等话题展开。所提供的所有话题对于每位考生来说都可以接触到,不需要具备到北美各大院校学习的经历。

阅读文章会有很多可选内容。比如说,有可能是学校管理处贴出的有关新的停车规定的公报,或者是写给校园新闻编辑处的一篇关于在宿舍内限制对收音机使用新条例的回应,也许是校园报纸的一篇关于提议修建新的足球体育场的文章。在陈述提议的同时,阅读的段落同时会有2个原因或理由来支持或反对那个提议。阅读的文章比较短,通常在75-100字左右,有充足的时间阅读这些文章。

对话(或独白)将在你读完段落之后播放,你会听见1-2个谈话人——通常是学生——谈论刚刚读过的段落相同的话题(如书信,通知)。如果有2个谈话人,那么一般其中一个对这个话题有强烈感想,另一个则与他的观点相反。这个简短的讨论通常在60-80秒之内。

读完段落听完讨论后,会问到跟它们有关的一个问题。例如,这里的阅读材料是描述一个大学新的计划规定,对话为一个教授和学生在讨论这些计划规定。假设在对话中,那个学生觉得这个计划规定很不合适,那么有可能将被问到那个学生的意见以及要求解释相关原因,你将会用到读过和听过的材料。

Example

The following sample question consists of an announcement of a university's decision to increase tuition and a discussion between students about whether the increase is justified. This example shows how a question of this type will be presented to you on your computer.

You will hear:

Narrator:

In this question you will read a short passage about a campus situation and then listen to a talk on the same topic. You will then answer a question using information from both the reading passage and the talk. After you hear the question, you will have 30 seconds to prepare your response and 60 seconds to speak.

Then you will hear this. . .

Narrator:

City University is planning to increase tuition and fees. Read the announcement about the increase from the president of City University. You will have 45 seconds to read the announcement. Begin reading now.

Announcement from the President

The university has decided to increase tuition and fees for all students by approximately 8% next semester. For the past 5 years, the tuition and fees have remained the same, but it is necessary to increase them now for several reasons. The university has many more students than we had five years ago, and we must hire additional professors to teach these students. We have also made a new commitment to research and technology and will be renovating and upgrading our laboratory facilities to better meet our students' needs.

The reading passage will appear on the screen.

When the passage appears, a clock at the top of your computer screen will begin counting down the time you have to read. When reading time has ended, the passage will disappear from the screen and will be replaced by a picture of two students engaged in conversation.

You will then hear:

Narrator:

Now listen to two students as they discuss the announcement.

Then the dialogue will begin.

Man: Oh great, now we have to come up with more money for next semester.

Woman: Yeah, I know, but I can see why. When I first started here, classes were so much smaller than they are now. With this many students, it's hard to get the personal attention you need. . .

Man: Yeah, I guess you're right. You know, in some classes I can't even get a seat. And I couldn't take the math course I wanted to because it was already full when I signed up.

Woman: And the other thing is, well, I am kind of worried about not being able to get a job after I graduate.

Man: Why? I mean you're doing really well in your classes, aren't you?

Woman: I'm doing ok, but the facilities here are so limited. There are some great new experiments in microbiology that we can't even do here. ., there isn't enough equipment in the laboratories, and the equipment they have is out of date. How am I going to compete for jobs with people who have practical research experience? I think the extra tuition will be a good investment.

When the dialogue has ended, the picture of the students will be replaced by the following:

Now get ready to answer the question.

The question will then appear on your computer screen and will also be read aloud by the narrator.

3. The woman expresses her opinion of the announcement by the university president. State her opinion and explain the reasons she gives for holding that opinion.

Preparation Time: 30 Seconds

Response Time: 60 Seconds

After you hear the question, you will be told when to begin to prepare your response and when to begin speaking. A "Preparation Time" clock will appear below the question and begin to count down from 30 seconds (00: 00: 30). At the end of 30 seconds you will hear a short beep. After the beep, the clock will change to read "Response Time" and will begin counting down from 60 seconds (00: 00: 60). When the response time has ended, recording will stop and a new screen will appear alerting you that the response time has ended.

In giving your response to this question, you should state what the woman's opinion about the tuition increase is, and then explain her reasons for holding that opinion. You will probably have noticed as you listened to the conversation that the woman's reasons are essentially the same as those of the university president but are drawn from her own experience as a student, so in your answer you would probably want to connect information from the two sources. You could perhaps begin by saying that the woman agrees with the announcement and thinks that the university is right to increase its fees. In describing her reasons, you might say that she thinks the tuition increase is necessary because the university can then hire more teachers. She feels that classes are getting too crowded and more teachers are needed. You might also want to mention that she has found it hard to get personal attention from her professors. You could also point out that she agrees that the money should be spent to improve laboratory facilities because they are out of date, and that this has made it hard for her to get the practical laboratory experience she feels she needs to get a good job. Your response should be complete enough that someone listening to your response who has not read the announcement or heard the conversation would understand what the new policy is, what the woman's opinion about it is, and the reasons she has for her opinion. There is a great deal of information in the reading passage and the conversation, and you are not expected to summarize all of the information in giving your response.

Question 4

Question 4 is the second of the Integrated Speaking Tasks. For this task you will read a short passage about an academic subject and listen to a professor give a brief excerpt from a lecture on that subject. You will then be asked a question which you will answer based on what you have read and heard. You will have 60 seconds in which to give your spoken response.

The topics for this question are drawn from a variety of fields: life science, social science, physical science, and the humanities. Although the topics are are academic in nature, none of the written passages, lectures, or the questions themselves requires prior knowledge of any academic field in particular. The language and concepts used are designed to be accessible to you no matter what your academic specialization may be.

The reading passage is usually between 75 and 100 words in length. It provides background or context to help you understand the lecture that will follow. The reading passage will usually treat the topic in somewhat general and abstract terms, and the lecture will treat the topic more specifically and concretely, often by providing an extended example, counterexample, or application of the concept presented in the reading. To answer the question that follows the lecture, you will need to draw on the reading as well as the lecture, and integrate and convey key information from both these sources.

For example, some tasks will contain a reading passage that gives the definition of a general principle or process and a lecture that discusses a specific instance and/or counterexample of the principle or process. For a pairing like this, you might be asked to explain the principle or process using the specific information from the listening. Or another pairing might include a reading passage that describes a problem and a lecture that presents the success, failure, or unintended consequences of an attempt to solve the problem, together with a question that asks you to explain the attempt to solve the problem and account for its results.

The sample question 4 task presented below is a typical example. It begins with a reading passage discussing a general concept—the domestication of animal species—by describing two characteristics that make an animal species suitable for domestication. This passage is coupled with a lecture in which the professor talks about the behavior of two species of animals—a familiar domesticated animal that has both of the characteristics and a common, undomesticated species that lacks these characteristics. The question asks you to apply the more general information you have learned in the reading to the examples discussed in the lecture, and explain how the behavior of the two species of animals is related to their suitability for domestication.

问题4

问题 4 是综合题的第 2 道。在这部分中,您会读一篇学术话题的文章,然后听一篇关于教授讲座的摘要部分,然后根据所读和所听,回答一道问题。有 60 秒的时间来回答。

问题的话题涉及各个方面:生活科学,社会科学,自然科学或人类等等。虽然话题是有关自然界的学术问题,但所有的段落讲座都不需要考生具备任何专业学术知识。不管你的专业是什么,这些问题都能够回答。

阅读的段落大约有 75 – 100 词。通常会提供相应的知识背景内容来帮助了解下面所要听到的讲座。阅读的段落中会有抽象也会有具体,讲座部分则会用举例子、概念诠释等方法来叙述得更具体。回答问题时,段落和讲座两部分都会有帮助,你需要综合两部分主要内容及信息来回答问题。

举例来说,在一些问题中,阅读部分会给出一些普遍原则或进程的定义,讲座部分则会讨论一些具体的例子(或对应事例),像这样的问题,或许会被要求利用听到的具体信息来解释这些原则或进程,或者阅读部分描述一个问题,讲座部分会涉及试图解决问题的成、失败或一系列连锁后果。问题会是要求你解释尝试问题的方法和可能的结果。

以下关于问题4的例子是个典型的例子。它的阅读段落从讨论一个普遍观点开始——动物种类的驯化——描述它的二种使一个动物种类适合驯化特点，讲座中教授会谈到这二个物种的行为——一个适合驯化的动物会具备这二种特点，而一般不适合驯化的动物则不具备这些特点。问题将会要求你根据学到的知识解释那二个动物种类的行为与它们驯化的适应性之间的关系。

Example:

The following example shows how a question of this type will be presented to you on Your Computer. Question 4 will be presented visually in the same way as Question 3.

First You will hear the narrator say this:

Narrator:

In this question you will read a short passage on an academic subject and then listen to a talk on the same topic. You will then answer a question using information from both the reading and the talk. After you hear the question, you will have 30 seconds to prepare your response and 60 seconds to speak.

Then you will hear this:

Narrator:

Now read the passage about animal domestication. You have 45 seconds to read the passage.

Begin reading now.

The reading passage will then appear on the screen.

Animal Domestication

For thousands of years, humans have been able to domesticate, or tame, many large mammals that in the wild live together in herds. Once tamed, these mammals are used for agricultural work and transportation. Yet some herd mammals are not easily domesticated.

A good indicator of an animal's suitability for domestication is how protective the animal is of its territory. Non-territorial animals are more easily domesticated than territorial animals because they can live close together with animals from other herds. A second indicator is that animals with a hierarchical social structure, in which herd members follow a leader, are easy to domesticate, since a human can function as the "leader".

A clock at the top of your computer screen will count down the time you have to read. When reading time has ended, a picture of a professor in front of a class will appear on the screen.

And you will hear this:

Narrator:

Now listen to a lecture on this topic in an ecology class.

Then you will hear the lecture:

Professor:

So we've been discussing the suitability of animals for domestication... particularly animals that live together in herds. Now, if we take horses, for example... in the wild, horses live in herds that consist of one male tand several females and their young. When a herd moves, the dominant male leads, with the dominant female and her young immediately behind him. The dominant female and her young are then followed immediately by the second most important female and her young, and so on. This is why do-mesticated horses can be harnessed one after the other in a row. They're "programmed" to follow the lead of another horse. On top of that, you often find different herds of horse in the wild occupying overlapping areas—they don't fight off other herds that enter the same territory.

But it's exactly the opposite with an animal like the uh, the antelope . . . which . . . well antelopes are herd animals too. But unlike horses, a male antelope will fight fiercely to prevent another male from en-tering its territory during the breeding season, OK — very different from the behavior of horses. Try keeping a couple of male antelopes together in a small space and see what happens. Also, antelopes don't have a social hierarchy — they don't instinctively follow any leader. That makes it harder for humans to control their behavior.

When the lecture has ended, the picture of the professor will be replaced by a screen instructing you to get ready to answer the question. Then the question will appear on the screen and will be read aloud by a narrator as well.

4. The professor describes the behavior of horses and antelope in herds. Explain how their behavior is related to their suitability for domestication.

Preparation Time: 30 Seonds

Pesponse Time: 60 Seconds

After you hear the question, you will be told when to begin to prepare your response and when to begin speaking. A "Preparation Time" clock will appear below the question and begin to count down from 30 seconds (00: 00: 30). At the end of 30 seconds you will hear a short beep. After the beep, the clock will change to read "Response Time" and will begin to count down from 60 seconds (00: 00: 60). When the response time has ended, recording will stop and a new screen will appear alerting you that the re-sponse time has ended.

To answer this question, you would use information from both the reading passage and the lecture, linking the specific information the professor provides in the lecture with the more general concepts in-troduced in the reading. For example, you could begin your response by saying that herd animals can be easily domesticated if they have a hierarchical social structure and are not territorial, and that this is why it is easier to domesticate horses than antelopes. You would want to provide some details about the behavior of horses, pointing out that their hierarchical social structure makes them willing to follow one another and thus allows a human being to act as their leader. You could also say that because horses are not territorial, they can be harnessed together without fighting. You would probably want to contrast horses' behavior with that of antelopes, which are territorial. You could explain that unlike horses, male antelopes fight if they are together, and that because antelopes do not have a social hierarchy, humans can't control them by acting as their leader. Notice that you are not asked to summarize all the information in the reading and in the lecture about animal domestication and horses and antelopes. But you should provide enough infor-mation so that even a listener who had not read the passage or listened to the lecture would be able to understand your explanation.

Other question 4 tasks include such pairings as a reading passage about malaria that discusses, in general terms, what is now known about the casues of this disease, how it is spread, and how it can be prevented, coupled with a lecture about the history of malaria research that describes the work of one particular doctor in the 1800s. The question that follows this lecture asks you to describe the doctor's beliefs about the cause of malaria and the recommendations he made to prevent its spread, and then to explain why his recommendations were effective. To answer this question, you would tell how the doctor's recommendations were in line with what is now known to be true about the disease. Here, as in all speaking questions that are based on academic content, you are provided with all the facts necessary to give your response, and no outside knowledge is assumed.

INTEGRATED LISTENING/SPEAKING: QUESTIONS 5 AND 6

Question 5

The Integrated Listening/Speaking tasks in questions 5 and 6 do not have a reading passage associated with them. For question 5, you will listen to a short conversation about a campus-related situation and respond to a question based on what you have heard. In the conversation, two people will typically discuss a problem and two possible solutions. The problem is one that concerns one of them or both of them directly. After you listen to the conversation, you will be asked to briefly describe the situation that was discussed in the conversation and to give your own opinion about solutions to the problem. You will have 60 seconds in which to give your spoken response. The topics for this task are based on common, everyday situations or problems that might arise at a college or university.

Typically, the speakers in the conversation will be two students, or a student and a professor, or a student and an university staff member(e. g., a teaching assistant, librarian, administrator, etc.). The problems may involve such issues as scheduling conflicts, unavoidable absences, unavailable resources, student elections, financial difficulties, and so forth. In some cases, the problem is one that affects both speakers equally, and they must decide on a single, common solution. In other cases, the problem may involve only one of the speakers, and in this situation that speaker will present his or her problem and the other speaker(or both of them) will propose the two possible solutions. The conversations are usually between 60 and 90 seconds long.

The question you are asked when the conversation has ended has several parts: you are asked first to describe the problem that the speakers are discussing, then to state which of the two solutions you prefer, and finally to explain why you prefer that solution. The reasons you give for your preference can include information provided by the speakers in their discussion as well as your own experiences. For example, if your own experience with a similar or related problem is relevant to your choice of one solution over the other, you may draw on that experience when explaining your reasons. Here, as in other Speaking tasks in which you are asked to choose between two alternatives and give reasons for your choice, it does not matter which of the two proposed solutions you choose, and there is no "right" solution or "wrong" solution. Your response will be rated not on which solution you choose but rather on how well you describe the problem, state the solution you prefer, and explain the reasons for your preference.

The types of problems discussed by the speakers in these conversations will vary. The problem could be that one of the speakers needs to arrange transportation for a class field trip and does not know whom to ask. Or the problem could be that a student has a doctor's appointment scheduled at the same time as a meeting with job recruiters. Another could be about a student who is not getting along with other members of his or her study group. In the following sample question, the speakers are discussing a problem that you may find very familiar: too much schoolwork and not enough time to do it.

问题 5

综合听力和口语部分中的第 5 题和第 6 题没有需要阅读的文章。第 5 题中，你会听到一个关于校内情景的短对话，然后回答一个问题。对话中，2 个人通常会讨论一个问题和两种解决办法，问题是与其中一个或两个有直接联系的。听完对话后，要求简要描述一下刚才所听到的情景，然后陈述你所认为的解决办法。有 60 秒的回答时间。这些问题所讨论的话题都是大专院校内每天所发生的情景问题。

通常，对话中的人物会是两个学生或一个学生和一个教授，也有可能是一个学生和一个校内人员(例如助教,馆员)等等。可能发生的问题会包括日程冲突，缺勤，无法获取的资源，学生竞选，财政困难等等。在某些情况下，那个困难很有可能是困扰两个谈话人的，所以他们必须想出一个办法解决。其他情况下，只有一个谈话人有困难，那么另一个人将会提出 2 个可能的解决办法。对话通常为60 – 90 秒钟。

这个问题是在对话结束后提出的：首先会让你描述谈话人讨论的困难，然后陈述你喜欢的解决途径，最后解释为什么喜欢。你所陈述的理由可以你包括谈话人所说的加上自己的看法。例如，当与你的经历与问题类似时，根据你的经验来作出选择。同样，这里没有"对"或"错"的选择，关键在于如何对答案解释的全面易懂，让人信服。

对话中的问题将是多种多样的。问题可能是谈话人需要安排一个班级外出的，但不知道该问谁，或者是一个学生的时间冲突事件，也有可能是一个学生和他的学习小组成员之间的相处问题。请看下面的例子，下列中的谈话人讨论的话题你也许会觉得非常熟悉——太多的作业没有时间做。

Example:

The following example shows how you would hear and see this task on your computer:

You will hear:

Narrator:

In this question, you will listen to a conversation. You will then be asked to talk about the information in the conversation and to give your opinion about the ideas presented. After you hear the question, you will have 20 seconds to prepare your response and 60 seconds to speak.

Then a picture of two students will appear on the screen.

Then you will hear the conversation:

Man: Hey Lisa, how's it going?

Woman: Hi Mark. Uh, I'm OK, I guess, but my schoolwork is really stressing me out.

Man: [impathetically] Yeah? What's wrong?

Woman: Well, I've got a paper to write and two exams to study for. And a bunch of math problems to finish. It's just so much that I can't concentrate on any of it. I start concentrating on studying for one of my exams, and then I'm like, how long's it gonna take to finish that problem set?

Man: Wow. Sounds like you've got a lot more work than you can handle right now. It wanting to sound too pushy Look, have you talked to some of your professors..., mean, you know, try to explain the problem. Look, you could probably get an extension on your paper, or on the math assignment . . .

Woman: You think? It would give me a little more time to prepare for my exams right now.

Man: Well, I mean another thing that you might do . . . I mean have you tried making yourself a schedule? I mean that's what I do when I'm feeling overwhelmed.

Woman: What does that do for you?

Man: Well, I mean it helps you to focus your energies. You know, you make yourself a chart that shows the next few days and the time till your stuff is due and. . .

Woman: Uh-huh . . . [meaning "I'm listening"]

Man: I mean think about what you need to do and when you have to do it by. You know then start filling in your schedule—like, all right 9: 00 [nine] to 11: 30 [eleven-thirty] A. M., study for exam. 12: 00 [twelve] to 3: 00 [three], work on problem set. But I mean don't make the time periods too long. Like, don't put in eight hours of studying—you know, you'll get tired, or start worrying about your other work again. But if you keep to your schedule, you know you'll just have to worry about one thing at a time.

Woman: Yeah, that might work. [me what noncommitally]

When the conversation has ended, the picture of the two students will be replaced by a screen instructing you to get ready to answer the question. Then the question will appear on the screen and will be read aloud by the narrator.

5. The students discuss two possible solutions to the woman's problem. Describe the problem. Then state which of the two solutions you prefer and explain why.

Preparation Time: 30 Seonds

Pesponse Time: 60 Seconds

After you hear the question, you will be told when to begin to prepare your response and when to begin speaking. A "Preparation Time" clock will appear below the question and begin to count down from 20 seconds (00: 00: 20). At the end of 20 seconds you will hear a short beep. After the beep, the clock will change to read "Response Time" and will begin to count down from 60 seconds (00: 00: 60). When the response time has ended, recording will stop and a new screen will appear alerting you that the response time has ended.

To answer this question, you should begin by briefly describing the woman's problem, giving just enough details so that someone listening to your response but who has not heard the conversation would know what you are talking about. Then you would state which solution you prefer, and explain why. If you believe the second solution is preferable, you would probably begin by saying that you think it would be better if the woman prepared a schedule, and then you would proceed to explain why. There are any number of reasons you can give: you might say, for example, that the problem of too much work to do is something that the woman is going to confront in the future as well, and that if she learns how to organize a schedule now, this will help her throughout her academic career. You could also speak about the disadvantages of the other solution: for example, even though her professors might be willing to give her an extension, they might somehow penalize her for it by grading her assignments more severely. If your own personal experiences are relevant to your reasons for choosing one solution over the other, you may wish to mention those experiences, but you should keep in mind that the focus of the question is the problem faced by the speaker or speakers, not your own situation. Remember, too, a question like this can be answered in many different ways, and there is no "right" or "wrong" choice.

Question 6

This integrated task, the last of the six Speaking tasks, is based on academic content.

For this task you will first listen to a professor present a brief excerpt from a lecture on an academic subject and then you will be asked a question about what you have heard. You will have 60 seconds in which to give your spoken response.

As with question 4 (the other Speaking task that is based on academic content), the topics for this question are drawn from a variety of fields within the life sciences, social sciences, physical sciences, and the humanities. Here too, no prior knowledge of any academic field in particular is required for you to understand the lecture or answer the question.

The lecture excerpt is between 60 and 90 seconds long, and focuses on a single topic. Usually the professor will begin the lecture by defining a concept, by highlighting an issue, or by introducing a phenomenon, and will then go on to discuss important aspects of it or perspectives relating to it. The lecture will contain illustrative examples that help explain or clarify the main concept or issue. The question you are asked after you have heard the lecture will typically ask that you explain the main concept or issue of the lecture, using points and examples that were given in the lecture.

The lectures can be about processes, methods, theories, ideas, or phenomena of any type natural, social, psychological, etc. If a lecture is about a process, the professor might explain the process by describing some of its functions. In a lecture about a theory, the professor might explain the theory by describing its applications. In a lecture about a phenomenon, the professor might explain it through examples that illustrate its causes or its effects.

In the sample question 6 given below, the lecture is about a social phenomenon—the emergence of a national culture in the United States in the early twentieth century. The professor illustrates this phenomenon by describing two of its causes — radio and the automobile and how they contributed to it. After you hear the lecture, you are asked to use information from the lecture to explain how the two causes contributed to the formation of a national culture.

问题6

这是综合问题中的最后一道,以学习内容为主。首先,你会听到一个教授讲座中的摘要,然后据此有一个问题。有60秒钟的时间来做答。

就如同问题 4 一样,这个问题的话题范围也较广泛,如生活科学,社会科学,自然科学或人类。同样,不需要具备特殊的专业知识。

这个讲座的摘要有 60-90 秒左右,只有一个话题。通常教授会用事实或介绍现象的方式来先定义一个概念,然后会讨论它的重要方面和不同角度。讲座中会配有图文和示例来更好地解释主要概念。通常随后的问题会要求利用讲座中的要点和实例对主要概念进行解释。

讲座可能是发展过程、方法、理论,概念或现象等等,类型会涉及到自然、科学、心理等等。如果讲座是一个发展过程,教授可能会描述这个不断发展过程的作用。在理论的讲座中,教授可能会通过描述它的应用来解释这个理论。在现象的讲座中,教授会通过适当的例子来解释现象的起因和影响。

下面的例子中,是关于一个社会现象的——美国 20 世纪早期的国家文化危机。教授通过描述它造成的影响——收音机和移动电话以及它们是如何做出贡献的——这一例子来解释这个现象。在听完讲座后,需要利用其中的信息来回答这两个影响是怎样对国家文化的构成做出贡献的。

Example:

The following example shows how a question of this type will be presented to you on your computer. First you will hear the narrator say this:

Narrator:

In this question, you will listen to part of a lecture. You will then be asked to summarize important information from the lecture. After you hear the question, you will have 20 seconds to prepare your response and 60 seconds to speak.

Then a picture of a professor standing in front of a class of students will appear on your screen, and you will hear the narrator say:

Narrator:

Now listen to part of a talk in a United States history class.

The professor will then begin the lecture.

Professor:

Because the United States is such a large country, it took time for a common national culture to emerge. One hundred years ago there was little communication among the different regions of the United States. One result of this lack of communication was that people around the United States had very little in common with one another. People in different parts of the country spoke differently, dressed differently, and behaved differently. But connections among Americans began to increase thanks to two technological innovations: the automobile and the radio.

Automobiles began to be mass produced in the 1920's, which meant they became less expensive and more widely available. Americans in small towns and rural communities now had the abillity to travel with ease to nearby cities. They could even take vacations to other parts of the country. The increased mobility provided by automobiles changed people's attitudes and created links that had not existed before. For example, people in small towns began to adopt behaviors, clothes, and speech that were popular in big cities or in other parts of the country.

As more Americans were purchasing cars, radio ownership was also increasing dramatically. Americans in different regions of the country began to listen to the same popular radio programs and musical artists. People repeated things they heard on the radio — some phrases and speech patterns heard in songs and radio programs began to be used by people all over the United States. People also listened to news reports on the radio. They heard the same news throughout the country, whereas in newspapers much news tended to be local. Radio brought Americans together by offering them shared experiences and information about events around the country.

When the lecture has ended, the picture of the professor will be replaced by a screen instructing you to get ready to answer the question. Then the question will appear on the screen and be read aloud at the same time by the narrator.

5. Using points and examples from the talk, explain how the automobile and the radio contributed to a common culture in the United States.

Preparation Time: 30 Seonds

Pesponse Time: 60 Seconds

After you hear the question, you will be told when to begin preparing your response and when to begin speaking. A"Preparation Time" clock will appear below the question and begin to count down from 20 seconds (00: 00: 20). At the end of 20 seconds you will hear a short beep. After the beep, the clock will change to read "Response Time" and will begin to count down from 60 seconds (00: 00: 60). When the response time has ended, recording will stop and a new screen will appear alerting you that the response time has ended.

To answer this question, you might begin with a little background and mention that the United States did not have a common culture 100 years ago because people in different regions of the country did not communicate much with each other: Then you could say that the automobile and the radio changed this situation, and go on to summarize the information from the lecture that explains how they caused this change. For example, you could say that when automobiles became inexpensive, people from small towns could travel easily to cities or to other parts of the counto; and that when they began to do this, they started acting like people from those other regions and started to dress and speak in the same way. As for the role that radio played in the emergence of a national culture, you could point out that when radio became popular, people from different parts of the country began listening to the same programs and the same news reports and began to speak alike and have similar experiences and ideas. If you have time, you could conclude by saying that these similar ways of speaking and dressing and thinking became the national culture of the United States. You should remember that you do not need to repeat all of the details provided in the lecture. There is simply too much information in the lecture to allow you to do that. You should, however, convey enough information so that someone who has not heard the lecture would be able to form a good idea of what the professor was explaining to the class.

Other lectures for question 6 could include such topics as how people learn, and the central concept might be that learning occurs when two events are associated in the brain. The professor would illustrate that concept by describing two different ways that events can be associated in the brain, and you would be asked to use points and examples from the lecture to explain how these two ways of associating events result in learning. Or in a lecture about money, the professor might provide two different definitions of the concept and illustrate them with two examples, and you would be asked in your response to explain the two definitions, using the two examples. The question that follows a lecture like this would typically ask you to use points and examples that you heard in the lecture to explain how people learn or what the definitions of money are.

Strategies for Raising Your iBT TOEFL Speaking Score

When you take the Practice iBT TOEFL Speaking section in this chapter, listen carefully to each of your recorded responses. Create a set of guiding questions to help you evaluate your performance. Here are some examples of the kind of questions ou may want to include:

1. Did I complete the task?

2. Did I speak clearly?

3. Did I make grammatical errors?

4. Did I use words correctly?

5. Did I organize my ideas clearly and appropriately?

6. Did I provide a complete response?

7. Did I use the time effectively?

Once you have completed your evaluation, decide what changes you want to make to your response. Then try again, making a new recording. Compare the two recordings and determine if any further revisions are necessary.

1. Try to periodically analyze your strengths and weaknesses. Try to understand what you are and are not able to do well and why.

2. When you monitor your speaking practice, try to evaluate the pace of your speech.

   After each practice ask yourself the following questions:

   A. Did I speak too fast?

   B. Did I speak too slowly?

   C. Did I pause too often?

3. You may want to monitor your own progress by keeping an audio journal, which entails keeping samples of your speaking activities or practices. You can also ask for feedback from one or more friends, tutors, or teachers.

HINTS FOR THE DAY OF THE TEST

1. Remember that taking notes on the reading and listening material in the integrated Speaking tasks on the iBT TOEFL is allowed.

2. Listen to the item directions carefully to understand exactly what you are being asked to do.

3. Use your preparation time as effectively as possible. Plan your response by thinking about the important ideas you want to convey in a simple, organized fashion.

4. Do not begin speaking until you are told to do so.

5. Answer each question as completely as possible in the time allowed.

6. Make sure to adjust your microphone and volume carefully.

7. Speak into the microphone at an appropriate volume. Do not put your mouth directly onto the microphone. If you touch your mouth to the microphone, scorers may find it difficult to understand what you are saying.

8. Avoid whispering. If you whisper, scorers may find it difficult to understand what you are saying.

提 醒

提高新托福考试口语的方法

当你作这部分口语练习时,认真听你的回答录音,提出一些问题以便帮你评估自己的口语表现。以下的问题可予考虑。

1. 我是否完成了口语任务?

2. 我说的是否清楚?

3. 我是否犯了语法错误?

4. 我的用词是否正确?

5. 我的思路组织的是否清晰?

6. 我的回答是否完整?

7. 我的用时是否有效?

当你完成了自我评估后,看你对自己的回答需要做哪些改变。然后再试一遍,重新录音。把两次录音进行比较,看是否还需要进一步的修改。

1. 定期分析你的优势和劣势,尽量明白你能做什么和不能做什么的原因。

2. 当你听口语练习时,尽量评估你的口语速度,当完成每个口语练习时,可问以下几个问题:

(1)我是否说得太快?

(2)我是否说得太慢?

(3)我是否停顿过多?

3. 你可以通过录音来监听你的口语进展情况,你还可以寻问朋友、老师以得到他们的反馈意见。

※ 考试当日提示

1. 记住在综合口语考试过程中可以就听力和阅读材料做笔记。

2. 仔细听每道题的指令,准确理解口语任务。

3. 有效使用准备时间,重要观点可以在脑子中以简单有序的方式思考。

4. 在未听到开始指令前,不要开口说话。

5. 在有限时间内尽量全面回答每个问题。

6. 适当调整麦克风音量。

7. 对准麦克风以适当音量讲话,不要把嘴贴到麦克风,如果这样做口语评分员将很难听清你讲话的内容。

8. 不要低声细语,如果这样做评分员听不见你在讲什么?

Part 4

iBT TOEFL Writing
新托福写作

（一）Introduction to the Writing Section

There are two tasks in the Writing section of the iBT TOEFL: an Integrated Writing Task and an Independent Writing Task.

The Integrated Writing Task comes first because it involves some listening, and when you are taking the real iBT TOEFL you will wear your headphones. When you are finished with the Integrated Writing Task, which takes about 20 minutes, you will be free to take your headphones off to work on the Independent Writing Task. You will have 30 minutes to complete the Independent Writing Task.

This part discusses each of the writing tasks in detail and the scoring criteria that readers will use to evaluate your writing. It includes samples of each task, sample responses to each task, and specific advice on how to approach writing your own response.

For both the writing tasks on the iBT TOEFL, the people evaluating your writing recognize that your response is a first draft. You are not expected to produce a well-researched, comprehensive essay about a highly specific, specialized topic. You can earn a high score with an essay that contains some errors.

（一）写作简介

新托福的写作分为两个部分：综合论文题和独立写作题。

综合论文题为第一题，因为要求您听一些材料，所以到时会带着耳机进行。当完成这部分时（大约 20 分钟），您可以摘下耳机来进行大约 30 分钟的独立写作题。

本节详细讨论写作的两道题目以及评分标准。这部分包括例题、范文以及关于写作的一些建议。

对于新托福写作的两部分来说，并不要求您的文章写得非常完美，有一些小错误的文章同样会得高分。

（二）The Integrated Writing Task

You will read a passage about an academic topic for three minutes, and then you will hear a lecture related to the topic. Then you will be asked to summarize the points in the reading passage and explain how they relate to specific points in the reading passage.

This task gives you the opportunity to demonstrate your abiiity to show that you can communicate in writing about academic information you have read and listened to.

（二）综合写作部分

您将需要用 3 分钟时间读一篇关于学习上的文章，听一个与此有关系的讲座，然后在文章中写出这两部分是怎样联系在一起的。

在这部分，您将展现自己把所听到的和读到的信息综合起来写作的能力。

Example:

A reading passage like the following will appear on your computer screen. You will have 3 minutes to read the passage.

In many organizations, perhaps the best way to approach certain new projects is to assemble a group of people into a team. Having a team of people attack a project offers several advantages. First of all, a group of people has a wider range of knowledge, expertise, and skills than any single individual is likely to possess. Also, because of the numbers of people involved and the greater resources they possess, a group can work more quickly in response to the task assigned to it and can come up with highly creative solutions to problems and issues. Sometimes these creative solutions come about because a group is more likely to make risky decisions that an individual might not undertake. This is because the group spreads responsibility for a decision to all the members and thus no single individual can be held accountable if the decision turns out to be wrong.

Taking part in a group process can be very rewarding for members of the team. Team members who have a voice in making a decision will no doubt feel better about carrying out the work that is entailed by that decision than they might doing work that is imposed on them by others. Also, the individual team member has a much better chance to "shine"; to get his or her contributions and ideas not only recognized but recognized as highly significant, because a team's overall results can be more far-reaching and have greater impact than what might have otherwise been possible for the person to accomplish or contribute working alone.

Then you will hear:

Narrator:

Now listen to part of a lecture on the topic you just read about.

Professor:

Now I want to tell you about what one company found when it decided that it would turn over some of its new projects to teams of people, and make the team responsible for planning the projects and getting the work done. After about six months, the company took a look at how well the teams performed.

On virtually every team, some members got almost a "free ride" . . ., they didn't contribute much at all, but if their team did a good job, they nevertheless benefited from the recognition the team got. And what about group members who worked especially well and who provided a lot of insight on problems and issues? Well. . . the recognition for a job well done went to the group as a whole, no names were named. So it won't surprise you to learn that when the real contributors were asked how they felt about the group process, their attitude was just the opposite of what the reading predicts.

Another finding was that some projects just didn't move very quickly. Why? Because it took so long to reach consensus; it took many, many meetings to build the agreement among group members about how they would move the project along. On the other hand, there were other instances where one or two people managed to become very influential over what their group did. Sometimes when those influencers said "That will never work" about an idea the group was developing, the idea was quickly dropped instead of being further discussed. And then there was another occasion when a couple influencers convinced the group that a plan of theirs was "highly creative". And even though some members tried to warn the rest of the group that the project was moving in directions that might not work, they were basically ignored by other group members. Can you guess the ending to this story? When the project failed, the blame was placed on all the members of the group.

The reading passage will then reappear on your computer screen, along with the following directions and writing task.

You have 20 minutes to plan and write your response. Your response will be judged on the basis of the quality of your writing and on how well your response presents the points in the lecture and their relationship to the reading passage. Typically, an effective response will be 150 to 225 words.

Summarize the points made in the lecture you just heard, explaining how they cast doubt on points made in the reading.

The writing clock will then start a countdown for 20 minutes of writing time.

(三)How the task is phrased

If the lecture challenges the information in the reading passage, the writing task will usually be phrased in one of the following ways:

1. Summarize the points made in the lecture, being sure to explain how they cast doubt on specific points made in the reading passage.

2. Summarize the points made in the lecture, being sure to explain how they challenge specific claims/arguments made in the reading passage.

3. Summarize the points made in the lecture, being sure to specifically explain how they answer the problems raised in the reading passage.

If the lecture supports or strengthens the information in the reading passage, the writing task will usually be phrased in one of the following ways:

(1)Summarize the points made in the lecture, being sure to specifically explain how they support the explanations in the reading passage.

(2)Summarize the points made in the lecture, being sure to specifically explain how they strengthen specific points made in the reading passage.

(三)如何陈述写作任务
如果讲座者不同意文章作者的观点,写作任务通常是以下陈述中的一种:
1. 总结讲座者的观点,解释他是如何对文章作者观点产生怀疑的。
2. 总结讲座者的观点,解释他是如何反驳文章观点的。
3. 总结讲座者的观点,解释他是如何对文章中的问题作出解答的。

如果讲座者支持文章中作者的观点,写作任务通常是以下陈述中的一种:
1. 总结讲座者的观点,解释他是怎样支持文章的观点的。
2. 总结讲座者的观点,解释他是怎样巩固文章中具体要点的。

(四)**Strategies for raising your score on the integrate writing task 如何提高综合部分得分**

1. As you read:

(1)Take notes on your scratch paper.

(2)Look for the main idea of the reading passage. The main idea often has to do with some policy or practice or some position on an issue. Or it may have to do with proposing some overall hypothesis about the way some process or procedure works or should work or how some natural phenomenon is believed to work.

(3)See how this main idea is evaluated or developed. Usually it will be developed in one of two ways:

① Arguments or explanations are presented that support the main position, for example, why there are good reasons to believe that some policy or practice will be beneficial or prove useful or advisable or perhaps why it has been a good thing in the past.

② Arguments or explanations or problems are brought up concerning why some policy or practice or position or hypothesis will not or does not work or will not be useful or advisable.

(4)Don't worry about forgetting the reading passage. It will reappear on your computer screen when it is time to write.

(5)Note points in the passage that either support the main idea or provide reasons to doubt the main idea. Typically the main idea will be developed with three points.

2. As you listen:

(1)Take notes on your scratch paper:

(2) Listen for information, examples, or explanations that make points in the reading passage seem wrong or less convincing or even untrue. For instance, in the example just given, the reading passage says that working in teams is a good thing because it gives individuals a chance to stand out. But the lecture says that often everyone gets equal credit for the work of a team, even if some people do not do any work at all. The reading passage says that work proceeds quickly on a team because there are more people involved who each brings his or her expertise. But the lecture completely contradicts this claim by stating that it may take a long time for the group to reach consensus. The lecture brings up the idea that the whole team can be blamed for a failure when the fault lies with only a few team members. This casts doubt on the claim in the reading that teams can take risks and be creative because no one individual is held accountable.

3. As you write your response:

(1)You may take off your headset if you wish. You will not need your headset for the remainder of the iBT TOEFL test.

(2) Before you start writing, briefly reread the passage, consult your notes, and make a very brief outline of the points you wish to make. You can write this outline on your scratch paper or draw lines between the notes you took on the reading and the notes you took on the lecture. You can even type your outline and notes right into the answer area and then replace these by sentences and paragraphs as you compose your response.

(3) Rmember that you are NOT being asked for your opinion. You ARE being asked to explain how the points in the listening relate to points in the reading.

(4) Write in full English sentences. You can write either one long paragraph or a series of short paragraphs listing the points of opposition between the reading and the lecture. Occasional language errors will not count against you as long as they do not cause you to misrepresent the meaning of points from the reading and the lecture.

(5) Remember that your job is to select the important information from the lecture and coherently and accurately present this information in relation to the relevant information from the reading. Your response should contain the following:

① The specific ideas, explanations, and arguments in the lecture that oppose or challenge points in the reading.

② Coherent and accurate presentations of each point that you make; that is, the language you use should make sense and should accurately reflect the ideas presented in the lecture and the reading.

③ A clear, coherent structure that enables the reader to understand what points in the lecture relate to what points in the reading.

(6) Suggested length is between 150 and 225 words. You will not be penalized if you write more, so long as what you write answers the question.

(7) CAUTION: You will receive a score of zero if all you do is copy words from the reading passage. You will receive a score of if you write ONLY about the reading passage. To respond successfidly, you must do your best to write about the ways the points in the lecture are related to specific points in the reading.

(四)综合写作高分战略

1. 阅读的时候:

(1) 在草稿纸上作笔记。

(2) 找出阅读材料的大意。通常大意和一些政策或实践问题有关。

(3) 注意主要大意是怎样发展的。通常会有两种发展方法:

① 用争论和解释的方式来支持观点。例如,我们为什么相信一些政策活动是有益的,或被证明是有用的,或是为什么在过去它是一件好事。

② 反面来说,即为什么这些政策活动对我们是没有帮助和建设性的。

(4) 在写作时,阅读段落会自动显示在屏幕上,所以无需担心遗忘。

(5) 为文章提供支持的依据,或是陈述原因说明为什么反对。通常需分三个方面对你的观点进行叙述。

2. 当听的时候:

(1) 在草稿纸上做出笔记。

(2) 注意听讲中感觉错误甚至不正确的信息、例子等等。例如,就像刚刚举的例子一样,阅读文章中说团队工作非常好,因为它给了每个人发表意见的机会,但讲座中却说团队工作中每个人的得分都一样,就算不工作也是如此。阅读文章中说工作进程因为团队工作加快了很多,因为会有更多的人参与其中发表观点,讲座却完全反对这一观点,还说团队工作可能很久都完成不了任务等等。

3. 回答的时候:

(1)可以取下耳机。

(2)写之前,再读一遍文章,如需要,写出简要的提纲。可以把提纲打在计算机上,然后在写的时候继续补充其他的部分。

(3)记住这里不是让你发表观点看法,而是要求解释听力部分的观点和阅读部分观点的关系。

(4)写出完整的句子。可以写一个长段落或是一系列短段落来表达。只要所表达的观点没有歪曲原文或讲座的内容,偶尔的语言错误将不会影响得分。

(5)记住从讲座中选取有用的信息,然后和阅读文章中的信息结合起来。你的回答需包括以下内容:

①讲座中的具体观点、解释或辩论与阅读文章中对立的地方。

②所写的文章必须通顺,合乎情理并且反映文章中的观点。

③在讲座和阅读文章之间建立清晰易懂的结构。

(6)建议写文章的长度在约 150 - 225 字左右,内容长不会影响得分。

(7)注意:如果你的文章全部抄自阅读文章,那将以 0 分计算。如果只写阅读文章的内容,那只得 1 分。为了取得理想的成绩,应该尽力描述讲座与阅读文章内容之间的关系。

(五)Integrated writing scoring rublic

Here is the official Scoring Guide used by raters when they read the Integrated Writing Task.

Score Task Description

5 A response at this level successfully selects the important information from the lecture and coherently and accurately presents this information in relation to the relevant information presented in the reading. The response is well organized, and occasional language errors that are present do not result in inaccurate or imprecise presentation of content or connections.

4 A response at this level is generally good in selecting the important information from the lecture and in coherently and accurately presenting this information in relation to the relevant information in the reading, but it may have minor omission, inaccuracy, vagueness, or imprecision of some content from the lecture or in connection to points made in the reading. A response is also scored at this level if it has more frequent or noticeable minor language errors, as long as such usage and grammatical structures do not result in anything more than an occasional lapse of clarity or in the connection of ideas.

3 A response at this level contains some important information from the lecture and conveys some relevant connection to the reading, but it is marked by one more of the following:

A. Although the overall response is definitely oriented to the task, it conveys only vague, global, unclear, or somewhat imprecise connection of the points made in the lecture to points made in the reading.

B. The response may omit one major key point made in the lecture.

C. Some key points made in the lecture or the reading, or connections between the two, may be incomplete, inaccurate, or imprecise.

D. Errors of usage and/or grammar may be more frequent or may result in noticeably vague expressions or obscured meanings in conveying ideas and connections.

2 A response at this level contains some relevant information from the lecture, but is marked by significant language difficulties or by significant omission or inaccuracy of important ideas from the lecture or in the connections between the lecture and the reading; a response at this level is marked by one or more of the following:

A. The response significantly misrepresents or completely omits the overall connection between the lecture and the reading.

B. The response significantly omits or significantly misrepresents important points made in the lecture.

C. The response contains language errors or expressions that largely obscure connections or meaning at key junctures, or that would likely obscure understanding of key ideas for a reader not already familiar with the reading and the lecture.

1 A response at this level is marked by one or more of the following:

A. The response provides little or no meaningful or relevant coherent content from the lecture.

B. The language level of the response is so low that it is difficult to derive Meaning.

(五)写作评分标准

分值	评 分 标 准
5分	→ 圆满完成写作任务,完整表达出讲座中的信息。 → 将讲座中的主要观点与阅读材料中的信息准确地结合。 → 结构完整,表达连贯。 → 语法和词汇使用得当,有个别拼写错误。
4分	→ 表达了讲座中的大部分信息,但也有小部分遗漏。 → 能将讲座中的主要观点与阅读材料中的信息大部分结合在一起,但在观点的衔接以及内容表达上不够准确和清晰。 → 结构基本完整。 → 语法和词汇大致上使用得当,有明显的小错误,但不影响内容表达。
3分	→ 部分表达了讲座中的信息,但展开不够。 → 能将讲座的主要观点和阅读材料中的信息部分地结合在一起,但内容不够完整,观点衔接不够准确。
2分	→ 有部分语法错误,影响了主要观点的表达和阐述。 → 包含与讲座相关的部分信息,但遗漏主要观点。 → 有明显的信息理解错误,主要观点展开不够。 → 只能使用初级词汇和简单的句子结构。
1分	→ 几乎没有包含讲座中的信息。 → 无法将讲座中的观点和阅读材料中的信息结合在一起。 → 语法和词汇的掌握极其有限,偶尔有几句完整句。 → 章及短。

(六)Sample scored responses for the integrated writing task

The following were written in response to the task "Working in Teams" shown in the example about

Score 5 Response

The lecturer talks about research conducted by a firm that used the group system to handle their work. He says that the theory stated in the passage was very different and somewhat inaccurate when compared to what happened for real.

First, some members got free rides. That is, some didn't work hard but got recognition for the success nontheless. This also indicates that people who worked hard was not given recognition they should have got. In other words, they weren't given the oppotunity to "shine".

This derectly contradicts what the passage indicates.

Second, groups were slow in progress. The passage says that groups are more responsive than individuals because of the number of people involved and their aggregated resources. However, the speaker talks about how the firm found out that groups were slower than individuals in dicision making. Groups needed more time for meetings, which are necessary procceedures in decision making. This was another part where experience contradicted theory.

Third influetial people might emerge, and lead the group towards glory or failure. If the influent people are going in the right direction there would be no problem. But in cases where they go in the wrong direction, there is nobody that has enough influence to counter the decision made. In other words, the group might turn into a dictatorship, with the influential party as the leader, and might be less flexible in thinking. They might become one-sided, and thus fail to succeed.

Rater's Comments

There are several errors of spelling, word formation, and subject-verb agreement in this response; however, most of these errors seem to be the result of typing errors common to first drafts. This writer does an excellent job of presenting lecturer's points that contradict the arguments made in reading passage. The writer is very specific and has organized his points so that they are parallel with one another: in each of the supporting paragraphs, the lecturer's observation of what really happened is given first, then explicitly connected to a theoretical point from the reading. The final paragraph contains one noticeable error ("influent"), which is then used correctly two sentences later ("influential"). Overall, this is a successful response and earns a score of 5.

Score 4 Response

The lecture that followed the paragraph on the team work in organizations, gave some negative views of the team work itself,

Firstly, though it was said in the paragraph that the whole team idea would probably be faster than the individual work, it was said in the lecture just the opposite: it could actually be a lot slower. That is because team members would sometimes take more time than needed just to reach the same conclussions, or just even to simply decide where to go from certain point to the next on.

Secondly, paragraph suggests that by doing work as a team might give you an "edge", the lecture suggests that that might also be a negative thing as well. The people who made themselves leaders in the group may just be wrong in certain decisions, or just simple thing something is so creative, when in reality it is not and it would not work, but the rest of the people would nevertheless still follow them, and end up not doing well at all.

And lastly, paragraph says that everyone feels responsible for their own part, and all together they are all more effective as a team. The lecture suggests quite the opposite in this case as well. It suggests that some team members are there only for the "free ride," and they don't do much of anything to contribute, but still get the credit as a whole.

Rater's Comments

The writer of this response is clearly attempting to interweave the points from the passage and lecture and does a good job of discussing what the lecturer says about group decision-making and the issue of some group members failing to contribute. The writer's second point, however, is not as clearly stated as the first and third points. The key sentence in this paragraph ("The people who made themselves leaders in the group may just be wrong in certain decisions, or just simple thing something is so creative, when in reality it is not and it would not work, but the rest of the people would nevertheless still follow them, and end up not doing well at all") is difficult to follow. This is what the Scoring Guide calls "an occasional lapse of clarity" in a response that earns a score of 4. Overall, this is still a very strong response that directly addresses the task and generally presents the relevant information from the lecture.

Score 3 Response

The lecturer provide the opposite opinion concerning what the article offered. The team work often bring negative effet. As we all know superficially, team work and team spirits are quite popular in today's business world and also the fashionable terms. However, the lecturer find deeper and hiding results.

Firstly, the working results of team members can't be fully valued. For example, if a team member does nothing in the process of team discussion, decision making and final pratice, his or her work deliquency will not be recognized because we only emphasize team work. Also, the real excellent and creative member's work might be obliterated for the same reason.

Secondly, the team work might lose its value when team members are leading by several influential people in the group. One of the essential merits of team is to avoid the individule wrong. But one or two influential or persuasive people will make the team useless.

Thirdly, team work oftem become the excuse of taking responsibillity. All in charge, nobody care.

All in all, what we should do is the fully distinguish the advantages and disadvantages of a concept or widely used method. That is to keep the common sense.

Rater's Comments

This response frames the issue well. The first point is clearly stated and accurately conveys the lecturer's comments about team members who contribute very little and team members who contribute a great deal. However, the writer discusses the second point about influencers in somewhat error-prone or vague and non-idiomatic language ("hiding results", "working results" and "when team members are leading by . . . influential people"). The point about influencers drops off at making the team "useless" and does not fully explain the reason these influencers create problems. The final point beginning with the word "thirdly" is not fully related to the passage and lecture, and the meaning of it is unclear. This response illustrates many of the typical features that can cause a response to receive the score of 3.

Score 2 Response

In a company's experement, some new projects were planed and acomplished by different teams. Some teams got very good results while some teams didn't. That is to say it's not nessesary for teams to achieve more than individuals do because some team members may only contribute a little in a team for they may relying on the others to do the majority.

Another thing is the recognition for the achievement by the team is for the whole team, for everyone in the team. It's not only the dicision makers in the team feel good after successfully finishing the project, but also every member in the team.

It is also showed in the lecture that in a team with one or two leaders, sometimes good ideas from some team member are dropped and ignored while sometimes they may be highly creative. In some teams decisions were made without collecting ideas from all team members. Then it would be hard to achieve creative solutions.

For those failed projects, blames are always given to the whole team even though it's the leader or someone in the team who caught the unexpected result.

Rater's Comments

Although it has the appearance of a stronger response, on close reading, this example suffers from significant problems with connecting ideas and misrepresenting points. For instance, the third sentence of paragraph 1 seems to be getting at a point from the lecture ("some team members may contribute only a little however, it is couched in such a way that makes it very unclear how it relates to the point of the task ("That is to say it's not necessary for teams to achieve more than individuals do because some team members may only contribute"). In addition, it is not clear where the information in paragraph 2 is coming from and what point the writer is trying to make. In paragraph 3 the writer tries to make a point about influencers, but again, it is not clear what information relates to what. For all these reasons, this response earns a score of 2.

Score 1 Response

In this lecture the example shows only one of the group succeed the project. Why the group will succeed on this project it is because of few factor.

First of all, a group of people has a wider range of knowledge, expertise, and skills than single individual is like to prossess, and easier to gather the information and resources to make the work effectively and the group will willingly to trey somethIng is risky decision to "make the project for interesting and suceessful it is because all the member of the group carries the differnt responsibility for a decision, so once the decision turn wrong, no a any individual one will be blame for the whole responsiblity.

On the other way, the groups which are fail the project is because they are lay on some more influence people in the group, so even the idea is come out. Once the inflenced people say that is no good, then the process of the idea will be drop down immediately instead taking more further discussion! So the idea will not be easy to settle down for a group.

The form of the group is very important, and each of the member should be respect another and try out all the idea others had suggested, then it will develop a huge idea and the cooperate work environment for each other for effectively work!

Rater's Comments

The level of language used in this response is fairly low, and it is lowest in the second paragraph, which is the only reference to the lecture. Because the reader has difficulty gleaning meaning from that paragraph, the response contributes little coherent information and therefore earns a score of 1.

(六)综合写作任务评分示例

以下是"团队作战写作任务"5分得分学生的回答:

考官评语:

该生的写作中有几处拼写错误,并有组词以及主谓不一致原则。尽管这样大多数错误似乎是打字错误。本文作者全面总结了讲座人的观点,这些观点与阅读材料的观点正好相反,该生组织能力强,在支持段落中,先给出了讲座人的观点,然后明确与阅读中的理论进行联系。最后一致有一个显而易见的单词拼写错误,而这个单词在后两句又使用正确。总的来说,这是一篇优秀的作文,可以得5分。

4分作文

考官评语:

该生努力把阅读中的观点与讲座的观点进行联系,并讨论了讲座人所谈到的集体做出决定和其他一些观点。该生的第二个观点没有第一个和第三个陈述得清楚,本段的关键的一句话让人十分费解,这就是4分作文中所描述。"偶尔有不清楚的地方"。总的来说本文比较好的完成了写作任务。

3分作文

考官评语:

本文可以基本回答问题,第一个观点陈述的清楚,并精确表达了讲座人关于团队作战中,哪些人贡献大,哪些人贡献小的评论。但是,该考生在讨论第二个观点时,有些语言错误和表达不清的情况。最后一点与讲座关系不大,并表述不清,本文可以得3分。

2分作文

考官评语:

本文尽管看起来表面还可以,但是仔细阅读后发现举例与主要观点不相符合,主要论点陈述错误。另外,第二段的信息来源不明,不知想表达什么意见。第三段内容也不十分清楚。由于以上原因该生可得2分。

1分作文

考官评语:

该生语言水平低,尤其是第二段,读者无法看懂该生的作文,另外作文缺乏连贯信息,因此该生可得1分。

(七)The Independent Writing Task

This second task in the Writing section of iBT TOEFL is the Independent Writing Task. You are presented with a question, and you have 30 minutes to write an essay in response. The question asks you to give your opinion on an issue. Here is how the uestion is typically phrased:

Do you agree or disagree with the following statement?

[sentence or sentences that present an issue appear here.]

Use specific reasons and examples to support your answer.

An effective response is typically about 300 words long. If you write fewer than 300 words, you may still receive a top score, but experience has shown that shorter responses typically do not demonstrate the development of ideas needed to earn a score of 5. There is no maximum word limit. You may write as much as you wish in the time allotted. But do not write just to be writing; write to respond to the topic. The number of ideas you express is important, but it is the quality of your ideas and the effectiveness with which you express them that will be most valued by the raters.

(七)独立写作部分

这部分会有一个问题,有 30 分钟时间来写一篇文章,表达你自己的观点。以下是通常问法:

您同意下面的陈述吗? 用具体的实例来支持您的观点。

通常,文章的长短在 300 字左右。字数较少不会影响得分,但经验显示,较短的文章通常会表达不完全。这里没有字数限制,您可以在时间允许的情况下去尽量多写,但要围绕主题写。你表达观点的不同方面很重要,但是质量高和表达好的文章通常会得到高分。

Example

Do you agree or disagree with the following statement?

Always telling the truth is the most important consideration in any relationship.

Use specific reasons and examples to support your answer.

ESSAY-WRITING HINTS

1. Think before you write. Make a brief outline or some notes on scratch paper to help you organize your thoughts. You can even type your outline and notes right in the answer area on the computer and then replace your outline with sentences and paragraphs.

2. Keep track of your time. Try to finish writing your essay by the time the clock counts down to 4 or 5 minutes. Use the remaining time to check your work and make final changes. At the end of 30 minutes your essay will be automatically saved.

3. ETS/TOEFL ScoreItNow is an excellent way to practice for the Independent Writing Task on iBT TOEFL. ScoreIt Now is scored on a scale of 1 to 6, but to get an idea of how your essay would be scored on the iBT TOEFL 1 – 5 scale, you can just subtract 1 from the ScoreItNow score assigned by the software program. To find out how you can get your copy of ScoreIt Now, visit the ETS Web site.

‖ 提 醒 ‖

1. 写作之前要思考,可在草稿纸上列出简要提纲和要点。同时也可以把它们打在计算机上然后再填补其他内容。

2. 注意时间。最好提前 4、5 分钟写完,然后检查,作最后修改。30 分钟后你的文章将被自动储存。

3. 托福在线评分系统可用于自己练习独立写作进行任务评估。它的写作分值范围为 1 – 6 分。详情可登陆 ETS 官方网站。

（八）How essays are scored

Raters will judge the quality of your writing. They will consider how well you develop your ideas, how well you organize your essay, and how well you use language to express your ideas.

Development is the amount and kinds of support (examples, details, reasons) for your ideas that you present in your essay. To get a top score, your essay should be, according to the rater guidelines, "well developed, using clearly appropriate explanations, exemplifications, and/or details". The raters will judge whether you have addressed the topic and how well your details, examples, and reasons support your ideas.

Do not "memorize" long introductory and concluding paragraphs just to add words to your essay. Raters will not look favorably on wordy introductory and concluding paragraphs such as the following:

"The importance of the issue raised by the posed statement, namely creating a new holiday for people, cannot be underestimated as it concerns the very fabric of society. As it stands, the issue of creating a new holiday raises profound implications for the future. However, although the subject matter in general cannot be dismissed lightheartedly, the perspective of the issue as presented by the statement raises certain qualms regarding practical application. "

"In conclusion, although I have to accept that it is imperative that something be done about creating a new holiday for people and find the underlying thrust of the implied proposal utterly convincing, I cannot help but feel wary of taking such irrevocable steps and personally feel that a more measured approach would be more rewarding. "

Likewise, raters will not look favorably on paragraphs like the following, Which uses a lot of words but fails to develop any real ideas:

"At the heart of any discussion regarding an issue pertaining to creating a new holiday, it has to borne in mind that a delicate line has to be trod when dealing with such matters. The human resources involved in such matters cannot be guaranteed regardless of all the good intentions that may be lavished. While it is true that creating a new holiday might be a viable and laudable remedy, it is transparently clear that applied wrongly such a course of action could be calamitous and compound the problem rather than provide a solution. "

In your writing, make sure you develop some solid ideas about the given topic. Don't just use a lot of words saying that a certain issue exists. Your essay may be 300 or even 400 words long, but if it consists largely of the sorts of empty or contentfree paragraphs shown above, you'll probably earn a score of just 1 or 2.

Organization is really something that raters notice — when you fail to organize. If an essay is organized, a reader will be able to read it from beginning to end without becoming confused. Writing in paragraphs and marking transitions from one idea to another in various ways usually helps the reader to follow your ideas. But be aware that just using transition words such as first or **second** does not guarantee that your essay is organized. The points you make must all relate to the topic of the essay and to the main idea you are presenting in response. In other words, your essay should be unified. The scoring guide mentions "unity" as well as "progression" and "coherence" —these are terms that all have to do with how well your essay is organized and how easy it is for the reader to follow your ideas. To earn a top score, you need to avoid redundancy(repetition of ideas), digression(points that are not related to your main point, that take away from the "unity" of your ideas), and unclear connections (places where it is hard for the reader to understand how two ideas or parts of your writing are related).

Language use is the third criterion on which your essay will be judged, To get a top score, an essay must display "consistent facility in the use of language". There should be a variety of sentence structures, and word choice should be appropriate. If your essay includes a few minor lexical or grammar errors, you can still get a high score. However, if you make a lot of grammar errors and if those errors make it hard to understand your meaning, you will get a lower score. Raters will also judge your essay based on the complexity of sentence structures and on the quality and complexity of your vocabulary. If you use very simple sentences and very basic vocabulaw, you will probably not be able to express very complex ideas. If your language is hard to follow, your sentences are overly simple, and your vocabulary is limited, you may score no higher than a 3 no matter how impressive your ideas may be.

(八)如何评分

评分员会评断你的写作质量。他们会看你如何陈述自己的观点,如何安排你的文章,以及你对语言的运用能力。

文章是靠各种各样的支持(例子,细节,原因)而展开的。要得到高分,根据评分员所说,"你的文章要自然的展开,利用清晰合适的解释、例证或是细节。"评分员会评断你的文章是否扣题以及你所举的例子、细节、原因等等是如何为你的文章服务的。

不要为了增加字数而自己死记较长的介绍段落和总结段落。评分员将不会对类似于以下的冗长的介绍段落和总结段落给与高分:

"给大家创造一个新的假期这件事,由于关系到社会的组织因此不能低估其重要性。正如其言,创造一个新的假期对将来的生活有深远涵义。虽然这个问题不能被轻易忽视,但在考虑到实际操作时,它还是十分让人头疼的。"

"所以,尽管我觉得创造一个新假期这个建议十分必要,这个提议很有说服力,但我依然对采取这些无法取消的步骤感到担心。我个人觉得,一个更正规的方案会更加有益。"

同样,像以下运用大量单词却未表达其真正含义的文章,也不会得到高分:

"我们在讨论关于创造一个新假期这个问题的时候,一定要细致谨慎。不管那些可能会被浪费的好的意图,牵扯这个问题的人力资源将得不到保证。虽然,创造一个新假期可能会是个不错可行的建议,但若错误的适用此行,不但没能提供解决的办法,反而会使其更加复杂甚至不幸。"

在你的文章中,一定要对所给话题提出具体的论点。不要用一大堆的词来证明一个本来就存在的问题。文章大约在300-400字,但如果其中出现很多无论点或无具体内容的段落,你或许只能得1-2分。

如何组织文章是评分员所关注的,尤其当你在组织失败的时候。如果一篇文章很有条理,那么读者从头读到尾将不会感到困惑。成段写作,在话题转换处用大量不同的方式来表示过度会很有帮助。但同时要注意,只是简单的用第一,第二等过度词并不表示文章就很好的组织起来了。所有你写的要点必须紧扣或围绕文章的话题和大意。也就是说，你的文章是统一的，因为它在表达一个意思。得分要点在于"统一性，渐进性和一致性"——这些都和你文章是否组织好有关系。同时，关注读者觉得你所表达的意思清晰易懂的程度。要得到高分，你需要避免冗长（对同一观点的重复），离题（和你文章没有关系的观点，这也脱离了一致性）和模糊的连接（读者觉得理解困难即不清楚2个观点是如何联系起来的）。

语言的运用是评断文章的第三个标准。要得到高分，你的文章需展现出"在语言运用上一致的熟练性"。运用的句式要多种多样，选词也需准确合适。如果你的文章出现一些不太重要的词汇或语法错误，你仍然能拿到高分。当然，若是语法错误太多达到了对理解文章大意造成困难的时候，分数自然会较低。评分员同时会根据你文章中句型和单词的复杂性来评分。你若是使用十分简单的单词和句型，可能在表达复杂观点时会有困难。若你的文章很难令人理解，句子过于简单，词汇十分有限，那么无论你的观点多么新颖难忘，分数将不会超过3分。

(九)Independent writing scoring rubric

5. An essay at this level largely accomplishes all of the following:

(1)Effectively addresses the topic and task.

(2) Is well organized and well developed, using clearly appropriate explanations, exemplifications, and/or details.

(3)Displays unity, progression, and coherence.

(4) Displays consistent facility in the use of language, demonstrating syntactic variety, appropriate word choice, and idiomaticity, though it may have minor lexical or grammatical errors.

4. An essay at this level largely accomplishes all of the following:

(1)Adresses the topic and task well, though some points may not be fully elaborated.

(2) Is generally well organized and well developed, using appropriate and sufficient explanations, exemplifications, and/or details.

(3) Displays unity, progression, and coherence, though it may contain occasional redundancy, digrJession, or unclear connections.

(4)Displays facility in the use of language, demonstrating syntactic variety and range of vocabulary, though it will probably have occasional noticeable minor errors in structure, word form, or use of idiomatic language that do not interfere with meaning.

3. An essay at this level is marked by one or more of the following:

(1) Addresses the topic and task using somewhat developed explanations, exemplifications, and/or details.

(2) Displays unity, progression, and coherence, though connection of ideas may be occasionally obscured.

(3) May demonstrate inconsistent facility in sentence formation and word choice that may result in lack of clarity and occasionally obscure meaning.

(4) May display accurate but limited range of syntactic structures and vocabulary .

2. An essay at this level may reveal one or more of the following weaknesses:

(1)Limited development in response to the topic and task.

(2)Inadequate organization or connection of ideas.

(3) Inappropriate or insufficient exemplifications, explanations, or details to support or illustrate generalizations in response to the task.

(4)A noticeably inappropriate choice of words or word forms.

(5)An accumulation of errors in sentence structure and/or usage.

1. An essay at this level is seriously flawed by one or more of the following weaknesses:

(1)Serious disorganization or underdevelopment.

(2)Little or no detail, or irrelevant specifics, or questionable responsiveness to the task/topic.

(3)Serious and frequent errors in sentence structure or usage.

0. An essay at this level merely copies words from the topic, rejects the topic, or is otherwise not connected to the topic, is written in a foreign language, consist' of keystroke characters, or is blank.

(九)独立写作评分说明

分值	评 分 标 准
5分	→ 观点表达简洁有力,结构完整,理由和细节恰当。 → 用词准确得体,句式使用得当。 → 有个别小错误,不影响内容表达。
4分	→ 表达基本充分,但某些论点论证不足。 → 结构完整,理由和细节恰当。 → 用词准确,句式使用得当。 → 有一些小错误,但不影响内容表达。
3分	→ 内容完整,表达前后一致,但观点之间衔接不太好,表达不够清晰。 → 语言不一致,有语法和用词错误,有时表达不准确。 → 句式和词汇准确,但表达不够丰富。
2分	→ 文章的观点展开不够,缺乏合适和充分的信息。 → 衔接不连贯,结构不完整。 → 使用简单的语法和词汇时也会犯明显的错误。
1分	→ 文章组织无序,表达没有展开。 → 有一些或几乎没有细节。 → 严重的语法错误频繁出现,仅能使用一些基本词汇。
0分	→ 与主题无关。 → 用非英语语言进行写作。 → 什么也没写。

Chapter Four

Model Test
模拟测题

READING

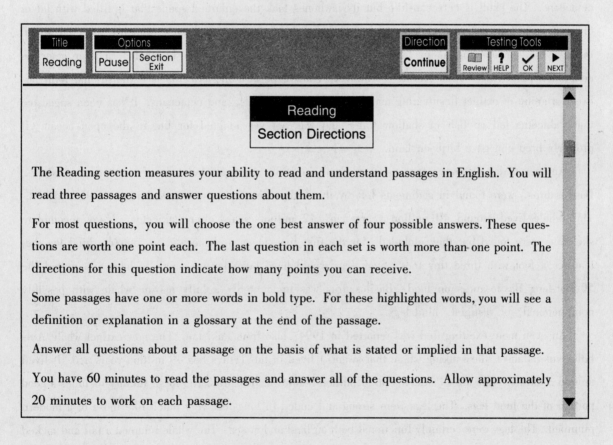

The Reading section measures your ability to read and understand passages in English. You will read three passages and answer questions about them.

For most questions, you will choose the one best answer of four possible answers. These questions are worth one point each. The last question in each set is worth more than one point. The directions for this question indicate how many points you can receive.

Some passages have one or more words in bold type. For these highlighted words, you will see a definition or explanation in a glossary at the end of the passage.

Answer all questions about a passage on the basis of what is stated or implied in that passage.

You have 60 minutes to read the passages and answer all of the questions. Allow approximately 20 minutes to work on each passage.

The Origins of Cetaceans

Paragraph

It should be obvious that cetaceans—whales, porpoises, and dolphins—are mammals. They breathe through lungs, not through gills, and give birth to live young. Their streamlined bodies, the absence of hind legs, and the presence of a **fluke** and **blowhole** cannot disguise their affinities with land-dwelling mammals. However, unlike the cases of sea otters and pinnipeds (seals, sea lions, and walruses, whose limbs are functional both on land and at sea), it is not easy to envision what the first whales looked like. Extinct but already fully marine cetaceans are known from the fossil record. How was the gap between a walking mammal and a swimming whale bridged? Missing until recently were fossils clearly intermediate, or transitional, between land mammals and cetaceans.

Very exciting discoveries have finally allowed scientists to reconstruct the most likely origins of cetaceans. In 1979, a team looking for fossils in northern Pakistan found what proved to be the oldest fossil whale. The fossil was officially named Pakicetus in honor of the country where the discovery was made. Pakicetus was found embedded in rocks formed from river deposits that were 52 million years old. The river that formed these deposits was actually not far from an ancient ocean known as the Tethys Sea.

The fossil consists of a complete skull of an archaeocyte, an extinct group of ancestors of mod ern cetaceans. Although limited to a skull, the Pakicetus fossil provides precious details on the origins of cetaceans. The skull is cetacean-like but its jawbones lack the enlarged space that is filled with fat or oil and used for receiving underwater sound in modern whales. Pakicetus probably detected sound through the ear opening as in land mammals. The skull also lacks a blowhole, another cetacean adaptation for diving. Other features, however, show experts that Pakicetus is a transitional form between a group of extinct flesh-eating mammals, the mesonychids, and cetaceans. It has been suggested that Pakicetus fed on fish in shallow water and was not yet adapted for life in the open ocean. It probably bred and gave birth on land.

Another major discovery was made in Egypt in 1989. Several skeletons of another early whale, Basilosaurus, were found in sediments left by the Tethys Sea and now **exposed** in the Sahara desert. This whale lived around 40 million years ago, 12 million years after Pakicetus. Many incomplete skeletons were found but they included, for the first time in an archaeocyte, a complete hind leg that features a foot with three tiny toes. Such legs would have been far too small to have sup ported the 50-foot-long Basilosaurus on land. Basilosaurus was undoubtedly a fully marine whale with possibly nonfunctional, or vestigial, hind legs.

An even more exciting find was reported in 1994, also from Pakistan. The now extinct whale Ambulocetus natans ("the walking whale that swam") lived in the Tethys Sea 49 million years ago. It lived around 3 million years after Pakicetus but 9 million before Basilosaurus. The fossil **luckily** includes a good portion of the hind legs. The legs were strong and ended in long feet very much like those of a modern pinniped. The legs were certainly functional both on land and at sea. The whale retained a tail and lacked a fluke, the major means of locomotion in modern cetaceans. **The structure of the backbone shows, however, that Ambulocetus swam like modern whales by moving the rear portion of its body up and down, even though a fluke was missing.** The large hind legs were used for propulsion in water. On land, where it probably bred and gave birth, Ambulocetus may have moved around very much like a modern sea lion. It was undoubtedly a whale that linked life on land with life at sea.

Glossary

Fluke: the two parts that constitute the large triangular tail of a whale

Blowhole: a hole in the top of the head used for breathing

Questions

P1   It should be obvious that cetaceans—whales, porpoises, and dolphins are mammals. They breathe through lungs, not through gills, and give birth to live young. Their streamlined bodies, the absence of hind legs, and the presence of a fluke and blowhole cannot disguise their affinities with land-dwelling mammals. However, unlike the cases of sea otters and pinnipeds (seals, sea lions, and walruses, whose limbs are functional both on land and at sea), it is not easy to envision what the first whales looked like. Extinct but already fully marine cetaceans are known from the fossil record. How was the gap between a walking mammal and a swimming whale bridged? Missing until recently were fossils clearly intermediate, or transitional, between land mammals and cetaceans.

(Note: The letter "P" stands for paragraph. P1 means paragraph 1.)

Directions: Mark your answer by choosing the correct choice.

1. In paragraph 1, what does the author say about the presence of a blowhole in cetaceans?

    A. It clearly indicates that cetaceans are mammals.

    B. It cannot conceal the fact that cetaceans are mammals.

    C. It is the main difference between cetaceans and land-dwelling mammals.

    D. It cannot yield clues about the origins of cetaceans.

2. Which of the following can be inferred from paragraph 1 about early sea otters?

    A. It is not difficult to imagine what they looked like.

    B. There were great numbers of them.

    C. They lived in the sea only.

    D. They did not leave many fossil remains.

    P3   The fossil consists of a complete skull of an archaeocyte, an extinct group of ancestors of modern cetaceans. Although limited to a skull, the Pakicetus fossil provides **precious** details on the origins of cetaceans. The skull is cetacean-like but its jawbones lack the enlarged space that is filled with fat or oil and used for receiving underwater sound in modern whales. Pakicetus probably detected sound through the ear opening as in land mammals. The skull also lacks a blowhole, another cetacean adaptation for diving. Other features, however, show experts that Pakicetus is a transitional form between a group of extinct flesh-eating mammals, the mesonychids, and cetaceans. It has been suggested that Pakicetus fed on fish in shallow water and was not yet adapted for life in the open ocean. **It** probably bred and gave birth on land.

3. The word **precious** in the passage is closest in meaning to _____ .

    A. exact   B. scarce   C. valuable   D. initial

4. Pakicetus and modern cetaceans have similar _____ .

A. hearing structures   B. adaptations for diving   C. skull shapes   D. breeding locations

5. The word **it** in the passage refers to _____ .

A. Pakicetus   B. fish   C. life   D. ocean

P4   Another major discovery was made in Egypt in 1989. Several skeletons of another early whale, Basilosaurus, were found in sediments left by the Tethys Sea and now **exposed** in the Sahara desert. This whale lived around 40 million years ago, 12 million years after Pakicetus. Many incomplete skeletons were found but they included, for the first time in an archaeocyte, a complete hind leg that features a foot with three tiny toes. Such legs would have been far too small to have supported the 50-foot-long Basilosaurus on land. Basilosaurus was undoubtedly a fully marine whale with possibly nonfunctlonal, or vestigial, hind legs.

6. The word **exposed** in the passage is closest in meaning to _____ .

A. explained   B. visible   C. identified   D. located

7. The hind leg of Basilosaurus was a significant find because it showed that Baailosaurus _____ .

A. lived later than Ambulocetus natans   B. lived at the same time as Pakicetus

C. was able to swim well   D. could not have walked on land

8. lt can be lnferred that Basilosaurus bred and gave birth in which of the following locations?

A. On land.   B. Both on land and at sea.

C. In shallow water.   D. In a marine environment.

P5   An even more exciting find was reported in 1994, also from Pakistan. The now extinct whale Ambulocetus natans ("the walking whale that swam") lived in the Tethys Sea 49 million years ago. It lived around 3 million years after Pakicetus but 9 million before Basilosaurus. The fossil **luckily** includes a good portion of the hind legs. The legs were strong and ended in long feet very nuch like those of a modern pinniped. The legs were certainly functional both on land and at sea. The whale retained a tailand lacked a fluke, the major means of locomotion in modern cetaceans **The structure of the backbone shows however that Ambulocetus swam like modern whales by moving the rear portion ot its body up and down even though a fluke was missing.** The large hind legs were used for **propulsion** in water. On land, where it probably bred and gave birth, Ambulocetus may have moved around very much like a modern sea lion. It was undoubtedly a whale that linked life on land with life at sea.

9. Why does the author use the word **luckily** in mentioning that the Ambuloc etus natans fossil included hind legs?

A. Fossil legs of early whales are a rare find.

B. The legs provided important information about the evolution of cetaceans.

C. The discovery allowed scientists to reconstruct a complete skeleton of the whale.

D. Until that time, only the front legs of early whales had been discovered.

10. Which of the sentences below best expresses the essential information in the highlighted senntence in the passage?

Incorrect choices change the meaning in important ways or leave out essential information.

A. Even though Ambulocetus swam by moving its body up and down, it did not have a backbone.

B. The backbone of Ambulocetus, which allowed it to swim, is missing fluke.

C. Although Ambulocetus had no fluke, its backbone structure shows that it swam like modern whales.

D. By moving the rear parts of their bodies up and down, modrn whales swim in a different way from the way Ambulocetus swam.

11. The word **propulsion** in the passage is closest in meaning to _____ .

A. staying afloat   B. changing direction

C. decreasing weight   D. moving forward

P1&2   Extinct but already fully marine cetaceans are known from the fossll record. ■How was the gap between a walking mammal and a swimming whale bridged? ■ Missing until recently were fossils clearly intermediate, or transitional, between land mammals and cetaceans.

Very exciting discoveries have finally allowed scientists to reconstruct the most likely origins of cetaceans. ■In 1979, a team looking for fossils in northern Pakistan found what proved to be the oldest fossil whale.

12. Look at the four squares ■ that indicate where the following sentence can be added to the passage.

This in a question that has puzzled scientists for ages.

Where would the sentence best fit?

A. Extinct but already fully marine cetaceans are known from the fossil record. This is a question that has puzzled scientists for ages. How was the gap between a walking mammal and a swimming whale bridged? ■Missing until recently were fossils clearly intermediate, or transitional, between land mammals and cetaceans.

■Very exciting discoveries have finally allowed scientists to reconstruct the most likely origins of cetaceans. ■In 1979, a team looking for fossils in northern Pakistan found what proved to be the oldest fossil whale.

B. Extinct but already fully marine cetaceans are known from the fossil record. ■ How was the gap between a walking mammal and a swimming whale bridged? This is a question that has puzzled scientists for ages. Missing until recently were fossils clearly intermediate, or transitional, between land mammals and cetaceans.

■Very exciting discoveries have finally allowed scientists to reconstruct the most likely origins of cetaceans. ■ In 1979, a team looking for fossils in northern Pakistan found what proved to be the oldest fossil whale.

C. Extinct but alreacly fully marine cetaceans are known from the fossil record. ■ How was the gap between a walking mammal and a swimming whale bridged? ■ Missing until recently were fossils clearly intermediate, or transitional, between land mammals and cetaceans.

This is a question that has puzzled scientists for ages. Very exciting discoveries have finally allowed scientists to reconstruct the most likely origins of cetaceans. ■ In 1979, a team looking for fossils in northern Pakistan found what proved to be the oldest fossil whale.

D. Extinct but already fully marine cetaceans are known from the fossil record. ■ How was the gap between a walking mammal and a swimming whale bridged? ■Missing until recently were fossils clearly intermediate, or transitional, between land mammals and cetaceans.

■Very exciting discoveries have finally allowed scientists to reconstruct the most likely origins of cetaceans. **This is a question that has puzzled scientists for ages.** In 1979, a team looking for fossils in northern Pakistan found what proved to be the oldest fossil whale.

13 – 14. Directions: An introductory sentence for a brief summary of the passage is provided below. Complete the summary by selecting the THREE answer choices that express the most important ideas in the passage. Some answer choices do not belong in the summary because they express ideas that are not presented in the passage or are minor ideas in the passage. **This question is worth 2 points.**

This passage discusses fossils that help to explain the likely origins of cetaceans — whales, porpoises, and dolphins.

Answer Choices

(1) Recent discoveries of fossils have helped to show the link between land mammals and cetaceans.

(2) The discovery of Ambulocetus natans provided evidence for a whale that lived both on land and at sea.

(3) The skeleton of Basilosaurus was found in what had been the Tethys Sea, an area rich in fossil evidence.

(4) Pakicetus is the oldest fossil whale yet to be found.

(5) Fossils thought to be transitional forms between walking mammals and swimming whales were found.

(6) Ambulocetud hind legs were used for proputsion in the water.

Desert Formation

Paragraph

The deserts, which already occupy approximately a fourth of the Earth's land surface, have in recent decades been increasing at an alarming pace. The expansion of desertlike conditions into areas where they did not previously exist is called desertification. It has been estimated that an additional one-fourth of the Earth's land surface is **threatened** by this process.

Desertification is accomplished primarily through the loss of stabilizing natural vegetation and the subsequent accelerated erosion of the soil by wind and water. In some cases the loose soil is blown completely away, leaving a stony surface. In other cases, the finer particles may be removed, while the sand-sized particles are accumulated to form mobile hills or ridges of sand.

Even in the areas that retain a soil cover, the reduction of vegetation typically results in the loss of the soil's ability to absorb substantial quantities of water. The impact of raindrops on the loose soil tends to transfer fine clay particles into the tiniest soil spaces, sealing them and producing a surface that allows very little water penetration. Water absorption is greatly reduced, consequently runoff is increased, resulting in accelerated erosion rates. The gradual drying of the soil caused by its diminished ability to absorb water results in the further loss of vegetation, so that a cycle of progressive surface deterioration is established.

In some regions, the increase in desert areas is occurring largely as the result of a trend toward drier climatic conditions. Continued gradual global warming has produced an increase in aridity for some areas over the past few thousand years. The process may be accelerated in subsequent decades if global warming resulting from air pollution seriously increases.

There is little doubt, however, that desertification in most areas results primarily from human activities rather than natural processes. The semiarid lands bordering the deserts exist in **a delicate** ecological balance and are limited in their potential to adjust to increased environmental pressures. Expanding populations are subjecting the land to increasing pressures to provide them with food and fuel. In wet periods, the land may be able to respond to these stresses. During the dry periods that are common phenomena along the desert margins, though, the pressure on the land is often far in excess of its diminished capacity, and desertification results.

Four specific activities have been identified as major contributors to the desertification processes: overcultivation, overgrazing, firewood gathering, and overirrigation. The cultivation of crops has expanded into **progressively** drier regions as population densities have grown. These regions are especially likely to have periods of severe dryness, so that crop failures are common. Since the raising of most crops necessitates the prior removal of the natural vegetation, crop failures leave extensive tracts of land devoid of a plant cover and susceptible to wind and water erosion.

The raising of livestock is a major economic activity in semiarid lands, where grasses are generally the dominant type of natural vegetation. The consequences of an excessive number of livestock grazing in an area are the reduction of the vegetation cover and the trampling and pulverization of the soil. This is usually followed by the drying of the soil and accelerated erosion.

Firewood is the chief fuel used for cooking and heating in many countries. The increased pressures of expanding populations have led to the removal of woody plants so that many cities and towns are surrounded by large areas completely lacking in trees and shrubs. The increasing use of dried animal waste as a substitute fuel has also hurt the soil because this valuable soil conditioner and source of plant nutrients is no longer being returned to the land.

The final major human cause of desertification is soil salinization resulting from overirrigation. Excess water from irrigation sinks down into the water table. If no drainage system exists, the water table rises, bringing dissolved salts to the surface. The water evaporates and the salts are left behind, creating a white crustal layer that prevents air and water from reaching the underlying soil.

The extreme seriousness of desertification results from the vast areas of land and the tremendous numbers of people affected, as well as from the great difficulty of reversing or even slowing the process. Once the soil has been removed by erosion, only the passage of centuries or millennia will enable new soil to form. In areas where considerable soil still remains, though, a rigorously enforced program of land protection and cover-crop planting may make it possible to reverse the present deterioration of the surface.

Questions

Para 1   The deserts, which already occupy approximately a fourth of the Earth's land surface, have in recent decades been increasing at an alarming pace. The expansion of desertlike conditions into areas where they did not previously exist is called desertification. It has been estimated that an additional one-fourth of the Earth's land surface is **threatened** by this process.

(Note: The letter "P" stands for paragraph. P1 means paragraph 1.)

Directions: Mark your answer by choosing the correct choice.

15. The word threatened in the passage is closest in meaning to _____ .

    A. restricted   B. endangered   C. prevented   D. rejected

Para 3   Even in the areas that retain a soil cover, the reduction of vegetation typically results in the loss of the soil's ability to absorb substantial quantities of water. The impact of rain-drops on the loose soil tends to transfer fine clay particles into the tiniest soil spaces, sealing them and producing a surface that allows very little water penetration. Water absorption is greatly reduced' consequently runoff is increased, resulting in accelerated erosion rates. The gradual drying of the soil caused by its diminished ability to absorb water results in the further loss of vegetation, so that a cycle of progressive surface dete rioration is established.

16. According to paragraph 3, the loss of natural vegetation has which of the following consequences for soil?

    A. Increased stony content.   B. Reduced water absorption.

    C. Increased numbers of spaces in the soil.   D. Reduce water runoff.

Para 5   There is little doubt, however, that desertification in most areas results primarily from human activities rather than natural processes. The semiarid lands bordering the deserts exist in a **delicate** ecological balance and are limited in their potential to adjust to to increased environmental pressures. Expanding populations are subjecting the land to increasing pressures to provide them with food and fuel. In wet periods, the land may be able to respond to these stresses. During the dry periods that are common phenomena along the desert margins, though, the pressure on the land is often far in excess of its diminished capacity, and desertification results.

17. The word **delicate** in the passage is closest in meaning to _____ .

    A. fragile   B. predictable   C. complex   D. valuable

18. According to paragraph 5, in dry periods, border areas have difficulty _____ .

    A. adjusting to stresses created by settlement

    B. retaining their fertility after desertification

    C. providing water for irrigating crops

    D. attracting populations in search of food and fuel

Para 6   Four specific activities have been identified as major contributors to the desertification processes: overcultivation, overgrazing, firewood gathering, and overirrigation. The cultiation of crops has expanded into **progressively** drier regions as population densities have grown. These regions are especially likely to have periods of severe dryness, so that crop failures are common. Since the raising of most crops necessitates the prior removal of the natural vegetation, crop failures leave extensive tracts of land devoid of a plant cover and susceptible to wind and water erosion.

19. The word progressively in the passage is closest in meaning to _____ .

    A. openly   B. impressively   C. objectively   D. increasingly

20. According to paragraph 6, which of the following is often associated with raising crops?

    A. Lack of proper irrigation techniques.

    B. Failure to plant crops suited to the particular area.

    C. Removal of the original vegetation.

    D. Excessive use of dried animal waste.

21. The phrase **devoid of** in the passage is closest in meaning to_____ .

    A. consisting of   B. hidden by   C. except for   D. lacking in

Para 9   The final major human cause of desertification is soil salinization resulting from overirrigation. Excess water from irrigation sinks down into the water table. If no drainage system exists, the water table rises, bringing dissolved salts to the surface. The water evaporates and the salts are left behind, creating a white crustal layer that prevents air and water from reaching the underlying soil.

22. According to paragraph 9, the ground's absorption of excess water is a factor in desertification because it can _____ .

    A. interfere with the irrigation of land   B. limit the evaporation of water

    C. require more absorption of air by the soil   D. bring salts to the surface

23. All of the following are mentioned in the passage as contributing to desertification EXCEPT_____

    A. soil erosion.   B. global warming.

    C. insufficient irrigation.   D. the raising of livestock.

Para 10   **The extreme seriousness of desertification results from the vast areas of land and the tremendous number of people affected as well from the great difficulty of reversing or event slowing the process.** Once the soil has been removed by erosion, only the passage of centuries or millennia will enable new soil to form. In areas where considerable soil still remains, though, a rigorously enforced program of land protection and cover-crop planting may make it possible to reverse the present deterioration of the surface.

24. Which of the sentences below best expresses the essential information in the highlighted sentence in the passage?

    Incorrect choices change the meaning in important ways or leave out essential information.

    A. Desertification is a significant problem because it is so hard to reverse and affects large areas of land and great numbers of people.

    B. Slowing down the process of desertification is difficult because of population growth that has spread over large areas of land.

    C. The spread of deserts is considered a very serious problem that can be solved only if large numbers of people in various countries are involved in the effort.

D. Desertification is extremely hard to reverse unless the population is reduced in the vast areas af-fected.

25. It can be inferred from the passage that the author most likely believes which of the following about the future of desertification?

A. Governments will act quickly to control further desertification.

B. The factors influencing desertification occur in cycles and will change in the future.

C. Desertification will continue to increase.

D. Desertification will soon occur in all areas of the world.

P7 ■ The raising of livestock is a major economic activity in semiarid lands, where grasses are generally the dominant type of natural vegetation. ■ The consequences of an excessive number of live-stock grazing in an area are the reduction of the vegetation cover and the trampling and pulverization of the soil. ■ This is usually followed by the drying of the soil and accelerated erosion. ■

26. Look at the four squares ■ that indicate where the following sentence can be added to the passage.

This economic reliance on livestock in certain regions makes large tracts of land sus-ceptible to overgrazing.

Where would the sentence best fit?

A. **This economic reliance on livestock in certain regions makes large tracts of land sus-ceptible to overgrazing.** The raising of livestock is a major economic activity in semiarid lands, where grasses are generally the dominant type of natural vegetation. ■ The consequences of an excessive number of live-stock grazing in an area are the reduction of the vegetation cover and the trampling and pulverization of the soil. ■ This is usually followed by the drying of the soil and accelerated erosion. ■

B. ■ The raising of livestock is a major economic activity in semiarid lands, where grasses are generally the dominant type of natural vegetation. **This economic reliance on livestock in certain re-gions makes large tracts of land susceptible to overgrazing.** The conse-quences of an excessive number of livestock grazing in an area are the reduction of the egetation cover and the ~ rampling and pulverization of the soil. ■ This is usually followed by the drying of the soil and accelerated erosion. ■

C. ■ The raising of livestock is a major economic activity in semiarid lands, where grasses are generally the dominant type of natural vegetation. ■ The consequences of an excessive number of live-stock grazing in an area are the reduction of the vegetation cover and the trampling and pulverization of the soil. **This economic reliance on livestock in certain regions makes large tracts of land susceptible to overgrazing.** This is usually followed by the drying of the soil and accelerated erosion. ■

D. ■ The raising of livestock is a major economic activity in semiarid lands, where grasses are generally the dominant type of natural vegetation. ■ The consequences of an excessive number of live-stock grazing in an area are the reduction of the vegetation cover and the trampling and pulverization of the soil. ■ This is usually followed by the drying of the soil and accelerated erosion. **This economic reliance on livestock in certain regions makes large tracts of land susceptible to overgrazing.**

27 – 28   Directions: An introductory sentence for a brief summary of the passage is provided be-

low. Complete the Summary by selecting the THREE answer choices that express the most important ideas in the passage. Some answer choices do not belong in the summary because they express ideas that are not presented in the passage or are minor ideas in the passage. This question is worth 2 points.

Many factors have contributed to the great increase in desertification in recent decades.

Answer Choices

(1) Growing human populations and the agricultural demands that come with such growth have upset the ecological balance in some areas and led to the spread of deserts.

(2) As periods of severe dryness have become more common, failures of a number of different crops have increased.

(3) Excessive numbers of cattle and the need for firewood for fuel have reduced grasses and trees, leaving the land unprotected and vulnerable.

(4) Extensive irrigation with poor drainage brings salt to the surface of the soil, a process that reduces water and air absorption.

(5) Animal dung enriches the nutrients for plant growth.

(6) Grasses are generally the dominant type of natural vegetation in semiarid lands.

Artisans and Industrialization

Paragraph

Before 1815 manufacturing in the United States had been done in homes or shops by skilled artisans. As master craftworkers, they imparted the knowledge of their trades to apprentices and journeymen. In addition, women often worked in their homes part-time, making finished articles from raw material supplied by merchant capitalists. After 1815 this older form of manufacturing began to give way to factories with machinery tended by unskilled or semiskilled laborers. Cheap transportation networks, the rise of cities, and the availability of capital and credit all stimulated the shi to factory production.

The creation of a labor force that was accustomed to working in factories did not occur easily. Before the rise of the factory, artisans had worked within the home. **Apprentices were considered part of the family, and masters were responsible not only for teaching their apprentices a trade but also for providing them some education and for supervising their moral behavior.** Journeymen knew that if they perfected their skill, they could become respected master artisans with their own shops. Also, skilled artisans did not work by the clock, at a steady pace, but rather in bursts of intense labor alternating with more leisurely time.

The factory changed that. Goods produced by factories were not as finished or elegant as those done by hand, and pride in craftsmanship gave way to the pressure to increase rates of productivity. The new methods of doing business involved a new and stricter sense of time. Factory life necessitated a more regimented schedule, where work began at the sound of a bell and workers kept machines going at a constant pace. At the same time, workers were required to discard old habits, for industrialism demanded a worker who was alert, dependable, and self-disciplined. Absenteeism and lateness hurt productivity and, since work was specialized, **disrupted** the regular factory routine. Industrialization not only produced a fundamental change in the way work was organized; it transformed the very nature of work.

The first generation to experience these changes did not adopt the new attitudes easily. The factory clock became the symbol of the new work rules. One mill worker who finally quit complained revealingly about "obedience to the ding-dong of the bell—just as though we are so many living machines". With the loss of personal freedom also came the loss of standing in the community. Unlike artisan workshops in which apprentices worked closely with the masters supervising them, factories sharply separated workers from management. Few workers rose through the ranks to supervisory positions, and even fewer could achieve the artisan's dream of setting up one's own business. Even well-paid workers sensed their decline in status.

In this newly emerging economic order, workers sometimes organized to protect their rights and traditional ways of life. Craftworkers such as carpenters, printers, and tailors formed unions, and in 1834 individual unions came together in the National Trades' Union. The labor movement gathered some momentum in the decade before the Panic of 1837, but in the depression that followed, labor's strength collapsed. During hard times, few workers were willing to strike * or engage in collective action. And skilled craftworkers, who spearheaded the union movement, did not feel a particularly strong bond with semiskilled factory workers and unskilled laborers. More than a decade of agitation did finally bring a workday shortened to 10 hours to most industries by the 1850's, and the courts also recognized workers' right to strike, but these gains had little immediate impact.

Workers were united in resenting the industrial system and their loss of status, but they were divided by ethnic and racial antagonisms, gender, conflicting religious perspectives, occupational differences, **political party loyalties, and disagreements over tactics.** For **them**, the factory and industrialism were not agents of opportunity but reminders of their loss of independence and a measure of control over their lives. As United States society became more specialized and differentiated, greater extremes of wealth began to appear. And as the new markets created fortunes for the few, the factory system lowered the wages of workers by dividing labor into smaller, less skilled tasks.

＊**strike**: a stopping of work that is organized by workers

Questions

Para 1　Before 1815 manufacturing in the United States had been done in homes or shops by skilled artisans. As master craftworkers, they imparted the knowledge of their trades to apprentices and journeymen. In addition, women often worked in their homes part-time, making finished articles from raw material supplied by merchant capitalists. After 1815 this older form of manufacturing began to give way to factories with machinery tended by unskilled or semiskilled laborers. Cheap transportation networks, the rise of cities, and the availability of capital and credit all stimulated the shi to factory production.

Directions: Mark your answer by choosing the correct choice.

29. Which of the following can be inferred from the passage about articles manufactured before 1815?

　　A. They were primarily produced by women.

　　B. They were generally produced in shops rather than in homes.

　　C. They were produced with more concern for quality than for speed of production.

D. They were produced mostly in large cities with extensive transportation networks.

Para 2   The creation of a labor force that was accustomed to working in factories did not occur easily. Before the rise of the factory, artisans had worked within the home. Apprentices were considered part of the family, and masters were responsible not only for teaching their apprentices a trade but also for providing them some education and for supervising their moral behavior. Journeymen knew that if they perfected their skill, they could become respected master artisans with their own shops. Also, skilled artisans did not work by the clock, at a steady pace, but rather in bursts of intense labor alternating with more leisurely time.

30. Which of the sentences below best expresses the essential information in the highlighted sentence in the passage?

Incorrect answer choices change the meaning in important ways or leave out essential information.

A. Masters demanded moral behavior from apprentices but often treated them irresponsibly.

B. The responsibilities of the master to the apprentice went beyond the teaching of a trade.

C. Masters preferred to maintain the trade within the family by supervising and educating the younger family members.

D. Masters who trained members of their own family as apprentices demanded excellence from them.

Para 3   The factory changed that. Goods produced by factories were not as finished or elegant as those done by hand, and pride in craftsmanship gave way to the pressure to increase rates of productivity. The new methods of doing business involved a new and stricter sense of time. Factory life necessitated a more regimented schedule, where work began at the sound of a bell and workers kept machines going at a constant pace. At the same time, workers were required to discard old habits, for industrialism demanded a worker who was alert, dependable, and self-disciplined. Absenteeism and lateness hurt productivity and, since work was specialized, **disrupted** the regular factory routine. Industrialization not only produced a fundamental change in the way work was organized; it transformed the very nature of work.

31. The word disrupted in the passage is closest in meaning to _____.

    A. prolonged   B. established   C. followed   D. upset

Para 4   The first generation to experience these changes did not adopt the new attitudes easily. The factory clock became the symbol of the new work rules. One mill worker who finally quit complained revealingly about "obedience to the ding-dong of the bell — just as though we are so many living machines". With the loss of personal freedom also came the loss of standing in the community. Unlike artisan workshops in which apprentices worked closely with the masters supervising them, factories sharply separated workers from management. Few workers rose through the ranks to supervisory positions, and even fewer could achieve the artisan's dream of setting up one's own business. Even well-paid workers sensed their decline in status.

32. In paragraph 4, the author includes the quotation from a mill worker in order to _____.

    A. support the idea that it was difficult for workers to adjust to working in factories

B. to show that workers sometimes quit because of the loud noise made by factory machinery

C. argue that clocks did not have a useful function in factories

D. emphasize that factories were most successful when workers revealed their complaints

33. All of the following are mentioned in paragraph 4 as consequences of the new system for workers EXCEPT a loss of _____.

    A. freedom

    B. status in the community

    C. opportunities for advancement

    D. contact among workers who were not managers

Para 5   In this newly emerging economic order, workers sometimes organized to protect their rights and traditional ways of life. Craftworkers such as carpenters, printers, and tailors formed unions, and in 1834 individual unions came together in the National Trades' Union. The labor movement gathered some momentum in the decade before the Panic of 1837, but in the depression that followed, labor's strength collapsed. During hard times, few workers were willing to strike ✱ or engage in collective action. And skilled craftworkers, who **spearheaded** the union movement, did not feel a particularly strong bond with semiskilled factory workers and unskilled laborers. More than a decade of agitation did finally bring a workday shortened to 10 hours to most industries by the 1850's, and the courts also recognized workers' right to strike, but these gains had little immediate impact.

34. The phrase **gathered some momentum** in the passage is closest in meaning to _____.

    A. made progress   B. became active   C. caused changes   D. combined forces

35. The word **spearheaded**, in the passage is closest in meaning to _____.

    A. led   B. accepted   C. changed   D. resisted

36. Which of the following statements about the labor movement of the 1800's is supported by paragraph 5?

    A. It was most successful during times of economic crisis.

    B. Its primary purpose was to benefit unskilled laborers.

    C. It was slow to improve conditions for workers.

    D. It helped workers of all skill levels form a strong bond with each other.

Para 6   Workers were united in resenting the industrial system and their loss of status, but they were divided by ethnic and racial antagonisms, gender, conflicting religious perspectives, occupational differences, **political party loyalties, and disagreements over tactics.** For **them**, the factory and industrialism were not agents of opportunity but reminders of their loss of independence and a measure of control over their lives. As United States society became more specialized and differentiated, greater extremes of wealth began to appear. And as the new markets created fortunes for the few, the factory system lowered the wages of workers by dividing labor into smaller, less skilled tasks.

37. The author identifies **political loyalties, and disagreements over tactics** as two of several factors that _____.

    A. encouraged workers to demand higher wages.

    B. created divisions among workers.

C. caused work to become more specialized.

D. increased workers' resentment of tbe industrial system.

38. The word **them** in the passage refers _____ .

A. workers   B. political party loyalties

C. disagreements over tactics   D. agents of opportunity

Para 1   Before 1815 manufacturing in the United States had been done in homes or shops by skilled artisans. ■ As master craftworkers, they imparted the knowledge of their trades to apprentices and journeymen. ■ In addition, women often worked in their homes part-time, making finished articles from raw material supplied by merchant capitalists. ■ After 1815 this older form of manufacturing began to give way to factories with machinery tended by unskilled or semiskilled laborers. ■ Cheap transportation networks, the rise of cities, and the availability of capital and credit all stimulated the shift factory production.

39. Look at the four squares ■ that indicate where the following sentence can be added to the passage.

This new form of manufacturing depended on the movement of goods to distant locations and a centralized source of laborers.

Where would the sentence best fit?

A. Before 1815 manufacturing in the United States had been done in homes or shops by skilled artisans. **This new form of manufacturing depended on the movement of goods to distant locations arid a centralized source of laborers.** As master craftworkers, they imparted the knowledge of their trades to apprentices and journeymen. ■ In addition, women often worked in their homes part-time, making finished articles from raw material supplied by merchant capitalists. ■ After 1815 this older form of manufacturing began to give way to factories with machinery tended by unskilled or semiskilled laborers. ■ Cheap transportation networks, the rise of cities, and the availability of capital and credit all stimulated the shift to factory production.

B. Before 1815 manufacturing in the United States had been done in homes or shops by skilled artisans. ■ As master craftworkers, they imparted the knowledge of their trades to apprentices and journeymen. **This new form of manufacturing depended on the movement of goods to distant locations and a centralized source of laborers.** In addition, women often worked in their homes part-time, making finished articles from raw material supplied by merchant capitalists. ■ After 1815 this older form of manufacturing began to give way to factories with machinery tended by unskilled or semiskilled laborers. ■ Cheap transportation networks, the rise of cities, and the availability of capital and credit all stimulated the shift to factory production.

C. Before 1815 manufacturing in the United States had been done in homes or shops by skilled artisans. ■ As master craftworkers, they imparted the knowledge of their trades to apprentices and journeymen. ■ In addition, women often worked in their homes part-time, making finished articles from raw material supplied by merchant capitalists. **This new form of manufacturing depended on the movement of goods to distant locations and a centralized source of laborers.** After 1815 this older form of manufacturing began to give way to factories with machinery tended by unskilled or semiskilled laborers.

■ Cheap trans portation networks, the rise of cities, and the availability of capital and credit all stimulated the shift to factory production.

D. Before 1815 manufacturing in the United States had been done in homes or shops by skilled artisans. ■ As master craftworkers, they imparted the knowledge of their trades to apprentices and journeymen. ■ In addition, women often worked in their homes part-time, making finished articles from raw material supplied by merchant capitalists. ■ After 1815 this older form of manufacturing began to give way to factories with machinery tended by unskilled or semiskilled laborers. This new form of manufacturing depended on the movement of goods to distant locations and a centralized source of laborers. Cheap transportation networks, the rise of cities, and the availability of capital and credit all stimulated the shift to factory production.

40. Directions: Complete the table below by indicating which of the answer choices describe characteristics of the period before 1815 and which describe characteristics of the 1815 – 1860 period. **This question is worth 3 points.**

Before 1815	1815 – 1850
►	►
►	►
	►

Answer Choices

(1) A united, highly successful labor movement took shape.

(2) Workers took pride in their workmanship.

(3) The income gap between the rich and the poor increased greatly.

(4) Transportation networks began to decline.

(5) Emphasis was placed on following schedules.

(6) Workers went through an extensive period of training.

(7) Few workers expected to own their own businesses.

LISTENING

Listening Comprehension
Section Directions

This section measures your ability to understand conversations and lectures in English.

You will listen to 1 conversation and 2 lectures. You will hear each conversation and lecture one time. After each conversation or lecture, you will hear some questions about it. Answer all questions based on what the speaker state or imply.

You may take notes while you listen. You may use your notes to help you answer the question. Some questions have special directions, which appear in a gray box. Most questions are worth one point. If a question is worth more than one point, special directions will indicate how many points you can receive.

In some questions, you will see this icon: 🎧 . This means that you will hear, but not see, part of the question.

You have approximately 40 minutes to complete the Listening section. This includes the time for listening to the conversations and lectures and for answering the questions.

You will now begin this part of the Listening section.

Questions 1 – 5

Listen to a conversation between two students.

1. What are the students mainly discussing?

    A. Summer jobs.

    B. Summer classes.

    C. Renting an apartment off campus.

    D. The man's difficulty in finding a job.

2. Listen again to part of the conversation. Then answer the question.

    What can be inferred about the woman when the man says this:

    A. She spends a lot of time in finding campus news.

    B. She loves the news business.

    C. She would be famous in the campus newspaper.

    D. She's looking for a new job in the news business.

3. What kind of job does the woman have now?

A. A summer intern in a news agency.

B. A reporter for the campus newspaper.

C. An amateur journalist.

D. No fixed job yet.

4. What does the man suggest the woman do?

Click on two correct answers.

A. Phone the recruiter directly.

B. Bring some work samples.

C. Advertise her resume in the campus newspaper.

D Take a summer class instead.

5. What can be concluded about the woman's feeling about her job outlook?

A. Frustrated.   B. Confident.   C. Uncaring.   D. Encouraged

Questions 6 – 10

Listen to a conversation between a student and a student advisor.

6. Why does the student go to see the advisor?

A. To discuss an idea for online study opportunities.

B. To find help with his financial status.

C. To register for the advisor's class.

D. To look for advice on registering for a course.

7. According to the advisor, what is the department's policy on taking courses fro partments?

A. It's not allowed.

B. It's allowed but students have to seek approval.

C. Students must take required courses first.

D. Students must take similar courses offered within the department first.

8. When is Statistics I offered?

A. summer.   B. fall.   C. spring.   D. year-round.

9. What does the advisor suggest the man do?

Click on two correct answers

A Talk to the Professor before registering for the course.

B. Take the class in spring.

C. Choose a course within the department.

D. Register as soon as possible.

10. Listen again to part of the conversation. Then answer the question.

What can be inferred about Professor Gordon's class when the advisor say this:

A. Professor Gordon is very likely to reject those on the waiting-list.

B. Professor Gordon is very likely to accept those on the waiting-list.

C. Students are very likely to be put on a waiting-list for Professor Gord on class.

D. Late enrollment is very likely to result in one being put on the waiting-list.

Questions 11 – 16

Listen to a lecture in an American history class.

11. What is the lecture mainly about?

    A. Sweden's population pressure resulting in mass emigration to America.

    B. Sweden's societal and economic difficulties in the eighteenth century.

    C. Swedish emigration to America and some of the causes behind the move.

    D. The history of American emigration from Europe.

12. The professor explained various reasons for the Swedish emigration to America. Indicate for which

    reasons the term falls into _____ .

    A. Less developed industry

    B. Agricultural Crisis Population Pressure and communications "Peace, vaccination and potatoes"

    C. The state-supported en-closure movement

    D. City beggars and prosti-tutes

13. Listen again to part of the lecture. Then answer the question.

    Why does the professor use the word "exodus"?

    A. To compare the Swedish emigration to an ancient story.

    B. To emphasize the significant number of Swedes that left.

    C. To state the emigration movement more precisely.

    D. To introduce some real figures to prove his argument.

14. When did the first Swedish immigrants arrive at the New Continent?

    A. In the middle of the nineteenth century.

    B. In the late nineteenth century.

    C. Prior to the landing of the "Mayflower".

    D. Before the establishment of the United States as a country.

15. According to the professor, what was the primary intent of the first Swedish?

    A. Establishing a colony.

    B. Staying away from the prevailing diseases in Europe at the time.

    C. Looking for new opportunities.

    D. Fleeing the prisons in Sweden.

16. Listen again to part of the lecture. Then answer the question.

    What can be inferred about people going to Stockholm at the time?

    A. Most were farmers without technical knowledge.

    B. Most were beggars and prostitutes.

    C. Probably people enjoying city lives.

    D. Penniless people who couldn't even afford a ticket.

Questions 17 – 22

Listen to a lecture in a biology class.

17. Listen again to part of the lecture. Then answer the question.

     Why does the professor say doubt-with-the-hole-filled-in shape"?

     A. To illustrate the similarity of two different things.

     B. To describe osmosis.

     C. To show a connection between bod and blood cells.

     D. To illustrate the shape of blood cells.

18. Which of the following does the professor NOT mention in the lecture?

     A. Single cells living in sea water.

     B. Blood cells flooded in sea water.

     C. Single cells living in freshwater lakes.

     D. Blood cells bathed in mineral water.

19. Listen again to part of the lecture. Then answer the question.

     What is probably true about the "lake inhabitants" (single cells living in the lake)?

     A. They usually do not keep a balanced concentration of solutes with the lake water.

     B. They don't have a solute inside the cells at all.

     C. They usually have to pump excess water out of the cells.

     D. They usually have to absorb lake water to sustain life.

20. According to the professor, determine what is/are true or false about the cell membrane?

     True or False

     Selectively permeable.

     Has some gaps.

     Permeable only to water molecules.

     Protect the cell from harmful chemicals.

21. Why is the professor discussing this topic?

     A. He is lecturing about something that the students will see tomorrow.

     B. He is discussing something that the students will be required to read.

     C. He is preparing the students for an exam tomorrow.

     D. He is explaining something that the students have just seen.

22. Listen again to part of the lecture. Then answer the question.

     What does the professor imply about "Paramecia", a single cell inhabitant in a fresh water lake?

     A. Paramecia probably need some organic features to keep them alive from the osmosis effect.

     B. Paramecia can't exist in a freshwater environment.

     C. Paramecia survive the environment because of osmosis.

     D. The osmosis effect is the most prevailing danger for Paramecia.

Questions 23 - 28

Listen to a lecture in a geology class.

23. Listen again to part of the lecture. Then answer the question.

     Why does the professor say this:

A. The predictions might not be valid because there is no way to prove it now.

B. The plates might move in different directions from what the theory has suggested.

C. The predictions will be proved in the future.

D. Scientists don't need predictions because there is a theory to explain why.

24. According to the lecture, where was North America located millions of years ago?

Click on two correct answers

A. To the north of its present location.

B. To the south of its present location.

C. To the west of its present location.

D. To the east of its present location.

25. Listen again to part of the lecture. Then answer the question.

What does the professor mean when she says this:

A. You have to guess.   B. I'll explain it.

C. You must have known it.   D. How silly you are!

26. According to the professor, determine whether the following information is true or false?

True False

Atlantic Ocean will be larger.

Australia will move farther north.

The Pacific Ocean will be larger.

North and South America will move farther west.

27. What is the Pangaea?

A. A prehistoric super-continent.

B. A prehistoric super-ocean.

C. A hypothesized super-continent.

D. The 12 earth plates above the mantle.

28. What conclusion can be drawn about the Continental Drift Theory?

A. It's been confirmed by many observations so its validity is unarguable.

B. The theory has many flaws.

C. It's only a hypothetical theory yet to be further tested.

D. No one can wait for 50 million years to see how valid the theory is.

Questions 29 – 34

Listen to a lecture in a geology class.

29. What is the main idea of the lecture?

A. Damages that a tsunami can cause.

B. Ocean waves resulting from a tsunami.

C. Technical features about a tsunami.

D. General knowledge on the causes and effects of a tsunami.

30. According to the professor, what can be an approximate term for a tsunami?

A. Seismic waves.   B. Tidal waves.

C. Wave trains.   D. Single waves.

31. Why does a tsunami travel thousands of miles without losing much of its energy?

    A. Because of its large wavelength.

    B. Because Of the distance from where the earthquake occurs to the coast.

    C. Because of its speed.

    D. Because of the series of waves a tsunami holds.

32. According to the professor, determine whether the following can cause a tsunami?

    True False.

    A volcanic action in the open sea.

    A landslide along the coastline.

    An inland explosion near the coast.

    A meteorite landing in the ocean.

33. Listen again to part of the lecture. Then answer the question.

    How does the professor seem to feel about the student's answer?

    A. Highly encouraged.

    B. Conditionally accepted.

    C. Mildly irritated.

    D. Openly indifferent.

34. What point does the professor make about the energy of a tsunami?

    A. It's in good proportion to the degree of earthquake that causes the tsunami.

    B. The features of the land beneath the water influence its actual weight.

    C. It does not lose much weight even after the tsunami hits the coast.

    D. It remains powerful although the speed of the wave diminishes.

SPEAKING

Speaking

Section Directions

In this section of the test, you will be able to demonstrate your ability to speak about a variety of topics. You will answer six questions. Answer each of the questions as completely as possible.

In questions 1 and 2, you will speak about familiar topics. You need to demonstrate your ability to speak clearly and coherently about the topics.

In questions 3 and 4, you will first read a short text. You will then listen to a talk on the same topic. You will then be asked a question about what you have read and heard. You will need to combine appropriate information from the text and talk to provide a compete answer to the question. You need to demonstrate your ability to speak clearly and coherently and to accurately convey information about what you read and heard.

In question 5 and 6, you will first listen to part of conversation or a lecture. You will then be asked a question about what you heard. You need to demonstrate your ability to speak clearly and coherently and on your ability to accurately convey information about what you heard.

You may take notes while you read and while you listen to the conversations and lectures. You may use your notes to help you prepare your response.

Listen carefully to the direction for each question. The direction will not be written on the screen.

Question 1

Please Listen Carefully.

Describe a teacher that has had a great influence on you and explain why the teacher was so important to you. Include details and examples to support your explanation.

Preparation Time: 15 seconds

Response Time: 45 seconds

Please begin speaking after the beep.

Question 2

Please Listen Carefully.

Some people think it is a good idea for students to take part-time jobs while in university, while other believe having a job will influence their studies. What is your opinion on this issue? Include details and examples in your explanation.

Preparation Time: 15 seconds

Response Time: 45 seconds

Please begin speaking after the beep.

Question 3

Please Listen Carefully.

Read the announcement about foreign language classes. You have 45 seconds to read the announcement. Begin reading now.

Reading Time: 45 seconds

Announcement from the President

All students enrolled in foreign language classes are now also required to register for a one-credit language lab. In the past, this was only a requirement for students who were recommended by a professor. However, effective on the first day of the second semester, all students attending foreign language classes will be asked to enroll. These laboratory sessions will be taught by a graduate teaching assistant. Students will receive a final grade for the laboratory work that will be kept separate from the final grade of the language classes.

Now listen to two students as they discuss the announcement.

The woman expresses her opinion about the new requirement for students taking foreign language classes. State her opinion and explain the reasons she gives for holding that opinion.

Preparation Time: 30 seconds

Response Time: 60 seconds

Please begin speaking after the beep.

Question 4

Please Listen Carefully.

Now read the passage about health. You have 45 seconds to read the passage. Begin reading now.

Reading Time: 45 seconds

Diabetes (or diabetes mellitus) is a serious disease. It is basically a problem with the pancreas, in which it prevents the body from producing the hormone insulin so that sugars can not be used properly. Sufferers of diabetes can be treated with shots of insulin and/or with a strict diet. According to a current statistics, about seven percent of the American population suffer from diabetes. There are many symptoms of diabetes. These include frequent urination, excessive fatigue, excess thirst, extreme hunger, unusual weight loss, irritability and blurry vision. If these symptoms are detected early enough, the chance of having complications down the road remains low.

Now listen to part of a lecture on this topic in a health class.

The professor poses the question of why so many people with diabetes go undiagnosed.

Explain what is being done to help build awareness of the disease.

Preparation Time: 30 seconds \Response Time: 60 seconds

Please begin speaking after the beep.

Question 5

Please listen carefully.

Describe the woman's problem and the suggestions her classmate gives her. What do you think the woman should do, and why?

Preparation Time: 30 seconds

Response T me: 60 seconds

Please begin speaking after the beep.

Question 6

Please Listen Carefully.

Now listen to part of a talk in an Intercultural Communication class.

Using points and examples from the talk, explain the different stages in culture shock.

Explain why it is important for people to be aware of the different stages.

Preparation Time: 20 seconds

Responsesponse Time: 60 seconds

Please begin speaking after the beep.

WRITING

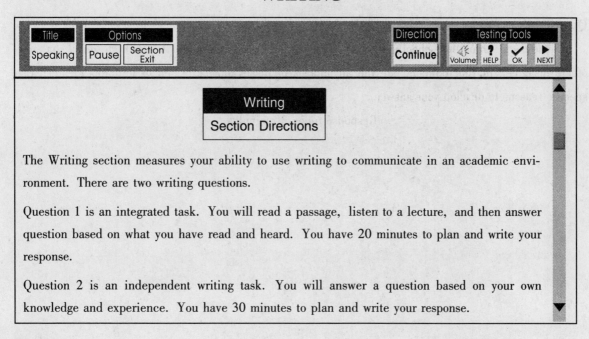

Title	Options		Direction	Testing Tools
Speaking	Pause	Section Exit	Continue	Volume HELP OK NEXT

Writing
Section Directions

The Writing section measures your ability to use writing to communicate in an academic environment. There are two writing questions.

Question 1 is an integrated task. You will read a passage, listen to a lecture, and then answer question based on what you have read and heard. You have 20 minutes to plan and write your response.

Question 2 is an independent writing task. You will answer a question based on your own knowledge and experience. You have 30 minutes to plan and write your response.

Question 1

Read the passage. On a piece of paper, take notes on the main points of the reading passage.

Readng time: 3 minutes.

In the past century, the equality of men and women has grown from a few rebellious voices to an increasingly accepted universal principle. Unlike in times past, where women were often viewed with prejudice as inferior, second-class citizens, today's women have broken free of old dogmas and showcased their abilities in all fields. And the world is a better place for it. Take, for instance, the corporate world: in the past it was dominated with macho thinking boardrooms and a "guys only" mentality. Today, however, women are changing that and making valuable contributions and bringing different perspectives to the table. Some multi-nationals, like HP, have even chosen female CEOs, showing that women are not only capable workers, but also outstanding leaders. In fact, the working dynamic has changed so much, that many companies and governments have actively introduced laws and practices, such as affirmative action and workers' unions, to promote and maintain a more gender-balanced, harmonious, work environment. Nowadays, ask a young girl what she wants to be when she grows up and you might hear: lawyer, businesswoman, architect and anything in between—a far cry from a few decades ago. Today's women are realizing their career dreams. In today's workplace, where the bottom-line is still measured in dollars and cents, there has been a fundamental recognition that a variety of voices and skills is an asset, not a liability. For those who still cling to outdated notions that men can do things better than their female counterparts, the workplace of the 21st century will be a serious wake-upcall.

Listen to part of a lecture on the topic you just read about. Take notes on the main points of the following lecture.

Now answer the following questions:

Summarize the points made in the lecture, being sure to explain how they challenge the arguments made in the reading passage.

Question 2

Some people think that school uniforms can have a positive effect on middle and high school students, others disagree. In your opinion, are the advantages or disadvantages of school uniforms greater? Use specific reasons to develop your answer.

Response time: 30 minutes

Tapescript

录音稿

Chapter Two   Basic Skills Needed for iBT TOEFL

Part 2   Basic Skills Needed for Listening

Section A   Short Conversations

Directions: In this part, you will hear 150 short conversations between two people. After each conversation, you'll hear a question about what has been said. The conversations and the questions will not be repeated. Listen carefully and decide which of the four choices is the best answer to each question you've heard.

1. W: I am amazed you are still driving that old car of yours. I thought you would have gotten rid of it years ago.

   M: It runs well. And I've actually grown quite attached to it.

   Q: What does the man mean?

2. W: Tom has tried so hard to win a race since he first joined the track team. But it's two years later, and he still hasn't.

   M: I know. And it takes so much time from his class work. Maybe he should just forget about sports for now.

   Q: What does the man mean?

3. M: Don't you just love the hot mid-day sun?

   W: I sure do. Unfortunately, it doesn't like my skin.

   Q: What does the woman mean?

4. W: I'm not going swimming in the lake unless it warms up outside today.

   M: Me, either. Unfortunately, I think it is supposed to stay this cold all day.

   Q: What can be inferred about the speakers?

5. M: That sweater is so unusual, and yet it looks familiar. Did I just see you wearing that yesterday?

   W: Well, not me. But it belongs to my roommate, Jane, and she is in your physics class.

   Q: What does the woman imply?

6. M: You know my car hasn't been the same since I had bumped into that telephone poll.

   W: You'd better have that looked into before you drive to Florida.

   Q: What does the woman mean?

7. M: I notice that you don't buy your lunch in the cafeteria any more.

W: When prices went up I decided to bring my own.

Q: Why doesn't the woman buy food in the cafeteria?

8. M: If I don't find my wallet pretty soon, I'm going to have to report it stolen.

W: Hold on. Before you call campus security office, have you checked your car or your jacket pocket, everywhere?

Q: What does the woman suggest the man do?

9. W: I've been calling David for the past half hour, but I keep getting a busy signal.

W: Well, if you don't get him soon we'll just have to go to the movies without him.

Q: Why are the women trying to call David?

10. M: Are you ready to go jogging?

W: Almost. I have to warm up first.

Q: What does the woman mean?

11. M: You did an excellent job on that presentation.

W: Thanks. I put a lot of time into it.

Q: What does the woman mean?

12. M: Got the time?

W: It's a little after ten.

Q: What does the woman mean?

13. W: Excuse me, could you bring me a glass of water, please?

M: Sorry, but I am not a waiter.

Q: What does the man mean?

14. W: My cousin Bob is getting married in California and I can't decide whether to go.

M: It's a long trip but I think You will have a good time.

Q: What does the man imply?

15. W: Thanks a lot, this scarf will be perfect with my blue jacket.

M: Made a good choice, did I?

Q: What does the man mean?

16. M: I think I'll add that information to my paper.

W: You really should check it out in your reference book.

Q: What does the woman imply?

17. W: Do you know when Thomas was born?

M: Don't ask me. I'm not good with dates.

Q: What does the man mean?

18. M: The forecast is for a severe winter. Are you prepared?

W: Hardly. I'm waiting for the next sale to get a down jacket.

Q: What does the woman imply?

19. M: How long has it been since you saw Becky?

W: I bumped into her at the market just last week.

Q: What does the woman mean?

20. M: Pam says she likes art museums.

    W: But she doesn't often visit them, does she?

    Q: What does the woman imply about Pam?

21. M: Why did you come to the meeting late? I left a message with your roommate about the time change.

    W: She has a very short memory and it really gets on my nerves sometimes.

    Q: What does the woman imply?

22. M: You know, every time I talk to Mary I get the feeling she's been critical of me.

    W: Don't you think you are overreacting a bit?

    Q: What does the woman mean?

23. W: Would you like to come to Janet's surprise party tomorrow night?

    M: I'm going to a concert tomorrow. I wish I could be in two places at once.

    Q: What does the man mean?

24. W: There is a great antique show at the grand auditorium. Let's go see it this evening.

    M: I have worked really hard all day long. Won't it be there for a while.

    Q: What does the man imply?

25. M: Bill has only been on the job a week and already he's acting like he is the boss.

    W: He's not going to last long with that attitude.

    Q: What does the woman imply?

26. M: Did you pick up your letter at the post office?

    W: No. I got my roommate to do it.

    Q: What happened to the letter?

27. W: Debra says she is going to stay up all night studying for her exam tomorrow morning.

    M: Wouldn't she be better off getting a good night sleep, so she'll feel fresh in the morning?

    Q: What does the man imply?

28. M: Your little nephew is growing by leaps and bounds.

    W: Yes. He must be at least three feet tall already.

    Q: What do the speakers say about the woman's nephew?

29. W: That's a nice computer you have.

    M: Now all I have to do is figure out how to use it.

    Q: What does the man imply?

30. W: You know the noise in my dorm has really gotten out of control. My roommate and I can rarely get to sleep before midnight.

    M: Why don't you take the problem up with the dorm supervisor?

    Q: What does the man suggest the woman?

31. M: This machine has so many buttons. I can't figure out which one makes it run.

    W: You'd better read the instructions first. Pressing the buttons randomly may cause the machine to break down.

Q: According to the woman, what should the man do first?

32. M: Has today's mail arrived? I'm anxious to know about the result of my application.

W: I've checked the mail-box. There is nothing in it, but a postcard from our daughter.

Q: What do we learn from this conversation?

33. W: Was Robert elected to the committee?

M: Yes, in fact he was made chairman. But he only agreed to take the job if they let him have the final say.

Q: What does Robert intend to do?

34. W: Could you help me, sir? My flight got in fifteen minutes ago. Everyone else has picked up-their luggage, but mine hasn't come through.

M: I'm sorry, Madam. But I'll go and find out if there is any more to come.

Q: What's the woman's problem?

35. M: Could you give me your office phone number or fax number, so that we can contact each other more often?

W: But I've been trying to find a new job in another company. You see, I've worked here for three years without a raise. That's unfair to me.

Q: What does the woman mean?

36. M: These watches are outrageously expensive.

W: You think they are bad? You should see the ones in the jewelry store.

Q: What does the woman imply?

37. W: What we need is a roommate who is neat and considerate.

W: That's right. Let's write that in the ad neatness and consideration a must.

Q: What do the speakers hope to do?

38. W: I'm bored with the same food all the time. Let's try something different Saturday night.

M: How about an Italian Place?

Q: What does the man suggest they do?

39. W: I found a perfect book bag but I'm about 20 dollars short.

M: Don't look at me. I don't get paid for another week.

Q: What does the man imply?

40. M: Here are two seats.

W: Don't you think these are too close to the movie screen?

Q: What does the Woman imply they should do?

41. M: Is Louis going to join us for a short break?

W: Yes, if she can tear herself away from her studies.

Q: What does the woman imply about Louis?

42. M: Hi, Ann. Where are you rushing off to?

W: I'm on my way to pick up the text for American history. I'm in shock. It's going to be 65 bucks.

Q: What does the Woman mean?

43. W: I'm way behind in my letter writing. I've got to get started.

M: Who's got time to write letters? Exams are coming up, remember?

Q: What does the man imply the woman should do?

44. W: John, I'm sorry. But I forgot to bring your tape player back.

M: Well, as long as I get it by Friday.

Q: What does the man mean?

45. W: I just saw an ad on television that said men's suits were on sale today and tomorrow at Conrad's men's

ware.

M: Great! That's just what I've been waiting for.

Q: What will the man probably do?

46. W: Do you want to go on a trip with us to Florida this spring ? It will cost about 300 dollars a person.

M: Three hundred dollars? Do you think I just inherited a fortune?

Q: What can be inferred about the man?

47. W: My watch stopped again, and I just got a new battery.

M: Why don't you take it to Smith's Jewelry? They can check it for you. And they are pretty reasonable.

Q: What does the man mean?

48. W: We're going to change our meeting from Monday to Tuesday.

M: It's all the same to me.

Q: What does the man mean?

49. M: We planned to go to the beach after class. Want to come?

W: I'd love to. But Professor Jones wants to speak with me.

Q: What will the woman probably do?

50. W: Janet sounds worried about her grades.

M: But she's getting As and Bs, isn't she?

Q: What does the man imply about Janet?

51. M: I'm really having trouble with this calculus course. If I can start soon, I'm going to have to drop it.

W: Why don't you get some help from the graduate assistant? That's what he is there for.

Q: What does the woman suggest the man do?

52. W: Hey, don't forget to drop that book at the library on your way home.

M: Oh, thanks for reminding me. I'm on my way.

Q: What will the man probably do next?

53. W: I sure wish I had a metric meter with me. I need the measurements in millimeters not in inches,

and I'm tired of converting.

M: Would it make things go faster if you borrowed mine?

Q: What does the man imply?

54. M: Good news. I'm not going to need surgery after all. The doctor says I can start working out again

soon, and maybe play soccer again in a few weeks.

W: That's terrific. It would be great if you could get back in shape in time for the tournament.

Q: What does the woman mean?

55. M: I already know what I want to take next semester, so why do I have to make an appointment to see

my advisor? All I need is a signature on my call sheet. I'm afraid it doesn't work that way. She has to talk with you to make sure everything's on the right track.

Q: What does the woman mean?

56. W: Prof. Smith sure was acting strangely today.

M: I noticed that, too. She was talking so quietly and then not giving us any homework. Can you believe that?

Q: What can be inferred about Prof. Smith?

57. M: It's been pouring for three days now. I begin to wonder if it'll ever stop.

W: And tomorrow was gonna be my day at the beach. But if it doesn't clear up by then, I'll just have to forget about that.

Q: What does the woman imply?

58. M: What a boring speaker! I could hardly keep from falling asleep.

W: Oh, I don't know about that. In fact, it's been a long time since I've heard anyone as good.

Q: What does the woman mean?

59. W: Gee, Tom, I hear you are working as a house painter this summer. It's got to be awfully hard working up there on a ladder in the blazing sun all day.

M: Well, it's hard, but I get to be outdoors and the pay is decent.

Q: What does the man imply?

60. W: I've been working on this report all day and I've still got twelve papers to write. At this rate, I'll never get it done by tomorrow.

M: Oh, that's right. You weren't in class today, so you probably haven't heard the deadline has been extended a week.

Q: What does the man imply?

61. W: You look great since you've been taking those exercises classes.

M: Thanks. I've never felt better in my life.

Q: What does the man imply?

62. M: I had a hard time getting through this novel.

W: I know how you feel. Who can remember the names of 35 different characters?

Q: What does the woman imply?

63. M: That's a long line. Do you think there'll be any tickets left?

W: I doubt it. Guess we'll wind up going to the second show.

Q: What does the woman mean?

64. W: This course is much too hard for me.

M: Sorry you decided to take it, huh?

Q: What does the man ask the woman?

65. M: Are you going home for winter vacation?

W: I've agreed to stay on here as a research assistant.

Q: What can be inferred about the woman?

66. M: Can you believe the way Larry was talking to his roommate? No won der they don't get along.

W: Well, maybe Larry was just reacting to something his roommate said. There're two sides in every story, you know.

Q: What does the woman mean?

67. M: I just called the travel agent, it's all set. On June 1st I'm heading for the mountains for an entire week.

W: Have you checked the academic calendar? Because my classes aren't over till the 7th.

Q: What does the woman imply?

68. M: What sort of grade did you get on your research paper? I know how hard you worked on it.

W: Yeah. Well, I was hoping for something really good. But the professor said I made too many broad claims that weren't supported enough.

Q: What can be inferred about the woman's paper?

69. W: The state ballet's coming to town next weekend, and I can't find a ticket anywhere.

M: You know my sister just happens to have one and she can't go. She's got some sort of conflicts in her schedule.

Q: What does the man imply the woman should do?

70. M: Have you found out yet what hotel you'll be staying in? I'm at the Gordon, right across the street from the conference center.

W: Oh, lucky you. I'm at the Apple Gate, 6 miles away.

Q: What does the woman mean?

71. W: Joe, I thought your article on the school newspaper was right on target. You certainly convince me, anyway.

M: Thanks, Mary. Unfortunately, based on the general response, you and I are definitely in the minority.

Q: What does the man mean?

72. W: Why didn't you go to the hockey finals last weekend? You missed a great game.

M: Oh, come on. You know how sensitive I am to loud noise.

Q: What can be inferred about the man?

73. W: I know I promised to drive you to the airport next Tuesday, but I'm afraid something has come up. They've called a special meeting at work.

M: No big deal. Karen said she was available as the backup.

Q: What does the man mean?

74. M: My telephone doesn't seem to be working, and I have lots of calls I have to return this afternoon.

W: Feel free to use mine if you want. I'll be in a meeting till five.

Q: What does the woman suggest the man do?

75. M: I don't think we have nearly enough information for our financial plan. But it's still tomorrow. So I guess there's not a lot we can do about it.

W: Guess not. At this point, we'll just have to make do with what we've got.

Q: What will the speakers probably do?

76. M: Did you know that Arthur has three brothers living on three different continents?

W: He must get an incredible phone bill every month.

Q: What does the woman imply about Arthur?

77. M: This calculator isn't working right.

    W: I think you've got the battery in upside down.

    Q: What does the woman mean?

78. W: We should buy a good guide book and study it before our trip to Montreal.

    M: We should. But they are so overpriced. What about the library?

    Q: What does the man imply?

79. W: I always want a little something to eat about this time of day.

    M: So do I. Let's have a snack now and then have a light lunch later.

    Q: What are the speakers discussing? Being hungry.

80. M: I've just been over to my friend Tom's new apartment. It's much bigger than my place. . .

    W: But more expensive I bet.

    Q: What does the woman mean?

81. M: Prof. Parker, maybe you'd better find another actor to play this role. The lines are! so long, sometimes I just completely forgot them.

    W: Look, Mike. It's still a long time before the first show and I don't expect you to know all the lines yet. Just keep practicing and I'm sure you'll get them.

    Q: What does the woman suggest the man do?

82. M: Come on, Kate. The sun is shining, the flowers are blooming, maybe you're missing the point of life.

    W: Maybe you're missing the point of this chemistry study group.

    Q: What does the woman mean?

83. W: Could you give me a ride to the engineering building?

    M: I would, but I'm late for an appointment on the other side of town.

    Q: What does the man mean?

84. W: Excuse me, Professor. Since class is cancelled on Thursday, when are we going have the quiz?

    M: It will be postponed until next week's class.

    Q: What does the man mean?

85. W: I can't believe I still have this pain in my back. This medicine the doctor gave me was supposed to make me feel better by now.

    M: Maybe you should start taking it three times a day, like you were told.

    Q: What does the man suggest the woman do?

86. M: I'm not sure what I'm in the mood for. Pizza and hamburger, they're both really good here.

    W: Oh, the movie starts in an hour, and we still have to go there and park, so just make a decision.

    Q: What does the woman suggest the man do?

87. M: The basketball team is in the playoffs and I don't have a ticket, I guess I'll just watch it on TV. Do you want to come over?

W: Actually, I have a ticket, but I'm not feeling well. You can have it for what it cost me.

Q: What does the woman mean?

88. M: Don't you ever go home? Every time I see you, you're here in the library, ponder over your books.

W: What do you mean? I thought this was home.

Q: What can be inferred about the woman?

89. M: Doctor, I haven't been able to get to sleep lately and I'm too tired to concentrate during classes.

W: Well, you know, spending too much time indoors with all that artificial lighting can make you ill. Your body loses track of whether it's day or night.

Q: What does the doctor imply the man should do?

90. M: I'm having trouble drawing the model's right arm. It's supposed to look like he pointing at me;

W: To get the perspective you want, you need to use what we call "foreshortening". Here, give me your pencil.

Q: What will the woman probably do next?

91. W: Could you mail these letters for me, please?

M: More letters? Your friends are going to be very happy to hear from you.

Q: What does the man imply about the woman?

92. W: Does Professor Ford always come to class?

M: Is ice cold?

Q: What does the man imply about Professor Ford?

93. W: Would you have some time this week to go over these questions with me?

M: How does tomorrow sound?

Q: What does the man mean?

94. M: Hey? John! John!

W: Save your breath. He's out of earshot.

Q: What does the woman mean?

95. W: You only have water to serve your guests?

M: This isn't just water. This is imported mineral water.

Q: What does the woman imply?

96. M: Could I borrow a twenty to tide me over till payday next Tuesday?

W: You are in luck. I just cashed the check.

Q: What will the woman probably do next?

97. M: Jean, didn't you get my messages? I left two on your answering machine.

W: Hmm? Oh, sorry, Tom. I've been meaning to get back in touch with you. It just slipped my mind.

Q: What does the woman mean?

98. W: I'm sorry, sir, but you're allowed only one piece of luggage on the plane. You'll have to check in one of your suitcases at the package center.

M: Actually, one of these belongs to the woman up ahead. I'm just giving her a hand.

Q: What does the man mean?

99. W: We need to drive to the city tonight, but the doctor said this medicine might make me drowsy.

M:In that case, I'd better drive.

Q:What does the man think the woman should do?

100. M:Look at all the pollution going into the air from those factories. Do you think they'll ever get under control?

   W:With the new laws and social awareness, we'll turn things around.

   Q:What does the woman predict will happen?

101. W:Aren't you cold? Why aren't you wearing a jacket?

   M:I overslept this morning, so I ran out of the house without listening to the forecast.

   Q:What does the man mean?

102. M: Prof. Jones, last night when I was putting the finishing touches on my paper that electric storm completely wiped out my computer files. Do you think I could have another day to retype it?

   W:I'm sorry, Steven. I'm leaving for a conference tomorrow, and I'll be away 2 weeks. I suppose you could send it to me there.

   Q:What will the professor probably allow the student to do?

103. W:Do you know if Mary has come by the office this morning?

   M:I just got here myself, so I'm not the one to ask.

   Q:What does the man mean?

104. M:I really enjoyed that TV special about "wealth" last night. Did you get to home in time to see it?

   W:Well, yes. But I wish I could have stayed awake long enough to see the whole thing.

   Q:What does the woman mean.

105. W:Take two of these pills three times a day and you shouldn't take them on an empty stomach.

   M: What if I don't have an appetite?

   Q: What does the man imply?

106. W:I want to play tennis tomorrow, but I didn't bring my racket with me this weekend. Do you have one I could borrow?

   M:I do. But it has a broken string.

   Q:What does the man imply?

107. M:I thought this shirt was a great deal. But I washed it once and it's shrunk so much that I can't wear it.

   W:Some bargain. You should ask for a refund.

   Q:What does the woman mean?

108. M:I broke my ankle last Tuesday. And now I have to be on crutches for six weeks.

   W:I'm sorry to hear that. Is there anything I can do for you?

   Q:What does the woman mean?

109. W:Why didn't you call me last night like you were supposed to?

   M:I did. Your line was busy.

   Q:What does the man mean?

110. M:Sue, would you like a sandwich or something?

W:Oh, please don't bother. I can get something later.

Q:What does the woman mean?

111. M:This looks like the way to Susan's house, but I don't know. I wish I'd written down the directions.

W:At this rate, we'll be lucky to get there in time for dessert.

Q:What does the woman imply?

112. W:So, did you pick up that orange juice for me like you said you would?

M:I meant to, but I was short on cash. I'll be going back later, though, after I stop by the bank, if you can wait that long.

Q:What does the man imply he will do?

113. M:That's a great dress, Cindy. I don't think I've ever seen you wear it before.

W:Oh, I haven't. It's just been at the back of my closet. My sister gave it to me like ages ago and I had totally forgotten about it.

Q:What does the woman imply?

114. W:Just look at this apartment, Karen. What a mess! Your stuff is all over. How I wish your roommate put up with it.

W: I know. I haven't been doing my share this week, but I have three reports due on Friday and I haven't even started one of them.

Q:What can be inferred about Karen?

115. W:I wish we had better stuff to read for our literature class. That novel she assigned us is so boring.

M:Really? I started it yesterday afternoon and I couldn't put it down until I finished it.

Q:What does the man mean?

116. W:Wow. You seem to be in a really good mood today. What's the secret?

M:Don't know. I guess some mornings you wake up feeling great, some mornings you don't.

Q:What does the man mean?

117. W:If you're planning to take the train when you leave next Friday, remember that I drive right past the station on my way home from campus.

M:Say, I think I'll take you up on that.

Q:What will the man probably do next Friday?

118. M:I need to ask John about the Chemistry assignment for tomorrow, but his phone has been busy for the last hour and a half. Who could he be talking to for so long?

W: It may not be him, you know. It could be one of his housemates. Why don't you just get down over there if it's important?

Q:What does the woman suggest the man do?

119. W:Jim, I don't know if you know this, but I've decided to run for class president, and I was wondering if I could count on your vote.

M:Oh. Maybe if you'd asked me sooner but my roommate is running too, and I've already promised him my support.

Q:What does the man mean?

120. M:I might argue with some of the details, but I basically agree with this author's thesis about manag-

ing the economy.

　　W：Sure, it sounds great in theory. My concern is whether it applies in practice.

　　Q：What does the woman mean?

121. M：I'd like to try to sell some of my textbooks from last semester.

　　W：You and a few hundred other people.

　　Q：What does the woman imply?

122. M：Could I talk to you for a minute about the discrepancy I found in this graph?

　　W：I'm kind of in the middle of things right now.

　　Q：What does the woman mean?

123. W：Do you know if George is coming to the meeting?

　　M：Oh, no. I was supposed to tell you that he's sick and can't come.

　　Q：What does the man mean?

124. W：Dick, please don't tie up the phone. I need to make a call.

　　M：I'll be off in a minute.

　　Q：What will the man do?

125. M：Sally says we should meet her in the park at noon.

　　M：I thought we were meeting at the library.

　　Q：What do the speakers disagree about?

126. M：I'm coming about the job you advertised in the paper.

　　W：You need one of those forms over there. On the table next to the file cabinet.

　　Q：What does the woman imply the man should do?

127. M：I know I ought to call home, but I've got a plane to catch, and I'm already late.

　　W：Well, I know you have to hurry, but it'll only take a minute.

　　Q：What does the woman suggest the man do?

128. W：I have to drive into Chicago next week. Do you have a map I could borrow?

　　M：Sorry, I don't, but I can pick one up for you at the bookstore.

　　Q：What does the man mean?

129. W：What did you think of the paintings showed last week?

　　M：I never made it to the exhibit.

　　Q：What does the man mean?

130. M：Did you hear about the big snowstorm in Iowa yesterday? Three feet in 12 hours.

　　W：Yeah, and I hear it's heading our way. We're supposed to get the same thing tonight.

　　Q：What does the woman mean?

131. M：You're joining us for dinner tonight, aren't you?

　　W：Oh, I'm really sorry, but I have the wrong day for my geometry test. I just found out it's tomorrow, and I need all the time I can get to prepare.

　　Q：What does the woman imply?

132. W：I can't decide whether I should take physics now or wait till next semester.

　　M：You might as well get it over with if you can.

Q: What does the man suggest the woman do?

133. W: You look different today. Did you get a haircut?

    M: It's funny. You're the third person to ask me that. But all I did was get new eyeglass frames.

    Q: What does the man imply?

134. W: Dr. Eliot, I'd like you to check the way you calculated my grade for this test. I think you may
    have made a mistake in adding up the number of questions I got right. When I added them up,
    I came up with a slightly higher grade than you did.

    M: I'll be happy to check it for you, and if I made a mistake in determining the grade, I'll be sure to
    correct it. Don't worry.

    Q: What does the man imply?

135. M: That last speaker was pretty boring, but he did make a few good points at the end.

    W: Really? I didn't catch them. I must have dozed off for a minute.

    Q: What does the woman mean?

136. W: I'm sort of upset with my brother. He hasn't answered either of my letters.

    M: Well, just remember how hectic your freshman year was. Give him a chance to get settled.

    Q: What does the man imply?

137. W: I wonder what this new flavor of ice cream tastes like?

    M: I tried it last week. If I were you, I would stick with an old favorite.

    Q: What can be inferred from the conversation?

138. M: Peter had hoped to have his apartment painted by this time.

    W: But he hasn't even started yet, has he?

    Q: What does the woman imply about Peter?

139. W: You don't believe in diets, do you?

    M: There is nothing wrong with them perse but they have to be combined with exercise to do any good.

    Q: What does the man mean?

140. W: I'm amazed that you still haven't gotten to know your neighbors.

    M: They tend to keep to themselves.

    Q: What does the man mean?

141. W: How did your job interview go?

    M: I don't think I came across as well as I could have.

    Q: What does the man mean?

142. W: Care for any of these cookies? My roommate made them.

    M: Don't mind if I do.

    Q: What will the man probably do?

143. W: Oh, my. You still don't look too good. Didn't you take the pain-reliever I gave you?

    M: Yeah, an hour ago, guess I've got a headache that just won't quit.

    Q: What does the man mean?

144. M: Oh, you must be sad when your best friend is taking a job in Texas. It's so far away.

    W: Yeah. I'm rally gonna miss her, but at least I have a good reason to visit a new part of the country now.

Q: What does the woman imply?

145. M: My fingers are sticky from that candy bar. Do you mind if I use the rest room to wash up befor we leave?

   W: Sure, I'll be over at the bus-stop.

   Q: What will the speakers probably do next?

146. W: This strap on my briefcase is broken. Do you think you could replace it, say by next Tuesday?

   M: Let's see. Oh, sure, that won't be a problem. It won't even take that long.

   Q: What does the man mean?

147. M: So my advisor wants me to take the creative writing class that meets on Wednesday instead of the Monday class, because the instructor on the Wednesday class is supposed to be great. But that means I have to spend a whole day on campus, every Wednesday.

   W: Well, but ... especially in creative writing, the instructor can make a big difference in how much you get out of the class.

   Q: What does the woman imply the man should do?

148. W: Have you finalized of your plans for spring break yet?

   M: Well, I could visit some friends in Florida, or go to my roommate's home. It's a tough choice.

   Q: What does the man mean?

149. W: This is such a great time to buy winter clothes, so many stores are having sales now and the price reductions are pretty substantial.

   M: Yes. It's just what I have been waiting for. There are so many things I need.

   Q: What does the man imply?

150. M: Where have you been? I was just about to give up on you.

   W: Sorry, my bus was delayed, but I'm glad you were patient. It would be hard for us to find another time to meet this week.

   Q: What does the woman mean?

Section B   Longer Conversations and Lectures

Directions: In this part, you are going to hear some lectures and longer conversations. Each lecture or conversation is followed by some questions. Below each question, there are four options marked A, B, C, and D. Listen carefully and choose the best answer to each question.

Lecture 1

More than one million students from all over the world have once studied in the United States since 1945. In a recent single year, there were more than 150 thousand foreign students who came to the United States' institutions of higher learning. They were welcomed and most were successful in their academic studies. Foreign students who study in the United States benefit a lot from the educational system of the United States.

Three developments in the United States higher education that the students are benefiting from today started more than a century ago following the Civil War. The first of these was the rapid growth of the technological and professional education to meet the urgent demands of a complex industrial and urban society. New schools of technology, engineering, architecture, law and medicine flourished. The second was the provision for graduate study, such as what had long existed in France and Germany. Harvard and John Hopkins Universities quickly took the lead in this field, but the state universities did not lag far behind. The third was the increased provision for the education of women. This included the establishment of new women's colleges, such as Vassar, Wellesley and Smith, and the adoption of co-education in all the new state universities outside the South as well as in many private institutions. These developments, the growth of the technological and professional education, the provision for graduate study, and the increased educational opportunities for women began over a century ago, well over thirteen decades since the end of the Civil War.

Lecture 2

Finding the right place to live can help guarantee a most rewarding experience in the United States for international students. Depending on your situation, whether you are here alone or with a family, the duration of your stay, the amount of privacy you would like, anything from living on campus in a residence hall to private accommodation in a motel could suit your needs. As an ESL student, your housing may or may not be included in the study program. The basic choice to make is whether to live on or off campus. There are advantages and disadvantages to both.

The advantages for living on campus are as follows: you will have furnished rooms, easy access to campus facilities such as libraries, computer labs, sports facilities and cafeterias, access to social activities and peers, and maximum interaction with other students. Eating on campus is usually cheaper, and you don't have to worry about transportation to and from classes. There are also some disadvantages. You may be sharing a bedroom with other students, so you will not have much privacy. You must be flexible in living with others.

The advantages for living off campus are as follows: you will have privacy, more real-world experiences, your own bathroom and kitchen facilities, and furnished rooms. It is possible to have visitors at any time and suitable for students with their families. However, there are some disadvantages. The rooms are not always furnished. Unless you are living with a host family, there is a lack of spontaneous social activities with people and transportation is inconvenient. You may waste some time in transit to and from classes.

Lecture 3

Welcome to Yellowstone National Park. Before we begin our nature walk today, I'd like to give you a short history of our National Park Service. The National Park Lesson Twelve Environmental Protection Service began in the late 1800's. A small group of explorers had just completed a month long exploration of the region that is now Yellowstone. They gathered around the campfire and after hours of discussion, they decided that they should not claim this land for themselves. They felt it should be accessible to everyone. So they began a campaign to preserve this land for everyone's enjoyment. Two years later, in the late 19th Century, an act of congress signed by President Ulysses S. Grant proclaimed.

Yellowstone region a public park. It was the first national park in the world. After Yellowstone became a public park, many other areas of great scenic importance were set aside. And in 1916 the National Park Service was established to manage these parks. Today, there are more than 360 parks in the US

National Park System and more than 3,600 areas under similar protection around the globe. National parks and other public lands shelter well over half of the plant and animal species in North America. And today more than 80 countries have also established several hundred similar reserves specifically to protect biological diversity. As a park ranger, I'am an employee of the National Park Service. In the national park, park rangers are on duty at all times to answer questions and help visitors in any difficulty. Nature walks, guided tours and campfire talks are offered by specially trained staff members. The Park Service also protects the animals and plants within the parks.

Lecture 4

Up to now in this course on American authors, we have studied American novelists, but next class we'll move on to short story writers. We'll begin with the man who is probably the most famous American short story writer of all, edgar Allan Poe. To truly understand an author, it is important to have knowledge in advance of his life and times and how they affected his works. In Poe's case, we'll see that the major tragedy in his life, particularly, the untimely death of his wife after a long illness, exerted a major influence on his work. In addition to studying Poe's life and times, we'll read several of his short stories, including the "Fall of the House of Usher", and the "Masqure of the Red Death" and write a short analysis of one of the stories. Poe is best for his symbolism, his impressionist style and his ability to create and maintain an errie tone. And those two short stories are excellent examples of his style. For the next class, you should read the "Fall of the House of Usher' thoroughly", and be prepared for a discussion.

Lecture 5

Each year, millions of people around the world apply to study at American colleges or universities. The most widely used college admissions test is called the SAT. More than 3,000,000 of the tests were given in 2001.

The SAT was first used for college admissions in 1926. Its purpose was to help college officials identify which students would be successful in college. Critics say the test has not always done this. Research suggests that students from rich families do better on the SAT than students whose parents are poor. For example, many rich students are able to improve their scores on the test after taking costly preparation classes.

Critics also say many African-American and Hispanic teenagers score lower on the test than students of other ethnic groups.

The College Board is a non-profit higher education association that owns the SAT. It recently announced major changes in the test. It says the new SAT will better test a student's reasoning and thinking skills. Education experts say the new test will show how well students have learned material taught in high school.

The first change will end analogy questions on the SAT. Analogies are words with meanings that are linked. Critics have said that such' questions show only a knowledge of words, not reasoning skills. The analogy questions will be replaced with questions that better show the student's reading ability. The second major change will add higher level mathematics questions. The final change will add a writing test. Students will have about thirty minutes to write about their reactions to a question or statement.

In 2001, the president of the University of California, Richard Atkinson, called on his school to stop using the SAT as an entrance requirement. He said the skills it tests are not taught in high school. He said the results of the test do not show if students are prepared to attend college.

College Board officials say those comments caused them to move quickly to change the test. However, they say they had been discussing such changes for some time. They say students will begin taking the new SAT in March, 2005. It will affect students planning to enter college in the fall of 2006.

Lecture 6

There are many different kinds of taxes paid in the US. The most common tax is sales tax. When someone buys something, he pays the price of his purchase plus a small additional percentage. This percentage is the sales tax. The revenue from the sales tax goes to the state government to help pay for public schools, public safety, roads, parks and benefits for the poor. Each state sets its own tax percentage. Some states are considerably lower than others. In some states there is no sales tax.

A second type of tax is income tax. This tax is a percentage of all the money earned by a family each year. Americans pay income taxes to the federal government which uses the revenue for national expenses such as defense, help for the needy and other public services. Some states also have a state income tax. Income tax, like other taxes, is usually graduated. This means the tax percentage increases as a family's income increases.

A third kind of tax is property tax. This tax is paid by anyone who owns land or a house. The amount of the tax is based on the property's value. The revenue from this tax goes to the local governments for schools and community services. In addition people must pay luxury tax when they purchase certain things such as cigarettes and alcoholic beverages.

A fifth kind of tax is inheritance tax. When someone dies, usually his family inherits the dead person's wealth and property. However, those who inherit must pay a percentage of this wealth to the government as an inheritance tax.

As we have heard, there are five kinds of taxes that Americans pay. Most Americans don't want any more taxes.

Lecture 7

The United States is rich in most of the metals and minerals needed to supply its basic industries. The nation produces more than 75 million tons of iron a year in its steel mills.

Steel is vital to the manufacture of some 200,000 other products. Three-quarters of the iron ore comes from the Lake Superior region of the Great Lakes. Although much of the high-grade ore has been used, there remains enough low-grade ore to last for centuries. Industry already has developed practical methods for getting iron from taconite a hard, ore-bearing rock found in virtually unlimited quantities in the Lake Superior region.

Coal is the second major natural resources found in large quantities in the United States.

There are sufficient reserves to last hundreds of years. Most of the coal is used by steam plants to produce electricity, with about half of the nation's electric power coming from such plants. Much coal also is used in chemical industries for the manufacture of plastics and other synthetics.

Oil wells in the United States produce more than 2,700 million barrels of petroleum a year. The production, processing and marketing of such petroleum products as gasoline and oil make up one of

America's largest industries. The Alaska pipeline, completed in 1977, stretches for 1,290 kilometers and pipes 1.2 million barrels of petroleum a day from the northern oil fields to a port on the state's south coast. Natural gas and manufactured gas furnish more than one-third of the nation's power. Natural gas is carried by huge pipeline thousands of kilometers from oil and gas fields to heat homes and buildings and to operate industrial plants.

Other basic metals and minerals mined on a large scale in the United States include zinc, copper, silver and phosphate rock which is used for fertilizers.

Lecture 8

A hutong is an ancient city alley typical of Beijing. Surrounding the Forbidden City, many were built during the Yuan, Ming and Qing dynasties. In the prime of these dynasties the emperors, in order to establish supreme power for themselves, planned the city and arranged the residential areas according to the etiquette systems of the Zhou Dynasty. The center of the city of Beijing was the royal palace—the Forbidden City. One kind of hutong, usually referred to as the regular hutong, was near the palace to the east and west and arranged in orderly fashion along the streets. Most of the residents of these hutongs were imperial kinsmen and aristocrats. Another kind, the simple and crude hutong, was mostly located far to the north and south of the palace.

The main buildings in the hutong were almost all quadrangles—a building complex formed by four houses around a quadrangular courtyard. The quadrangles varied in size and design according to the social status of the residents. The big quadrangles of high-ranking officials and wealthy merchants were specially built with roof beams and pillars all beautifully carved and painted, each with a front yard and back yard. However, the ordinary people's quadrangles were simply built with small gates and low houses. Hutongs, in fact, are passageways formed by many closely arranged quadrangles of different sizes. The specially built quadrangles all face south for better lighting; as a result, a lot of hutongs run from east to west. Between the big hutongs many small ones go north and south for convenient passage.

In recent years, the houses in many hutongs have been pulled down and replaced by modern buildings. Many hutong dwellers have moved to new housing. In the urban district of Beijing today, houses along hutongs still occupy one third of the total area. The hutong today is fading into the shade for both tourists and inhabitants.

Lecture 9

The Federal Bureau of Investigation is the main investigating agency of the United States Department of Justice. The Justice Department recently announced new measures to help the FBI fight terrorism. For many years, FBI agents investigated threats to national security. Now, however, FBI Director Robert S. Mueller has told Congress that the Bureau's main responsibility must be to protect the United States from terrorist attacks.

The Justice Department recently announced a major reorganization of the FBI. The size of the agency will be increased. FBI agents also will have new powers to invest igate inside the United States. Most of the reforms are to improve the FBI's ability to gather and study intelligence information about terrorists planning attacks on the United States.

The changes are in reaction to recent criticism of the FBI. Many people have questioned its actions in relation to the terrorist attacks on the United States on September llth, 2001.

The FBI plans to hire 900 more agents. They include people skilled in computer technology, science and languages. They will join about 11,500 other FBI agents. A central Office of Intelligence will be established in the FBI's Washington headquarters. The FBI has already appointed a number of officials to intelligence positions.

FBI Director Mueller and Justice Department officials say the new rules will greatly improve FBI performance. For example, commanders at agency offices will now be able to order investigations that are limited in time. In the past, they needed permission from FBI headquarters to do this. The commanders can also start limited investigations when no crime has taken place. Evidence gathered during this time could help launch extended investigations.

In addition, agents will be able to gather information about religious and political organizations from the internet computer system and from libraries. And agents will be able to observe activities in public places, including religious centers.

Some civil rights groups, however, say the new rules interfere with traditional American rights. They say privacy and free speech might be threatened. Critics of the new rules say the FBI might investigate political dissenters without any evidence of wrongdoing. Many American Muslims say they fear the possibility of FBI agents targeting them unfairly.

Lecture 10

Tree experts have begun an effort to rebuild forests near the home of America's first president, George Washington. Earlier this month, workers gathered buds from tall, old trees on the grounds of George Washington's home, Mount Vernon. It is in the state of Virginia, near Washington, D. C. The experts hope to produce genetic copies, or clones, of the trees and plant them on the property.

Tree experts David Milarch and his son, Jared, are leading the efforts. As a special project, David and Jared Milarch offered to make clones of the thirteen oldest trees at Mount Vernon. They are huge, beautiful trees. George Washington supervised the planting of these trees more than two hundred years ago.

The Milarch family plans to grow fifty copies of each tree in tree nurseries in Alabama and Oregon. They will return the trees to be planted at Mount Vernon in two years. Some copies of the trees will be sent to the Arnold Arboretum at Harvard University in Cambridge, Massachusetts for safe keeping.

Grafting is the name of the process used to clone trees. It has been done for thousands of years. A method called the T-bud technique often is used to copy trees. Workers begin by cutting the bark, or covering, on the side of a young tree. The cut is made in the shape of a cross, or the letter T. Next, the workers find a bud, or small growth, on the tree to be copied. A small piece of wood under the bud is carefully removed from the tree. The bud is then put into the hole on the other tree. The bud is tightly tied in place and begins to grow.

Mount Vernon officials say George Washington was interested in his tree collection. The officials add that he was a strong environmentalist. They say the old trees are important because they existed when America's first president was alive.

Longer Conversation 1

Student: Dear Professor, can you tell me what is the first thing that I should do to start my college search? Thank you.

Professor: Finding the best college for you begins with you. With thousands of colleges and universities out there, the best way to choose the one for you is by process of elimination. First, ask yourself some very important questions:

What are you looking for in a school? Do you want to attend a large university or a small private college? Or would you rather go to a junior college or a technical college?

Do you want to stay close to home? Or is it time for a change, a new city, a new state?

What can you afford to spend on education? How much can your parents afford to pay? Are you going to receive any scholarships? Are you willing to take out a student loan if needed?

What are you thinking about as a major? If you change your mind, will your school of choice have a wide range of majors for you to choose from?

This list could go on and on but I hope you get the idea. Start looking atthose schools that have characteristics that are important to you! Once you've narrowed the search, take advantage of college representatives who visit your school by asking them questions and getting literature from them.

Finally, visit your top choices. Seeing the campus, its students and some of its faculty should give you a good idea if it's right for you. Hope this helps. Good luck.

Student. Thanks a lot, professor.

Longer Conversation 2

M: Come in, Come in! What can I do for you?

W: Prof. Donner, are you giving your Advanced Geology course again next semester?

M: Yes, I'm planning on it.

W: I wonder if I could enroll in it. I know it's a graduate course and I'm only a junior, but. . .

M: Aren't you a bit young? I've allowed qualified seniors to take the course and they usually have a hard time keeping up.

W: I know, but the geology of the American West is my favorite interest and I've done a lot of reading in the field. Last semester I took Prof. Burman's course and I didn't find it nearly chanllenging enough.

M: I see. You certainly aren't one of those students who are out for easy grades.

W: I should say not. I really want to learn something.

M: Well, I'll speak to Prof. Burman. If he thinks you're ready, I'll let you enroll.

W: Oh, thanks. Professor Donner, that's really very nice of you.

Longer Conversation 3

M: What's that book you just picked up?

W: The Sociology text professor Maynor uses in his course.

M: You had better read it if you want to pass the course. Manynor swears by it.

W: But it costs 30 dollars. I simply can't afford it.

M: Did you check the used book secion here? Maybe they have it.

W: No they don't, I asked.

M: Why don't you get it from the library?

W: Are you kidding? I've been trying for months and it's always out. There are over 50 students in the course and every single one wants the book.

M: Listen, you know my roommate, Henry, don't you? He took the same course last year and I believe he owns the book. I'll ask him if he'll lend it to you.

W: Oh, Jim, that would solve everything.

Longer Conversation 4

M: What are you doing in the library on Saturday?

W: I've got a term paper due before Christmas.

M: What's in if on?

W: Oh, it's a language subject I dreamed up. I had no idea the bibliography would be so big. I've got a lot of notes though.

M: If the bibliography's too big, maybe the subject's too broad. What's your title now?

W: "Language and Culture".

M: No wonder! You couldn't have picked a broader subject. Let's see your outline.

W: Here it is. I've already got 10 pages.

M: Why don't you just take Part VI on "Bilingualism" and make a paper out of that. You speak two languages and can make a good contribution.

W: That's a good idea. Then I won't need to use any books, either.

M: On the contrary, you'll have to back up your ideas by looking up a lot of references.

W: Would you take a look at it when I get my rough draft?

M: Sure, I'm going to be on the campus next weekend. I'll look at it then.

Longer Conversation 5

M: How do you do, Miss Li! Please have a seat.

W: Thank you.

M: Now then, let's look at your transcript. You got your Bachelor of Arts in Enlish and now want to get your Master's in Education, right?

W: Right.

M: You'll need 36 credit hours, of which 15 must be from the English Department and 15 from the Education Department. For the remaining six credit hours, you can either write a thesis or take two more selected courses.

W: Right now, this is very confusing to me, but I'm sure it will straighten itself out in my mind as I learn more about it.

M: Let's program your courses. Since you have had English Literature, you should take American Literature and American Prose and Fiction. Your transcript indicates that your English background is strong, so I don't think you will have any problem with it.

W: How many credits do I earn for each course?

M: Three. You also should take two three-credit courses in the Education Department. I suggest E-

289

ducational Psychology and Audiovisual Methods and Aids. That will give you 12 hours altogether which is the minimum for a full-time student.

W: Excuse me, sir. Actually I am part-time student so I would like to audit one course.

M: That's right. You have been appointed Assistant Head Resident at Western. How many hours do you have to work?

W: Twelve hours a week. Since this is my first time in the United States, I don't want to fail at class and would therefore prefer a somewhat lighter program.

M: That's correct. In fact, you must maintain a "B" average to earn your Master's. In other words, if you get a C, you will need an A to balance it. If you get a D, it takes two A's to raise it to a B average.

W: I surely don't want to get any D's or F's. Therefore, like the tortoise in the fable, I'd better go slowly but surely.

M: That's a good idea. Which course do you want to audit?

W: American Prose and Fiction.

M: Are you aware that even though you won't receive any credit for an audited course, you still pay the same for the other caurses?

W: Yes, I am. I know that the professor will keep track of my attendance but that I won't have to do any papers or take any exams.

M: Fine. You're all set now. Jim will show you to the Administration Builing. Good luck, and I hope you'll enjoy studying here at Miami.

W: Thank you, sir. I'm sure I will.

Longer Conversation 6

M: Margaret, I could use your advice.

W: What about, Ron?

M: Well. I've put off doing my science requirement for three years.

W: And if you want to graduate this year, you've got to take a science course.

M: Right. I figure since you are doing pre-med, you know about the various courses.

W: Well, I've had to take Bilolgy, Chemistry, Math and Physics. What you need is a good introductory course for nonscience majors.

M: Yes. I'm really weak in Math. I did poorly in it in high school.

W: Then you'd better aviod Chemistry and Physics. How about Bilolgy?

M: The problem is lab. I'm a little squeamish about dissecting things.

W: That is a problem. What about astronomy? Everybody says Dr. Kuli is great. I'd take that course myself if I had the time.

M: That is what I thought I'd take. But it meets at the same time as my modern drama course.

W: Geology is pretty interestig and cutting up rocks shouldn't bother you.

M: That's a good idea. It even fits in with my hobby of mountain climbing. Thanks a lot.

Longer Conversation 7

W: It was exactly two years ago today that we moved to this town. You started working on your degree, and I started working down at the lab.

M: It seems like only yesterday. I suppose that I am so busy I don't even notice how the time passes.

W: I'd expect the opposite. I mean, the way you've been studying, working on experiments and writing dozens of papers, it might seem more like four years than two.

M: Haven't you ever noticed how time seems to crawl when you have nothing to do? But how time flies when you are busy with what you really like to do.

W: That's ture. Those days when there is not much to do at the lab don't ever seem to end.

M: Just wait a little longer. As soon as I finsh my degree we will open our own laboratory. Marston and Marston's Biochemical Analyses.

Longer Conversation 8

W: Well, John, how was your vacation? Did you visit all the places you wanted to see?

M: Oh, hardly, but we had a good time just the same. We managed to stop at the old Ghost Town near Virginia City. That's what Jimmy was all excited about.

W: Did you go to Denver like your wife wanted to?

M: Yes, we stayed with her cousin for two days. We had to pass up the Grand Canyon though, because Jimmy got sick from eating too mant grapes.

W: How about the stop at Indian Falls? Did you have any time for that?

M: Yes, but we almost didn't. We left Denver on Highway 14 when we should have taken Hihway 90. When we got straightened out, it was almost dark. Still we got there in time to take a few pictures.

W: Where else did you go?

M: Well, we went through Phoenix, Arizona. We all liked that. But we had some trouble with the car there. We had to stay an extra day because of that.

W: I bet that made you mad.

M: It sure did, especially because I had the guy at the garage give the car a checkup just before we left home, and he said it was in top shape. Still I can't complain. I was able to get in some extra fishing because of the delay. I went out with a guy who was staying in the hotel we were at.

W: All in all, you did quite a lot.

M: Yes, we certainly did. But after we got home, it took us two days to rest up. All that driving around was murder.

Longer Conversation 9

M: Are you ready for the trip to the Big Apple? I can hardly wait.

W: The Big Apple. What are you talking about?

M: The Big Apple is the nickname for New York City. You are going to New York with us, aren't you?

W: Yes, I'm going. I'm especially looking forward to seeing the Museum of Modern Art. There's a special show of 20th century American painters there. But tell me, where does the nickname the Big Apple come from?

M: The jazz musicians of the 1920's are responsible for the name. They played a concert in a city like an apple. Of course. New York was the biggest city in the country, and the best place for a jazz concert. So the musicians called it the Big Apple.

W: Amazing! New York is such a fascinating place. And it evenhas an interesting nickname, one that it's had for more than 50 years.

Longer Conversation 10

M: Have you ever visited a redwood forest? I recently had a chance to go to Muirwoods, National Monument north of san Francisco.

W: I've never seen a redwood tree. I really can't imagine how big they are.

M: The coastal redwoods are the tallest living things. Some are more than three hundred and fifty feet high. But none of the trees at Muirwoods is that high. You have to go further north in California to see the tallest trees.

W: You said that Muirwoods is near san Francisco? I guess it must be quite a tourist attraction.

M: Yes, it's less than an hour's drive away, so it's easy to go to.

W: I've heard that many redwood trees are thousands of years old. Are the ones in Muirwoods that old?

M: The oldest documented age for a coastal redwood is more than 2,000 years. The trees at Muirwoods are 400 to 800 yeards old.

W: Why have they survived so long?

M: They have remarkable resistance to forest fires. Their tough thick bark protects the trees during a fire. The coastal redwoods also like a damp, foggy climate.

W: Then since Muirwoods is near foggy San Francisco, it must be ideal for the trees' survival. I can't wait to go there and see them!

Tapescript for the Sample Test

Listening

Questions 1 – 5

Narrator: Listen to a conversation between two students.

M: Hi, Rachel! I haven't seen you around for ages. What's happening?

W: Hi, Jeff. Good to see you, too. I live off campus now, in Forest Chapel. How about you? What have you been up to?

M: Busy with school and work. Hey, what are you taking for the summer?

W: No, I don't take any courses in the summer uh... I'm hoping to do something in the newspaper, maybe some sort of internship. I don't know.

M: Fantastic! I didn't know you were into news. What do you have in mind?

W: Well, there's a student journal I just found out about in the Western Campus. I went there a couple of times. They're an interesting group. They do intensive reports about campus life... and... you know

I'm really impressed and would love to work with them in some way.

M: Do you write for them?

W: Yes, of course. I took journalism class last spring. We had a couple of tough assignments for the course.

M: Like what? Reporting live from the scene?

W: No, not actually. But we did some interviews, held news conferences and all the other stuff. It was kind of fun.

M: It sounds like you are going to work for them this summer.

W: I'd like to. . . but as far as that goes. . . my problem is I don't know if I should go there full-time. Do you know anything about the summer internship?

M: Better go see your advisor about this. Doesn't the advising department post a list of internships that are available?

W: Yeah, there's a list. I already checked it, but there was nothing in news agencies. But I'll talk to Susan, of course. She's always got some pretty good ideas.

M: Oh. . . I remembered. How about the Post-Gazette? They offer a summer internship program. I saw their ads in campus last week.

W: Are they still around?

M: I'm not sure. You know what you could do? What I did — how I got started for my last summer intervals, I picked up the phone and then just talked to the recruiter on the phone. I told her I was a student, and had to do a report for my classes, and asked if I could meet with them in their workplace?

W: What happened?

Li. The lady I talked to said just come with your CV.

W: Wow! You make it sound so easy. I wonder if that'd work for me.

M: Then. . . Oh. . . they said it'll be a plus if you have some college newspaper experience. And they are looking for some work samples that show your talent and promise to be a journalist.

W: How can I reach them?

M: I'll send you an email with their contacts. It's worth a try, isn't it?

W: Absolutely. Hey, I'm glad to run into you!

Question 1. What are the students mainly discussing?

Question 2. Listen again to part of the conversation. Then answer the question.

W: No, I don't take any courses in the summer uh. . . I'm hoping to do something in the newspaper, maybe some sort of internship. I don't know.

M: Fantastic! I didn't know you were into news. What do you have in mind?

What can be inferred about the woman when the man says this:

M: I didn't know you were into news.

Question 3. What kind of job does the woman have now?

Question 4. What does the man suggest the woman do?

Question 5. What can be concluded about the woman's feeling about her job outlook?

Questions 6 – 10

Narrator: Listen to a conversation between a student and a student advisor.

Student: Hi, Erin. How are you?

Advisor: Fine, thanks, Martin. How can I help you today?

Student: I tried to register a course on line but couldn't get through the system. I wonder if I can register for that course in person. Where should I go?

Advisor: Can you tell me what course you're trying to register for?

Student: It's Statistics II by Professor Jeremy Smith of the Business School.

Advisor: Oh, then it's outside of the department I guess. Do you know that if you wish to register for courses outside of the department, you must have prior approval from the Academic Committee?

Student: No. I kind of forgot how it works. Then do I have to fill out a form or something?

Advisor: That'll be good. Here it is... While you are filling out the form, I can check it on my computer that... Oh, Statistics II is not available for online registration. You have to apply for it in person with the Registrar of the Business School. Be aware that to be accepted into the class, there's a prerequisite course, Statistics I, offered only in the spring.

Student: Really? I didn't notice that. Then I need to complete Statistics I before I can register for the II?

Advisor: Definitely.

Student: Too bad I missed that class this spring. Does that mean I have to start it all over again next year since it's fall and I have no way to get in the II class?

Advisor: I'm sorry but I'm afraid that's the reality. If you do wish to work on such a subject, probably you can take a similar course in our department. Let me check. Oh... It's the Fundamentals in Statistics by Professor Gordon. It's a good one too.

Student: Do you think so? Probably I'll consider that. Can I register for it now, in your office?

Advisor: I'm sorry I can't help you here. You'll have to go to the registrer office if you wish to register inperson, or you can log on to the course registration website. It'll be much quicker that way.

Student: Well then, I'll have a try tomorrow morning.

Advisor: Keep in mind that it's always true that the earlier, the better. Professor Gordon's class is one of the student's favorites. You'd better act early before a waiting scenario occurs.

Student: Oh... OK. Thank you, Erin. Thanks for your help.

Advisor: No problem. Have a nice day!

Question 6. Why does the student go to see the advisor?

Question 7. According to the advisor, what is the department's policy on taking courses from other departments?

Question 8. When is Statistics I offered?

Question 9. What does the advisor suggest the man do?

Question 10. Listen again to part of the conversation. Then answer the question.

Student: Well then, I'll have a try tomorrow morning.

Advisor: Keep in mind that it's always true that the earlier, the better. Professor Gordon's class is one of
the student's favorites. You'd better act early before a waiting scenario occurs.

What can be inferred about Professor Gordon's class when the advisor says this:

Advisor: You'd better act early before a waiting scenario occurs.

Questions 11 – 16

Narrator: Listen to a lecture in an American history class.

Professor: What we' re going to talk about today is the history of Swedish emigration to America. The
history of Swedish emigration to America goes further back in time than that of the United States. Swedes
started to come in 1638, just eighteen years after the landing of the "Mayflower" . Unlike the Pilgrim
Fathers, the Swedes were not religious dissenters but rather an organized group of colonizers. They had
been sent out by the government in Stockholm in order to establish a colony under the Swedish Crown in
Delaware. The era of New Sweden ended in 1655, when the colony was lost to the Dutch. But the original
settlers remained and kept up their language and culture for a long time. Many of the descendants of the
Delaware Swedes became distinguished fighters for freedom in the war against England in 1776.

The tidal wave of Swedish emigration began in the mid 1840s, when the first organized emigrant
groups started to arrive in New York. These farmers, destined to Lowa and Illinois, were followed during
the period up to 1930 by almost 1. 3 million countrymen. In proportion to the population of their home
countries, only the British Isles and Norway surpassed Sweden in the number of immigrants. The effect of
this exodus from Sweden reached its climax around 1910, when 1. 4 million Swedish first and second
generation immigrants were listed as living in the U. S. . Compare this to Sweden's population at the time:
5. 5 million. Roughly one fifth of all Swedes had their homes in America right before World War II.

So, we'll review some of the primary reasons behind the Swedish emigration to America. The first
reason is the agricultural crisis. In the middle of the nineteenth century, Sweden was a land of poverty and
social frustration. Some advanced landholders tried to reorganize agriculture through the state-supported
enclosure movement, farm schools and refined methods of farming, but it was difficult to reform the
thousand-year-old "Mother economy" on a wider scale. The liberals were disappointed. Many of them,
like "the father of Swedish emigration", Gustav Unonius, saw no future in Sweden and left for America.

Another reason for the mass emigration was population. Swedish emigration primarily had the same
causes as the contemporary population surge from Northern and Western Europe: population pressure. The
famous Swedish bishop and poet Esaias Tegne'r explained the population pressure in three words: "peace,
vaccination and potatoes". He thereby referred to the fact that Sweden had not been in war since the fatal
Russian war of 1809 and the successful Danish one of 1814. Smallpox vaccination had reduced the infant
mortality from 21% in 1750 to 15% in 1850. Potatoes became a nutritious supplement to the poor man's
bread. The combined affects of such benefits resulted in a growth in population which in turn produced
other problems for society. The number of Swedes doubled between 1750 and 1850, and the growth
continued. In a country with few industries and cities, the burden had to be carried by the primitive a-
gricultural society.

Yet another reason for the emigration was Sweden's less developed industry and communications. By the middle of the nineteenth century, Sweden had experienced an increasing series of technical inventions and improvements. It is true that the industrial era seemed to promise a new future for most of them, but the frames around the splendid expectations proved to be cut too short. For instance, it was easy to buy a ticket to Stockholm, but where does one find housing and a job in a city suddenly over-crowded with job-hungry unskilled laborers? The labor market of the small, backward country was too limited. Many young people were therefore drawn down into the social swamp of Stockholm, ending up as beggars or prostitutes. Others read the advertisements about America. Therefore, a large portion of the Swedish emigrants came from cities in 1850 – 1920.

Well, that's all for today's class. Next week we're going to examine other issues about the Swedish emigrants in America. See you next week.

Question 11. What is the lecture mainly about?

Question 12. The professor explained various reasons for the Swedish emigration to America. Indicate for which reason the term falls into.

Question 13. Listen again to part of the lecture. Then answer the question.

Professor: In proportion to the population of their home countries, only the British Isles and Norway surpassed Sweden in the number of immigrants. The effect of this exodus from Sweden reached its climax around 1910, when 1. 4 million Swedish first and second generation immigrants were listed as living in the U. S.. Compare this to Sweden's population at the time: 5. 5 million.

Why does the professor use the word "exodus"?

Question 14. When did the first Swedish immigrants arrive at the New Continent?

Question 15. According to the professor, what was the primary intent of the first Swedish immigrants?

Question 16. Listen again to part of the lecture. Then answer the question.

Professor: For instance, it was easy to buy a ticket to Stockholm, but where does one find housing and a job in a city suddenly over-crowded with job-hungry unskilled laborers? What can be inferred about people going to Stockholm at the time?

Queestions 17 – 22

Narrator: Listen to a lecture in a biology class.

Professor: Good morning, class. Today, we'll be looking at one of the most important aspects of a live cell, osmosis. As you know, we'll have a lab tomorrow. And we're going to use some of the knowledge we discuss today for it.

In the previous class we examined how the cell membrane of a plant—the thin skin that holds a cell all in place—is formed. Do you still remember how the cell membrane exchanges substance with the outer world? Well, the cell membrane presents a barrier to large molecules, including harmful chemicals that may occur in its environment. But temporary gaps in the membrane make the cell permeable to water molecules. Therefore, the cell membrane is said to be a selectively permeable membrane. Being surrounded by a selectively permeable membrane has consequences. If more water enters the cell than leaves, the cell swells up. If more water leaves than enters, the cell shrinks. This movement of water through a selectively permeable membrane is known by one of the big words of biology—osmosis.

There is, of course, water on both sides of the cell membrane, so it is other molecules, dissolved in the water that cause a cell to shrink, grow, or stay the same. These dissolved substances are called solutes. Whether more water enters or leaves a cell can be predicted by knowing the concentration of solutes inside and outside of the cell.

I'll give you some examples on how osmosis is useful in our lives. One such example is red blood cells, which contain about one percent solutes and 99% water. The blood plasma in which they are bathed also contains about 1% solutes. Under these balanced conditions, inflow and outflow, due to osmosis, is equal, and the red blood cells retain their donut-with-the-hole-filled-in shape. If we flood the blood cells with distilled water — water in which all solutes have been removed—what do you think will happen?

As you probably guessed, the cells blow up as water rushes in. But why? It's because the solute molecules inside have a tendency to trap water molecules, holding them, or at least slowing them down. Therefore more water molecules come in than go out and the cell swells up. Under these extreme conditions some blood cells rupture, leaving empty membrane ghosts. But can the opposite effect occur?

Sea water contains a lot of solutes, 3.5 percent by weight. This is the picture when normal shaped red blood cells are flooded with sea water. So, if you are lost at sea, and dying of thirst, you better hope for rain, because there may be water, water, everywhere, but nary a drop fit to drink.

Our kidneys keep the concentration of solutes in blood plasma just right most of the time, so our cells stay in shape. But this is not the case with the lake inhabitants. A freshwater lake contains a very low percentage of solute molecules, and this creates a problem for single cells living there. If osmosis were the only factor at work, the inflow of water would balloon them up until their internal solutes reached the same concentration as the water around them. If you collect some Paramecia from a lake, and observe one for a minute or so, you will see a star-shaped organelle pumping water out of the cell. This "contractile vacuole" is getting rid of the excess water entering by osmosis.

So osmosis explains how water enters plant roots, why people dehydrate if they drink sea water, and why body cells normally maintain their shapes. I hope that from our discussion of osmosis you've developed a clearer understanding of how it really is.

Question 17. Listen again to part of the lecture. Then answer the question.

Profesor: One such example is red blood cells, which contain about one percent solutes and 99% water. The blood plasma in which they are bathed also contains about 1% solutes. Under these balanced conditions, inflow and outflow, due to osmosis, is equal, and the red blood cells retain their donut-with-the-hole-filled in shape. Why does the professor say "donut-with-the-hole-filled-in shape"?

Question 18. Which of the following does the professor NOT mention in the lecture?

Question 19. Listen again to part of the lecture. Then answer the question.

Profesor: Our kidneys keep the concentration of solutes in blood plasma just right most of the time, so our cells stay in shape. But this is not the case with the lake inhabitants. What is probably true about the "lake inhabitants" (single cells living in the lake)?

Question 20. According to the professor, determine what is/are true or false about the cell membrane?

Question 21. Why is the professor discussing this topic?

Question 22. Listen again to part of the lecture. Then answer the question.

Professor: If osmosis were the only factor at work, the inflow of water would balloon them up until their internal solutes reached the same concentration as the water around them. What does the professor imply about "Paramecia", a single cell inhabitant in a freshwater lake.

Questions 23 – 28

Narrator: Listen to a lecture in a geology class.

Professor: Good morning, everyone. Welcome to the lesson "From Pangaea to the Present". For class today, we'll be looking at the movements of earth plates. As you have known, the earth is a dynamic or constantly changing planet. The thin, fragile plates slide very slowly on the mantle's upper layer.

Student 1: Excuse me, Professor, but can you please explain what a mantle is? I don't quite get it.

Professor: You bet. A mantle refers to the earth that lies beneath the crust and above the central core. This sliding of the plates is caused by the mantle's convection currents slowly turning over and over. This overturn is like a conveyor belt that moves the plates of the crust. These plates are in constant motion causing earthquakes, mountain building, volcanism, the production of "new" crust and the destruction of "old" crust. Then what are the plates? Well, the Earth's crust is broken into many pieces. These pieces are called plates. There are twelve main plates on the Earth's surface. The red lines on this map of the world represent the plate boundaries. A plate boundary occurs where two plates come together. There are three kinds of plate boundaries:

1. Convergent boundary—where two plates collide to form mountains or a subduction zone. Convergent is named in the sense that the two plates come together.

2. Divergent boundary—where two plates are moving in opposite directions as in a mid-ocean ridge. Divergent is named in the sense that the two plates move apart.

3. Transform boundary—where two plates are sliding past each other as in the San Andreas Fault of California. Transform is in the sense that the two plates go over each other.

The Earth's plates are in constant, but very, very slow motion. They move at only 1/2 to 4 inches per year! This does not seem like much, but over millions of years it adds up to great distances of movement. The Continental Drift Theory states that the continents have moved and are still moving today. In1912 Alfred Wegener introduced this theory, but hedid not fully understand what caused the plates to move. The motion of the Earth's plates help scientists to understand why earthquakes, volcanoes, and mountain building occur. You will learn more about why the plates are moving in the next lesson, "How Plates Move".

Scientists believe these plates have been moving for millions of years, and 250 million years ago the Earth's seven continents were all grouped together into a super-continent called Pangaea. This huge super-continent was surrounded by one gigantic ocean called Panthalassa. Scientists believe that the North American Continent was located much farther south and east of its position today. In fact, much of North

America was in or near the tropics!

Student 2: Then, how do scientists know this?

Professor: Good question. How do scientists know this? They have found fossils from this period of time. These fossils are of tropical plants and animals. The fossils have been found in cold regions like North Dakota and Greenland!

Today, the plates are still moving making the Atlantic Ocean larger and the Pacific Ocean smaller. The yellow arrows on the world map indicate the direction of plates movements today. Notice the position of the Indian Subcontinent today. It moved hundreds of miles in 135 million years at a great speed (4 inches per year.) The Atlantic Ocean will be much larger 50 million years from now and the Pacific Ocean will be much smaller. North and South America will have moved farther west while Greenland will be located farther west but also farther north. Australia will move farther north into the tropics, while New Zealand will move to the south of Australia.

All of these predictions are just that, predictions. These movements of the continents may happen if the plates continue to move in the same direction and with the same speed as they are moving today. Scientists are not certain of the movement today, let alone 50 million years into the future.

What do you think the world will look like in 50 million years? Well, that's the topic of your new assignment for this week. It's due on the 3rd Wednesday from now. That's...uhmm... November the 19th. That's all for now. See you next week.

Question 23. Listen again to part of the lecture. Then answer the question.

Professor: All of these predictions are just that, predictions. These movements of the continents may happen if the plates continue to move in the same direction and with the same speed as they are moving today. Scientists are not certain of the movement today, let alone 50 million years into the future. Why does the professor say this:

Professor: All of these predictions are just that, predictions.

Question 24. According to the lecture, where was North America located millions of years ago?

Question 25. Listen again to part of the lecture. Then answer the question.

Student 1: Excuse me, Professor, but can you please explain what a mantle is? I don't quite get it.

Professor: You bet... What does the professor mean when she says this:

Professor: You bet...

Question 26. According to the professor, determine whether the following information is true or false?

Question 27. What is the Pangaea?

Question 28. What conclusion can be drawn about the Continental Drift Theory?

Questions 29 – 34

Narrator: Listen to a lecture in a geology class.

Professor: Good morning, class. We'll be looking at the major cause behind one of the Mother Nature's tremendous revenge on human beings: the tsunami. We'll also talk about how it can accumulate such a devastating force against our lives. As you may have known, a recent earthquake off the coast of

Sumatra jolted the ocean floor, which caused a tsunami. This was a devastating one that raced across the Indian Ocean sweeping coastal areas in Thailand, Malaysia, Indonesia, Sri Lanka and India. The effects were felt as far away as the east cost of Africa. So, what is a tsunami? How is it formed? Anyone in class?

Student 1: A tsunami is a large destructive ocean wave, or a series of waves I guess, resulting from sudden vertical movement of the Earth's crust.

Professor: Uh, you're almost there! A tsunami may also be caused by volcanic action, a landslide, an explosion, or even a meteorite landing in the ocean, although the most common cause is an earthquake occurring on the ocean floor.

The word tsunami (pronounced tsoo-NAH-mee) means "harbor wave" in Japanese. Some people call tsunamis "tidal waves", but this term is misleading. Tsunamis are not related to tides. The level of the tide at the time a tsunami reaches land has some effect on how much damage takes place, but that is the only connection. Another name for tsunamis is "seismic waves". This term is not accurate either, since earthquakes are not the only events that cause these waves.

So, when an earthquake or other major disturbance causes a section of the ocean floor to rise or sink abruptly, the mass of water above the affected area is also suddenly displaced. As the water tries to regain its equilibrium, waves are formed. Because of the depth of the water, the wavelengths of these waves are much greater than that of normal waves that occur where the ocean meets the land. A tsunami wave may be hundreds of miles in length. It moves out in a circle from the spot where it started, similar to the way circles of water move out from the place where a rock has been dropped into apond. Many people have the mistaken belief that tsunamis are single waves. They are not. Insteadtsunamis are "wave trains" consisting of multiple waves.

Because of the large size of its wavelength, a tsunami moves at high speed across great distances without losing much of its energy. In deep ocean, the surface swells marking the wave are hardly noticeable. In fact, they are often less than three feet high. However, as the wave approaches land and moves into more shallow water, it slows down and increases in size. The features of the land beneath the water influence its actual height. The waves generated by the eruption of Krakatoa in 1883 reached a height of 120 feet. In 1737, a tsunami estimated to be 210 feet high struck Cape Lopatka in northeast Russia.

In the open ocean, a tsunami can travel as fast as 435 mph, approximately as fast as a jet aircraft. It loses speed as it approaches land, but it does not lose much energy. As its speed diminishes, the height of the wave increases. When it reaches land, it may behave like a series of breaking waves, a rapidly rising and falling tide, or a large, powerful wave called a bore. The tremendous energy of the wave can cause great quantities of water to surge inland, far beyond where even the highest of high tides would commonly reach.

Ordinary waves — the type that normally occurs at an ocean beach or lakeshore — are generated by the wind. These waves, which typically roll in one right after another, might last about ten seconds and have a wavelength of 490 feet or so. In contrast, when a tsunami wave reaches shore, its wavelength might be iBRe than 50 miles, and it might last for more than an hour.

A tsunami moving onto the shore is usually traveling at about 45 mph with tremendous force that can stripsand off beaches, undermine trees, and crush buildings. People and boats are powerless against its turbulence. The quantity of water carried inland is capable of flooding vast areas of normally dry land.

Ok, so much for today. Next week we'll be discussing about more technical aspects of the tsunamis.

Please look at Chapter 3 and complete all the questions after the text. Thank you and have a nice weekend.

Question 29. What is the main idea of the lecture?

Question 30. According to the professor, what can be an approximate term for a tsunami?

Question 31. Why does a tsunami travel thousands of miles without losing much of its energy?

Question 32. According to the professor, determine whether the following can cause a tsunami?

Question 33. Listen again to part of the lecture. Then answer the question.

Student 1. A tsunami is a large destructive ocean wave, or a series of waves I guess, resulting from sudden vertical movement of the Earth's crust.

Professor: You're almost there! How does the professor seem to feel about the student's answer?

Question 34. What point does the professor make about the energy of a tsunami?

Speaking

Question 1

Please Listen Carefully.

Describe a teacher that has had a great influence on you and explain why the teacher was so important to you. Include details and examples to support your explanation.

Please begin speaking after the beep.

Question 2

Please Listen Carefully.

Some people think it is a good idea for students to take part-time jobs while in university, while other believe having a job will influence their studies. What is your opinion on this issue. Include details and examples in your explanation.

Please begin speaking after the beep.

Question 3

Please Listen Carefully.

Read the announcement about foreign language classes. You have 45 seconds to read the announce-ment. Begin reading now.

Now listen to two students as they discuss the announcement.

M: What do you think about the new requirement? As of the first day of class next semester, we have to start enrolling in a language lab for every language class we are taking.

W: I know, isn't it great? We just don't get enough time to practice using the language in the other classes. Hopefully this will help us improve.

M: How can you be ok with this? Now I won't have enough time to study.

W: Time spent in the language lab will be much more beneficial than your "study sessions" with your girlfriend.

M: Very funny. I just don't think it's fair. If we don't need extra help, I don't know why we have to sit in a lab.

W: Face it; none of us are very fluent in our second languages. I'm glad they're changing the policy and respect them for taking a stand on the issue.

The woman expresses her opinion about the new requirement for students taking foreign language classes. State her opinion and explain the reasons she gives for holding that opinion.

Please begin speaking after the beep.

Question 4

Please Listen Carefully.

Now read the passage about health. You have 45 seconds to read the passage. Begin reading now.

Now listen to part of a lecture on this topic in a health class.

Professor: So, as I was saying, diabetes is a fairly common disease. You probably all know someone with the disease. But you probably know more people than you think, because diabetes often goes undiagnosed. Approximately 1/3 of those who have diabetes are not aware of that fact. Why? Well, quite simply, the symptoms of diabetes seem quite harmless. They could be connected to pregnancy, the common flu, stress, or even from just being busy. The only difference is, for those problems, the symptoms eventually go away. For diabetes, they only get worse.

So, what is being done to bring awareness to society, you might ask. There are quite a few things. The first and foremost is simple education. If you pay attention to the papers, you will see lots of workshops that are being put out by public hospitals, Red Cross, and other diabetes organizations. Also, if you look online, you will find that there are plenty of websites designed to give people the information they need about the symptoms, as well as quizzes to take to find out what your chances are of getting the disease. There has also been quite a lot of news about it recently.

The professor poses the question of why so many people with diabetes go undiagnosed. Explain what is being done to help build awareness of the disease.

Please begin speaking after the beep.

Questions 5

Please listen carefully.

M: How are your classes going, Sarah?

W: Well, they are going alright. It's just my English Literature class that is giving me a problem.

M: Oh? What's wrong?

W: Well, with my part-time job at the coffee shop, I don't really have much time to do my homework. My professor assigned a 20-page paper to us at the beginning of the semester. It's due next Monday, and I've barely started.

M: Oh dear. That is a problem. Have you talked to your professor about it? Since it's your first paper, maybe he'll give you an extension.

W: To be frank, I'm a bit scared of my professor. He's known on campus for his strict policies.

M: Well, I still think you should talk to him about it, but if you don't want to do that, then you're going to have to make some time to write the paper in the next week. Are you scheduled to work at the coffee shop this week?

W: Unfortunately, I am.

M: Maybe you could find someone else to cover some of your shifts so that you can just focus on the paper.

W: Yeah, that might be difficult though. The other employees are all students, too. They're busy.

M: Well, unless you want to fail, you're going to have to think of something!

Describe the woman's problem and the suggestions her classmate gives her. What do you think the woman should do, and why?

Please begin speaking after the beep.

Question 6

Please Listen Carefully.

Now listen to part of a talk in an Intercultural Communication class.

Professor: Culture shock is what people experience when they go to live in another country for extended periods of time. There are many different stages to culture shock. Some stages last longer than others. Sometimes, people can experience the same stage more than once.

The first stage of culture shock is the "honeymoon" stage. In this stage, a person may feel euphoric and have a good feeling about everything encountered. Everything at this time is new and exciting.

After a while, the person will stop feeling excited about everything and start to feel frustrated with the new culture. This is the beginning of the second stage. Some common feelings at this point include discontent, impatience, anger, sadness, and a feeling of incompetence. This is a stage of transition from the old ways and the new ways of life for the person.

The third stage begins with a feeling of some understanding of the new culture. At this point, people might start to laugh at the differences. People want to belong and start to feel some sense of belonging.

In the fourth stage, people can see both the positive and negative aspects of the new culture. The sense of belonging that people feel here increases.

The fifth stage is called "re-entry shock". This is when people move back to their original country. When this happens, people might find that some of the new habits and customs acquired in the new country can not be found in the original country. People often see their original country with a new perspective.

Everyone experiences culture shock differently. Things that might effect this is one's personality, prior experiences of living abroad, and one's mental state. Whether you are the one traveling or if you are friends with someone who is traveling, knowing the different stages of culture shock can be helpful for everyone.

Using points and examples from the talk, explain the different stages in culture shock. Explain why it's important for people to be aware of the different stages.

Please begin speaking after the beep.

Writing

Question 1

Read the passage. On a piece of paper, take notes on the main points of the reading passage.

Listen to part of a lecture on the topic you just read about. Take notes on the main points of the following lecture.

When we consider the changing role of women in the work place and society in general, it is important to consider not only quantitative changes, but also qualitative. We must consider the matter not only in terms of ideals and moral principles, but also in terms of feasibility.

Recently I spoke with a human resource manager for an international company who complained that his job has become a delicate juggling act of finding the best person for the job while maintaining some kind of gender and ethnic equilibrium. In the past, it was simply a matter of trying to objectively find the best candidate: nowadays, there are gender quotas and ratios to maintain, and the whole process can make for an overly sensitive work environment.

For one thing, recent studies show that when it comes to promotions and assigning tasks, regardless of the basis for reaching decisions by mangers, employees are likely to attribute such decisions to "political correctness", or gender favoritism. As well, complications can arise with language and behavior. A slap on the back between a male manager and employee would be seen as friendly and a sign of encouragement or support. A pat on the shoulder or prolonged eye contact between a male and female co-worker, however, could be interpreted as flirtatious and even harassing. Moreover, numbers show that while there has been a substantial increase in the number of women entering the workforce, those able to reach management and senior management positions are the exception, not the norm. Also, workplaces with a more balanced mix of male and female employees did not show higher productivity or work efficiency. As well, salary discrepancies for the same work, between men and women, do exist. It should come as no surprise, therefore, that while many women have found careers, many are less than enthusiastic about their odds for finding equality.

iBT TOEFL

Answer Key

答　案

Chapter Two　　Basic Skills Neended for iBT TOEFL

Part 1　　Basic Skills Needed for Reading

Passage 1	1. C	2. B	3. A	4. C	5. C
Passage 2	1. C	2. A	3. C	4. B	5. D
Passage 3	1. C	2. D	3. A	4. D	5. D
Passage 4	1. A	2. D	3. A	4. A	5. B
Passage 5	1. A	2. B	3. B	4. D	5. C
Passage 6	1. C	2. A	3. B	4. C	5. A
Passage 7	1. C	2. D	3. A	4. B	5. C
Passage 8	1. D	2. C	3. A	4. A	5. A
Passage 9	1. D	2. B	3. D	4. A	5. A
Passage 10	1. D	2. C	3. B	4. D	5. A
Passage 11	1. D	2. C	3. A	4. C	5. C
Passage 12	1. C	2. A	3. D	4. D	5. A
Passage 13	1. C	2. A	3. B	4. D	5. A
Passage 14	1. C	2. B	3. C	4. C	5. C
Passage 15	1. C	2. D	3. C	4. A	5. D
Passage 16	1. C	2. D	3. B	4. D	5. A
Passage 17	1. D	2. A	3. D	4. A	5. B
Passage 18	1. B	2. A	3. C	4. D	5. B
Passage 19	1. C	2. D	3. B	4. D	5. A
Passage 20	1. B	2. C	3. C	4. C	5. A
Passage 21	1. D	2. C	3. D	4. A	5. C
Passage 22	1. A	2. B	3. C	4. A	5. A
Passage 23	1. B	2. D	3. B	4. C	5. A
Passage 24	1. A	2. B	3. B	4. C	5. C
Passage 25	1. C	2. D	3. C	4. C	5. B	6. B	7. A	8. A	9. D	10. B

Passage 26 1. B   2. C   3. A   4. D   5. C   6. A   7. B   8. D   9. A   10. C
Passage 27 1. A   2. C   3. B   4. D   5. C   6. B   7. D   8. C   9. D   10. A
Passage 28 1. A   2. B   3. C   4. D   5. D   6. A   7. B   8. C   9. D   10. C
Passage 29 1. A   2. B   3. C   4. C   5. D   6. B   7. C   8. A   9. D   10. D
Passage 30 1. C   2. D   3. B   4. C   5. A   6. C   7. B   8. A   9. D   10. D

Part 2   Basic Skills Needed for Listening

Section A : Short Conversations

1. D 2. C 3. D 4. B 5. B 6. D 7. C 8. A 9. C 10. A 11. D 12. A 13. B 14. B 15. C 16. C 17. A 18. D 19. B 20. B 21. C 22. C 23. D 24. B 25. D 26. A 27. C 28. A 29. D 30. A 31. A 32. B 33. C 34. C 35. B 36. D 37. B 38. B 39. C 40. A 41. D 42. C 43. D 44. A 45. D 46. D 47. D 48. B 49. C 50. C 51. D 52. B 53. A 54. D 55. B 56. C 57. D 58. A 59. B 60. D 61. A 62. A 63. A 64. D 65. B 66. D 67. D 68. B 69. D 70. A 71. A 72. D 73. A 74. B 75. C 76. A 77. A 78. B 79. A 80. A 81. C 82. D 83. B 84. A 85. A 86. B 87. D 88. B 89. A 90. C 91. D 92. C 93. C 94. A 95. B 96. A 97. A 98. C 99. C 100. D 101. C 102. B 103. C 104. A 105. D 106. C 107. C 108. A 109. A 110. D 111. C 112. A 113. A 114. C 115. B 116. C 117. A 118. D 119. A 120. A 121. C 122. B 123. D 124. A 125. A 126. A 127. D 128. C 129. B 130. D 131. D 132. A 133. B 134. B 135. C 136. D 137. C 138. D 139. C 140. B 141. A 142. A 143. D 144. B 145. A 146. D 147. D 148. B 149. B 150. A

Section B: Longer Conversations and Lectures

Lecture 1   1. B   2. B   3. C   4. D   5. D
Lecture 2   1. C   2. D   3. A   4. B   5. D
Lecture 3   1. C   2. A   3. A   4. B   5. D
Lecture 4   1. C   2. C   3. C   4. D   5. B
Lecture 5   1. C   2. A   3. C   4. D   5. D
Lecture 6   1. D   2. A   3. B   4. D   5. B
Lecture 7   1. C   2. D   3. A   4. D   5. B
Lecture 8   1. A   2. D   3. C   4. B   5. A
Lecture 9   1. A   2. D   3. B   4. C   5. A
Lecture 10   1. C   2. D   3. B   4. B   5. C
Longer Conversation 1 1. A   2. B   3. B   4. D   5. B
Longer Conversation 2 1. C   2. D   3. A   4. B   5. D
Longer Conversation 3 1. B   2. D   3. B   4. A   5. D
Longer Conversation 4 1. B   2. D   3. B   4. D   5. B
Longer Conversation 5 1. B   2. A   3. B   4. C   5. D
Longer Conversation 6 1. C   2. D   3. B   4. C   5. A
Longer Conversation 7 1. B   2. 考 3. D   4. A   5. A

Longer Conversation 8 1. C   2. B   3. B   4. D   5. B

Longer Conversation 9 1. A   2. D   3. D   4. B   5. A

Longer Conversation 10 1. C   2. D   3. B   4. D   5. B

Part 3   Basic Skills Needed for Writing

Exercise 1

Two examples are given for each item. The controlling idea is underlined. Your controlling ideas may be different.

1. Owning a large car has many <u>advantages</u>.

    The <u>disadvatnages</u> of owning a large car are many.

2. The <u>reason</u> a person lives in a remote area may be one of the following.

    A person who lives in a remote area may face many <u>problems</u>.

3. Before applying to a foreign university, one should consider the <u>disadvantages</u> of studying abroad.

    The <u>advantages</u> of studying abroad outweigh the disadvantages.

4. Car accidents can be avoided or minimized if the driver takes certain <u>precautions</u>.

    Although a person thinks it is safe at home, many different <u>kinds</u> of accidents occur there.

5. An international airport is divided into different <u>sections</u>.

    There are several <u>kinds</u> of airports.

6. Teachers can list many <u>reasons</u> why students are absent from their classes.

    Absenteeism causes the employer many <u>problems</u>.

7. Taking exams is required of all students, and to do their best, students should use the following <u>methods</u> to prepare themselves.

    One should follow these <u>procedures</u> when taking an exam.

8. Computers have brought many <u>changes</u> to our way of life.

    Many <u>educational games</u> can be played on computers.

9. Rice can be prepared in many <u>ways</u>.

    Rice can be put to many <u>uses</u>.

10. Preparing to go camping is easy when you organize your trip using these <u>steps</u>.

    Camping has changed in many <u>ways</u>.

Exercise 2

The following topic sentences are only examples. Your sentences may be different.

1. This is a strong topic sentence.

2. This is a weak topic sentence because the rest of the paragraph describes what the writer does when he or she goes to the beach. A better topic sentence would be: "Whenever I have the opportunity to go to the beach, I always follow the same rountine."

3. This is a weak topic sentence because the rest of the paragraph describes the various ways students can get to class. A better topic sentence would be: "For the many students who cannot afford a car, there

are several alternative ways of getting to class. "

Exercise 3

These are only examples. Your topic sentences may be different.

1. A dormitory room is cold and impersonal until several changes have been made to make it more inviting.

2. American telephone books are divided into several sections.

3. The fast-food restaurant has become popular for various reasons.

Exercise 4

1. D 2. B 3. D 4. A 5. C

Exercise 5

1. Students who need extra money can hold down a full-time temporary job during their summer vacation.

2. A person can also meet other people by going to parties.

3. In my opinion, people should write clearly.

Exercise 6

These supporting ideas are based on the examples given in the Answer Key for Exercise 1. Yours may be different.

1. Disadvantages of large cars

    A. expensive to buy

    B. expensive to maintain

    C. use more gasoline

    D. difficult to park

2. Reasons for living in a remote area

    A. get away from city noise

    B. live in unpolluted area

    C. remaining where one has been

    D. be closer to nature

3. Disadvantages of studying abroad

    A. Far from family and friends

    B. difficult in understanding a foreign language

    C. more expensive

    D. hard to get home in an emergency

4. Kinds of home accidents

    A. falls

    B. poisoning

    C. burns

    D. cuts

5. Kinds of airports

    A. international

    B. national

    C. rural

    D. private

6. <u>Problems</u> caused by absenteeism

    A. lost production

    B. missed deadlines

    C. mistakes made by substitutes

    D. expenses for training substitutes

7. <u>Methods</u> to prepare for taking exams

    A. study on a rgular basis

    B. review appropriate material

    C. anticipate questions

    D. get good night's sleep the night before

8. <u>Changes</u> brought by computers

    A. better telephone services

    B. information easier to obtain

    C. easier inventory procedures in business

    D. helpful in education

9. <u>Ways</u> to prepare rice

    A. rice with vegetables

    B. fried rice

    C. curried rice

    D. rice salad

10. <u>Steps</u> to organize a camping trip

    A. make list of necessary items to take

    B. get maps of area

    C. have car in good condition

    D. check weather report

Exercise 7

These are only a few examples. Your paragraphs will be different. Have a fluent English speaker check your pragraphs.

1. The disadvatages of owning a large car are many. First, they are much more expensive to buy. After having purchased a large car, the owner is then faced with the expense of maintaining it. It uses more gasoline than a small car. Also, it is frequently hard to find a parking place for large cars.

2. The reasons a person lives in a remote area may be one of the following. Cities are usually very noisy, and a person may want to get away from the noise. Another attraction of a remote area might be that it is unpolluted. If a person was born and raised in a remote area, he or she may want to rmain in the place that is best known. Finally, some people like to be closer to nature, and this is easier away from a city.

3. Before applying to a foreign university, one should consider these disadvantages of studying

abroad. First, a student may feel alone by being far from family and friends. Also, difficulties in understanding a foreign language can be very frustrating and can affect the student's grades. It can be very expensive to pay the costs of travel and housing in a different country. Finally, if there is an emergency at home, it is hard to get home in a hurry.

4. Although a person thinks it is safe at home, many different kinds of accidents occur there. Falls are perhaps the most common accident among both young children and older adults. Poisoning is a danger, especially if an adult leaves medicines or cleaning chemicals within the reach of a small child. Burns frequently occur in the kitchen area during meal preparation. Finally, people cut themselves when using kitchen knives, trimming equipment in the yard, and power tools in the workshop or garage.

5. There are several kinds of airports. From an international airport, flights go to other countries as well as to cities in the same country. A national airport usually only serves the cities within its nation. Rural airports usually link a town with a nearby national airport. Private airports are those on a military base or a hospital. Individuals and companies own their own private airports.

Exercise 8

These are only examples. Your answers may differ greatly.

1. It is the largest and most interesting city in the country.

2. I read on the bus on my way to class, while I'm waiting for my friends, and before I go to sleep.

3. People can choose the movie they want and watch it in the comfort of their own homes.

4. The university that I want to attend requires that I get a score of at least 500.

5. The sound of the water along the shore calms one's nerves.

6. They can be both psychologically and physically addictive.

7. Had my brother been paying attention instead of changing the CD in the CD player while he was driving, he wouldn't have crashed into the tree and broken his leg.

8. A building such as the Pompidou Center in Paris has had as many people criticize its design as it has had people praise its modern features.

9. In fact, it's still possible to find ancient relics in parks and other undeveloped spaces.

10. Many city centers are not bustling with shoppers anymore. Instead, the streets are empty except when workers are leaving or returning to their offices.

Exercise 9

The following answers are only one way that you could add details. Your answers may be different.

1. When you plant a tree, you are helping your environment in many ways. Your tree will provide a home and food for other creatures. Birds may build nests in the branches. The flowers will provide honey for insects, and the fruits or nuts may feed squirrels or other small animals. Your tree will hold the soil in place. This will help stop erosion. In addition, your tree will provide shade in the summer. This will provide welcome relief on hot days. You can watch your tree grow and someday show your children or even grandchildren the tree you planted.

2. Airplanes and helicopters can be used to save people's lives. Helicopters can be used for rescuing people in trouble. For example, when a tall building is on fire, people sometimes escape to the roof, where a helicopter can pick them up. Passengers on a sinking ship could also be rescued by helicopter.

Planes can transport food and supplies when disasters strike. This is very important when there is an earthquake, flood, or drought. Both types of aircraft can transport people to hospitals in emergencies. Getting a victim of an accident or heart attack to a hospital quickly could save the person's life. Helicopters and airplanes can be used to provide medical services to people who live in remote areas. They can be used as a kind of ambulance service in cases where getting to the hospital by car would take too long.

3. Studying in another country is advantageous in many ways. A student is exposed to a new culture. This exposure teachers him or her about other people and other ways of thinking, which can promote friendships among countries. Sometimes students can learn a new language. This language may be beneficial for keeping up with research after the student has finished studying. Students can often have learning experiences not available in their own countries. For example, an art history student studying in Rome would get to see works of art that can only be seen in Italian museums and churches. A student may get the opportunity to study at a university where a leading expert in his or her field may be teaching. A leading expert can introduce the student to the most up-to-date findings of the top researchers in the field. Exposure to such valuable knowledge and insights into the field can aid the student in becoming an expert as well.

Exercise 10

The following are possible questions to simulate details.

1.   What kind of scenery do you like?

Why would you want to stop along the road?

Where and when have you met interesting people on your travels?

How much luggage can you carry on airplanes?

Why don't you have to worry about missing flights?

2.   What are the poor and inhumane conditions?

Why don't the animals get exercise?

What is an example of neurotic behavior?

Why is it a problem for animals not to breed?

Why is it a problem for animals to breed with a related animals?

3.   Why is knowing the matrial important?

Why should teachers be able to explain their knowledge?

Why are patience and understanding important?

What should teachers do to show their patience and understanding?

How can teachers make the subject matter interesting?

Exercises 13 and 15

The following are complete student essays using the questions in Exercise 12. There are several other ways these essays could be written. As long as the arguments are well reasoned, it does not matter whether or not the examiner agrees with their content.

1. Our world today is faced with many major threats. The most dangerous threat of all is war. Everyone in the world fears the outbreak of a war, especially another world war in which nuclear weapons may be used. With the use of nuclear weapons there is the possibility of the destruction of our entire

planet. Each war starts for a particular reason, but there are a number of steps countries can take to prevent its outbreak.

One main reason for war is a difference in ideology. For example, nations have engaged in struggles over the merits of communist and capitalist systems of government. They frequently aided other countries in wars in order to topple governments that have not agreed with their principles.

Land ownership is also a reason that countries declare wars on their neighbors. Frequently, these conflicts are economic in nature. For example, if oil is found on land in one country and that land can be claimed by another country for historical reasons, that country may declare war in order to recover the land containing oil. A landlocked country needing access to the sea may claim the territory between itself and the sea. When a border between two countries lies in an important food growing area such as, for example, a border formed by rivers, disputes over the water rights and the fertile land can turn into war.

To prevent the destruction of our Earth in a nuclear catastrophe, countries should try to resolve their differences through international organizations such as the United Nations. All countries need to educate their citizens to be more tolerant of other ideologies. After all, no ideology is worth total annihilation of the planet. In adition, the countries that are better off need to give more assistance to those countries that suffer severe economic troubles. So that those countries will not try to solve their problems through violence. In conclusion, there are solutions to the world's problems, and they should be put into practice now before it is too late.

2. For centuries, the roles of women and men in any particular country remained unchanged. However, modern technology has spread into most societies. This has made it possible for men and women to enter into new roles. Some of these changes in roles have been very beneficial.

The role of women has shifted from the homemaker/nurturer to the outside working world. This change has widened women's point of view. Women can now better understand men and the problems they face every day in their jobs. Because women are more prepared to take on decision-making roles. Their solutions to problems may be very different from those of men.

Men's roles have changed dramatically as well. It is no longer a man's world. Husbands find that with their wivies helping to support the family, they are helping to do many chores that were not considered manly before. However, in activities such as taking care of children, men have learned more nurturing habits. Men also no longer view women as helpless, mindless grown children, but as adults with decision-making abilities. Such experiences have helped men acquire a different, more positive attitude toward women and children.

In conclusion, these changes have been very beneficial. The two sexes are able to understand each other better and, therefore, help each other as a team. However, as with all change, there are conflicts. Some men resent the intrusion of women into their domain, and some women resent being forced out of their homemaking role. But it is with the raising of new generations acustomed to these roles that these conflicts will eventually smmoth themselves out for the benefit of all.

3. Nowadays, we have many conveniences in our society which have been brought about through technology and science. However, these same advancements in technology and science have caused some very dangerous problems. These problems won't go away easily because people don't want to give up the conveniences of a modern lifestyle. The most critical problems which should be dealt with immediately are

those of pollution.

Pollution caused by chemicals is a very serious problem because it causes the loss of the ozone layer. Without our ozone, not only we ourselves but all plant and animal life are exposed to dangerous rays from the sun. Aerosol cans emit chemicals which break down our ozone layer. Refrigeration and air-conditioning systems and cars also have dangerous emissions.

Perhaps the most serious threat to the planet is the warming of the earth's atmosphere, primarily through carbon dioxide emissions. Many scientists think that the warming could be sufficient to melt the polar ice caps, thus raising the sea levels. This would mean that many parts of theworld would be submerged below sea level.

There are other problems caused by pollution. Factories which make our modern conveniences emit poisonous gases into the air we breathe. The chemicals we use for cleaning and wastes from factories go into our water systems and pollute the water we drink and the fish we eat. They also kill much of the wildlife we depend on for food. Some of the pesticides we have sprayed on our crops have been found to be dangerous. This kind of pollution may stay in the ground for a very long period of time.

In conclusion, the problems created by pollution are growing daily. Because people do not want to change their lifestyles, we must invent a way to neutralize the pollutants we are putting into our environment. People need to be educated so they will stop damaging the planet. Furthermore, governments must take action to prevent individuals and companies from harming their environment.

Chapter Four   Answer and Explanations to the Sample Test

Reading

1. B 2. A 3. C 4. C 5. A 6. B 7. D 8. D 9. B 10. C 11. D 12. B 13 – 14. (1) (2) (5) 15. B 16. B 17. A 18. A 19. D 20. C 21. D 22. D 23. C 24. A 25. C 26. B 27 – 28. (1) (3) (4) 29. C 30. B 31. D 32. A 33. D 34. A 35. A 36. C 37. B 38. A 39. D 40. (2) (3) (5) (6) (7)

Listening

1. A 2. D 3. D 4. A/B 5. D 6. D 7. B 8. C 9. C/D 10. D 11. C

12.

	Agricultural Crisis	Population Pressure	Less developed industry and communications
"Peace, vaccination and potatoes"		√	
The state-supported enclosure movement	√		
City beggars and prositutes			√

13. B 14. D 15. A 16. A 17. D 18. A/D 19. A

20.

	Ture	False
Selectively permeable.	√	
Has some gaps.	√	
Permeable only to water molecules.		√
Protect the cell from harmful chemicals.	√	

21. A 22. A 23. A 24. B/D 25. B

26.

	Ture	False
The Atlantic Ocean will be larger.	√	
Australia will move farther south.		√
The Pacific Ocean will be larger.		√
North and South America will move farther west.	√	

27. C 28. C 29. D 30. C 31. A

32.

	Ture	False
A volcanic action in the open sea.	√	
A landslide along the coastline.		√
An inland explosion near the coast.		√
A meteorite landing in the ocean.	√	

33. B 34. D

Speaking

Sample Answers

Question 1

Though I have almost always admired my teachers for what they have taught me, there is one teacher that has had a greater influence on me than others have. Her name was Miss Baymler and she was my 4th grade teacher. I think that being a teacher for her was very natural. It was easy for us to see that she cared about each and every one of my classmates. She didn't just teach us facts; in fact, what she taught us was much more important — she taught us how to think and how to be proud of who we were.

Question 2

Though I can See the benefits of both options, I think that having a part-time job is an important part of university. I think jobs not only teach people how to manage time and money, but it also teaches them about human behavior. I've had a job since I was 15 years old and I've never regretted it. Instead, I've always pitied the people who didn't have a job and still depended on their parents for support. Though it's important to keep the hours to a minimum, having some kind of job during university has more benefits than downfalls.

Question 3

The woman basically believes that the new requirement for students taking foreign language classes is a marked improvement. First of all, she thinks that it will not only be beneficial for her studies, but that it is a sign of respect for the students as well. Secondly, she doesn't agree with her friend that it will be a waste of money. She strongly feels that most students could use more time practicing and that the laboratory sessions will be more worthwhile than individual study sessions. Furthermore, she finds that there isn't enough time to practice using the language in the other classes. So, unlike her friend, she believes that it will help foreign language students to become more fluent in their language of choice.

Question 4

Diabetes is a disease that often goes undiagnosed. The main reason for this is that the symptoms are similar to that of such problems as the common flu. Examples of these symptoms include fatigue, hunger, thirst, weight loss, irritability, and the need to go to the bathroom often.

There are many things that are being done to build awareness of this disease. Most importantly, is the education that is being offered by hospitals and diabetes organizations. Besides this, there is also information and quizzes online for people who might be at risk. Finally, news agencies have been writing about diabetes in the news a lot lately.

Question 5

The woman's problem is that she has a 20-page paper due the following week, and she doesn't think she'll be able to finish it in time. Her classmate gave her a few suggestions. One suggestion was that she talk to her professor about it and ask for an extension. The other suggestion was to find another worker to work her shifts at the coffee shop for a week so that she could simply concentrate on finishing her paper.

I think that the best thing for her to do is to talk to her professor. If her professor wanted her to write a paper in a week, he wouldn't have given her such a long time to write it in the first place. Though there's a chance that her professor might get angry at her for procrastinating for such a long time, there's also a chance that he might give her an extension.

Question 6

There are five main stages in culture shock. Some people take longer to go through some stages than others. Some people even go through one (or more) of the stages more than once.

The first stage is the 'honeymoon stage'. At this stage, people generally feel excited about everything new. The next stage is a transition stage. At this point, people often feel frustrated and displeased with things they encounter in the new culture. The third stage is where people start to understand what's going on in the new culture a little. The next stage is where people are able to judge the new culture more carefully; people can see the good side as well as the bad side. The final stage is called 're-entry shock'. It happens when people go back to their original culture. People often find that things are not the same as they used to be and that new customs and habits learned are different there.

It's important for people to be aware of these different stages so that they can understand what they or their friends are going through when in a new country.

Writing

Model Answers

Question 1

The lecturer begins by telling us that the idea of women working in the workforce is not as positive or clear cut as the article would have us believe. He suggests that a qualitative look at the issue reveals that there are practical difficulties in achieving real gender equality in the workplace and that the progress made is sometimes misleading.

To begin with, companies have a more difficult time when hiring new employees. They must not only consider a person's professional qualities and skills, but sometimes must make decisions based on gender. Trying to keep this balance, while at the same time finding excellent workers, can be difficult. This point is quite different from the optimism mentioned in the reading passage.

Another issue is that employees may become overly sensitive about treatment by other co-workers. If someone is given a better position, or treated differently in any way, it is likely to be interpreted as some kind of gender bias. Also, it can be easy for colleagues of the opposite sex to offend one another, meaning that the work environment is not always "harmonious" as mentioned above.

The lecturer also tells us that while more women are working, they are not necessarily being treated equally. Their pay is often lower and few women can enter high-level positions, showing that the example of HP's female CEO is not typical. As well, a more equal mix of male and female employees, the lecturer says, does not mean the company performs better. This directly contradicts the view in the passage that a better balance of men and women in the workplace is an "asset".

Question 2

In my native country, China, it is not uncommon for schools to require students to wear uniforms. When I was younger, I also had to wear a school uniform and I have thought a lot about the issue and experienced it personally. To begin with, it is important to acknowledge that our opinions on this issue can be influenced by perspective. Generally speaking, students dislike the concept whereas parents and educators, at least in China, tend to be in favor of it. I shall talk about the issue from my perspective, realizing that perhaps when I am older, my attitude may change.

Generally, I dislike the idea of school uniforms, and that we even have the idea of school uniforms suggests that they serve some purpose(s). So let's begin by considering the reasons for school uniforms and then determining whether or not the reasons are sound.

Educators often claim that school uniforms are an effective way to create equality between students. But in my opinion, people are still different. We look different, our parents make different amounts of money, and teachers give us different scores. Therefore, I reject this argument of creating equality.

Some say that by drawing attention away from fashion, school uniforms help students focus more effectively on learning. But in my experience, this is simply not true. Firstly, students will still discover ways to show their personality, whether it's with haircuts, shoes, or other accessories. As well, not focusing on fashion does not mean that students will like learning more. If anything, being told what to wear is likely to make them rebellious.

While I am unaware of any other so-called advantages for school uniforms, I can think of further disadvantages. For example, teachers will have a more difficult job distinguishing students, especially in China where classes can be quite large. As well, parents have a more difficult job keeping the same outfit clean day in and day out and hygiene would improve if students could change their clothes daily. Therefore, if schools want to create a harmonious environment and really promote learning, they should do it in ways that won't restrict a healthy amount of personal expression. School uniforms are not the answer.

Explanations to Reading

1. (B) This is a Factual Information question asking for specific information that can be found in paragraph 1. Choice B is the best answer. It is essentially a rephrasing of the statement in paragraph 1 that blowholes cannot disguise cetaceans' affinitis with other mammals. The other three choices are refuted, either directly or indirectly, by that paragraph.

2. (A) This is an Inference question asking for information that can be inferred from paragraph 1. Choice A is the best answer beause paragraph 1 says that sea otters are unlike early mammals whose appearances are not easy to imagine. By inference, then, the early appearance of sea otters must be easy (or not difficult) to imagine.

3. (C) This is a Vocabulary question. The word being tested is precious. It is highlighted in the passage. The correct answer is choice C, "valuable". Anything that is precious is very important and therefore valuable.

4. (C) This is a Factual Information question asking for specific information that can be found in the passage. Choice C is the best answer. Paragraph 3 describes the differences and similarities between Pakicetus and modern cetaceans. Sentence 3 of that paragraph states that their skulls are similar. The other three choices describe differences, not similarities.

5. (A) This is a Reference question. The word being tested is It. That word is highlighted in the passage. This is a simple pronoun referent item. Choice A, "Pakicetus" is the correct answer. The word It here refers to a creature that probably bred and gave birth on land. Pakicetus is the only one of the choices to which this could apply.

6. (B) This is a Vocabulary question. The word being tested is exposed. It is high-lighted in the passage. The correct answer is choice B, "visible". Exposed means "uncovered". A skeleton that is uncovered can be seen. Visible means "can be seen".

7. (D) This is a Factual Information question asking for specific information that can be found in the passage. Choice D is the best answer because it is the only detail about the skeleton of Basilosaurus mentioned in paragraph 4, meaning that it is significant. Choice A is true, but it is not discussed in the detail that choice D is, and does not represent the significance of the discovery. Choice C is not mentioned, and choice B is not true.

8. (D) This is an Inference question asking for a conclusion that can be drawn from the entire passage. Choice D is the best answer based on the last sentence of paragraph 4, which describes Basilosaurus as a fully marine whale. That implies that everything it did, including breeding and giving birth, could have been done only in a marine environment.

9. (B) This is an Inference question asking for a cnclusion that can be drawn from the passage. Paragraph 5 explains that this discovery provided important information to scientists that they might not have been able to obtain without it. Therfore, you can infer that the discovery was a "lucky" one. The passage offers no support for the other choices. Therefore, choice B is the best answer.

10. (C) This is a Sentence Simpoification question. As with all of these items, a single sentence in the passage is highlighted: The structure shows however that Ambulocetus swam like modern whales by moving the rear portion of its body up and down even though a fluke was missing Choce C is the best answer becarse it contains all of the essential information in the highlighted sentence. Choice A is not true becarse Ambulocetusdid showed how the Ambulocetus swam, not that it was missing a fluke. Choice D is untrue because the sentence states that Arnbulocetus and modern whales swam in the same way.

11. (D) This is a Vocabulary question. The word being tested is propulsion. It is high-lighted in the passage. Choice D, "moving forward" is the best answer because it means the action of propelling. The whale in the sentence used its hind legs to push itself forward in the water.

12. (B) This is an Insert Text question. You can see the four black squares in paragraphs 1 and 2 that represent the possible answer choices here.

Extinct but already fully marine cetaceans are known from the fossil record. ■ How was the gap between a walking mammal and a swimming whale bridged? ■ Missing until recently were fossils clearly intermediate, or transitional, between land mammals and cetaceans.

■ Very exciting discoveries have finally allowed scientists to reconstruct the most likely origins of cetaceans. ■ In 1979, a team looking for fossils in northern Pakistan found what proved to be the oldest fossil whale.

The sentence provided is "This is a question that has puzzled scientists for ages." The best place to insert it is at square 2.

The sentence that precedes square 2 is in the form of a rhetorical question and the inserted sentence explicitly provides a response to it. None of the other sentences preceding squares is a question, so the inserted sentence cannot logically follow any one of them.

13 – 14. (1) (2) (5) This is a Prose Summary question. It is completed correctly below. The correct choices are 1, 2, and 5. Choices 3, 4, and 6 are therefore incorrect.

Correct Choices

Choice 1, "Recent discoveries of fossils have helped to show the link between land mammals and cetaceans," is correct because it represents the major idea of the entire passage. The bulk of the passage consists of a discussion of the major discoveries(Pakecitus, Basilosaurus, and Ambulocetus) that show this link.

Choice 2, "The discovery of Ambulocetus natans provided evidence for a whale that lived both on land and at sea," is correct because it is one of the major discoveries cited in the passage in support of the passage's main point, that mammals and cetaceans are related.

Choice 5, "Fossils thought to be transitional forms between walking mammals and swimming whales were found," is correct because like choice 1, this is a statement of the passage's major theme as stated in paragraph 1: these fossils were "clearly intermediate, or transitional between land mammals and cetaceans." The remainder of the passage discusses these discoveries.

Choice 3, "The skeleton of Basiosaurus was found in what had been the Tethys Sea, an area rich in fossil evidence," is true, but it is a minor detail and therefore incorrect.

Choice 4, "Pakicetus is the oldest fossil whale yet to be found," is true, but it is a minor detail and therefore incorrect.

Choice 6, "Ambulocetus' hind. legs were used for propulsion in the water," is true, but it is a minor detail and therefore incorrect.

15. (B) There is a Vocabulary question. The word being tested is threatened. It is highlighted in the passage. To threaten means to speak or act as if you will cause harm to someone or something. The object of the threat is in danger of being hut, so the correct answer is choice B, "endangered".

16. (B) This is a Factual Information question asking for specific information that can be found in paragraph 3. The correct answer is choice B, reduced water absorption. The paragraph explicitly states that the reduction of vegetation greatly reduces water absorption. Choice D, reduced water runoff, explicitly contradicts the paragraph, so it is incorrect. The "spaces in the soil" are mentioned in another context: the paragraph does not say that they increase, so choice C is incorrect.

17. (A) This is a Vocabulary question. The word being tested is delicate. It is highlighted in the passage. The correct answer is choice A, "fragile", meaning "easily broken". Delicate has the same meaning as "fragile".

18. (A) This is a Factual Information question asking for specific information that can be found in paragraph 5. The correct answer is choice A: border areas have difficulty "adjusting to stresses created by settlement". The paragraph says that "expanding populations", or settlement, subject order areas to "pressures," or stress, that the land may not "be able to respond to". Choice B is incorrect because the paragraph does not discuss "fertility" after desertification. Choice C is also incorrect because "irrigation" is not mentioned here. The paragraph mentions "increasing populations but not the difficulty of attracting populations," so choice D is incorrect.

19. (D) This is a Vocabulary question. The word being tested is progressively. It is highlighted in the passage. The correct answer is choice D, "increasingly". Progressively as it is used here means "more," and "more" of something means that it is increasing.

20. (C) This is a Factual Information question asking for specific information that can be found in paragraph 6. The correct answer is choice C, "removal of the original vegetation". Sentence 4 of this paragraph says that "the raising of most crops necessitates the prior removal of the natural vegetation," an explicit statement of answer choice C. Choice A, lack of proper irrigation techniques, is incorrect because the paragraph mentions only "overirrigation" as a cause of desertification. No irrigation "techniques" are dicussed. Choice B and D, failure to plant suitable crops and use of animal waste, are not discussed.

21. (D) This is a Vocabulary question. A phrase is being tested here, and all of the answer choices are phrases. The phrase is "devoid of ". It is highlighted in the passage. "Devoid of " means "without", so the correct answer is choice D, "lacking in". If you lack something, that means you are without that thing.

22. (D) This is a Factual Information question asking for specific information that can be found in paragraph 9. The correct answer is choice D, "bring salts to the surface". The paragraph says that the final human cause of dertification is salinization resulting from overirrigation. The paragraph goes on to say that the overirrigation causes the water table to rise, bringing salts to the surface. There is no mention of the process "interfering" with or "limiting" irrigation, or of the "amount of air" the soil is required to absorb, so choices A, B, and C are all incorrect.

23. (C) This is a Negative Factual Information question asking for specific information that can be found in the passage, Choice C, "insufficient irrigation", is the correct answer. Choice A, "soil erosion", is explicitly mentioned in paragraph 2 as one of the primary causes of dertification, so it is not the correct answer. Choice B, "global warming", is mentioned as a cause of dertification in paragraph 4, so it is incorrect. Choice D, "raising of livestock", is described in paragraph 7 as another cause of desertification, so it is incorrect. The passage includes excessive irrigation as a cause of desertification, but not its opposite, insufficient irrigation, so that is the correct answer.

24. (1) This is a Sentence simplification question. As with all of these items, a single sentence in the passage is highlighted. The correct answer is choice A. That choice contains all of the essential information in the highlighted sentence and does not change its meaning. The only substantive difference is

between choice A and the tested sentence is the order in which the information is presented. Two clauses in the highlighted sentence, "The great difficulty of reversing the process" and "the number of people affected", have simply been reversed; no meaning has been changed, and no information has been removed. Choices B, C, and D are all incorrect because they change the meaning of the highlighted sentence.

25. (C) This is an Inference question asking for an inference that can be supported by the passage. The correct answer is choice C; the passage suggests that the author believes "Desertification will continue to increase. " The last paragraph of the passage says that slowing or reversing the erosion process will be very difficult, but that it may occur in those areas that are not too affected already if rigorously enforced anti-erosion processes are implemented. Taken together, this suggests that the author is not confident this will happen; therefore, it can be inferred that he thinks erosion will continue. The passage provides no basis for inferring choices A, B, or D.

26. (B) This is an Insert Text question. You can see the four black squares in paragraph 7 that represent the possible answer choices. The sentence provided, "This economic reliance on livestock in certain regions makes large tracts of land susceptible to overgrazing, " is best inserted at Square 2. The inserted sentence refers explicitly to relying on livestock in certain regions. " Those regions are the ones described in the sentence preceding square 2, which states that raising livestock is " a major economic activity in semiarid lands. " The inserted sentence then explains that this reliance " makes large tracts of land susceptible to overgrazing. "The sentence that follows square 2 goes on to say that "The consequences of an excessive number of livestock grazing in an area are. . . Thus, the inserted sentence contains references to both the sentence before square 2 and the sentence after square 2. This is not true of any of the other possible insert points, so square 2 is correct.

27 – 28. (1) (3) (4) This is a Prose Summary question. It is completed correctly below. The correct choices are 1, 3, and 4. Choices 2, 5, and 6 are therefore incorrect.

Many factors have contributed to the great increase in desertification in recent decades.

◇ Growing human populations and the agricultural demands that come with such growth have upset the ecological balance in some areas and led to the spread of desets.

◇ Excessive numbers of cattle and the need for firewood for fuel have reduced grasses and trees, leaving the land unprotected and vulnerable.

◇ Extensive irrigation with poor drainage brings salt to the surface of he soil, a process that reduces water and air absorption.

Correct Choices

Choice 1, "Growing human populations and the agricultural demands that come with such growth have upset the ecological balance in some areas and led to the spread of deserts, " is correct because it is a recurring theme in the passage, one of the main ideas. Paragraphs 5, 6, 7, and 9 all provide details in support of this statement.

Choice 3, "Excessive numbers of cattle and the need for firewood for fuel have reduced grasses and trees, leaving the land unprotected and vulnerable, " is correct because these are two of the human activities that are major causes of desertification. The causes of desertification is the main theme of the passage. Paragraphs 6, 7, and 8 are devoted to describing how these activities contribute to desertification

Choice 4, "Extensive irrigation with poor drainage brings salt to the surface of the soil, a process that reduces water and air absorption," is correct because it is another of the human activities that is a major cause of desertification, the main theme of the passage. Paragraph 6 mentions this first, then all of paragraph 9 is devoted to describing how this activity contributes to desertification.

Incorrect Choices

Choice 2, "As periods of severe dryness have become more common, failures of a number of different crops have increased," is incorrect because it is a supporting detail, not a main idea of the passage.

Choice 5, "Animal dung enriches the soil by providing nutrients for plant growth," is incorrect because it is contradicted by paragraph 8 of the passage.

Choice 6, "Grasses are generally the dominant type of natural vegetation in semi-arid lands," is incorrect because it is a minor detail, mentioned once in passing in paragraph 7.

29. (C) This is an Inference question asking for an inference that can be supported by the passage. The correct answer is choice C, "They were produced with more concern for quality than for speed of production." A number of statements throughout the passage support choice C.

Paragraph 1 states that "Before 1815 manufacturing in the United States had been done in homes or shops by skilled artisans... After 1815 this older form of manufacturing began to give way to factories with machinery tended by unskilled or semiskilled laborers." Paragraph 2 states that "Before the rise of the factory.., skilled artisans did not work by the clock, at a steady pace, but rather in bursts of intense labor alternating with more leisurely time." Paragraph 3 states, "The factory changed that. Goods produced by factories were not as finished or elegant as those done by hand, and pride in craftsmanship gave way to the pressure to increase rates of productivity." Taken together, these three statements, about production rates, the rise of factories after 1815, and the decline of craftsmanship after 1815, support the inference that before 1815, the emphasis had been on quality rather than on speed of production. Answer choices A, B, and D are all contradicted by the passage.

30. (B) This is a Sentence Simplification question. As with all of these items, a single sentence in the passage is highlighted. The correct answer is choice B. Choice B contains all of the essential information in the highlighted sentence. The highlighted sentence explains why (part of the family) and how (education, moral behavior) a master's responsibility went beyond teaching a trade. The essential information is the fact that the master's responsibility went beyond teaching a trade. Therefore, choice B contains all that is essential without changing the meaning of the highlighted sentence.

Choice A changes the meaning of the highlighted sentence by stating that masters often treated apprentices irresponsibly.

Choice C contradicts the essential meaning of the highlighted sentence. The fact that "Apprentices were considered part of the family..." suggests that they were not actual family members.

Choice D, like choice C, changes the meaning of the highlighted sentence by discussing family members as apprentices.

31. (D) This is a Vocabulary question. The word being tested is disrupted. It is highlighted in the passage. The correct answer is choice D, "upset." The word "upset" here is used in the context of "hurting productivity". When something is hurt or damaged, it is "upset".

32. (A) This is a Factual Information question asking for specific information that can be found in paragraph 4. The correct answer is choice A, "support the idea that it was difficult for workers to adjust to working in factories." The paragraph begins by stating that workers did not adopt new attitudes toward work easily and that the clock symbolized the new work rules. The author provides the quotation as evidence of that difficulty. There is no indication in the paragraph that workers quit due to loud noise, so choice B is incorrect. Choice C (usefulness of clocks) is contradicted by the paragraph. The factory clock was "useful," but workers hated it. Choice D (workers complaints as a cause of a factory's success) is not discussed in this paragraph.

33. (D) This is a Negative Factual Information question asking for specific information that can be found in paragraph 4. Choice D, "contact among workers who were not managers," is the correct answer. The paragraph explicitly contradicts this by stating that "factories sharply separated workers from management," The paragraph explicitly states that workers lost choice A (freedom), choice B (status in the community), and choice C(opportunities for advancement) in the new system, so those choices are all incorrect.

34. (A) This is a Vocabulary question. The phrase being tested is "gathered some momentum". It is highlighted in the passage. The correct answer is choice A, "made progress". To "gather momentum" means to advance with increasing speed.

35. (A) This is a Vocabulary question. The word being tested is spearheaded. It is high-lighted in the passage. The correct answer is choice A, "led". The head of a spear leads the rest of the spear, so the craftsworkers who "spearheaded" this movement led it.

36. (C) This is a Factual Information question asking for specific information that can be found in paragraph 5. The correct answer is choice C, "It was slow to improve conditions for workers. " The paragraph states, "More than a decade of agitation did finally bring a workday shortened to 10 hours to most industries by the 1850's, and the courts also recognized workers' fight to strike, but these gains had little immediate impact. " This statement explicitly supports choice C. All three other choices are contradicted by the paragraph.

37. (B) This is a Factual Information question asking for specific information about a particular phrase in the passage. The phrase in question is highlighted in the passage. The correct answer is choice B, "created divisions among workers. " The paragraph states (emphasis added): "... they (workers) were divided by ethnic and racmi antagonisms, gender, conflicting religious perspectives, occupational differences, political party loyalties, and disagreements over tactics. " So "political party loyalties and disagreements over tactics" are explicitly stated as two causes of division among workers. The other choices are not stated and are incorrect.

38. (A) This is a Reference question. The word being tested is them. It is highlighted in the passage. This is a simple pronoun-referent item. The word them in this sentence refers to those people to whom "the factory and industrialism were not agents of opportunity but reminders of their loss of indepen-

dence and a measure of control over their lives." Choice A, "Workers," is the only choice that refers to this type of person, so it is the correct answer.

39. (D) This is an Insert Text question. You can see the four black squares in paragraph 1 that represent the possible answer choices here.

Before 1815 manufacturing in the United States had been done in homes or shops by skilled artisans. ■ As master craftworkers, they imparted the knowledge of their trades to apprentices and journeymen. ■ In addition, women often worked in their homes part-time, making finished articles from raw material supplied by merchant capitalists. ■ After 1815 this older form of manufacturing began to give way to factories with machinery tended by unskilled or semiskilled laborers. ■ Cheap transportation networks, the rise of cities, and the availability of capital and credit all stimulated the shift to factory production.

The sentence provided, "This new form of manufacturing depended on the movement of goods to distant locations and a centralized source of laborers," is best inserted at square 4. The inserted sentence refers explicitly to "a new form of manufacturing." This "new form of manufacturing" is the one mentioned in the sentence preceding square 4, "factories with machinery tended by unskilled or semiskilled laborers." The inserted sentence then explains that this new system depended on "the movement of goods to distant locations and a centralized source of laborers." The sentence that follows square 4 goes on to say, "Cheap transportation networks, the rise of cities, and the availability of capital and credit all stimulated the shift to factory production." Thus the inserted sentence contains references to both the sentence before square 4 and the sentence after square 4. This is not true of any of the other possible insert points, so square 4 is the correct answer.

40. This is a Fill in a Table question. It is completed correctly below. The correct choices for the "Before 1815" column are 2 and 6. Choices 3, 5, and 7 belong in the "1815 – 1850" column. Choices 1 and 4 should not be used in either column.

Before 1815	1815 – 1850
◇ Workers took pride in their Workmanship. ◇ Workers went through an extensive period of training.	◇ The income gap between the rich and the poor increased greatly. ◇ Emphasis was placed on following Schedules. ◇ Few workers expected to own their own Businesses.

Correct Choices

Choice 2: "Workers took pride in their workmanship" belongs in the "Before 1815" column because it is mentioned in the passage as one of the characteristics of labor before 1815.

Choice 3: "The income gap between the rich and the poor increased greatly" belongs in the "1815 – 1850" column because it is mentioned in the passage as one of the characteristics of society that emerged in the period between 1815 and 1850.

Choice 5: "Emphasis was placed on following schedules" belongs in the "1815 – 1850" column because it is mentioned in the passage as one of the characteristics of labor in the factory system that emerged between 1815 and 1850.

Choice 6: "Workers went through an extensive period of training" belongs in the"Before 1815" column because it is mentioned in the passage as one of the characteristics of labor before 1815.

Choice 7: "Few workers expected to own their own businesses" belongs in the "1815 – 1850" column because it is mentioned in the passage as one of the characteristics of society that emerged in the period between 1815 and 1850.

Incorrect Choices

Choice 1: "A united, highly successful labor movement took shape" does not belong in the table because it contradicts the passage.

Choice 4: "Transportation networks began to decline" does not belong in the table because it is not mentioned in the passage in connection with either the pet'od before 1815 or the period between 1815 and 1850.

Appendix

TOEFL Score Comparisons 托福成绩换算表

Score Comparison		Score Comparison, cont.	
Internet-based	Paper-based	Internet-based	Paper-based
TOEFL Total	Total	TOEFL Total	TOEFL Total
120	677	51	467
120	673	49 – 50	463
119	670	48	460
118	677	47	457
117	660 – 663	45 – 46	450 – 453
116	657	44	447
114 – 115	650 – 653	43	443
113	647	41 – 42	437 – 440
111 – 112	640 – 643	40	433
109	630 – 633	39	430
106 – 108	623 – 627	38	423 – 427
105	617 – 620	36 – 37	420
103 – 104	613	35	417
101 – 102	607 – 610	34	410 – 413
100	600 – 603	33	407
98 – 99	597	32	400 – 403
96 – 97	590 – 593	30 – 31	397
94 – 95	587	29	390 – 393
92 – 93	580 – 583	28	387
90 – 91	577	26 – 27	380 – 383
88 – 89	570 – 573	25	377
86 – 87	567	24	370 – 373
84 – 85	563	23	363 – 367
83	557 – 560	22	357 – 360
81 – 82	553	23	363 – 367
79 – 80	550	22	357 – 360
77 – 78	547	21	353
76	540 – 543	19 – 20	347 – 350
74 – 75	537	18	340 – 343
72 – 73	533	17	33 – 337
71	527 – 530	16	33
69 – 70	523	15	330
68	520	14	317 – 320
66 – 67	523	13	313
65	513	12	310
64	507 – 510	11	310
62 – 63	503	9	310
61	500	8	310
59 – 60	497	7	310
58	493	6	310
57	487 – 490	5	310
56	483	4	310
54 – 55	480	3	310
53	477	2	310
52	470 – 473	1	310
		0	310
		0	310

Range Comparison

New Internet – based	Paper – based
TOEFL total	TOEFL Total
111 – 120	640 – 677
96 – 110	590 – 637
79 – 95	550 – 587
65 – 78	513 – 547
53 – 64	477 – 510
41 – 52	437 – 473
30 – 40	397 – 433
19 – 29	347 – 393
9 – 18	310 – 343
0 – 8	310

Note: The paper-based total score does not include writing.

TOEFL Score Comparison for Reading

New Internet – based	Paper – based
TOEFL Reading	Reading
30	67
29	66
28	64 – 65
27	63
26	61 – 62
24	59 – 60
23	58
21	57
20	56
19	54 – 55
17	53
16	52
15	51
14	50
13	48 – 49
12	47
11	46
10	44 – 45
9	43
8	41 – 42
7	40
6	38 – 39
5	36 – 37
4	34 – 35
3	32 – 33
2	31
1	31
0	31
0	31
0	31
0	31

Range Comparison

New Internet – based	Paper – based
TOEFL Reading	TOEFL Reading
28 – 30	64 – 67
26 – 28	59 – 63
21 – 24	56 – 58
17 – 20	52 – 55
14 – 16	48 – 51
11 – 13	44 – 47
8 – 10	40 – 47
5 – 7	34 – 39
1 – 4	31 – 33
0	31

TOEFL Score Comparisons for Listening

New Internet – based	Paper – based
TOEFL Listening	TOEFL Listening
30	67 – 68
30	66
29	65
28	63 – 64
27	62
26	60 – 61
25	59
23	58
22	56 – 57
21	55
19	54
18	53
17	52
16	51
15	50
14	49
13	48
12	47
11	46
10	45
9	44
7	42 – 43
6	41
5	40
4	38 – 39
2	36 – 37
1	34 – 35
1	32 – 33
0	31
0	31
0	31

Range Comparison

New Internet – based	Paper – based
TOEFL Listening	Listening
29 – 30	65 – 68
26 – 28	60 – 64
22 – 25	56 – 59
18 – 21	53 – 55
15 – 17	50 – 52
12 – 14	47 – 49
9 – 11	44 – 49
5 – 7	40 – 43
1 – 4	34 – 39
0 – 1	31 – 33

TOEFL Score Comparisons for Writing

New Internet – based	Paper – based Structure
TOEFL Writing	and Written Expression
30	68
29	67
28	65 – 66
26	63 – 66
24	61 – 62
22	59 – 60
20	58
19	56 – 57
17	55
16	54
14	52 – 53
13	51
13	50
12	48 – 49
11	47
11	46
10	44 – 45
10	43
9	42
9	40 – 41
8	39
8	37 – 38
7	35 – 36
7	33 – 34
6	31 – 32
5	31
3	31
1	31
0	31
0	31
0	31

Range Comparison

New Internet – based	Paper – based Structure
TOEFL Writing	and Written Expression
28 – 30	65 – 68
22 – 26	59 – 64
17 – 20	55 – 58
13 – 16	51 – 54
13 – 16	47 – 50
11 – 13	43 – 46
10 – 11	39 – 42
8 – 9	33 – 38
7 – 8	31 – 32
3 – 6	31
0 – 1	

Note: The new Internet-based TOEFL writing section is composed of two writing tasks: one independent essay and one integrated writing task. The paper-based Structure and Written Expression section consistes of multiple-choice questions only, and the required essay is reported separately from the total score. Therefore, the scores for these two sections are derived differently.